Lucky Me

Lucky Me

A Novel

DEBRA BORDEN

 THREE RIVERS PRESS • NEW YORK

Library of Congress Cataloging-in-Publication Data
Borden, Debra, 1957–
Lucky me : a novel / Debra Borden.—1st ed.
1. Married women—Fiction.   2. Middle-aged women—Fiction.
3. Midlife crisis—Fiction.   4. Parent and child—Fiction.   5. Young men—
Fiction.   6. Psychological fiction.   7. Domestic fiction.   I. Title.
PS3602.O68P37   2005
813'.6—dc22   2004026594

ISBN-13: 978-1-4000-8222-3
ISBN-10: 1-4000-8222-6

Printed in the United States of America

Design by Lynne Amft

10 9 8 7 6 5 4 3 2 1

First Paperback Edition

For my family,

Neal, Erika, and David . . . what else is there?

In memory of my parents,

Sid and Estelle Feldman,

with apologies for the exaggerations,

and

Michelle Lynn Feldman, who loved a good family story.

ACKNOWLEDGMENTS

A first novel unfolds like a first garden; with more bravado than brains, bursts of energy, pauses of thoughtful planning, and, finally, labors of revision, tweaking, and pruning. If one is lucky, the flowering, frantic mess is tamed into something worth looking at. It is with deep gratitude, humility, and respect that I acknowledge those who helped me, and this book, to grow.

First and foremost, to my friend *Ann Malbin,* for convincing me to let go, for hours of thoughtful, tireless, intelligent critique, but most of all, for calling me up while reading other novels to tell me mine was better.

To *Laura Zinn Fromm*, my e-mail muse. You have no idea (although I've told you) how amazing you are. Because of your insights and suggestions, this book exists. *Your turn.*

To *Janet Jacobs,* for honoring our friendship with a leap of faith.

To *Binnie Kirshenbaum,* not only a writer of acclaim and awe, but also one of generosity and kindness, who took time out for the most unknown of entities; an unpublished, fledgling writer.

To *Hertha, Grace, Kevin, Sally, Bob,* and *Caroline,* my writer's group, for your collective talent and never-ending support.

To the incredible *Lisa Bankoff,* who gives class and savvy to the title "agent," for calling me the Real Deal. Next to "fully dilated," those are the two sweetest words I've ever heard.

To *Shaye Areheart,* who defies the clichés and combines a strong business and literary sense with a heart and soul. You had me at hello.

To *Tina Dubois* and *Julie Will,* who assist with excellence, professionalism, and cheerfulness, to *Cindy Berman* and *David Wade Smith* for their humbling expertise, to *Debbie Natoli* for her artistry and imagination and *Darlene Faster, Campbell Wharton,* and *Kira Stevens* for their energy and spirit, many thanks.

Thanks to the following people who freely offered their contacts or advice: *Andrew Jacobs, Arlene Jacobs, Carole Stuart, Bernard Zipken, Baba Zipken, Mel Berger, Susan Wels, Jil Seligman, Doris Mortman, Carron Landau, Jo Ann Chaus, Randy* and *Jeffrey Pollack,* and *Leslie Berger Mendell.*

To my extended family for the opportunity to grow as your sister, aunt, or cousin: *Feldmans, Posners, Snipes, Spitulniks, Strauses, Baers, Schleifmans, Levenhar-Pearson-Cohens,* and *Spielfogels.* It would be difficult to write with any authenticity about family without the gift of being connected to all of you.

To my adopted family, *Jayne, David, Aaron,* and *Derek Petak.* If you fill in as family long enough, you become one.

To the many others who so sincerely supported, rooted, and cheered; every smile, clap, and prayer has meant so much.

Thank-you. Peace and love to all.

D.B. 2005

If you cannot get rid of the family skeleton, you may as well make it dance.

Sigmund Freud

All my life, I always wanted to be somebody. Now I see that I should have been more specific.

Lily Tomlin

Somewhere on this globe, every ten seconds, there is a woman giving birth to a child. She must be found and stopped.

George Bernard Shaw

Lucky Me

ONE

back to herself in no time

By the spring of 1956, on Long Island's North Shore, my mother had acquired many things: a husband; two boys, ages nine and thirteen; four bedrooms; one mink coat; a housekeeper and a miniature schnauzer named Pearlie and Bambi respectively; and, despite the palpable salve of these possessions, a dreadful black hole in the center of her soul where her dreams used to be. Perhaps Estelle Berman (née Esther Levin) was nothing more than a postwar cliché, one more survival-driven daughter of immigrant parents, two parts old-fashioned respectability and a dollop of modern movie glamour, inspired to grab at a life of security tinged with trips to Bermuda rather than one of possible passion and the dreadful results such frivolousness might invoke. Maybe it was the tediousness of too many lunches of nothing more than portioned-out Jujubes, or the shame of so many overheard hysterics; her mother was indignant over the price of day-old bread, fish, and fabric, and perpetually accused the butcher of cheating her; charging her for meat weighed with the bone. Or perhaps it was ultimately the dress, the blue silk dress with layers of sheer cobalt chiffon and delicate smocking across the chest; the dress we would hear about for years, the one that went not to my mother, who stood trans-fixed in front of Felterman's Dress Shop coveting it for weeks, but to Miriam, my aunt, her baby sister, because Miriam was "fragile." With a sister who had cornered the market on fragility and a mother adept at selective hysteria, Estelle was left with little choice except to embrace prac-ticality. So, in the summer of her nineteenth year, the belle of First Street on Manhattan's Lower East Side, the most popular girl in the apartment complex above the candy store (Ach! It's some boy calling for Esther again!), the featured actress in Singer's summer-stock production of *Showboat* that August of 1939, and a real "looker," as the fellows used to say, promptly withdrew from the theatrical and social scene, decisively put an end to all whimsy and girlish adventure, to marry my father and liter-ally subdue herself with the pursuit of perfect domesticity. Soon enough she bought her own blue dress, two in fact, and a full closet and an even fuller wallet went a long way. Such items were able to plump her spirit and fill her belly for many months, years even. But there came a time when compromise began to feed on resolve and poison satisfaction, and no doubt resentment was the secret at the root of my mother's unhappiness. Then again, perhaps it wouldn't have mattered. Perhaps laying blame is merely the folly of a daughter fighting to rewrite the truth, a truth that precludes self-determination and marks the women in this filial line for genetic doom.

Whatever the cause, by April of her thirty-sixth year, the surface in her inner blueprint opened and spread like an emotional fault line, creat-ing cracks in the façade that were impossible to ignore. She'd built her inner dream house with a diagram she'd adopted first from the movies, then from studying the uptown goyim, and finally by mimicking her aloof neighbors in tony Great Neck, New York. Now she was scrambling to repair the pretend foundation as it chipped and crumbled. She sobbed in the shower. The moment the warm water ran down her face the tears spilled out. Leaning against the cold tile, she liked the feeling of not know-ing where the water stopped and the tears began. Sometimes she cried in the car—not for any particular reason and never in front of the boys, but if it was perhaps a windy day, and the sun caught a pile of leaves in just such a way, well, there was something about the fluttering down that made her think of dreams dying. She didn't understand. She thought she'd done everything right, acquired all the symbols of happiness, from her VKP sticker (the Village of Kings Point was Great Neck's most exclusive) to her summer membership at the Fleetwood pool. She could run up a charge with Rudy at the Great Neck Pharmacy and with Don at Prime Meats. Stewie and Lyle spent a full eight weeks at sleep-away camp in the Catskills and she had a standing hair appointment each week with Frank at Expressions, on Friday at 9:30 a.m., too; prime time. Her friends seemed happy and she didn't dare discuss it with them. They thought her life was perfect and she wasn't about to destroy that illusion just because of a silly little phase. Still, it became harder and harder to pretend, to relax the muscles of her face into a smooth mask. She began to take naps every day, first at three o'clock, then earlier, until she questioned the sense of changing out of her morning gown. She took two Bufferin as soon as she woke up, taught Pearlie how to prepare her string-bean casserole and salmon croquettes and spent whole days watching television in her bed. Bill Cullen gave way to Virginia Graham, a span of six hours that felt like seconds. Then she dropped out of her card games, gave up her place in the Wednesday matinee carpool, and didn't even mind when Lena Shore opined that missing Gwen Verdon's performance in *Damn Yankees* was criminal. She realized she was in big trouble when she overheard her littlest son, Stewie, playing house with the girl next door.

"You're the dad so you have to get in the car and go to work." Leslie Frankel was ten going on thirty-two.

"Okay, smarty," she heard her delicious baby say, "then if you're the mom you have to take your pills and get into bed 'cause you have a headache."

My mother searched for strength. She had always been the reliable one, the dependable one; she would not give in to such nonsense. She forced herself to shower and dress each day. She forbade herself to nap, and only lay down for a little while on top of the covers each afternoon. She practiced several smiles in front of the three-panel makeup mirror Sol had installed for her, just the way she'd practiced smiling when Miriam had paraded and twirled for all of them in a cloud of perfect blue chiffon that should have been hers, and even though her heart wasn't in it, she went back to one of her card games. She tried hard. So hard, in fact, that when smiling and dressing and cards didn't really help, she was frantic enough to explore any option, which is where I come in.

In 1956 there were all kinds of female problems that could purportedly be solved by childbirth. Boredom and restlessness were not the worst among them. By the 1980s it had become common for children to be conceived, *farmed* really, for their genetically matched cells or blood or parts, to save the life of a relative. Still, I was shocked to learn that this twisted, newly improved logic applied to me. Of course, that may have been because of the slight variation. It was my psychological stem cells they were after. I was a new life-force, created to replenish my mother's ailing one.

IN WHAT I have come to regard as her typical misguided conviction, it is my mother herself who tells me the story, twenty-five years later and just days before I am about to give birth to a daughter of my own. She has come to stay with me in the final weeks of my first pregnancy, and, as is often the case near the end of her extended visits, I am testy with our superficial conversations and am probing her unmercifully for psychological introspection she is unable or unwilling to consider. I do not know her as the most popular girl on First Street or the coquette who posed seductively for my father on the library steps. I have my own nicknames, my own assessments, and my own grievances. At twenty-five I am unforgiving, not softened yet by years of living, parenting, screwing up. I am in what a baker calls "the hard crack stage," boiling, bubbling; I stiffen in just seconds. Years later I will tolerate more, I will challenge gently, with less guilt or bitterness, but now, in private, I make fun. She is the Grande Dame, Pout Princess, Calorie Queen. We are in the middle of a discussion about women who work versus women who don't and she is defensive, stating that she can't imagine a woman going through life without fulfilling her true purpose.

"What do you mean, 'her true purpose'? Are you saying women have no real purpose unless they reproduce?"

"Well, I certainly couldn't have. The boys gave me purpose and then Thank God I was able to have you when I needed to."

"What do you mean, when you needed to?"

Already my mother is nervous. I can tell. She begins to twist a napkin to shreds. "Well, I just didn't feel right, Jule, I was, I don't know, anxious, I guess, for a while. So your father took me to see someone—"

"Who?" I interrupt. I don't want a name; I want a better description of *someone*.

"I don't remember who." She squirms. "What's the difference? The point is, he helped us." Of course it was a "he." In 1956 it was always a "he."

"Did he?" I try not to sound cynical, not because I especially want to be kind, but because I want her to continue.

"He told daddy"—my mother's voice deepens as she tries to imitate him—"Sol, I want you to get her pregnant as soon as possible, that's the ticket, you'll see. She'll be back to her old self in no time."

A nerve ending in my left side, just under my arm, starts to twinge.

"And so," my mother exclaims sweetly, "we had you."

Well. I am frozen. Not sure what to feel, how to act, what she wants. This is the greasy engine of the machine in which I have been raised, spun, tumble-dried. Wanted, yes, but for the wrong reasons, harvested, surely, to fill a need, loved, albeit in the way an asthmatic loves her nebulizer, as a relief from pain or panic. She looks at me expectantly; she is waiting for my smile, my acknowledgment that I have joined her in happy acceptance. She wants my confirmation, no questions asked, that all is well. But as I have suspected for some time, all is not—nor am I—well. I am not my mother, to her regret, and even more, I am that worst of all pests, a prober, a challenger, a dreaded truth-seeker. And I am blown away by this news on so many levels, not the least of which is that my mother seems so proud. This is a marvelous way for a child to come into the world, her expression says. So I struggle, ambivalent about giving her what she needs, which I have done to hypocritical exhaustion, and expressing my own needs, which has become more necessary. I know that in another moment it will be a moment too long, and I will disappoint her, because of the unwritten mother/daughter conversation rules that not only state how to react but how quickly, and in a moment the false bonding will dissolve into disappointed pouting (hers) and eventual apologizing (mine). In that disturbed, unnerving beat of time, whole snippets of my childhood pass through my mind: Twelve years old, I am crying over a boyfriend and my mother frets. "Don't cry. Stop it. This is not okay. No boy is worth your tears." Flash to junior high, I don't make the cheerleading squad but I am being given a present, a stereo. "You're *our* best booster!" Then I am seventeen, complaining that high school is boring, and within a day there are brochures spread out on the table offering early admissions to college.

So there I was, with my own belly just weeks away from repeating the cycle, when the truth finally hit. My life was a present for my mother, assembly required, few instructions enclosed. I came into the world to combat her depression and allow my parents' lives to resume their everyday, peaceful sameness. There would be no crying, no sadness for little Julie Ann Berman; that was not part of the arrangement. There *would* be excessive cheerfulness, laughter, forced if necessary, and scripted gaiety. If I encountered any bumps in the road, I would not have time to feel them, as they would be removed swiftly. I would not need to learn to handle disappointment or hurt, because there simply wasn't to be any. This was their silent pledge that they adhered to rigidly and consistently. I believe they called it love.

Just before my daughter was born, I made a promise to her and to myself. No matter how screwed up I was on the inside, she wouldn't pay the price for it and I would fight like hell to make sure we were normal in a way my family never was. Since I now understood the dynamics of my childhood, I could rise above them. In fact, I planned to become healthier than ever before. It's said that mental illness, like diabetes or glaucoma, is genetic. I vowed to prove that theory wrong. And for the better part of twenty years I've been able to keep that promise. And yet, strong as my conviction was back then, I confess it to be a shabby opponent in the face of the forces of middle age, forces that, paranoia aside, seem to be gathering together in a kind of cosmic, vengeful, midlife Perfect Storm. I find myself upended, tossed, and, worst of all, forced to consider that I've done no better at evolving than my mother. It's one thing to ceremoniously stop opening cans of Del Monte corn and start steaming my own fresh vegetables, organic if possible, or grab the Dove, fragrance-free, and not the Dial deodorant soap of my childhood. But eradicating the hidden and overt messages, the not-so-subtle manipulations, and the hurtful directives? Much trickier. Even items on the back shelves of long-term memory occasionally make their way to the front, especially if life happens to grab hold of the cabinet and rip it out of the wall.

I suspect that in my urgency to disassociate myself from the disturbing needs of my mother, I exorcised nothing, only ignored the infection, which now, after years of neglect, has evolved into a deep, festering, *active* toxic volcano. I don't know exactly what might be bubbling inside; I doubt that I will take an Uzi to the top of a tower or poison the drinking supply, but I do know I'm afraid. It's like a secret between me and me. On the outside is Eric's wife and the kids' mom, the PTO Class Mother, Chairperson of the Literary Circle for Kids, the woman who is doing everything right, but on the inside is the little girl who didn't escape, who is still trying to get it right and failing miserably and just one desperate act away from being exposed and vilified.

Last week there was a terrible smell in the kitchen, coming from the garbage, but I was on my way out and didn't have time to empty it, so I scrunched the top closed, went overboard with some Lysol spray, and left, returning hours later to a smell that hit me the minute I opened the door. That's the way it is with covering up: short-term gain, long-term price. You can disguise with perfume, but only for so long. It took me an hour to wash out the pail, and eventually I had to clean the whole cabinet to make the odor go away. Now, at almost forty-five, I'm wondering how long it might take to go back and disinfect a life. The perfume is no longer sufficient. The odors have taken over, poisoning even my dreams. I wake up in the middle of the night and say strange things to Eric, things like "You know, instead of Julie, they should have just named me Paxil."

TWO

a most dreaded cliché

Perhaps if I'd had an inkling of what the New Year would bring, I could have prepared, but having trained myself not to look for incoming clouds, I didn't. At the very least I could have ordered *The Complete Works of Dr. Phil* or at least a gift certificate to Yoga Express, the latest in a series of health oxymorons popping up all over suburbia. (Can you imagine trying to de-stress by rushing to a thirty-minute yoga class on your forty-five-minute lunch break? Naturally the place is wildly overbooked, and you have to reserve a spot a full day in advance.) I should have done something, I know, not just let the new year wash in like one more expected wave along a familiar shore. And yet there I was, me, with my famous emotional antennae and my sixth sense for doom, taken completely by surprise and turned into a most dreaded cliché, a poster child for the sandwich generation. Me, perpetually unable to resist food metaphors, coming to think of myself as an innocent piece of semisoft cheese slapped between two slices of female bread, one right out of the oven, the other a day old.

Here's just some of what was lost this year: one mother, one daughter (almost), one virginity, a sense of humor, our way. I've always been a lister. I like lists for the simple structure of them, so utilitarian and one-size-fits-all; they seduce you into imagining you can master the job. Whether it's Funeral Arrangements or Topics to Avoid with Your Teenage Son (two subjects on which I have become an expert), a list grabs the problem by the balls. Just think about the things people will list. Reasons Not to Commit Suicide (sad but true), My Best and Worst Attributes (self-help is an epidemic), People I've Slept With (for memory's sake, fun. For any other reason, as in "notification," less so.), Dreams I've Had Involving Oprah (in my case, eleven).

I should have known there was a problem from the last Oprah dream. I am always a huge success when I'm on *Oprah* in my sleep, either publishing a Pulitzer-worthy book of poems or making Oprah laugh. In the last one, the mood soured, and it was then that it all started to unravel, the normalcy, the façade, the glossy magazine cover that was Our Family and My Life.

"And so . . ." Oprah continues, leaning forward, breaking eye contact not to check her notes but to tilt her face skillfully open so that the audience feels they are a part of our discussion, included as if we were at tea: me, her, and a few hundred of our friends. It appears to be an effortless move, but I know such casualness is incredibly scripted.

"And so you truly had never heard the phrase 'sandwich generation,' even though you'd been a mother for twenty years and a daughter for more than double that?"

She is incredulous, turning fully to face the audience with an expression of disbelief and a little laugh that the audience dances to, murmuring their mutual suspicions like complimentary lunges and feints. "Hardly!" "Oh, c'mon!" "I don't think so!" A wave of shame washes over me, dripping from my cheeks down my neck and into my chest. First, I check to see if I am fat. Even though it's been over thirty years since I had a weight problem, sometimes my dreams get confused. Then I look to see if I am naked. I know that sometimes people are naked in their dreams, but once again, I needn't worry. I am not only thin, I am impeccably dressed; black pants, lemon-yellow cashmere sweater set, my new Coach leather satchel at my feet. An outfit my mother would be proud of. (Apparently her influence is so far-reaching that even in my dreams I don't dare don a pair of sweats. I will think of this later, not in the dream.) So I look good, no problems there. Still, this would be an excellent time to wake up. I am starting to hyperventilate and I can't think clearly at all, can't come up with a single coherent sentence to defend myself. I don't really want to hate Oprah, but I am beginning to feel unkindly toward her. I am thinking that despite her personal chef and sculpted trainer and diet secrets and some success managing her weight, she is still not wearing an appropriate outfit, she is still not black-Spandex-with-blue-stripes material. Somehow, Oprah hears my thoughts. She calls for security. So this is it, I think, my big crack-up. I knew it was only a matter of time. I don't even fight; just hang my head as the audience cheers. Oprah's boyfriend, Steadman, and her producer, Gail, escort me out. Only having never seen Steadman, in my dream he is Denzel Washington. I look for my family in the audience, but I can't find them. Eric is gone; my kids are nowhere to be found. I look for Amy and Beth, my best friends, and I can't understand why they aren't there. I know I would definitely invite them to come with me if I was on *Oprah*. I realize mournfully that since my true self has been revealed, my ugly, unstable self, everyone has abandoned me. My last thought as I am urged off the stage and before I wake up is that I've spent thirty years (since hearing the song "Society's Child" when I was fourteen) vowing to be color-blind, only to find myself so racially clichéd that the only successful black man I can conjure up when I'm asleep is Denzel.

THREE

the panic is palpable

I wake up from the dream lying on my back, confused. There is no Eric, and my mind is coalescing at unsettlingly slow speed. Bold stripes of sunlight form an intricate, unfamiliar graphic over two walls and across the ceiling above my head. I stare, unable to orient myself, then turn my head to the side and see the suitcase, my suitcase, on the floor. The Oprah ghosts linger and I think, *Chicago*? But there is something else; something instantly recognizable and it has never been to Chicago. It is the smell. Distinct, pervasive, unique to one place only, it is a combination I have spent years inhaling and eventually deciphering. Mothballs and Lemon Pledge. Even though this isn't the bed or even the house where I grew up, even though the sun is sneaking in through wooden shutters instead of sheer pink curtains, and the dog barking is not the hearty, dependable Shetland sheepdog of my youth but a rather anemic-sounding, pink-bellied ball of orange-stained white fur, I know instantly that I am in my parents' home. Mothballs and Lemon Pledge are my mother's signature smells, her staunchest allies against the evils of time and dullness. I stretch and sigh, uneasy. No wonder I had such an awful dream. I'll bet most people enjoy waking up in their parents' homes. That they feel cocooned and blissfully dependent, freed from the burdens of adulthood by a safe, sleep-inspired, childhood déjà vu. I feel something else entirely. Obligation. Duty. I know instantly that I am not nine or seventeen, not safely cuddled in blankets of "what's ahead" and "who knows," but firmly mired in middle age. In a few weeks I will be forty-five. And this is another one of my obligatory, semiannual trips to Florida. Three days of mother/daughter bonding centered on unnecessary shopping and forced fun. Three days of pretending that my mother and I have the kind of close relationship that the ever-meticulous, astoundingly perfect Estelle Berman publicizes. Of at least one thing I am sure: there will be lunches. Lunches are sacred rites to my mother, the mainstay of her lifestyle, as evidenced by what happens when you suggest a late breakfast or an early dinner.

"No *lunch*?" The panic is palpable. We usually plan early, at breakfast.

"So," she begins, deliciously warming to the task, "where shall we have lunch today?" If you want to make my mother really happy, you have to name various places so she can overrule them.

"How about Marino's?"

"It's gone down, the owner's having marital troubles."

"Lemongrass?"

"The last time I was there the tomatoes were hard."

"The club?"

"I thought we'd go to the club tomorrow . . . they have the most delicious tortilla soup on Thursday."

"Any place new?"

"Well, now that you mention it . . . Helen Ruskin mentioned a lovely new café in Palm Beach." Ahh. This is what my mother lives for, exposing me to the newest, trendiest salad boutiques on the East Coast. I wouldn't dare tell her that I view most of them with disdain, each one an obvious marketing attempt to seduce overdressed "snowbirds" in overpriced pastel couture into overpaying for increasingly desperate renditions of designer lettuce tossed with the tropical fruit *du jour*. All this delivered by affected

Latino maître d's suspiciously named Giancarlo. My mother customizes the names anyway. "Thank you, Johnny, dear, the papaya sprouts were just delightful."

My mother also has an unnatural obsession with fruit in her salad. It's not so much that she *likes* it, it's that she feels vindicated by it. When she and my dad first moved to Great Neck, she was invited to lunch by a popular Kings Point matron and was introduced to her first Waldorf salad, which contained apples. After that lunch she decided that all the best families would be serving fruit with their meals, and she was always trying to work it in. Lamb chops with stewed fruit gave way to spaghetti with ketchup and raisins and finally mashed potatoes with canned mandarin oranges. Luckily, we had a dog.

Sometimes we lost our minds and tried to tease her—well, sort of. It wasn't really worth it to try to discern just how far you could go before she'd turn red, bite her lip, and make you feel like the ungrateful wretch you secretly feared you were. My brothers were even wimpier than I was; being older, they took the escape route of dates, studying, and finally marriage to get away from that hot spot of emotional brainwashing, the dinner table. Naturally, when restaurants began sporting duck with bing cherries as regular fare, my mother wore a self-satisfied little smile, as if she'd known it was only a matter of time till we heathens caught up. When mango chicken hit, the excitement was almost too much. We were in her favorite restaurant, Yesterdays, in Fort Lauderdale. "Mangoes!" she exclaimed proudly, as if she'd been in on the very creation of them. "In the *chicken*." Then she felt faint and had to be escorted to the ladies' room (by me) so she could unbutton her shirt and press a cool paper towel to her chest.

ALL THESE MEMORIES are activated by a whiff of furniture polish and preservative. Before I even raise my head to face the day, I am resigned. I am the only daughter, and the only one of Estelle and Sol Berman's children without a *real job*. The demands of my life as Homemaker, School Volunteer, and Literary Club Chairperson do not qualify as real demands, even if they seem full-blown to me. The fact that my pilot program of a literary club for kids has been praised, copied, and now implemented in elementary schools countywide does not elicit nearly the applause afforded my two older brothers who are rigidly ensconced in suitably impressive careers: Stewie, as a tax attorney in Chappaqua, New York, and Lyle, as an investment analyst on Long Island's North Shore. It is I who am expected to make the trip, which I do, twice a year, in the fall and spring. And each time it is exactly the same. Each time the routine varies only by details such as whether or not it is too humid to eat outside or who in the Berman's golf community of Wood Palms West has divorced, become demented, or died. Each time, until today.

I DRAG MYSELF up to a sitting position. Although it is only 8:10 in the morning, the house is in motion. Outside, the engine in the gardener's mower, obviously on loan from the space program, becomes so loud that I involuntarily sit up before it can slice off my head. As the noise recedes, I hear the vacuum whirring, the washing machine switching cycles, the poodle yipping or perhaps gagging, my mother's heels as they click along the obligatory white ceramic tiles and her voice as she calls to Lourdes, the Peruvian cleaning lady. Actually, my mother does not call her Lourdes and never has. She finds it an imposition. The girl is in America and should learn to fit in. "It's not going to help her if I learn Spanish ways. As it is, I've had to teach her everything. When she first came she didn't even know how to self-clean the oven! Trust me, Jule, if you don't expect anything of them, that's exactly what you'll get." Therefore my mother calls her Lorie, an American nickname she thinks is more appropriate. "Lorie," I discover, since I do speak Spanish and have taken the time to ask, needs the job to help support her two daughters and a sick father and would answer to most anything I suspect. "Yes, Meesis!" I hear her respond, which, although I hate to side with my mother, is a bit irritating in that it seems to be the extent of the English she's learned in two years. My mother's theories do not surprise me.

Growing up, we had many housekeepers and invariably she would alter their names to suit her own sensibility. One such exchange haunts me. Co'reen, (accent on the first syllable) was a slim, quiet black woman from the Deep South. My mother told her it was better to have a name that was easier for people to say. Co'reen started to protest but my mother cut her off. She'd had an inspiration, a seamlessly transitional name, Corinne. Corinne was preferable, she urged, mistaking the woman's silence for acquiescence. To me, she confided that she was relieved to have the matter settled.

"How would I ever have been able to call her that?" she wondered. "Coren, coo-ren, what was it?"

"*Co*'reen."

"No, I don't think you're saying it right either. Anyway, this is much better. It makes sense. Like Corinne Levine, the secretary at the temple, or Corinne Gartner, my canasta teacher." Except it didn't make sense to Co'reen. She left abruptly after one week, taking her indignation and two small pitchers from the sterling silver tea service with her. Which, my mother said, proved her point.

As I PAD into the kitchen amid the whirring and clicking, I have to sidestep the apoplectic toy poodle who is snarling at the poor gardener on the other side of the picture window. I pray for just five blissfully oblivious minutes to nurse my coffee and flip through the *Miami Herald*. I have a moment of guilt when I smell the coffee: hazelnut. She has remembered it's my favorite, or, as my daughter would say, my obsession. My mother has been drinking Instant Sanka for years and only makes a pot of coffee for guests, so the brewed hazelnut is a big deal. I smile as I pour myself a cup and sit down in the bright yellow breakfast nook. "Gretel! Stop that!" my mother snaps at the poodle, who whimpers, gives one more half-hearted bark, and stalks off. Then she turns back to me, all smiles. "Good morning, dear, how did you sleep?" This is not a nicety; it's a test. If you don't sleep well in Estelle Berman's house, she's quite surprised. She will double-check that the shades were drawn, the thermostat was working, and the mattress didn't inexplicably deflate between the time she checked it for the fifth time before your arrival and the time you actually lay down. If all is in order she will conclude that the problem must lie with you, with some defect in your inner clock or some inability on your part to appropriately relax. "Perfect." I offer it, as a gift. "Didn't wake up once." My mother visibly relaxes. "Oh, and thanks for the coffee, smells delicious." I take a sip. "Mmmm." I'm making her day. She's jubilant. I've slept well *and* noticed the coffee. I reach for a section of the paper and smile to myself. If only it was always this easy. I steal a glance at her across the table. She is already dressed for the day in white slacks and a matching red sweater set. I can't help noticing that her glasses, earrings, and lipstick are exactly the same shade of red as her sweater, and she smells so delicious that between the hazelnut and her perfume I feel like I've walked into Sephora. I turn away. It is just too early to take stock of her; she is too bright and shiny. Still, her clothing rituals awe me. It is not just that she makes lists of outfits to wear on vacation (these are actual lists, I've seen them) and keeps a record of outfits she's worn for occasions ranging from bar mitzvahs to funerals, but she has this habit of going monochromatic. She'll start with a coral suit and dyed coral shoes, then add a light coral bag, dark coral jewelry, and even peachy coral lipstick. But the real weird part is when we get to the restaurant. She'll order cantaloupe, or carrot soup, and penne in pink sauce or poached salmon. Once I pointed it out to her.

"Um, Mom, did you happen to notice that you're deeply involved with the color orange today?"

"Am I? Oh, Jules, you're overreacting." She grabs her bag and pops an orange Tic Tac into her mouth.

"Well, you know you're wearing everything orange and you're only eating orange food and you seem to be, well, stuck on orange."

My mother looks at her food and back at me.

"For your information, there were *red* sun-dried tomatoes in the pasta, and pasta itself is rather neutral, don't you think, although I suppose it does absorb the sauce . . ." She trails off, thinking, lost for a moment, and I am silent, watching her, waiting. Suddenly she snaps out of it. "What? Oh yes, well"—she looks down—"well, this suit is not orange, it's pumpkin or russet. Really Julie, may I ask why you have such a need to pick on me?"

So this morning I avert my eyes quickly, but not so quickly that I miss her standard signs of nervousness. I realize that I will not even make it through page two in peace, not with the hair-twisting, lip-biting, and finger-tapping that is creating a small symphony to my left. I purposely do not ask if anything is wrong, and pretend to read. When I hear my dad coming down the hall, I watch him enter, head down, shuffling slightly. He is not sleepy or feeble, but purposeful in his attempt to navigate the way, because his eyes are rapidly failing due to misdiagnosed glaucoma. "Misdiagnosed" is my parents' press release *du jour*, and this month they blame the doctor, even though my dad concedes that he ignored certain obvious signs (just some small signs like not being able to see to the left or right anymore). My belief is that he is so programmed to attend to my mother that neither one of them would even think to tune in to him. Now he has deteriorated past tunnel vision into actual legal blindness and is severely hampered by all side lighting. He enters the kitchen without seeing me and is immediately busy at the counter. I am completely overwhelmed with love. It is a familiar reaction. We were never close in the traditional way, never shared intimate father-daughter moments or even many activities. There were no bike rides or baseball catches; he had been-there-done-that with the boys. I was a different creature, alien, a girl. Still, I have come to think of him as the good one, or at least the gentle one.

This morning, in contrast to my mother, my dad wears a hodgepodge of his favorite items. Blue bathing suit, his "trunks" as he calls them, short-sleeved yellow shirt with a pocket for his tissues and eyedrops, black socks on his feet pulled up high onto his bony, blue-mottled calves, sunglasses to keep out the glare, and his trademark, the ever-present visor on his head. This one says Pfizer Chemical. I think he looks like an aging croupier who might work the blackjack table on an assisted-living cruise ship. ("Hold on there, Mrs. Hufnagel, you don't wanna separate nines! Somebody check her oxygen!") But he is humming as he begins to pour a variety of unidentifiable substances into what appears to be a brand-new blender. I wonder at the concoction, there are so many bottles, and I believe he has put both salt and sugar into the mix, but before I can open my mouth to ask, he secures the top and presses a button and the machine roars deafeningly to life. My mother is up in a flash. She hurries into the kitchen, looks at the mess, presses another button, and the noise stops.

"Oh, Sol, please! You're going to kill me before the cancer."

This, followed by a gasp and a hand to the mouth, a very long, silent pause punctuated only by a husband following his wife's gaze and becoming aware that his daughter is in the room. Well, I think to myself, well. But no other thoughts come. My mother is still silent, while my father shakes his head and looks at her as if to say, "Now see what you've done," and still I am not quite able to process what I've heard. Instead, I look admiringly at this man who gave me life. He can no longer tell the sugar from the salt, but he knows a gaffe when he hears it. In this gaping silence I have the strangest thought: I want one of the large cheese Danish I saw on the counter next to the fridge. I am horrified by this, of course, chastise myself and check to see if anyone's noticed. Before I can recover, my mother grabs my father's elbow, turns to me, and commands, "Don't say a word. We'll be right back." With this, she turns my father toward the living room and escorts him out, leaving me dumbfounded and too stunned to protest. I am unable to form a cohesive thought, let alone protest. Outside, through the picture window, I can see the pool, the perfect blue sky and waxy green Bermuda grass. I can feel the heat, that April-in-Florida heat. I felt it last night outside the airport, getting into the cab, heavy and weighted, heat that even darkness and a cool breeze or, for that matter, a perfectly programmed central air-conditioning system set precisely at sixty-eight degrees can't dispel.

The patio is landscaped to the max, a jungle of vegetation, and is an extension of an abundant foliage scheme that begins inside. The house is bursting with plants, all kinds. Great tropical trees in oriental urns on carved mahogany stands, their trunks the thickness and coloration of pineapples, and thin, willowy palms planted three to a pot, flanking the doors. Clusters of low, profuse shrubs, some flowering, others merely fanning out, ferns, corns, prickly cactus, and pungent hibiscus, all of them gorgeous, emerge at strategic locations, "accidentally on purpose" the decorator says, to soften a corner or warm a pathway. The plants are all thriving, thanks to Phyliss of Chlora-Phyliss, a weekly plant service. After losing two specimen Anthereum and a Desert Bloom orchid last year, my mother hired a certified expert to maintain her "tropical family." In the kitchen, on the shelf above the sink, is an aloe in a small terra-cotta pot. It is about a foot high and its name is Moises. Apparently there's a baseball player named Moises Alou, which sounds like Aloe to my parents. The aloe is always on active duty. Every time my mother gets a burn she makes a small slit in one of its fronds and joyfully carves out a clear, gooey substance to use as a salve. For that one moment she is a Jewish Clara Barton, nursing off the land. Upon further inspection I see that Moises is covered in slits. I think he must be running out of veins. The reason my mother continually burns herself is unclear to all of us, but she consistently becomes distracted when cooking and suddenly has to fling open the oven to save the roast or lunge for a pot on the stove before it erupts. Oh, and the oven has a name, too. She thinks it doesn't like her, that it's anti-Semitic because it's made in Germany, so she calls it Eva Braun. Before today I never thought this little game my parents have of naming the household items was actually irrational—quirky maybe, but not crazy. Now, as I sit and wait for them to return, I'm not so sure. I don't remember the appliances having personalities when we were growing up. I wonder when it occurred to my parents that they should.

Outside, the pool is bubbling slightly and I see the automatic pool cleaner swirling around inside. This white plastic motor also has a name—two, in fact. It's actually had a formal name change. At first they called it Polly, short for the manufacturer's brand name, Polaris. But then it got temperamental, spurted the water out in short drips instead of a steady stream, tangled itself up, and hugged the filter near the steps, so they changed its name to Her Highness. From my seat in the breakfast room I can see that, as my dad would say, "Her Highness is touchy this morning." She is flailing about the pool in obvious agitation that is beginning to match my own. I want to call my dad and have him calm her down the way he calms us all. As I grew up and began to unravel my mother's ministrations and scrutinize her theories, I came to regret that he was relegated to a supporting role in my life. With that regret came anger at his loyalty to *her*. When I was little I used to wait for the moment when he would finally explode, or at least admonish my mother for being oversensitive or unreasonable, but that moment never came. I denied the names my brothers used—*pushover, pussy-whipped*—but I shamefully feared they were right. She ran the show, managed their lives, decided whom they'd see, where they'd go, and when. How did he stand it? For all her aspirations to high society, she remained a ghetto girl, limited by the familiar. My dad wanted to travel exotically, to Africa or South America or Asia. They could more than afford it, but she refused to go. With a wave of her hand she dismissed the idea as "an invitation to disease." He wanted to own an apartment in the city so they could spend weekends seeing shows and going to museums, but she refused to leave her suburban home. "Why would I trade my beautiful backyard and garden for that noise and pollution?" And when he begged her to take up golf so they could play together, she claimed a bad back. "I need two Bufferin just from sitting to get my nails done, Sol, you want me start swinging clubs all day?" Their relationship has had so much influence on my own. For our honeymoon, Eric wanted to go to the Galápagos Islands and swim with the sea lions or some such thing. I agreed, not for any real undersea desire, but so as *not* to be my mother, and it was only some biological or ecosystem imbalance that closed the area to tourists that saved me. Instead, we experienced Machu Picchu, the Lost City of the Incas, which was quite enough of an adventure, thank you. The Peruvian wilderness is not my idea of romance, but I assume it was better than sea slime.

Over time I became less angry with my dad, more realistic. I began to appreciate his blandness, in a way. It was so un-grating that it was comforting. You could rely on it. If he had engaged in his own mood swings and turbulent tirades, I doubt I would have survived. But he never wavered in his calmness, absorbing the neuroses, my tantrums, and the boys' moodiness without complaint. It wasn't as if he was a fellow soldier, a compatriot, I made that mistake once when I tried to enlist him against her and he shot me down.

"She's crazy!" I was shouting and pacing, stamping my feet around my bedroom as if I wanted to break the floor with my fuzzy pink slippers.

"That's enough, Julie. Do not talk about your mother that way."

"But, Daddy, I'm fourteen years old. I'm not marrying him, for God's sake. Ooooh! I can't take it, I swear!" I took a throw pillow from my bed. It was shaped like a one-way sign, black and white, and it was overstuffed and hard, and I hurled it across the room. It hit the red lacquered armoire that held books on shelves at the top and clothes in drawers at the bottom. We heard the books inside fall down. I felt some satisfaction in that.

"There. Are you feeling better now?" He sat down on the bed with a sigh.

"No," I said, but only halfheartedly. I sat down next to him, crossed my legs Indian style, and hugged them to my chest around another pillow, a stop sign.

"Everyone exchanges ID bracelets. It doesn't mean anything, really, it just means we like each other. Last week I had Neil Lane's, and over the summer it was David Greenman's."

A remarkable thing had happened during the summer of my fourteenth year at camp. Puberty. As my body began to change, my appetite diminished, and instead of sucking down Oreos I began to seek and relish the praise and compliments of my peers. I had been the pudgiest of preteens, a source of endless embarrassment to my mother, but that summer in camp I lost my pudge and sprouted breasts and became not only a girl, but also one of the girls. We read *Love Story* and listened to Donovan and dreamed about our very own Ryan O'Neal. Karen Goodgold insisted that we practice saying "Shut the fuck up," over and over again on her tape recorder to see who sounded the most authentic. We begged the counselors to bring back cans of Tab and packs of Marlboros and, blissfully unaware of skin cancer, we spent every spare minute tanning with oversized sun reflectors on the baseball field behind our cabin. By the beginning of ninth grade I'd traded in my retainer for tampons, and the guys noticed my new figure. My mother, who was at first gleeful, became wary of the attention it sparked from the opposite sex.

"Well, your mother seems to think it means more. That it means you're going steady."

"So? What's wrong with that?"

"She thinks you're too young for that."

"Why?"

"I don't know why, that's your mother's department. She loves you and she wants what's best for you."

"Right."

"Jules, I don't like that tone."

"Oh, sure, *she* can say anything she wants. She can *do* anything she wants, too." My voice was choppy and accusing. "Like just *take* Richard Geller's bracelet out of *my* room and return it to his mother without asking me, or—" I could feel myself getting a little out of control, but I couldn't stop. I stood up and lashed out at him. "Or make *you* go to her Leukemia Society Ball, which I know you do not want to do because it's your gin rummy night and you have to rent a tux and you hate that Carl Estrich!"

There. I'd said it. I had overheard their conversation the night before. Well, I had sort of purposely overheard it since their bedroom door was partially open and I couldn't sleep because I couldn't stop thinking about how amazing it felt when Richard Geller reached for my hand at the ice rink on Friday night and slid his silver ID bracelet, all smooth and cool and slippery, into my hand. I still had a little trouble breathing when I thought about it. Now I stood there, hands on hips, every particle of my fourteen-year-old person shaking with challenge. But I had gone too far. My dad stood up and his voice became uncharacteristically hard.

"This conversation is over. You will do what your mother says and you will mind your own business and may I remind you that I love your mother very much and I will not hear you talk disrespectfully about her at any time. Good night."

And he walked out the door. I didn't exactly feel betrayed, because I'd never really thought he was on my side to begin with, but I got the message and I never tried to get him on my side again. Even through my disappointment, I was impressed. He never even flinched in his defense of her; you had to admire that kind of devotion. Or love.

And as much time as I've spent trying to run from every speck of my mother's emotional legacy, I've spent just as much time trying to find that kind of love. After I discovered that my body was a source of interest to boys, I became heady with all the attention. At first I flirted and teased and enjoyed a little harmless petting like everyone else. The boys were so needy, literally begging for more, and being desired was more than intoxicating, it was addictive, even better than the sugar high of a hidden stash of Twinkies. Each year in high school I went further and further, and though I don't think I was afraid that saying no would lead to rejection, I had been trained to please, I enjoyed being able to give so much pleasure. Here was this moaning, pleading, adorable human being, and I could make him so happy with so little. I thought I was like Joan of Arc or Eleanor Roosevelt, a true hero. By the end of high school I'd developed a nasty little reputation, although the truth is that I never went all the way with any of them. Instead, I had a sort of warped, individualized value system. If I used my hands or my mouth but there was no vaginal penetration, it wasn't sex. (Now known as the Bill Clinton Theory.) This went on for years. I kept thinking that one of these casual sexual trysts would metamorphose into true love because I was so giving, but it never did. The guys always left. Sometimes they would show up months later and beg for a quickie blow job, and sometimes I actually complied. Years of emptiness were still not enough to convince me that this method wouldn't lead to wholeness or love. My parents never suspected my promiscuity. By the time I went away to college, it was easy to pretend that I was a normal student. I'd lost contact with most of my friends from home and made very few at college, but my parents assumed that this was due to my going to school in the Midwest. Occasionally, reality intervened. There was the rock concert in '76. I was home for the summer and recklessly decided to sneak a boy into my bedroom when he brought me home. My mother caught us and screamed. Literally screamed. She didn't talk to me for a week, never even broached the subject. Later that summer, while doing the laundry, she found a joint in my pocket and we lost her for two days. She refused to get out of bed. I would peek in every few hours to see if she was all right, only to find her still in her nightgown, mascara smudges dramatically untouched by her trusty tub of Pond's cold cream, brochures for residential drug treatment centers in places like Provo and Quechee fanned out on the quilt.

By my last year in college I was bored, tired, and probably depressed, but I couldn't make the connection that my efforts to please everyone always failed to please me. I was so unsure of who to be that I somewhat ceased to be at all. I went through the motions, but that's all. I ate only out of need, and didn't date at all. Of course, that was exactly when I met Eric. He was my salvation, literally. I was a mess, but for some reason he interpreted my silences for calm, my reserved demeanor for composure. And as Eric began to court me, to want me, to fall in love with me, I began to renew. I began to believe I could be that girl he saw. And although he would never arbitrarily side with me over the kids (we're both too evolved for that!), I have to admit that Eric's allegiance to me is as strong as my dad's to my mom. Of course, Eric doesn't know the real me. Not the fat me, or the promiscuous me, or the ready-to-self-destruct-at-any-minute me. For twenty-two years he's seen the charade, the good mother and wife, the reasonable partner. I've done such a good job at simulating a well-adjusted person, I've begun to believe it's who I really am. There are no taboo subjects, no hysterical pronouncements, in our family we talk every issue to death, explore every person's motives, all possible angles. Even the kids participate in this analysis (well, Jake used to, before he developed the social skills of a CIA operative). But being with my dad brings up all kinds of fears and I wonder about Eric, even after twenty-two years. If he knew the real me, would he be so devoted? My dad knows exactly who my mom is, and he is content. He gets something from her that he needs, and though this baffles me, at least it's the truth. But Eric only knows the face I've let him see, the front.

When my parents come back into the kitchen, they are a united front. They stand at the counter together, facing me. My father looks grim; my mother wears a tight smile. She seems to be bracing herself for impact.

"Well, you must have some questions," she offers. "Go ahead, ask away."

Unbelievable. We have no displays of emotion. No tears, no hugging. Instead, we have a panel. Like a senate hearing. Or a game show. *Well, Alex, I'll take Debilitating Diseases for $100.* No choice but to play.

"Okay, let's take this from the top. You have cancer?"

"I don't want you to tell the children."

On some level I know this is not the right response, not the answer to my question, although it is. My mother has spit these words out, both confirming the news and avoiding it all at the same time. Still, the non sequitur sparks an image of my daughter, twenty-year-old Alexis at Branford College in upstate New York. She and my mother have a close relationship, the kind that transcends the generation gap, the kind that my mother and I do not have, but for which I continue to strive. Alexis, that rare confection of Drama Queen and Social Scientist, would be crushed to learn that there was something wrong with her Grammy, let alone something fatal. For all her maturity, my daughter remains solidly in denial that she or anyone she loves is mortal, won't even consider the concept. Yet she handles her grandmother with an ease I never could, undisturbed by her thinly veiled criticism or jabs. If my mother suggests that it might be cold, Alexis runs in to get a sweater; if Alexis picks a movie and Grammy wrinkles her nose, she'll whisper, "Oh, Gram, I really didn't want to see that, either." No matter what gift my mother sends, Alexis always gushes that it's perfect. It could be two sizes too big or her least favorite color, she still tells my mother it's perfect. Later, in private, when I address her as "Miss Gumby," she says, "Oh, Mom, she means well, I don't want to hurt her feelings." For her compliance, Alexis is rewarded with her grandmother's unending, boundless devotion. When they are together, my mother absentmindedly pets her—really pets her, rubbing her hair, her back, or her arm the way she strokes Gretel the Nazi poodle, all the while telling her that she is the most talented, beautiful, delicious girl in the whole world. And while this love fest goes on, I, of course, am at the nearest mall, returning and exchanging the grossly *imper-fect* gifts. This is not an arrangement that Alexis imagines as changeable or vulnerable, so naturally the idea of having to tell her Grammy's news is upsetting. And my son? At sixteen, he would hurt, too, but we'd never see it. Jake has dissolved into a full-blown, typical male adolescent whose dia-logue has regressed to unintelligible grunting and who Eric and I barely see, except, like a great grizzly, at feeding time.

But this is not important, not now. My mother, whose shoes are tucked into symmetrical seclusion, each pair visible in its own clear box, whose vases are filled not with water, which turns and discolors, but with smooth, iridescent marbles that perpetually shimmer, whose terra-cotta tiles remain eternally grouted because they are painstakingly scrubbed by only soft-bristled, gently used toothbrushes, obviously has cancer. Ugly, uncontrolled, mutating cancer. It is almost unimaginable. I think perhaps I will laugh at what is seriously the worst joke in the poorest taste. But something stops me. Possibly it is the bottle of shark cartilage in my father's hands or more likely the naked look of despair on my mother's face that even her little smile can't hide. One thing I do know is that I am seeing both for the very first time.

FOUR

one less folding chair this year

By ten-thirty we have muddled through all the obligatory material. "When did you . . ." "How did you . . ." and the dreaded "How long do you . . ." This last question has no definitive answer, but the statistics are not good. Estelle Berman has pancreatic cancer, a "bad" cancer, not one you're likely to see on the list of Top Ten Most Likely Cancers to Beat. Yes, my brothers know. No, they weren't allowed to tell me because my mother was afraid of how I would take the news. I think this over and am unsure whether to be flattered or insulted. Either I am the most loving daughter, who will be totally devastated, or a fragile child who will not be able to bear up. But what is this about the kids? She doesn't want any of the grandchildren to know? When exactly *am* I supposed to tell my children? A week? A month? How about over the holidays? That might work. I could just casually say, "Oh, Jake, bring up the nice folding chairs, and Lexie, help me get that coffeepot down and by the way Grammy is dead. That's right, Jake, one less folding chair this year."

I have already had that cheese Danish I wanted, as well as a brownie, followed by two Excedrin Migraine. Now, after two more cups of coffee and three pieces of Orbit gum, my stomach is speaking in foreign tongues. I need to calm down, to do something productive, like make a list. Medical Connections, Plan for Beating Mom's Cancer, anything will do. My mind is both a magnet and a sieve. Thoughts are flying in and out like midday at LaGuardia Airport. Naturally they will come to New Jersey and explore the various treatments in New York City. Is Steve Rosen still the head of anesthesiology at Mount Sinai? What about Ken Kaplan and his connections at Maimonides? Does Jake have a tennis tournament this Friday? How many calories are in one cheese Danish? I am wondering if there are fresh sheets in the guest bedroom when my mother announces that she will not be undergoing chemotherapy or radiation.

"Excuse me?"

"No, dear, Dr. Palmer has assured me that when the time comes there will be no torturous procedures, no bruises from repeated IVs, nothing . . ." She searches for the right word ". . . disgusting."

"When the time comes?"

"Yes, exactly. I'll be right here in my lovely home with Daddy and Gretel." She bends down and scoops up the toy poodle, who wheezes when picked up and looks to be suffering from some sort of canine cancer of her own. Her eyes are watery black and runny, oozing a gummy gunk. The gunk hardens into black scabs that adhere to the fur beneath the lower lids. My mother does not notice. She can spot a run in my sweater at thirty paces, but Gretel's toxic leakage is okay. Lucky dog. I realize I have sunk to a new low, engaging in sibling rivalry with the family pet as my mother details her exit from the world. She is methodically stroking the dog as she speaks, but her cadence belies the calm acceptance she professes. Soon she is less stroking Gretel than kneading her, and finally the poodle, in obvious discomfort, gives a little yelp and leaps to the floor. My mother is startled. She looks down at her hands, seems to realize that they are the culprits, and as she begins to massage each finger, I stand up to go to her. I need to touch her, hold her, swaddle her even. But as I approach she stiffens, sits up straight, holds up a hand to stop me, and resumes her speech.

Her tone is flat but firm. "Soft sheets," she states. "Five-hundred count. That's a priority. Soft sheets on the bed and flowers on the nightstand and what else . . . ? Oh yes, my nightgowns. Not those stiff paper smocks with strings in the back. Speaking of paper, did I show you the new grass cloth for the bedroom walls? It's called Old-fashioned Butter, and it's the most perfect shade of pale cream." I'm listening to my mother but staring at the poodle. Gretel has retreated to a quilted cushion in the corner, where she is licking her little paw, biting it really, and looking scornful.

"Mom, are you serious? You're concerned with the sheets and the flowers when your time comes?" Without thinking I add, "Do you think you're about to give birth?"

My mother purses her lips, shocked, and my dad is quick to snap, "Jules, that's enough!"

I am instantly sorry. Before I can say so, my mother speaks.

"No, no, it's not her fault, it's all this unpleasantness. Honey, let's not talk about this anymore. There's a new makeup boutique in the Palm Centre that I want you to see, and Muriel is there. You remember Muriel, don't you? She used to give pedicures at Franco's, but now she is practically famous for a natural line of cosmetics—"

"Mom—" I have to interrupt the rambling, but I will try to be more sensitive. "Mom, I really think you have to at least explore some type of treatment."

"She uses fruits as the base. It's delicious. Have you ever smelled a product that's eighty-percent grapefruit?"

"Mom, what are you talking about? Citrus? Fruit? You need to face this."

"I DON'T HAVE TO FACE ANYTHING!" Now she is standing and yelling and shaking. "I WANT TO TAKE YOU FOR MAKEUP, OKAY?"

I am stunned. My mother doesn't yell. A lady never yells. She has mentioned that only about a million times since I was three years old. A lady never yells or makes a scene or sweats ("perspires" she would say), but she is doing all three. She cannot stop.

"WE'LL GET OUR EYEBROWS TWEEZED AND YOU NEED SOME NEW BLUSH—THAT COLOR IS ALL WRONG FOR YOU— AND I WILL BUY A NAVY EYELINER! OKAY? IS THAT TOO MUCH TO ASK?"

Estelle Berman, wife, mother, homeowner, gardener extraordinaire, duplicate bridge champion, former president of the Ladies' Auxiliary of the Leukemia Society of America, and current recording secretary for the Wood Palms West Audubon Society of Greater Broward County, is losing it.

"Daddy?" I whisper.

Silence. He is not Daddy right now, not even the background Daddy I remember. He is merely a human male with more years in the past than in the future: He is a former real-estate executive, former gin rummy champ, husband of fifty-five years, who is losing both his vision and his wife. Suddenly I am aware that it will take all his strength to see her through this. He shrugs and rises, reaches out to grasp my mother's shoulders. She has tears in her eyes, but she allows his touch. Deflated, she slumps back into the chair.

"Jules, your mother and I have been over this. She doesn't want any pain. She doesn't want hospitals and needles."

"And hair loss and nausea." My mother sniffles, quieter but still shaking as she uses a napkin to wipe the smudged mascara from under her eyes. I try to understand, but nothing makes sense. The aspirin and sugar have made me racy and edgy, and an hour of maniacal gum-chewing has left me with a throbbing jaw. My parents are firm in their conviction to do nothing. I take deep breaths and will myself toward composure, and it begins to work. Still my frustration and outrage remain, like an air bag fitting nicely between the news and my fear. I have the sense that we are not unique but timeless characters in an Albee play, spouting practiced lies on perfect living room chairs while all our wormy dysfunctions squirm just beneath the glossy suburban surface. My mother wants to downplay, I struggle not to harangue, and my father just wants everyone to be happy, and we are all facing death the way we've faced life, civilly, pleasantly. Of all the bizarre moments I've spent as a daughter, I think this might be the ultimate. My mother has cancer. Bad cancer. As opposed to a good one. And instead of discussing how to save her life, we are going to make plans for smoother skin.

At this moment my cell phone rings. I take it as a sign from God. Whoever is on the phone will know what to do.

"Hello?" I am tentative. I do not want to sound too aggressive in case it is the Almighty.

"Julie?" Soft, crooning, sexual. Totally unfamiliar.

"Who's this?" I cup the phone secretively and stand up, automatically, although I've nothing to hide.

"Is this the sexiest soccer mom in the tri-state area?" Ah, recognition. Ted Ruben is the Suburban Life editor of the North Jersey newspaper *Suburban Sentinel*. He is attractive, witty, and single—a dangerous combination if you're the type to be easily tempted, which thank God I haven't been for over twenty years. I met Ted when the paper did a story on the Literary Club. He was intrigued by the lengthy poems I sent home to recap the stories and the kids' discussions. While the poems were quite a hit with the students and their parents, I never dreamed that they would be printworthy, but Ted loved them, even encouraged me to write more and try to have them published, something I've considered but have so far been afraid to do. Since then, Ted had managed to pop into my life every so often, not altogether serendipitously I suspect. Usually I get a harmless thrill from his calls, a mixture of overt compliments and more subtle come-ons. But his timing is off.

"Uh, Ted, this is a bad time, I'm out of town right now." He is all jovial and light.

"Nothing deadly serious, I hope?" Silence. I don't know how to answer that.

"Oh shit, Jule, I'm sorry. Something's really wrong?"

"Yeah, well, sort of, I mean my mom . . ." I glance back toward the kitchen.

"Geez, are you at a funeral?"

"What? No, no, not yet. I mean, oh God, that sounded awful. Look, I have to go. I'll be back in a couple of days."

"Okay, hon, take your time, I'm sorry. But listen, call me as soon as you get back. There's something very exciting going on, and I think you'd be perfect for it." Something in Ted's voice tells me this isn't another one of his lame attempts to get me to lunch. Despite everything else, I feel a little stab of curiosity and excitement. Is there a position opening up for assistant to the Children's Editor? A special issue with poems about kids? Or is it just a knee-jerk reaction to Ted's blond, playful looks, to the fact that there is no hint of his forty-eight years anywhere on his fit body except those damned adorable laugh lines at his eyes, and the knowledge that those looks often express blatant infatuation for me?

I CLOSE THE PHONE and long for home, to get away from this hotbed of psychological spelunking and set myself back down on the solid, suburban landscape that is my life, a landscape I truly adore, despite its widely criticized flaws of competitive yuppie fervor and conservative domestic values. I flourish there, amid the tennis lessons and the mega-malls and my little attempts at a writing career, in the Friday-night wait at the local Italian restaurant or on line for sushi at the A&P, but most of all amid the easy rhythms of a marriage to the same guy for twenty-two years and the achievements of everything I promised to myself: a normal, happy family. There is a peace, some might say an anesthetic, but I know where I stand. At 8:00 p.m. on the first Tuesday of each month, in the senior cafeteria of the high school where the PTO meets, my opinions are sought out. At the post office and the deli and the pharmacy, I am greeted with a smile, someone asks about the kids, the dog, or last week's flu, and someone else compliments me on my hair. And in my writing group and my golf clinic and my birthday lunch club, I am an enviable size eight. I know I've invented this comfortable womb, surrounded myself with people who don't assume my few flaws will be my undoing since I've hidden my big flaws and actually created the creature my mother always envisioned, but it works. I might even go so far as to say I'm happy. And I suppose it will all still be there when I get back. But I am not too disappointed when later in the day we reach a compromise that includes my parents' promise to at least explore treatments in New York and a suggestion that we cut this visit short. By the next morning, one lunch and two fruit facials later, I am in the cab on the way to the airport.

They will fly up next week. By then I will have researched various doctors and made appointments; they will keep an open mind and then decide what to do. Real interpretation: They will take the information to Elaine Mendelson's genius-doctor son, Jerry, who is head of something at Mount Somewhere. It is Dr. Jerry's advice that means the most to my mom. She consults him on all things medical, from Q-Tip safety to colonoscopy. After all, she's known him "since before he was born," which presumably qualifies him to chart her last course on earth.

FIVE

I am now Mommy

On the way to the airport, in the blissful backseat of the cab, my cell phone rings, and I am surprised to see Alexis's area code on the little screen. Not just because she is NEVER, EVER awake before noon, but because I am instantly convinced that cell phones are the New Age conductors of ESP. We have had a mother-daughter spiritual connection and since she has been compelled to call me, I think perhaps I should speak to her about Grams after all.

"Lex?" I whisper instinctively, even though I have been awake for hours.

"Goood MORning!" It is a singsong salutation that is way too energetic for 8:30 a.m. on a Sunday. Perhaps she never went to bed? I try to remember college bars and frat parties. "Mom, listen," she begins. Instantly I realize she has not called because of spiritual vibrations, and I feel a tug of sadness that quickly turns into familiar dread. Lexie is often the bearer of big news, dramatic proclamations, and passionate surprises, in part because she has a gift for making even the most mundane information sound like news (I slept through the entire night and didn't wake up once!), and in part because we allow it. She has the emotional elbow room I never had, elbow room I must have cultivated subconsciously in my efforts to be non-neurotic and allow her to individuate. This falls under the heading of Be Careful What You Wish For. Since her early teens, Lexie's ability to access a repertoire of personae has been both impressive and schizophrenic. There are no certainties, no constants. She is at once in desperate need of a pair of designer jeans and shortly thereafter compelled to sleep outside overnight on Main Street in Dewitt, New York, to experience the plight of the homeless. And although I should be used to it, to the duality, I never am. Raising Lexie is like slowly eating a value-sized jar of gourmet jelly beans, there's a certain leap of faith each time you partake; the red ones might just as easily be cinnamon as cherry, and sometimes the coffee-colored ones are really root beer, which I dislike, or, worse, licorice, which I detest. I have learned to absorb her phone calls in a half-frozen state of amorphous dread. I have learned to expect licorice.

"Oh, Mom, something wonderful has happened, but you might freak out at first, so just listen to me before you say anything, okay? Is Dad there? Maybe I better talk to Dad first, except, I don't know, it might be better if you tell him."

I will not stop breathing. I will purse my lips and force the air into the back of my throat, down my windpipe and into my lungs.

"Mom? Mom, are you still there?"

One breath, two. Ah, I remember.

"I'm here. I'm listening . . . I think."

"Mom, remember I told you about my Comparative Literature professor? The really cute one with the bloodhound and the blue eyes, you know, I said he sort of looked like Brad Pitt, but in a kind of preppie way, not, like, a movie-star way, you know, well, do you remember?"

I nod, because I think I actually do remember her telling me something about a cute professor, but of course she can't see me nodding, which is good, because I am also grimacing. It has taken only a second for me to grow certain that she is pregnant with a married professor's baby and wants to have it and name it Kipling Thackeray Pitt.

"Mom, are you there?"

"Um-hmm." It is a sound, not quite a word, but it is all that I can manage.

"Okay, listen. We've gotten, well, *close*, this semester, because he's going through a really rough divorce. His wife is this bitch who doesn't want kids and thinks he should do more than be a college professor, and, well, he says I'm really easy to talk to, which is so true, you know how everyone thinks so, and actually sometimes I tell him about you and Daddy and how you try to communicate and, well, anyway, I've been meeting him for coffee and stuff, and oh, I also help him with his novel, and then suddenly, today, he makes this big announcement. Are you ready?"

I am never ready. I always try hard to be ready and I am trying really hard now, but as usual, I am failing. Mostly I am trying to think like me and not like my mother, to separate myself again and be me, whoever that is, and I am wondering what I would say if I were me, which of course I am, but it does not help. Instead, I end up wishing that my daughter would care about making me happy instead of herself, the way I had to at her age, and I am simultaneously horrified and guilty and so I start yelling at myself for wanting the unthinkable to repeat itself.

"G-go on." A scared little voice, I suddenly have. It is not a ready voice.

"Mom, you sound funny. I knew you wouldn't be able to handle this. I haven't even told you the really amazing part yet and already you are falling apart. You know, I can't always live this perfect little life for you, Mother."

And there it is, she has said it. The worst of all possible accusations. My daughter has implied that I am my mother, but instead of being devastated I am energized. I suddenly realize that my clever little girl is playing me better than anyone else could. She is setting me up, and suddenly

I breathe a full, cleansing breath and I know that it has not been a waste, all the self-analytical crap I read, all the damn growth. I have evolved into what I'm not sure, but out of something closed and limiting. Not all of me is fake. I can access control. I morph back into Mom, and my mom's voice is firm, knowing, rational.

"Alexis, cut it out. This is not like when you asked me for an earring, then a tattoo, and then a sleepover date, just to soften me up for the sleepover, which was all you really wanted in the first place. Get to the point of your *wonderful news* and stop playing games."

I can hear the effect, as she is suddenly silent, then contrite.

"Mommy, I was just trying to tell you everything in order."

I am now Mommy.

"Um-hmm. And I'm sensing that this wonderful news might not be so wonderful, so what is it?"

"Well, the thing is, Russell, that's his name, Russell, is probably going to be appointed the head of the Semester Abroad Program in London and he'll be able to travel to all of the great literary sites in history, um, you know, like Avon and, uh, somewhere in Scotland, and I think maybe even to Greece. So . . . he was just telling me about it, and I was saying how great I thought it would be, and he said, 'Well, why don't you come?' and I was like oh my God that would be so amazing, and then I said of course I couldn't, that my parents would freak, and he said you sounded like pretty creative, open-minded people, and it was certainly educational to go abroad. After all, it's not like I'd be dropping out or anything, just studying in Europe. And I will be a junior. I'm not a hundred percent sure that Branford offers sociology in their London program, but I could definitely take art or architecture or, um, finance, I think. And you always said there's more to learning than being in the classroom . . ."

As I listen to my daughter ramble on, I remember when she was in fifth grade and she staged a full-blown campaign to get a second dog.

"Statistically, dogs who live with other dogs live longer," she read from an article, "which means that if we don't get another dog for Lacey, we're not doing everything we can to give her a healthy life."

This, at age eleven. Now here she was, after eight more years, a public-speaking course, and who knows how many victories from three years on the high school debate team, with her arguments ready, her points lined up, her rebuttals, I was sure, in the wings. I was at a disadvantage, of course, she had prepared. I could barely digest the data, let alone argue it. So many thoughts at once. The first? There was no way she was going. She hadn't mentioned a word about wanting to go abroad until now. And "finance"? Finance? Did she really expect us to buy that one? She hated anything to do with math. She got a 740 on her verbal SATs and just barely squeaked out a 600 in math. She had trouble figuring out the tip on a restaurant check. She still didn't "get the whole percent thing." Now this incredible concoction of brains and beauty, this child of the nineties, was suddenly willing to alter her academic plans, her very life strategies, like some lovesick heroine? I was not only offended on a personal level, but on a principled one. If Lexie could be so upended by the semantic stirrings of a man, then all our progress as self-actualized women seemed null and void. The one thing I knew for sure was that I hated this Russell, whoever he was. I hated him for the smooth, Keats-spouting lecher I imagined him to be. For being smug enough to use such a cliché as a wife who didn't understand him, and for the way it was working on my baby. My husband, Mr. Non-Confrontation, would have dark fantasies about chopping off his balls the moment I told him. This was not going to be easy for Eric. Family mess was comforting to him because so far the spills fell into a framework of all things normal and transitional, like Jake's adolescent withdrawals or Lexie's self-righteous hunger strikes. I'm not sure he'll embrace this latest surprise, ripe with seedy overtones, but there's no question that I will have to tell him. This is not a job for one person. Together we will have to craft a strategy for squelching this outrageous, possibly illegal, certainly immoral plan, while communicating our respect for our daughter's individuality, our celebration of her soul, and our unconditional love. Would that be page 53 in the Parent's Handbook?

I remind Alexis that I am in Florida and about to get on a plane, and she instantly apologizes. Score one for me on the Guiltometer. She is probably kicking herself for bad timing. We agree to discuss this later in the day or tomorrow. "How's my Grammy?" she asks in a voice so innocent that I am momentarily stunned. I change the subject for lack of a convincing answer and ask her why in the world she is up so early. "I'm just so happy, so ecstatic!" she exclaims. Great. Our work will now involve deflating said ecstasy and of course ruining her whole life. I take out a pen and paper.

Plan for Changing Lexie's Mind

1. *Procure Bill Cosby's home phone number, he knows a lot about raising kids.*
2. *Go to Barnes & Noble for* The Complete Works of Sigmund Freud *and a copy of* Brainwashing for Dummies.
3. *Send Eric to store for magic beans.*

SIX

she didn't communicate!

I pay the cabbie, still unnerved by Lexie's call, and make my way into the airport. Thanks to the extra security there is no curbside check-in, so I have to haul my own bags to the ticket counter, where the line is already four rows deep and reminiscent of the wait at Disney's Space Mountain. I half expect Goofy to make an appearance for a photo shoot. And then, for no apparent reason, something happens, and although it's never happened before, I know exactly what it is because I've been waiting for it for a long time.

First an unexpected wave of intense, unmanageable fear, followed instantly by palpitations of cartoonish proportions, and finally dizziness that is so pervasive I must drop to one knee and rest my elbow on top of my black canvas suitcase for support.

"Miss, are you okay?"

I have no idea who is asking the question, but of course I am not okay. Not even marginally. Still, even in the midst of what I will later learn is a panic attack, some sense of propriety prevails and I do not clutch desperately at the legs of the speaker, fat drumsticks in nude stockings and scuffed navy pumps, and I do not pound the cold, polished industrial gray floor with my fists and wail that I can't stop shaking and I think I might pass out and the line is too long and my mother is going to die.

"Um-hmm," I whisper instead, not looking up, praying to any superior being who might be on call to intervene and make this, whatever it is, go away. It doesn't and I do not get up, and after a time I have the sensation that all airport activity has diffused into an eerie slow motion. My ears are clogged as if I've just taken off and the background noise becomes an indistinct low hum and I imagine that every traveler, skycap, and reservations clerk has stopped what they are doing to turn and stare at the poor dying woman on the floor. And then, mercifully, there is a voice.

"Hon, I'm a supervisor. How're you doing?"

I suddenly find this funny. I will just tell myself that everything is okay now because a *supervisor* is here, as if her authority, an authority I apparently do not have, can banish a panic attack and a whole legacy of psychosis, too. This is it, I think to myself, the beginning. The virus of psychological sickness, dormant for years, has been activated. I start to laugh. I know that this will probably cause her to share a worried glance with the other passengers even if she is the most professional supervisor in the country, but I cannot stop giggling and I do not want to because for a moment I actually do feel better. Instead of calling for a straitjacket, the supervisor, whose name I see on her gold American Airlines nameplate is Bev, kneels down and talks soothingly to me, and although this is strange it is also somehow comforting and I realize that she is probably trained to do this! My God, I am now on the crazy end of a training class in subduing a distraught passenger, and I wonder if this is the first time she's had to use this skill since school or if maybe she does this several times a day. The idea sobers me a bit, and I begin to stand and assure her that I will be okay. She insists on taking me right to the gate, and as she hands me my boarding pass I begin to cry although I can't say why except it must have something to do with adrenaline, at least I hope so. I start to tell her about my mom and I think for a second that she is really amazing, this Bev, this empathic middle-management airline employee, until she glances briefly at her watch and I realize I am still the crazy passenger she *thought* she had subdued and she probably wants to go to lunch or get back to something else. It's a sobering realization, but I am grateful that I am still able to discern when I have gone from threatening to tedious.

BY THE TIME my plane sets down in Newark, I have come to several decisions. First, I realize that my genetic predisposition for emotional illness is not all bad. It feels slightly better to inherit a tendency toward chemical imbalance than to think it is my fault. After all, it wouldn't be my fault if I had diabetes or glaucoma. It wouldn't be my weakness. Not at all. If I am going to crack up and lose everything, at least it's because I didn't have a chance. Besides, there is a sense of relief mixed with the doom. I was getting tired of looking under the bed and in the closet, so to speak. Second, I will say nothing of this to Eric; no need for him to know just yet that his wife has begun her descent into madness. And finally, I resolve to discuss this gingerly with Alexis. She needs to know that there is this legacy in the Berman line in case it happens to her. If it does, I do not want her to feel singularly defective or flawed. Of course, I will probably use other words, although I'm sure Alexis is incapable of imagining herself as flawed anyway. And besides, since the age of five she has regarded my advice with some skepticism, traced specifically back to what I call "The Laney Incident."

I HAD ALWAYS stressed communication with Lexie, and she had tried to cooperate. But I realize now that this adult point of view set her apart from the other kids. Laney Pomerantz was Alexis's desk buddy in Miss Neelan's morning kindergarten class. Laney was a biter, so the kids quickly learned to watch themselves around her. You could always tell when Laney took another victim. There would be silence, kids happily playing with blocks or crayons, and then suddenly a loud wail would erupt. It was zero-to-sixty in two seconds flat. As Laney's desk buddy, Lexie figured she was safe, but just to be sure, she *communicated* with her all the time. Just like her mother said, she expressed her feelings all the time. "You would never bite me 'cause we're friends, right, Laney? You know biting really hurts, right, and I let you have the blue crayon whenever you want, right?" Except mostly it was Lexie communicating and Laney ignoring. Then one day, after assembling her Lincoln Logs in the most perfect way, Lexie sat back on the play carpet to admire her work, and suddenly thought she was going to die from the stinging pain in her little finger. It was not until she could take a breath that she could even scream her teacher's name, and by the time she yelled "MIIIIISSS NNEEEELLAAN!" her teacher was already coming and saying, "Oh let me see!" while glaring at Laney, who was crying as well. "What happened?" her teacher asked tenderly. "She—she—" Lexie sniffed and pointed at Laney. "She didn't communicate!" It was Miss Neelan who gave me the details of this event, along with a funny look. "Maybe you know what she means?" The young teacher looked at me quizzically as Alexis clung to my skirt, bandaged finger and all. At home, I consoled and comforted. I resisted the urge to call Mrs. Pomerantz and ask her what unspeakable family dysfunction would lead her daughter to act like a sadistic, vicious animal that clearly should be institutionalized.

"Oh, honey, you did the right thing. Laney just can't express her feelings as well as you, she's obviously hurting in a different way, and biting is her way of letting it out."

I know Lexie tried to believe me, but her finger still hurt. A few weeks later, Laney tried to bite Kim Brickman, but Kim saw it coming, grabbed Laney's finger, and bit down hard. "That's what my mother told me to do," Kim whispered to the group. After that, Lexie regarded Kim with unbridled admiration and me with something else. Not suspicion exactly, but something less, something different, something like the beginnings of doubt. In fact, after that she began to challenge me about everything.

We had just hired a Jamaican housekeeper named Donna, and I was unsure of myself, trying to navigate my own feelings about having live-in help with my mother's mangled blueprint. Donna was large and jolly, unabashedly patriotic. She spoke of her island home with such color and excitement you half expected to turn and see the market women coming up the driveway with fruit on their heads. And she dressed like a commercial for the Jamaican Tourism Board, even when she worked; long, printed skirts and turquoise peasant blouses exposing her broad, deep brown shoulders and ample cleavage. Her thick patois filled the house with warm, musical notes.

"No, mahm, I can't be swimmin in no ocean, dontcha know. Oooh, lordy, me bein' a country girl and all. We don't ahl know how to swim, mmm-hmm." She would laugh and pat her stomach, "Oooo-hoooo, that would be a sight, now, my big fat self sinkin' right to the bottom, dontch know, and that would be the end of Donna. Sure to get a nice visit from the Cooley mon . . ."

One day, I am setting the table for dinner and Alexis asks, "Mommy, how come Donna doesn't eat with us?"

I suppose I have been expecting this question and it is not really a problem for me. I grew up with housekeepers who never ate dinner with us, and accepted my mother's explanation of dinner being family time, so I think I am comfortable with this and can be clear.

"Well, sweetie," I say, in my pleasant, reasonable voice, "this is the time of day when Daddy comes home and we sit down together, you and Jakie and me and Daddy, and we get to be together as a family and talk about our day."

She digests this, is silent for a moment, and then, with five years and about a hundred thousand pounds of innocence in her dark brown eyes, she looks up at me and asks, "You mean Donna didn't have a day?"

I stare back at her. I start to speak. Then I go and set another place.

I do not want to set another place for Russell.

WHEN I SEE Eric waiting for me at the end of the ramp, I am overwhelmed. At six feet two, he would be hard to miss, but just the fact that
he is not hanging back, that he has positioned himself near the front of the
crowd, fills me with such a burst of love and gratitude I might cry. He
looks so handsome, too. His dark hair has hardly thinned at all, and there
are shiny streaks of silver running through both sides that offset his naturally dark skin. Alexis has inherited that skin, lucky girl. The two of them
could be mistaken for Greek or Middle Eastern. But where Lexie's eyes are
dark, Eric's are hazel. When he smiles, it's like watching time-lapse photog-
raphy of a bud opening. A progressive event. The light plays off his pupils
and onto his teeth and back up to his hair, where the silver streaks seem to
reflect it back down. A glow settles, then, into the crinkles, as if the face is
satisfied, as if it knows it's done its best work. I still get a thrill watching the
process, even from a distance. Perhaps Eric's nose is a bit too blunt and his
forehead a touch high for him to be considered drop-dead gorgeous. I
don't see it that way. I like the fact that he is imperfect; it attracts me.
Because it makes him real. Five minutes from now we will go back to being
an old married couple, but for one moment I glide forward on the industrial carpet in Newark's Terminal B as if I am in a Clairol commercial: long
hair flying, one arm gracefully raised, body tilted ever so slightly forward.

I cling to Eric as if I haven't seen him in years, as if I've lost him. If
Eric were the jealous type, he might wonder what I've done that makes me
shower him with love after being gone for such a short time. I have a scary
thought: I never want him to leave me. It is irrational, Eric adores me, but
as my girlfriends say, you never know. I do not want to be *that* wife, the one
who doesn't know, the one who is sitting at the kitchen table making plans
for a twenty-fifth-anniversary party on the very morning her husband
announces that he's leaving. As I clutch my husband, he continues to grin
and hold me, but I can sense he thinks I'm overdoing it. Mental note to
self: As insanity progresses, if multiple personalities develop, try to invent
one for Eric who is a sexy, confident woman. He deserves that, at least.
Clearly, airports have become conductors of strange sensations for me. I

think they smell of endings. I am so physically grateful to be home on this day, I do not care if I am a spectacle. Besides, this is nothing. He should have seen me in the other airport. But I will not speak of that, won't even think it. I fervently do not want to break the spell of loving him, having him. I want to stay in Clairol Land, where there is a perfectly warm wind blowing a swing between two perfectly sturdy trees. Where there is no Dr. Palmer and no Professor Russell and everything is sun-drenched and airbrushed. As we walk, I do tell him about my mother, but nothing else. He is soft, concerned, assures me I did the right thing by not freaking out, and volunteers to try to talk them into something. Despite the weight of actually speaking aloud my mother's poor prognosis, I hold on to shards of contentment for almost the entire car ride home, before I lose my grip on the fantasy and return to the real world where I must broach the subject of our daughter.

"There's something else. I heard from Lexie today."

"Already?"

"Well, she had a bit of news."

"Dean's list?"

"No, not exactly."

"What do you mean?"

"Well, it seems she's met someone. Someone she really likes."

"Great!"

I just look back at him, silent. He gets the message.

"Okay. Not so great?"

"Well . . ." I thought this would be easier. I decide to go with the-cat's-on-the-roof method:

"Well, he's an ax murderer and a—a terrorist and he has a drinking problem."

"What?" Okay, I've overdone it.

"He's a little older."

"How much?"

"I'm not sure."

Silence. Then the unexpected.

"Well, you and I are seven years apart."

"Yes, but I wasn't your student."

More silence.

"Okay, but you know Lexie, wise beyond her years. I guess it's not that surprising she'd be attracted to her teacher." I don't say a word.

"Uh-oh. There's more?"

I look at him. I can't find the words.

"He really is a terrorist?"

"No, not that." I go slowly. "And no drinking problem, at least not that I know of, he's just . . . *mmmmd*." I put my hand over my mouth and purposely muffle the word.

"He's what?"

"*Mmrrddd*."

"Jules?"

Oh, hell. "He's married, okay? Married."

Eric displays no emotion. He continues to drive, staring straight ahead. He does not appear outraged or horrified. He does not swear, cringe, or in any way appear tortured that his daughter wants to be the muse for some married college professor. Instead he appears reasonable.

"Maybe it'll blow over."

"Maybe."

"I mean, it could be just a crush, right?"

"It could."

"We don't know all the facts."

"You mean like how long he's been married? Or how many years older he is? Or how long he's been her goddamned professor?"

"I don't think we should overreact."

I look at my husband as if he's out of his mind, and suddenly I know what's going on. Eric is in major denial. I want to jump and skip. Aha! I am not the only one in this family riddled with powerful emotions. Eric is afraid to give weight to the idea of this Russell because it will kill him. Poor Eric. He and Lexie share a connection that transcends words. I have it with Jake, so I know how it feels, an unexplained primal bond. This happens quite a lot in families. We have neighbors who also have a son and a daughter, and they call themselves the Blonds versus the Browns. Eric has been overwhelmed with this connection since before Alexis was even born. During my pregnancy, he spoke to her through my stomach *by phone,* not just in person. He bought a Minnie Mouse telephone for the nursery and insisted I put it to my belly when he called, which was twice a day. Actually, it worked out pretty well for all of us. Lexie was a difficult baby, but she could always be soothed by Eric's voice. Today it's much the same, although the currency has changed. A typical argument between the two of them usually ends with Eric handing her two hundred dollars "in case she needs anything." I don't say anything, because I do think it's wonderful. All girls should be a little spoiled by their dads. There's something so comforting, so Father Knows Best, about it.

In my home, my dad wasn't allowed near me. As the oldest of four brothers, and with two sons born before I was, he did not have the slightest idea what to do with a baby girl, a fact my mother did not dispel, but instead parlayed into complete control. She was in charge of raising me. Occasionally I was paraded before him in JonBenet-like fashion with newly purchased school outfits. He applauded dutifully. Less often we engaged in an hour or so of homework help (torture) in "new" math, a subject I rarely mastered and he couldn't explain without reading practically the whole textbook and then exclaiming that the method in the book was wrong. (This same scene played out early on with Eric and Alexis, but Eric, being nonconfrontational, handled it differently; Lexie had a creative mind, he asserted, and he saw no reason to force her mind to work in a way it didn't naturally go.) The jury's still out for me on this one. I can't argue with the results; they have a great relationship and Lexie has done just fine, but it irks me still. There's something so escapist about it on Eric's part.

Don't we have to confront our children sometimes? Apparently Eric doesn't think so, although this latest event is sure to test him.

It wasn't until college that I began to relate to my father at all, after I began to think and challenge. My mother was disturbed or perhaps just bored by my ideas. Ideas were a by-product of my education that she had to tolerate. She was biding time for her next role as mother-of-the-bride and grandmother. By then she had married off two sons, a totally different, primarily disturbing ordeal. Daughters-in-law have this annoying habit of having their own opinions and, even worse, their own mothers. Estelle bit her tongue on more than one occasion, but she'd put her foot down about the color scheme. "Pastels? A whole medley of them? Really, Lyle, you and Barbara ought to rethink this. Pink, yellow, and blue are nice for a bowl of mints, but a bridal party?" Barb wouldn't budge and even insisted that my mother's dress conform. But my mother never wore pastels and wasn't about to commit a fashion error at her own son's wedding. In the end she did exactly what she wanted, calling it a compromise, but everyone knew better. "Pink is pink, dear," she'd said to Barb, "let's not split hairs." Which is how she came to look like the hot pink cherry on a pastel parfait in Lyle and Barb's wedding photos. But a daughter! Now *that*, she'd practically drooled, was different. With a daughter you can run the show.

As we turn into the driveway we both glance up at the house and exchange a look. Jake's shades are still drawn, and it makes Eric smile. I want to smile, but it makes me a little crazy that Jake sleeps whole days away. Eric thinks I'm not quite ready for my little boy, who is now taller than I am, to grow up. But he doesn't realize that I'm the one who gets those brochures from the school warning parents not to miss the signs of trouble. I'm the one who hears through the grapevine about this one on drugs and that one who tried suicide. I'm worried about him *surviving* in these crazy times, not growing up. Besides, he needn't worry. I don't seem to be having much success holding on to Jake's childhood. He's had the nerve to turn sixteen, and his usual sweet chatter has dissolved into a series of sullen grunts and slamming doors and it seems like the only time we ever see him continues to be when he surfaces for food. Jake can eat three full meals between the time he comes home from school and the time he goes to bed. Eric has adapted to the change, and so has his new potbelly. Whenever he wants to hang out with Jake, he takes him out to eat. "Hey, Jake, how 'bout we go get a pizza?" "Jakie, boy, whaddya say to you and me and a major banana split over at Scoops?" "Say, Jake, feel like takin' a ride to Taco Bell?" Total bribery. Totally works. When you want to know anything about Jake, just take him out to eat.

In the house, we go our separate ways, and a little guiltily, I call Ted on his cell phone. I haven't been able to stop thinking about what he said. "I think it'd be perfect for you."

"Hey there, back in town?" Ted's voice is silky smooth, and I decide to comment.

"How is it that you always sound like you just got out of bed?"

"Maybe I have. Better yet, I could get back in. Would you come over?" I laugh and begin to make a pot of coffee as we talk.

"Behave yourself, sir, or I might have to report you."

"Oh, so you're into those games? Do you have a policewoman's outfit? I make a very convincing felon, you know."

"That's not hard to believe. But I thought you actually had something serious to talk to me about. Something legitimate?" I ask it as if I think it's a stretch.

"Well, you're no fun, but that's the challenge, I guess."

"Everyone likes a good challenge."

"Hey, something tells me that behind those pearls and sweater sets is a tiger in leather tights, and I'm gonna find her if it kills me."

"Well, it just might. For your information," I purr lasciviously, "I'm just a simple country girl who doesn't know anything about all that." Ted laughs loud and long.

"Right. And I'm a Franciscan monk."

"Besides, I haven't worn pearls in years!" Our verbal volleyball continued, but the fun was beginning to wane. For one thing, I thought I heard Eric on the stairs, and Ted's insinuation that I had a secret sexual side had actually hit a nerve. He couldn't know it, but he was reminding me of earlier exploits and making me feel exposed and ashamed. And not just of past indiscretions. There was no doubt I was feeling something right then, something intoxicating, maybe just flirtation, or maybe something else, I couldn't tell. Either way, I decided to quickly change gears.

"Okay, you win. I'm actually a closet nymphomaniac with a steady stream of paying customers who satisfy my insatiable sexual appetite each and every day including weekends and school vacations. You found me out."

"Thought so."

"So does that disqualify me from this 'thing that's perfect for me'?"

"On the contrary. You put that so eloquently that it only affirms my contention that you'd be perfect."

"For what? And keep it clean," I warned.

"Always. Okay, here's the deal."

Ted went on to describe the plan for a new weekly feature in the Suburban Life section, a kind of literary cross fire called "Suburban Sparring" that would debate current hot issues in the suburbs. One side would feature a conservative opinion, called "Right Jab," the other a liberal slant, "Left Hook." He wanted me to apply for the job by submitting a series of rebuttals to five mock columns written by a committee of editors.

"But I write children's poems," I protested.

"They all have a moral or message, as I remember."

"But they're for kids."

"And the parents."

"But—"

"Jule, what do you have to lose? Give it a try. I'll e-mail you the columns."

"Ted, this better not be another one of your tricks to get me in your life or your bed or whatever."

"Oh, right. That's always front burner. Because clearly I have nothing else to do as senior editor of North Jersey's most respected newspaper but invent fictitious job openings to court married homemakers with cute butts and nice smiles. Just check your e-mail and get to work. Gotta go." And that was that. He hung up.

I am standing in front of the coffeemaker, about to pour, when I realize what he said. Cute butt and nice smile. Not bad for almost forty-five. I start to smile, then stop. What are you doing? I chastise myself. Your mother is dying, your daughter is self-destructing, and you are probably just one psychotic episode away from a breakdown yourself, get a grip! You will not apply for that job and you will not go anywhere near Ted Ruben. You don't need the rejection or the temptation. I open the cabinet and stare at our array of mismatched, message-bearing coffee mugs and find myself paralyzed by the choices. Suddenly, which mug I choose takes on ridiculously superstitious significance. I feel that I can subliminally affect the future. On some level I believe that I have special powers and if I pick the right cup with the right message I can influence my mother's cancer or my daughter's thoughts and even though I know this is nonsense I can't ignore it because now that I've thought it, what if it should actually be true? The yellow mug whose bright red letters announce YOU'RE THE BOSS has potential. After all, it's an inspiring message that could fill someone with confidence. Perhaps it will imbue my mother's red blood cells with strength. But what if it causes Lexie to become strong in her resolve? Since I'm not quite sure how this magic works, I decide not to take the chance. Next I contemplate a red and white striped mug, emblazoned with hearts. It promises that LOVE WILL FIND A WAY, and that is so touching I almost reach for it until I think that Alexis might interpret that as some sort of sanction, and my hand recoils as if burned. Now I am getting impatient and also starting to scare my rational self. Thoughts of a job at the *Sentinel* have not been entirely banished as I'd commanded. One mug advises me to GO FOR IT! but obviously I am not rational enough to apply for a major position on a newspaper if I cannot even pick out a coffee cup. But that's ridiculous. Why shouldn't I apply for that job? Who says I don't have the talent? Boldly, I reach for the college mug we purchased during opening weekend of Alexis's freshman year. It is covered with happy little smiling faces in Branford's colors, maroon and tan. Smiles are generically wonderful. As I turn the mug over in my hands, I know it is the simple, right choice. And when I sit down at the kitchen table and hold it full and hot between both hands, it is not just the coffee that warms me, it is the sensation that there is a connection between my mother, my daughter, and me. Maybe I can send my family silent, positive directives, even specifics. I close my eyes and telepathically instruct Alexis to forget this teacher. I wish for Russell to get a big pus blister. I speak to my mother's lymph nodes and suggest that they clear, I tell her good cells to be fruitful and multiply. And I implore my own left brain to start manufacturing its cleverest discourses. There, at the cherrywood table, the coffee mug becomes my personal voodoo doll, my medium. It never occurs to me that imagining my mugs as magical is at least as bizarre as my parents' personification of their household appliances. Oblivious, I decide that next week I will use the mug that says TENNIS IS MY RACKET and help Andy Roddick win the French Open.

SEVEN

try to steer clear of the rocks

To Do

1. *Cure mom's cancer.*
2. *Fix Lexie's love life.*
3. *Forget dream job.*

When I hear Jake's shuffling, I realize it was him that I heard on the stairs. Jake is supposed to be working on a big science project this weekend. I'm a little annoyed that he hasn't gotten up earlier because I'm sure he has reading to do. Jake always has reading to do. Unlike the rest of us, he is not a reader, unless you count the credits after the WWF match or the pornographic lyrics on his rapsta/gangsta/ice t-cube-biggie-puffie-music collection. My mother, who is an avid reader, doesn't understand how I can allow Jake to rot his mind. "Get him *Treasure Island* or *Robinson Crusoe*." That's her solution, and I confess to having tried it. Also Michael Crichton, Stephen King, and even those sports books like *Ball Four* and *The Wayne Chrebet Story*. Nothing doing. Jake insists that reading puts him to sleep. Now if someone could invent a machine whereby you'd have to read to eat, I might have a chance.

Since I haven't seen Jake in three days I promise myself not to bug him right away, even though I can't believe that four hours ago I was in Florida and have since traversed two thousand air miles and he is just waking up. Such is navigating the relationship with a teenage son. Of course, Eric and I never know which Jake to expect at any moment of the day, whether we bug him or not. He can quite literally leave a room in a good mood and return two minutes later in a bad one. In private, we call him the "mystery meat" of teenagers. What is it? Man, boy, animal? This morning I am treated to an incredibly warm and stimulating encounter.

"Hi, honey, good morning."

"Umm."

"How was your night?"

"Unh."

"Do you want me to make you something to eat?"

"Nnh."

I sit at the breakfast table and watch him, fascinated. He barely opens his eyes as he slides around the kitchen in ripped plaid sweatpants and a T-shirt I never bought him. First he retrieves his favorite cereal bowl, which is not a cereal bowl at all. I use it to serve pasta. He fills this with a combination of Frosted Flakes and Raisin Bran, two snack-sized boxes of Sunkist raisins, a banana he first slices, then chops at with his spoon, and finally at least a pint of whole milk. Jake is the only one in the family, maybe on the whole planet, who still drinks whole milk. I think he is remarkable, a candidate for a segment on the Discovery Channel. Not just because he consumes approximately four thousand calories a day and still has a size 26 waist, but because of the simplicity of his routine. Although completely incapable of speech, he still manages to assemble a bowl of cereal worthy of Sunday brunch at the Four Seasons before padding sleepily, obliviously into the family room.

I AM LEFT completely unfulfilled by his grunts and his exit and feel quite useless. I need to be planning something, doing something; I need to be busy having an effect. If I just sit here I feel like I'm waiting for my mother's cancer to get worse and my daughter to ruin her life. My parents never felt this compelled, I think, to craft a plan. Certainly my mother had an agenda, but it was never spelled out, least of all to her. It seems as if they were just sure, as though they parented strictly from instinct. They trusted their judgment and that was it. For Eric and me, it was the opposite. We researched and read, practiced and critiqued. We approached parenting as we did our rafting trip on the Snake River, with training and preparation, the best equipment and supplies. And of course we were blindsided and upended by that first set of rapids. Too late we realized that no class or insulated suit prepares you for the force of the water, the ineffectual flailing of your oars, and the secret fear that you've made an irreversibly perilous move. Where's the manual when your little angel decides to emulate Linda Blair in *The Exorcist* at kindergarten registration? Or your precocious four-year-old asks the lovely black woman in the elevator, "Where's your vacuum?" Parenting may be the single most humbling experience. You spend years terrified that you are just one wrong decision away from creating permanent damage. You doubt your courage, your ability, even your worth. Still you hang on, steer clear of the rocks, pray to avoid the ones you don't see, and hope somehow that you just make it down. Eric and I tried to map it, which is laughable. On the other hand, it's good to check each other once in a while. You never know when one person's baggage might bulge over the acceptable weight allowance. My parents never second-guessed each other, and my brothers and I are the end results of their mutual self-reliance, end results that are advertisement enough against such blatant confidence. Eric's parents, too, never brainstormed, but in a different way. He insists they didn't parent at all.

"Nonexistent, no other word for it," is the way Eric recounts his memories of parental instruction. "We never really talked, I just did my thing and they did theirs." Knowing the Resnicks, that isn't hard to believe. They're nice enough, certainly benign as in-laws go, but terminally boring would be a generous description. Besides, whoever heard of Jewish parents doing their thing and letting their only son do his? I'm sure there must be some sort of Talmudic law against this; at the very least they should be identified as carriers of a rare genetic disorder and entitled to pre-pregnancy testing along the lines of Tay-Sachs disease or sickle-cell anemia. Can you imagine that sad day in the doctor's office?

"I'm sorry to tell you this, Mr. and Mrs. Goldblatt, but you've tested positive for the Absence of Guilt chromosome. This means you will never be able to endow your son with neurotic behaviors, dysfunctional guilt issues, and worst of all, instead of being sure that you know exactly what he should do in every situation, you will"—the doctor's voice drops—"let him explore independently, making decisions for himself."

The couple breaks down, hugging each other, the mother wailing, "Oh God, why us? What have we done?"

Since even the idea of being disengaged from my children causes me to shudder physically, this scenario reminds me that I am a daughter and I have work to do. One of the nice things about aging is that you know a fair number of people who've had cancer. Cold as that sounds, in no time I have spoken with three friends, one of whom is an orthopedist, the other a huge contributor to the local Gilda's Club, all in some stage of radiation, chemotherapy, or remission. Suddenly this cancer thing doesn't seem so overwhelming. There are anti-nausea remedies, hair-loss preventions, even a whole line of clothing and accessories for the "active cancer patient." Not that my mother would be seen in active wear. She doesn't believe in it for anyone but professional athletes, "and even then . . ." She also doesn't believe in sweatshirts or sweatpants and don't even get her started on Lycra. When Chanel came out with a quilted, gold-buckled,

$560 version of the warm-up suit, she declared it a mockery and "disrespectful" to Coco's memory.

Still, I'm energized by the amount of information about recovery. At the recommendation of Alan Konig, our orthopedist (who has colon cancer and has been to the Mayo Clinic, but is now playing team tennis at the Swim Club), I decide to run over to Borders and pick up several books. He said I'd be amazed at the amount of information devoted to surviving cancer, and I am. It takes me a full hour just to wander from Deepak Chopra to Bernie Siegel. Who knew you could laugh yourself to health, imagine yourself well, or massage those nasty cancer cells away? My mother might not wear "deep-stimulating Derma-leggings, guaranteed to reach beneath the skin where the rejuvenating process may begin," but surely some remedy will feel like a good fit. If only I could find something called *How to Canasta Your Cancer Away*. That she'd read.

Two hundred sixty dollars later I walk back into the house. From the family room I hear the sounds of a slapstick movie, probably something by Adam Sandler that Jake knows every word to and has seen thirty-two times. It has been hours since he came downstairs and I'm afraid he's fallen back to sleep on the couch. I decide to investigate. Jake is stretched out on the sectional, covered with an old quilt, propped halfway up by two huge pillows. The pasta bowl is drained dry and sits, congealing, on the coffee table in front of him. It is Jim Carrey on the screen, and Jake's eyes are open. He has a dopey smile on his face.

"Jake, what are you doing?" Okay, this is a stupid question.

"Watching."

"I can see that." No response.

"Jake, don't you have some work to do?"

He looks up at me, irritated.

"I am."

"You are?"

"I will."

"You will? When?"

"*Mom!* Jeez, I'm just waking up, okay?"

Jim Carrey is singing. Jake is laughing. I am dismissed. I start to protest, then stop. I remind myself that he is sixteen and I am not supposed to smother him or micromanage him. I am supposed to give him room to self-motivate. To individuate. Okay, fine. He needs room? Piece of cake. I will give him so much room he will think he's in the Palace at Versailles. Besides, I have some work to do too. Approximately 2,700 pages of cancer reading. Back at the kitchen table I remember something I heard on *Dr. Phil.* Most psychiatrists don't like to work with teenagers because it's often too difficult to distinguish between normal adolescence and pathological illness.

EIGHT

isn't there some sort of harness?

I spend the afternoon unpacking, straightening, and reassuring myself that Jake, in his room, is studying. I really want to talk about Lexie and I want to call my friend Amy, but I feel a little guilty. Eric hates it when Amy gives her opinion before he does, but it's not like I haven't given him a chance. I mean, how long is he going to take to process his damned feelings? I've been sitting on a lot of news for hours. I could distract myself with my poems, the ones I've been putting together for preteens about social situations. My favorite is called "I Wish Melissa Would Move Away," about a sixth-grader having difficulty with a mean but popular girl in her class. Another is called "His Dad Is the Coach," and recounts the injustice of losing a spot on the middle-school basketball team because a less talented schoolmate's father is the coach.

Amy is a literary agent, and although she doesn't handle kids' stuff, she's promised to use her connections to help me if I ever get it done. I also use my friend Beth's girls, ages twelve and fourteen, as my unofficial critics/experts for the material. They basically like everything I write, which makes me wonder if I'm the next Shel Silverstein or simply in need of more objective critics. My latest piece is my most daring, a trilogy of rhymes about a boy with ADHD, called "If They Don't Want You to Touch It, Why Did They Paint It Red?" In addition to exploring the simple logic of children with attention deficits, it also openly criticizes the current trend toward overclassifying and medicating young children for what may simply be immaturity.

While I have always been interested in psychology, I find myself drawn to the latest research in the field of ADHD, possibly because my brother Stewie always says it's too bad they didn't know about Ritalin when he was a child. ("There was nothing wrong with you." My mother gets angry whenever Stewie says this. "You were just a typical boy—into everything!") For once I agree with her. But also I'm amazed at how many kids these days get special testing or other considerations for standardized tests like the SATs. When Lexie was applying to college, she was told by one admissions counselor that if she were to be classified as a special education student, it was akin to being a minority and schools had diversity quotas to fill. Can you imagine? Years ago you tried to hide it if a child was "slow." It was a shameful disgrace. Now it's something of a badge of honor, gaining in prestige and catching on in suburbia to the point of oversaturation. Like the family pet or a BMW, everybody's got one. In Jake's grade there are kids who are being classified for the edge it will give them at college time, and people think this is normal.

I turn on the computer, and sure enough there are several new e-mails, one of which I'm sure will be from Ted. A quick check reveals his screen name, which I'm pleased to see isn't loverboy or teddybear, just a simple, professional Ruben T. In the subject box are the words "Just Do It." I am about to open it, but I get cold feet, I'm just not ready. Perhaps I will surf the web for something interesting. Maybe there is a site that deals with May-December romances. Or mothers who put a stop to them with undetectable poisons. I decide to call Amy.

Amy is my most volatile friend. She can be a huge pain in the ass, so opinionated and stubborn that you can't tell her *anything,* but it's okay, because when you need her to understand your crisis, she does. If you are mad at your husband, she tells you he is a big asshole. If your kids screw up, she reminds you of all their terrific qualities. If you feel old and ugly, she tells you that all the men in town want to sleep with you. But don't try to change her mind about a subject she has ruled on, you'll have better luck creating world peace.

I met Amy right after I moved to the suburbs, when Lexie was three years old and Jake was six months old. We were seated together at a temple luncheon for new members of the community, and while there were many women in their late twenties or early thirties present, we weren't seated with them. We were the only two women under sixty-five at our table. I was trying to be polite and friendly to these women, but Amy had no patience. "Excuse me," she said loudly to the chairperson, "why aren't we sitting with people our own age?" She saw nothing wrong with the question, nothing rude. The chairperson blushed, mumbled something about space, and retreated. Amy talked me into ducking out as dessert was served. We drove around town and she showed me the schools where her older boys went and where Lexie would eventually go. She didn't stop talking for two hours, punctuating her rulings on life, her family, diets, everything, in fact, with great finality and even greater humor. By the time she dropped me back at the temple to pick up my car, I was exhausted. Naturally, when she called me a few days later to get together, I jumped at the idea.

Over time I've learned a little about Amy's mysteriously horrible childhood. Her mother died when she was a teen, her father struggled with alcohol, and Amy raised her younger sister and brother. I know the big facts, but none of the underlying aches. Even after eighteen years of friendship she maintains that I wouldn't understand, not after growing up, as she says, "like Caroline Kennedy."

Amy and my mother have a complicated relationship. Because of me they've been forced together for holidays, birthdays, and lunches for years. Initially, neither one could understand how I related to the other. Amy plays by different verbal rules, often saying exactly what's on her mind, which scares my mother to death. "Nobody taught her how to regulate herself," my mother says. She's not wrong. Of course, Amy says virtually the same thing about my mom. "Jesus Christ!" she'll exclaim. "How do you stand it? She can never just be *there,* it's like she has to make a comment about everything!" A few years ago, however, their relationship took an unexpected turn for the better. It happened by accident. We were in a restaurant and Amy made a slightly lascivious, appreciative comment about our waiter. "Check out the smoldering eyes on that one." My mother blushed, but looked anyway, and then she actually tried to join in. "Oh my, he's a regular Mellors, all right."

"No, not quite," Amy responded. "He's not hairy enough to be Mellors."

"Oh, you're wrong, dear. Lawrence used hair to symbolize the beastly quality of the gardener, to offset Catherine's gentility, but that one"— tipping her head toward the sexy waiter—"has the essence of animal magnetism even without the hair." Amy and I exchanged glances, but my mother seemed not to notice. She did, however, take out her compact and a tissue and blot her upper lip. Amy was impressed.

"Estelle, you've read *Lady Chatterley*?"

"Actually"—my mother lowered her voice to a whisper—"I've read everything D. H. Lawrence ever wrote. Why?"

"Well, me too. I'm obsessed with him." Amy seemed dazed.

"Really?" My mother smiled then, the kind of smile I rarely saw, a relaxed, open, unaffected smile. "What do you know?" She was truly pleased.

Hello, remember me? I look from one to the other. I've read *Lady Chatterley* too. I think. In high school or college maybe. Or maybe it was Lady Macbeth. But no one is listening to me anyway.

"Did *you* think *Lady* was his best work?" Amy asks.

"Oh, certainly not," my mother resumes whispering, "it was the controversy that propelled it, of course." She looks right and then left, as if the Literary Porn Task Force is going to swoop down at any minute. "And the class conflict was rich, but as for story line and depth, there's no contest, really, I'd say that *Sons and Lovers* set the standard for romantic sagas of the time . . ."

". . . and a generation of romance novels to come." They said the last part in unison. Then they both sat back and grinned. On that day my best friend and my mother forged an unlikely bond. They spent the whole lunch talking Lawrence, eventually confessing a mutual weakness for modern romantic trash. I wanted to puke.

"How can you read romance novels?" I blasted Amy in private. "You made me go back and read Sinclair and the *Iliad* and you never once said anything about Nora Roberts or—or"—I couldn't even think of a romance writer—"or that Devereaux or whatever her name is." I was indignant, really, but Amy smiled. She'd found a compatriot.

"Oh, Jule, it gets to be a headache sometimes, you know, it's great reading, great literature, but I mean just try to smile after spending a Saturday submerged in the depressing inner life of some Joyce Carol Oates wannabe followed by a nightcap of deep, dark cultural rifts that surpass Andre Dubus, and you know, you'd need a little fluff and levity too." I still couldn't understand it. And I said so. I could understand my mother reading those stories of knights and damsels, she lived in a fantasy world as it was, and as I remembered, those romances rarely had graphic sexual scenes, merely the suggestion of them, which would suit her, and which now that I think of it sounds a lot *like* her—a mere suggestion of a real person, a concept, without the cold, hard, mess.

Since "the D. H. Lawrence lunch," my mother and Amy have had their differences, but always their alliance. As Amy once confessed, "Your mother's a trip, but I'll tell you one thing, when I'm with her, I remember what it's like to be someone's little girl." Enough said. Even if I don't seem to be getting what I need, there's no reason to deny Amy of a sense of maternal security. Who doesn't need that from time to time?

THE REASON ERIC doesn't like Amy is that Amy comes off as anti-men. Which is understandable since she's got a house full of them. Besides her husband, Seth, there are three sons, ages sixteen through twenty-two, and two huge bull mastiffs. They have the biggest balls I've ever seen—the dogs, that is. Well, maybe her sons do, too, but I really couldn't tell you about that. The dogs, however, are gross. My mother gets embarrassed just looking at them. Last time she came to visit, Amy had us for brunch. When she left the room for a minute, my mother whispered to me, "Are their testicles supposed to swing all over like that?"

"What would you like her to do, Mom? Cut 'em off?"

"No, no, it's just, well, isn't there some sort of harness, I mean, don't you find them a little obscene?"

As if the dogs weren't primal enough, Seth has named them King and Butch. They both have a disgusting slobber problem. Along the walls and furniture of Amy's house are streaks of dog mucus at jowl level that she can never completely erase. Apparently, drooping cheeks is a highly desirable trait in mastiffs (too bad drooping cheeks is not a desired quality in forty-four-year-old women), so it's hard to feel sorry for Amy, since she searched the country for these exact dogs, paid a fortune for them, and must have known exactly what she was getting into. She has to leave rags strategically placed through the house so that guests can wipe the slobber from couches or more often, themselves. I call them "shlobba towels," and sometimes I even bring my own. You can imagine how lovely the situation appears to my mother. I guess Gudrun or Ruburt or whoever the men were in her precious Lawrence's England didn't have balls. Amy waves the whole mess away with her usual shrug and a disparaging remark. "Oh, what's the difference, slobber, sperm, snot—I've got their crap all over this house." Amy's got a good thing going. She lives in a world full of jockstraps and uncensored bodily noises, and survives by pointing out how primitive men are, so that her husband and sons, feeling guilty for being the slobs that they are, have come to believe that she is a saint for putting up with them. They happily keep making the messes and count on her to be the evolved one who just as happily cleans up. And it all seems to work—they adore her. First of all, she's great looking, classic even, in an outdoor healthy way. Her appearance bears no resemblance to the comments that come out of her mouth, which I guess makes them easier to take. Tall, with short blond hair, she has the squared-off shoulders of a swimmer and a broad, strong face—pretty in a healthy, no-nonsense way. She looks solid and trustworthy, like you'd buy your house from her or let her teach your kids to swim. And as much as she berates her boys, she is the one who drives four hours to see them if they are sick, stays up all night cooling their foreheads and scratching their backs, races to the supermarket to get ingredients for their favorite dish if they feel a little blue. Even the dogs (both of them) like to sleep on her bed. Ugh. Recently I discovered another thing about Amy. As much as she puts down guys, she's lived with them for so long that she's used to them, and even though their habits drive her crazy, it's their habits that she knows. A few months ago she was in the car with me when I had to pick up Lexie and three of her friends. The girls piled into the backseat and started chattering happily. Nothing seemed out of the ordinary to me, but after a minute I noticed a pained expression on Amy's face.

"What's wrong?" I asked, worried.

"How do you stand it?" she whined.

"Stand what?"

"The noise!" she cried, raising her hands to cover her ears. "They're giving me such a headache."

I looked in the rearview mirror at the girls. They were oblivious, laughing, talking, well, I guess maybe shrieking. But that's how they always sound. Poor Amy. She left the car mumbling ". . . never again . . . high-pitched . . . deafening . . . aspirin . . ." I think now she realizes that even though girls are a different species, they come with their own special liabilities. I can't wait to see how she processes my latest news.

"You see," she announces, right after I finish telling her exactly what Lexie plans to do, "this is why all men should have to take a pill to lower their testosterone. I don't see why we can't get this bill passed in Congress.

It's so easy. They take their pill, submit to a blood test to make sure they're doing it, or they just lose their fucking jobs. I'm telling you, that would be the end of date rape, of these child molesters, it's genius."

"For the first time I wholeheartedly agree with you," I say glumly.

"Oh, listen, don't get crazy. You know Lexie." I wait for more, but there is none. How have I gotten to a place where friends of mine get to say "You know Lexie" and it speaks volumes. What kind of creature have I raised?

"What exactly does that mean? 'You know Lexie, she's just trying to shock you' or 'You know Lexie, she'll probably change her mind by next week' or 'You know Lexie, she just has to get this out of her system, have a sexual foray through the English countryside and then she'll be just fine'?"

"Well, yes."

"Yes?"

"No, not yes to anything in particular. Yes, she's complicated and you have to expect these things with your daughter. I'm actually not at all surprised. My boys wouldn't have the ingenuity to invent such a disaster. They just smash their cars into trees and spend huge sums of money on jewelry for girls so they can get laid. At least Lexie has creativity and . . . and . . . artistic passion."

"You didn't just say that, right?"

"I think I did, let me see, did you buy it?"

"Not even for a second, and don't bullshit me, you can't be thinking this is a good thing in any way."

"No, no, of course not. In fact, if I were you, I'd get the little cock-sucker's wife on the phone and tell her what he's up to. Then I'd get his class lists and send everyone an FYI e-mail about the professor's after-class activities. Of course, I'm the shy, reserved type. You might be able to come up with something a little more toxic and vindictive."

"Oh, I'd love to do something like that, but what if Lexie found out? I could end up sending her right into his arms. You know how she is about causes."

Amy laughs. "Oh no, I forgot the starving babies saga."

When she was eleven, Lexie saw a story on the news about women in the ghetto who didn't have enough money to feed their babies, so they would dilute baby formula with water and the kids would only get half the nutrition they needed. She was so appalled she went on a partial hunger strike the next day and told us to take half the money we spent on her meals and send it to those women. Of course, she only lasted one day and a breakfast, but her heart was in it.

"So, what are you going to do?"

That's the question, isn't it?

"I don't know. I just told Eric and he's downstairs freaking out, but I guess we'll figure it out together."

"Oh God, don't let the penis make any decisions. Call me if he comes up with a suggestion you're thinking of taking."

"Okay, fine."

"Jules, you know I'm just kidding. About everything. This is a tough one, but it's not like cancer or anything, okay? We'll figure it out."

"Oh yeah, I forgot to tell you. My mother has cancer."

"What? Are you kidding?"

"No, she really does. Can you believe it? I'm not allowed to tell the kids, either. But I have to go. I hear Eric coming up."

"Do you want me to come over?"

"No, sweetie, I'll talk to you later. Maybe tomorrow we'll get Beth and go out for coffee. Or Seconal. Love ya, 'bye."

NINE

no dead relatives

Eric stands in the doorway and says "I'm hungry," and "Let's get dinner," and I think that is a great idea. Maybe we can both think clearly in a public place. All afternoon, walking through the house, there are reminders of Lexie at an earlier, innocent age. A stain on the chair from when the tennis team gathered for a pasta party, pencil marks on the wall that notched both kids' growth, plants and posters and pottery of varying ugliness, purchased from art shows and Latin Club fairs and fund-raisers for the high school soccer association. Our house is not a cold, rational place, and we need one. Neither one of us wants to fuss or dress and I assume we'll go to Janice's Bistro, our favorite local restaurant. Janice's is a godsend, New York quality food with local comfort. Eric and I find ourselves there every chance we get, but since the *Times* did a write-up on it, our little undiscovered gem has hit the big time. Eric is afraid we won't get in.

"It's early, I think we'll be okay."

"I don't want to put any pressure on John." John is the owner, who would build another table in order to seat us if he could, but Eric is sensitive to his situation, and the more I think about it, we don't really want to schmooze or run into anyone we know. So we agree on the diner, and even though I am fine with this, a part of me protests. Dinner at the diner feels awfully close to racing for the Early Bird Special. Can a house with a screened-in pool on the ninth fairway be far behind? Jake decides not to join us, and why would he? He had breakfast at two in the afternoon, and a half hour ago he made himself a snack of sixteen chicken nuggets and a frozen Milky Way.

As we pull out of our driveway, a burst of wind sends a pile of fallen blossoms scattering, and they swirl around us like mini-tornadoes. It is such a surprise that I laugh out loud, close my eyes, and duck instinctively as they spin into the front windshield. When the wind eases, the petals float gracefully down. I notice everything acutely this evening, and I decide this slice of nature is a good sign, as if someone were trying to tell me that there is a natural harmony in the world and everything will work out okay. I watch as the fading sunlight catches the bits of pink, purple, and gold, causing them to shimmer rapidly, as if from a wand, like the fairy dust that precedes the arrival of a magical being. We do not outwardly acknowledge this spectacle, let alone admire it. In fact, I don't know if Eric has even noticed. Instead we unceremoniously disperse the sparkles with our big, black, unfairylike SUV, and rudely turn them back into old leaves. We don't look back to see if Glenda or Tinkerbell has shown up. We are grown-ups with big things on our minds.

On the next street, I see the Walker. I don't know what else to call him. Almost bald, except for two tufts on either side of his head over which his headphones conveniently rest, he has the look of someone newly retired; his stride says that he is taking it easy, but in a purposeful, ener-gized way. No armchair and rocker for this fellow. He must take a walk four times a day, minimum. Whether I'm driving Jake to school at 7:00 a.m., grocery shopping at noon, carpooling at four, or returning from dinner at ten, there he is, walking. This is okay, I guess, he's allowed to do whatever he wants, but there is always that little problem of the wave. I am a friendly girl who likes the idea of neighborhoods and community. I stop to talk to the mail lady, and to the couple with the spaniel and the cactus garden, two doors down. So of course it is only natural that I would wave to the Walker. But it can get a little annoying. Now, every time I pass him, I feel like I'm stuck. If I don't wave I might hurt his feelings. He might take it personally and wonder what he's done to make a waver into a non-waver. And then sometimes I wonder if all this waving actually annoys the crap out of him. Maybe he just wants to be left alone to walk and he *hates* all the waving. What if everyone who passes him waves to him? Then he has to wave back at about thirty cars, four times a day. What kind of a relaxing walk is that? He might be afraid that if he doesn't smile that friendly smile and raise his hand, we might think *he* is unfriendly. Such a dilemma every time I get in the goddamn car. They should probably pass a law to ban walking altogether, too socially problematic. It could even lead to Wave Rage. This evening I wish the Walker would get a small bone spur on his heel and give us all a break.

We are driving into Park Ridge, to the Ridge Diner, and I notice new town houses on Grand Avenue, done in country style, very tasteful. It seems like every square inch of Bergen County is being developed, the homes being put up on "postage stamps," as Eric says. I went to school with Monique Levitt, who was related to the builder of Levittown, Long Island, one of the first cookie-cutter developments in the northeast. Monique had the best name. So French and exotic. We were all Debbies and Wendys and Sues, so Monique was enviable. I really liked her, too, right up until the day her father died and then I was so mad at her I stopped wanting to be her friend.

When you're eight years old, hardly anything really spectacular ever happens to you, so when it does, when you have *news,* it is a Big Deal. The news has to be about something extraordinary, to make you a celebrity in the third grade. Somebody has to die or have an accident, or your family has to move; only then will you have everyone talking about you, everyone listening to your tale. It is a rare and sought-after recognition. And on a winter day in 1965, I should have had it; it should have been mine, because my grandmother died. I don't mean to sound callous, but my father's mother was a stern, rather distant woman whom I barely knew, so I didn't feel especially sad. What I felt was so excited I couldn't sleep. I couldn't wait to go to school the next day and tell everyone my Big News. I could imagine the attention: "Ssh, ssh, she's coming, no don't say anything to upset her, *her grandma died.*"

But it was not to be. I enjoyed short-lived notoriety at the bus stop, with the neighborhood kids, only five of them, who were impressed with my status as "the kid who knows someone who died." Kids are so funny about things like death. A kid with a just-dead grandparent is instantly an object of curiosity and respect, as if she has graduated to a club, the club of special experience. It's a new, elevated status. And I had it for about ten minutes. Because as soon as we all boarded the yellow school bus to take us to Cherry Lane School, all the kids who were on the bus yelled out, "Did you hear? Monique Levitt's *father* died!" And I will tell you, shamefully, that I did not feel bad for Monique Levitt at that moment. I felt devastated. How could Monique's father go and die on the day of my Big News? If he had only waited even one more day, I could have had some of the spotlight. It wasn't fair. I mumbled something about my grandma and took my seat, furious, because, even at eight years old, I knew that a dead father trumps a dead grandmother any day.

IN THE DINER, we order waffles, both of us, and in between sips of coffee, swirling of syrupy forks, and memories of childhood, Lexie's and our own, we begin to talk it out. She has always wanted to move too quickly, grow up too fast, we agree. Eric remembers the high school English teacher who wrote in her yearbook, "Alexis, take your time, life will happen soon enough." She has wanted a Great Love, that is part of it, I say, she is a romantic. Eric cringes. He really does not want to think too long about her having a love, great or small, with anyone.

"Remember the college application?" I ask, to change the subject.

He does. We sigh. The college application, we agreed, was a metaphor for her whole life: full of surprises, moments of solemn depth, and a smattering of bullshit. One time, after she'd already gotten in to Branford, but had decided to apply to just one more school, she brought an application to me for a final check. I scanned it quickly, a weary veteran of the process. List of Honors Classes, check. Community Service Credits, check. Extracurriculars, Awards, Letters, check, check, check. Then, I almost missed it, written so casually, so faintly, in pencil, under the heading, Any Other Notable Distinctions. Beneath that heading, Alexis had chosen to say:

One of Only Three Virgins in the Senior Class.

I smile at Eric, we are both remembering, both wondering what, if anything, has changed in that category. It is his turn to change the subject.

"Well at least we got her to erase *that*, unlike the essay."

He holds his head and smiles, remembering the essay. Alexis was vehemently against the "essay hype," as she called it. Even though she enjoyed writing, she hated the pressure of having to advertise herself. Her favorite applications had a choice of essays, where one leaned more toward the creative and seemed less like a campaign promise. On these applications she used her favorite essay, the one we always called "No Dead Relatives." It was an anti-essay essay, which began,

"No dead relatives, no crippling diseases, have never been abandoned by my ____(father, best friend, collie). You fill in the blank."

Essentially, the essay detailed all the phony propaganda that high school students use to convince admissions counselors that they have learned life's great lessons. She concluded by saying that she had lived a fairly average life, and was hoping still to learn life's lessons, and that was why she was going to college. Her adviser advised us to talk her out of it, but we didn't. She got into plenty of schools. She also learned that sometimes you could be subversive and still be successful. This will not come in handy now, I think, and I can see by the way Eric is twisting his paper napkin that he has come to the same conclusion.

"Look, let's not bullshit each other about what's bothering us," I say. It is impossible not to notice the immediate discomfort on my husband's face, since even his eyelashes begin to contort.

"Worst case: This guy is a sleazy sexual predator who's attempting to persuade a young, nubile co-ed, our impressionable daughter, to accompany him on a lewd, irresponsible journey, under the pretense of a lofty literary sabbatical."

"Thanks, Jule, I feel much better about it now. Will you be publishing that synopsis or merely saving it to edit later? What will you name the file, Shitty Facts?"

"C'mon, Eric, we have to face it to deal with it."

"It's not even the idea of sex that bothers me the most, you know. I mean of course it's the sex, okay, but it's the manipulation." Eric is getting red in the face and his fist seems permanently clenched. He pounds it methodically as he speaks, punctuating his words.

"If this guy (thud), this, this, asshole (thud, thud), thinks he's just (almost thud, stops thud in midair) going to get away with this (pause, big thud), he can forget it. I am definitely going to bring him up on some kind of charges (double thud)." Eric leans back and half smiles—the public dunking of Professor Russell is a sweet dream—but his smile is less a smile than a grimace. Eric is stuck on Big Bad Russell. I am, too, of course, but not the way he is. He is her father and is supposed to protect her from men like Russell. This is one confrontation from which he cannot shy away. I am her mother and a woman and I know that if I am to help her I have to try to understand her, which is more complicated. The waitress comes over, tucks a tip into her apron, pulls out her pad and pencil, and asks cheerfully, "You folks okay over here?"

No, we are not. And usually we would share a silent look, but today we do not even bother.

"Eric," I begin, when the waitress leaves, "what do you think we should do?"

"Well, first thing tomorrow, I'm going to call Burt Fogel."

"Burt Fogel? Why?"

"You know Burt—he has ties."

"Ties?" I have no idea what Eric is talking about. Truly.

"Eric, what are you talking about? So what?"

"So if someone wanted to exert a little influence on a certain professor, Burt could probably help."

Ah. *Those* kinds of ties. I have a vision of James Gandolfini and Edie Falco overtaking our bodies. They must have gotten in through the waffles. You'd think we'd at least have had to order fettuccine. The conversation is so surreal that I start to laugh. We are about as close to accessing Mafia connections as we are to renouncing our worldly possessions. Then I start to hum the theme from *The Godfather*.

"Da da da da—da da—da da dummm . . ."

"Very funny. But things go on that you don't even know about, Julie."

"Oh, please. Are you out of your mind?"

I look at my husband, who is all puffed up, preening about Burt Fogel. He seems to have transformed himself for the moment. This man, who would rather iron his own shirts than tell the cleaning lady she is doing it wrong, is suddenly a tough guy, a player. I turn away disgusted, reminded of a certain type of man my father knew from the country club, the kind he played gin rummy with and golfed with and drank Bloody Marys with, but never invited home. We saw these men in passing, at a Friday-night dinner or a Sunday brunch. They greeted him warmly, wondered aloud when they were all going to get together as couples, but it never happened. My mother shrank from them, their loudness and their maleness. So did I. I remember them as a mass of obnoxious pushiness, their guts protruding proudly, like obscene signs of status, from shirts with too many buttons open, straining the white leather belts against green golf pants so that after a big meal their fat fingers had to hook into the front and make room for their stomachs to expand. The type of man who always had a big fat cigar or smelled of one, and who dangled his own importance like his car keys as he told "the kid" to bring his Cadillac around. Eric is nothing like that man except at this moment he is.

"What if Lexie found out? What if he told her and then she decided to go off with him just to spite you? What would you do then, have him rubbed out?"

Eric is ignoring me, or trying to. He thought he had a great idea, at least one that made him feel like a savior, and I have ruined it for him.

"Rubbed out?'

"Whatever."

"Rubbed out, huh? That's good. Obviously you're the one with the connections. Who is it? Your cousin Moshe? Uncle Aaron? Maybe Stewie is really 'Stewie the Stiff.'"

"Okay, okay. I get it. But you're the one who sounds like Mafia Man." I put on my street-thug voice. "First you're gonna have lunch with your golf buddy and youse guys will talk and then he's gonna make a few calls." I go back to my normal voice. "And then Russell's suddenly going to be threatened? What does the Jewish Mafia leave in lieu of a horse's head? Maybe a free suit hanging ominously in his closet?"

"Very clever for someone who's obviously done such a marvelous job in the mother-daughter department that our only daughter is . . . is . . ."

Ouch. He's right. Whatever Lexie is right now, it isn't great, and this doesn't reflect well on my maternal parenting skills. But Lexie has always been exceptional. And Eric and I are better than this, better than picking at each other. We both take a deep breath. I reach for his hands.

"Honey, I do agree with one thing. You do need to take care of this. You should go up there."

"Go up there? Why?"

"Because someone has to."

"So? What makes you think she'll listen to me?"

"Not Lexie, him. You have to go up there and see him."

"Yeah, right. Me and my wholesale suit."

"No, really. A minute ago you were going to bring him up on charges, and that's not totally insane. There's nothing wrong with confronting him and letting him know that this girl has parents who are involved and know what's going on. Think about it. It makes sense."

"I don't know . . ."

"You wouldn't have to actually threaten him or anything. Just seeing you would probably be enough. He'd get the message, don't you think? You could tell him you're not happy with the situation. Mention the university administration and stuff like that."

"If you know exactly what I should say, why don't you go?"

"Because you're the dad. He doesn't know you're a pussycat at heart; you're still a big guy. I doubt he'd feel very intimidated by me. And, besides, my parents are coming this weekend and I need every second to prepare."

We are silent as the waitress brings more coffee. We are silent as we sip it. Eric is trying to imagine himself as intimidating, I think. I am wondering why I haven't told Eric about Ted Ruben and the job at the *Sentinel*. It's nothing, I tell myself. I just don't want to complicate things. Let him debate about Lexie first, then I'll tell him. When we get up to pay the check and leave, Eric decides. "I'll go next Sunday night. See him first thing Monday."

"Good," I reply. "Good."

TEN

a wonderful place to raise a family

I spend the morning furiously writing a rebuttal to an essay titled "Doesn't Anyone Mow Their Own Lawn Anymore?" I'd opened the e-mail from Ted with the intention of just taking a look, and had never planned to actually write anything. Five minutes in, I was hooked. It didn't help that Ted began with a personal plea: *Jules—this column was made for you. In fact, it's slated to be just like you—a combination of highbrow and down-to-earth in a classy, friendly package.* Whoa. Try to ignore that sales job. I couldn't. And besides, the topic unnerved me just enough to get the juices going, and when I get a little angry I write about mundane issues with a passion that could save someone on death row. Before noon I'd reduced the holier-than-thou, eco-friendly plaintiff into a sniveling, fantasy-filled, time-wasting enemy of both the environment and all God-fearing suburbanites, not to mention little children and small animals.

After that diatribe, in need of a break, I look for something mindless and refreshing to do, something gentler. We've been thinking about putting in a koi pond, and there is a gardening center in Westchester that is supposed to have the largest selection of stones and fish; so I decide an afternoon wandering among plants, fountains, ponds, and nature will be the ideal diversion. I am just reaching the crest of the Tappan Zee Bridge when it happens—with so little warning I'm literally gasping for breath. As my chest squeezes shut, I am overcome with nausea and begin to gag. I'm sure that if I continue to drive I will pass out, lose control of the car, and plunge over the side of the bridge. I slow down, not a real popular move with my fellow drivers. Do not stop, I tell myself, just get over this bridge. The more I try not to panic, to think of some way to help myself, the less I breathe. Then I remember: breathing is good. I try it. It's less a breath than a wheeze, but it gives me something other than my eulogy to focus on. I am only going twenty miles an hour, the recipient of familiar gestures and some I've never seen before, but somehow, incredibly, I make it to the other side. I get off at the first exit in Tarrytown, and the knot in my chest begins to loosen and I do not pass out. I do, however, forget any plans to visit Outdoor Creations and I find a small café in town, where I sit for the next four hours over a chicken salad, six cups of coffee, and through a change in the staff's shift, wondering how to get both my car and myself back across the bridge without driving. Like a mantra, I recite, "Do not bother Eric," "Do not bother Eric," although this is less for him than for me. Eric might actually like to be bothered. He views our family entanglements as evidence that he has improved upon his childhood lack of them. One time, years ago when the kids were little, they both caught a stomach flu. In the middle of the night, Jake's fever spiked to 104 and we ended up standing in the shower with him to try to cool him down. Then Lexie woke up vomiting, and of course the new puppy thought all the activity was a cue to relieve herself all over the kitchen floor. At one point Eric and I passed each other in the hall with dirty sheets, wet towels, and plastic bags of puppy doo. I was harried and shell-shocked, but Eric was smiling, content even. This was family, his expression said. It's funny, but when I remember that night, I don't remember the mess or the smell, just Eric, smiling, squeezing my arm as we passed, making me feel like we were a team, like nothing could be more rewarding, more fulfilling than this chaotic mess. So, as the afternoon begins to edge closer to the evening rush and instead of finding strength I become convinced that Westchester is a wonderful place to raise our family, I do bother him, if not for guidance then so he can call the schools and have the children's records sent.

Remarkably, Eric is sure that I have the superhero powers it will take to drive back across the bridge. I, in turn, assure him that I will never make it and urge him to make sure they wash and style my hair after they fish me out of the Hudson. Eric reminds me that rush hour will bring bumper-to-bumper traffic and the trip will take twice as long, so I remind Eric that I hate his guts and just for good measure tell him that I think his penis is too small, which I don't. I think I'm hoping that if I can make him angry we will fight and maybe it will distract me from being afraid or him from wondering if I'm nuts. He doesn't bite, doesn't even take offense. "If you can still make jokes, I know you can make it." How's that for confidence? I begin.

"C'mon, sweetie, just look straight ahead, make up your mind and go." Easy for you, I think, but I pull onto Route 9 and with the cell phone on speaker and Eric reassuring me, I make it to New Jersey like a contestant straddling a log across a piranha-infested lagoon on TV's *Survivor*. "Here I go, I'm moving, I'm halfway there, I'm on the other side." What an accomplishment. That night it occurs to me that I should probably see someone; I've now had two panic attacks and I can't shake the nagging notion that I'm genetically predisposed to crack-up. Plus, I've been personifying the coffee cups; what's next? Will I imagine that the vacuum can hear my thoughts? See images in the dishwater? Though I secretly hope that there are some hormonal changes, physically based, that are causing these symptoms, and though I really don't want to own the kind of psychological weakness that causes panic attacks, even I have to face the facts. "Hey!" I want to scream. "You've got the wrong girl! I'm too open to discussion, too willing to look at myself, too *not* my mother for that!" Secretly, I hope that Eric will try to talk me out of it, tell me there is nothing wrong with me.

"You know what, in light of everything that's going on, I think it's a smart idea. You've got a lot to handle and it might help to talk to someone. You know, just to set yourself right."

Oh, thanks, Eric. Couldn't you be irrationally opposed to therapy like most husbands, or at least complain about the cost? But of course I love it that he is so emotionally available. And I am beginning to crave the emotional dissection. Let the games begin. It is no longer enough to distance myself, or satisfy myself with sarcasm, or use Eric to confirm my *mother's* dysfunction in our layperson's pillow talk. Enough with psychology books and talk shows; it's time for fieldwork, to take the jury to the actual scene of the crime, my own mind. Time to, as Eric says, "set myself right."

THE TRUTH IS, I always imagined that if I ever went to "see someone," as my mother would say, he would look exactly like Gregory Peck in *To Kill a Mockingbird*. Rugged but intellectual, exquisitely sexy because of his complete lack of awareness that behind the glasses he is smolderingly hot. I imagined that along with that look would be moral fiber as strong as Oklahoma, a needle-sharp, educated mind, and a screen star's confident style. But alas, here in this nondescript second-floor office on Thursday morning, Dr. Bob is no Gregory Peck, despite his black-rimmed glasses. He is pleasant enough, fatherly even, but soft. No hard edges to suggest rippling muscles or Great Thoughts or passion. His brown hair is tinged with white; he has pink skin and small hands. I suppose I should be grateful there is nothing distracting about Dr. Bob. Perhaps that is a prerequisite for therapists, part of the curriculum. A final course for one credit before you graduate where you learn what clothes, posture, and style to adopt so that you look completely benign. Dr. Bob is actually a social worker and not a doctor at all, but I feel better thinking of him as a doctor so I call him that, only not to his face. Suffice it to say that my need to think of him as a doctor probably says much more about me than I want to admit. Whatever his title, he's good; I'll give him that. He not only found time to see me this week, but in our very first session we are already at the heart of the matter, my mother's need for me to be happy as a way to ward off her depression and my secret: how I've always known I was just one trigger away from my own bipolar disorder. Dr. Bob remarks that it's curious the way I see my mother as so powerless in the face of her depression and yet so powerful that she could cause mine. That's what he says, "curious." And suddenly I am uncomfortable. She *has* caused me to fear for my sanity, Dr. Bob. She's made me a basket case with her criticism, her judgments, and her unrelenting insistence on perfection. But I don't say this; instead, I ask whether this is in our contract. We do have a contract, Dr. Bob and I, he insisted on it so he could measure our progress and so I would be able to measure the benefits of therapy. I had to define my goals and we had to agree on a plan, but right now I'm not completely clear on what it is. I know that when he first brought it up I was thinking that I would've liked to contract for a bigger bathroom, maybe a Jacuzzi, and perhaps a sunroom off the kitchen. I was lost in a vision of home improvement and was picturing the framed-out, glass-enclosed octagon when Dr. Bob interrupted.

"Are you having trouble conceptualizing your goals?"

"Conceptualizing," I would learn, was one of Dr. Bob's tactful words for "facing," but I didn't know it at the time.

"No, no," I responded, thinking I was quite funny. "I can see the sunroom now. White wicker furniture, wooden shutters . . ." I laughed, waiting for Dr. Bob to share my joke, but he was silent. Of course, I dug a deeper hole.

"Anyway, you should've *told* me you were a contractor. I could have brought my tile samples and we could have worked on something that could actually be fixed." Even though I was smiling when I began to speak, I finished with a sort of sad half smile and a feeling of foolishness.

"Do you usually do this?" he asked.

"Do what?" I asked weakly, not really wanting to know. Make a fool of myself? Tell stupid jokes? Feel uncomfortable?

"Break the tension when things get too serious?"

And I thought of a million things I could say, but just as quickly dismissed them and decided to try to just answer his question, which in itself was a new experience for me. I had to give up being witty and sparkly for Dr. Bob, and that was harder to do than be entertaining, but I did it because it hit me that the trade-off was the chance to actually get to a place, if there was one, at the core of it all, at the core of me. So I took a leap, right there, determined that the only thing to get framed was my point of view and instead of a Jacuzzi I could surely do with a Coping Mechanism.

Now I remember. We contracted to help me see myself as separate from the fat preteen and the promiscuous teenager, separate from the negative suggestions that once defined me, and more aligned with the productive, open-minded wife and mother I'd strived to become. My goal was not only to understand that I had control now, but to own that control, no matter what the script had been in the past.

"It's possible that in assigning blame, you gave up your right to choose."

"Say that again?"

"Mothers have so much influence, don't they? When we're young we use them to understand the world. How to act, what to wear, even how to feel. It's easy to feel programmed; sometimes it's comforting to feel that way. But we're human beings, not pieces of stone. No matter how deep the ruts, human beings always have the power to replant, re-sow, if you will. The deeper the grooves, the harder it is, but the human mind is malleable, it's always possible."

"So you're saying I just accepted the ruts, like I kept planting, uh, corn or whatever, when I actually had the ability to replow and plant, say, tomatoes?"

"I'm saying that there are genetic physical conditions we don't necessarily have to accept anymore. There are so many preventions, behaviors, and choices to lessen the odds. Why wouldn't there be steps one could take to prevent emotional illness?"

"So instead of taking steps to prevent a repeat of my mother's depression, I've just been blaming her. I've just been planting corn over and over again. God, I don't even like corn." Dr. Bob laughs. Apparently he likes a good metaphor as much as I do.

"Not necessarily."

"But that's what you just said. I'm not doing any of the real work. I didn't get out the tractor and rip up the ground and—and re-fertilize it or whatever, and then plant something new. I kept saying that corn sucked, but I kept growing corn."

"Actually, I think you've done quite a lot. Think about your life. You have a family you love, for one thing, and children you've vowed to raise based on their needs instead of yours."

"True, but what about me? I put on this act, but I haven't really done anything about me."

"I wouldn't say that." Dr. Bob smiled. "You're here, aren't you?"

ELEVEN

stay close to home for a while

Right from Dr. Bob I head for my own brand of therapy, an emergency lunch with Amy and Beth. Here's the plan: Amy will tell me that I'm perfectly normal and Beth will explain that my nurturing side is my sensitive side and I will be completely cured of all my problems halfway through my egg-white omelet. My plan is a good one because neither Amy nor Beth was raised in a very functional family. Also, both of them have dead mothers. Well, Beth's mother isn't really dead, but Beth says that she is. "I lost my mother years ago" is how she puts it. In fact, her mother is very much alive in body and thinks she and Beth have "a relationship," but Beth swears they haven't had a real conversation in thirty years. "It's April," Beth will say, checking her Palm Pilot, "my mother should be calling any day about her Passover knaidlach." By now Amy and I know the ritual, so we ask Beth, laughing, "Why Beth, what *is* the secret to those good balls?"

"Oh, girls," Beth answers, in mock surprise, "I thought you would remember, you must always, always, freeze the balls!"

The lunch is so lighthearted, just what I need, I hesitate to ruin the mood by sharing my dilemmas. Our waiter is a friendly young kid with a crewcut and blue eyes and I wonder why he is not in school of some sort and feel guilty that my own kids are safely tucked away in the educational system that will prevent them from having to take just this sort of job on a full-time basis, when he opens his mouth and says his name is Russell, and he's going to be our server today. It is my turn to almost choke, on my water, and as Beth slaps me on the back, the irony of it hits me full force and I start to laugh, but it is not a hearty laugh and by the third chuckle it is more of a sob and then the tears are just spilling out and Amy is looking at me like What is going on?

"I guess this means we're not ready to order," Amy says to Russell, who looks at me as if I were giving birth. He is not sure whether to go or to stay, and Beth says, "Just give us a few seconds okay?"

Russell, this one anyway, takes off. I stop crying long enough for Amy to catch Beth up on Lexie and my mother, and then I explain that Lexie's professor is also named Russell. The girls don't look nearly as horrified as I feel, until I finish wiping my eyes and say, somewhat offhandedly and with one last sniffle, "Oh yeah, and I don't do bridges or airports anymore."

"Wait a minute, wait a minute." Amy takes a breath. "Could we just deal with one of your fucked-up problems at a time?" Clearly, Amy is enjoying this new role. She is not used to my falling apart like this, and I don't understand my own willingness to be so exposed, but it actually feels good. I am so tired of striving for perpetual sunshine. In that instant I also begin to understand that friendship of any kind needs to be a give-and-take. No one can just be the normal one, or the ditsy one, and I see that Amy is relishing the task of helping me, of nurturing. Suddenly she tells Beth, "Okay, you call the hostess over and tell her we need a new waiter, one with a different name."

This cracks me up. "Stop. Don't you dare."

Beth asks me if anything else has gone on since we last spoke about this Russell, and I really like that she is calling him "this Russell" with a little disgust in her voice because that is what I've been doing and clearly we have come to the same assessment of his character and his place in Lexie's life. We talk about the details for a few minutes and I tell them about sending Eric up there and they both look at me like I'm crazy for a minute until Amy says, "Brilliant. Absolutely brilliant."

Beth is not so sure and frets, "Are you sure that's the best thing?"

But Amy is proud. "Kid, I didn't think you had it in you. Way to go."

I want to feel good about Amy's reaction, but of course this is also a cause for concern. Having Amy agree with you is not necessarily validation of the right move. But to her credit, she softens. "Look, whether Eric can make a difference or not, who knows. Our prediction? This is just a Lexie phase."

"That's right." Beth nods convincingly. "I'm sure it's a stage."

I look from one to the other.

"You think?"

They nod at each other. I am not so sure.

"Definitely," Beth says. "This is so Lexie. She wants to be different; she wants to be in control. I bet that the minute it starts to become a reality, she calls it off."

"Probably all blow over by the summer. And," Amy goes on, "that's why it's okay if Eric goes up there. Maybe it'll hurry things up."

"Yes," Beth agrees, if less heartily, "it could be a good thing."

They look pretty sure, my friends, and I want to believe them, to feel as certain as they do. Perhaps Eric and I are too close to it to see it as a phase or a statement. With Lexie, we've become so used to grand gestures that we take them at face value. Maybe a visit from Dad will indeed hasten this romance into losing some of its luster.

"Now about the—what did you say, airports?" They share a glance. "Maybe you should stay close to home for a while."

THAT EVENING WE are scheduled to have dinner with Graham Post and his wife, Liza, at their club. At the time we made the date it seemed like a good idea, a midweek break, but now I am dreading it. The last thing I need is a superficial social engagement. Eric and I have had little time to talk since Sunday. On the drive there, I want to tell him about my session with Dr. Bob or what the girls had to say, but he brings up one of his favorite subjects: How I Could Have Gone to an Ivy League School, by Eric Resnick. The kids and I tease Eric that most of his stories and lectures are repeats, cataloged by name or number. If they were in the car, Jake would probably groan and say, "Oh, here goes story number 122, how Dad was smarter than anyone knew." And Lexie would pipe in, "Yeah, the famous 'If My Parents Helped Me Like We Help You'!" Then they'd both start laughing and bust him by talking to each other. "Hey, Lex, did you know Dad probably could have gone to Harvard?" "Oh no, Jake, Wharton! Or MIT!" "What about Oxford?" They would be hysterical and Eric would smile, but he would be a little offended, too. This was actually a sensitive subject with him. No matter how well he did in business, he always felt excluded from that select cadre of Ivy League graduates who were so plentiful among his network of financial analysts and investors. Eric's situation is enviable. He successfully manages the portfolios of a diverse group of investors from an office just ten minutes from his home. His gift with numbers and figures is unparalleled, and he brings a creative, probing energy to every potential opportunity. But sit him around a conference table with three bankers who are comparing a restaurant to one of Princeton's eateries or reminiscing about sunny days on the banks of Boston's Charles River, and he cringes with pain. It is his Great Regret. Eric believes that he had the intelligence but never applied himself in school because of his lack of a normal home life. He often states, in one form or another, that it was his upbringing, not his gray matter, that landed him at the University of Miami. And it doesn't help that his "friend" Graham, his racquetball buddy, lords it over him. Graham was "a Princeton man" and he never lets Eric forget it. Which is why Eric takes special pleasure in beating the shit out of Graham on the court. I try to kid him about it. Every Sunday when he comes back from the Y, I ask him, "So, was your IQ higher than Graham's today?" This will produce a wry smile, but not the unabashed laughter I expect, which tells me just how sensitive my husband is. And it's why I decide to humor him now.

"So, if I'd had some guidance, or even some tutoring for the SATs, that might have made all the difference."

"I'm sure you're right, sweetheart."

"And if I *had* gone to Cornell or The U of P, maybe Lexie would have gone *there* instead of Branford and she never would have met this little bottom-feeding, scurvy piece of shit." Okay. I get it. He will think of every outlandish way that this could be his fault, every way to blame himself.

"Honey," I say gingerly, "I don't think that kind of thinking is exactly a hundred percent rational, do you?" I am the sweetest wife with the sweetest little voice.

"FUCK RATIONAL!" he shouts back. "OKAY? JUST FUCK EVERY-THING! JESUS!" Okay, then. So much for the sweet voice. How about no voice? I think I prefer silence to outbursts. Is this the new Eric? The once-repressed Eric? Could I have possibly found fault with the mild, old one? I am shaken up more than I expect. What is this Russell doing to Eric? To our family?

As we enter the Posts' club, I put on my game face. Eric and I briefly agree not to discuss Lexie with the Posts. But it takes mere minutes for Eric to unburden himself, and by the time our appetizers arrive I am ready to kill him. Instead of sticking to our plan, he has told the Posts the Whole Story of Alexis and the Professor, and asked for Graham's advice, despite my making serious, threatening eyes at him, and despite even my interrupting him with "I'm not sure talking about this publicly is the best thing, *dear*," which Eric clearly knows means "Shut up now or die." And he has ignored me and said, "Oh, it's just the *Posts*," and "I'm not taking out an ad in the *Sentinel*, for God's sake." This throws me for a moment—does he mean something more? Know something about Ted? My heart does a little dancing panic step, but no, Eric is just being emphatic. And so now I am all bound up with my anger and am silent and he knows it and doesn't care because he is somehow angry with me, after all, for this whole thing, which I should have expected. I talk him out of blaming himself, and I do it so well that he looks for someone else to blame and naturally I'm the next best target.

Liza Post has assumed her sympathetic face, which is not to say that she isn't sympathetic, just that I know the face she gets when Lexie pulls something that her precious Taylor would not. Both of her manicured hands are smoothing down her blond hair, which doesn't need smoothing at all since it is cropped into a perfect helmet and has been that way for thirty years. She is pursing her lips as if to say, *What a shame.*

Graham, in his argyle vest and pale pink Brooks Brothers shirt, is gesturing to the waiter as if the man were his personal valet, crooking his finger and tilting his head just so, in a gesture both intimate and confident, ripe with entitlement and showmanship, masterfully conveying to the waiter that he has a private but very urgent need, and, to us, his pride in what he obviously regards as his impressive power at the swiftness with which his needs are addressed. After whispering to the deferential Mexican, he turns back with a reserved smile and says with some collusion, "Coffee's cold. He'll bring a fresh pot."

Liza nods with approval, as if her husband has solved the world hunger crisis and they both bask for an unnecessarily long moment of mutual self-satisfaction until finally Graham shifts in his seat, suddenly remembering our problem. Then he begins to outline the issues and analyze Alexis as if she were a business glitch. This is so like a man, I think. If Amy were here, she'd be kicking me under the table, pantomiming a hand job.

"The way I see it," Graham offers, "you've got yourself a marketing challenge."

I roll my eyes, internally, and I continue to glare at my husband, willing him to look at me so I can drill a painful hole into the center of his forehead with my piercing stare. He is listening to Graham.

"See, right now, it's like this guy has got her business by painting a picture of a fabulous product, making promises that are right on target. He's done his research, knows his market. She's ready for excitement and romance and he's tapped into that. What you've got to do is find out what else she wants, and repaint the picture. Or find out what she doesn't want, and reframe his picture so that it's there. Are you with me?"

I look at Eric. Please do not be with him. Graham does not know Lexie. Graham does not know anything. We think he is a big phony, super-ficial, unable to connect, remember? Last year at his birthday party you said if he made one more speech about how lucky he was to have Liza, you would throw up in his Princeton Cup. But Eric is thinking, contemplating Graham's words and nodding his head. I now wish for superpowers, the kind that let you freeze a room, turn all the people in the restaurant into statues. I would get up, walk over to Graham, whose mouth would be open, mid-bite, and I would take his glass of red wine and spill it down the front of his shirt and all over his crotch. Then I would walk back to my seat and snap my fingers, and the restaurant would come back to life and Graham would stand up in horror, and they would have to leave because he is soaked. Oh yes, and I would also turn back time about a half hour, to before Eric told the Posts anything. That's all I want to happen. Well, maybe I would also put a little piece of spinach puff in Liza's hair because I am feeling pissy. And then, as a little flutter plays across my chest, I have another thought: The only thing worse than this would be to have a panic attack right here in the Posts' club. I am quickly mollified, and as I concen-trate on willing the flutter to be a onetime occurrence, I begin to negotiate with God. I am sorry for being so snotty, I will promise not to be nasty if only I can get control of my own body again. I do not even want to think about it, for fear of bringing it on. I am terrified, actually. What would Eric say? So far he's been supportive, but I don't think falling to the floor in front of Graham at prestigious Dell Creek would go over so well. This is much worse than diabetes or glaucoma, it is more like epilepsy. In subur-bia, a chronic disease is tragic, but not nearly as deplorable as making a scene.

By the time dinner ends, I am feeling stuffed and not just with food, although I did keep getting up to sample the buffet, more in an attempt to break up both conversations, the one at the table and the one in my head, than because I was hungry, but I couldn't very well keep bringing pasta and lamb chops back to the table and not eat them. Still, the stuffed feeling seems to have settled more in my heart than in my stomach. And I'm not just upset with myself. This whole dinner could have been an escape, if only Eric had stuck to the plan. Sometimes Eric is a huge disappointment and I find myself replaying a situation in my mind as if I were with one of my girlfriends and of course it always comes out better! They just get it. With Amy or Beth, there is that unspoken acknowledgment when something either shocks or amuses us. I have that with Eric, at times, but it's different, more conditional. Without warning, I think of Ted. There's something more than I've been willing to admit there, and it's not just his looks. We have a kind of synergy, a rhythm to our exchanges; I think Ted gets it, and that frightens me. Of course, I hardly know him. You don't make assumptions about a spiritual connection based on a few short meetings or conversations. Do you? Who knows, maybe it's actually better if you're *not* on the same wavelength as your husband; maybe that's where the balance comes, from different points of view. One thing is for sure: there aren't many married couples I've seen who have it all, who are best friends *and* in love. Still, Eric does not have to act like such a dick. Is he trying to give me a reason to look elsewhere? Or maybe I'm doing that all by myself.

In the car going home, I try to work off my frustration and beat Eric up with my silence, pummeling him with lusty uppercuts of anger and landing great, telekinetic jabs to his jaw. He doesn't even seem to know that anything is wrong. He is worried about something in the car, with the brakes.

"Has the car been giving you any trouble?"

I don't answer, just shake my head.

"What? Yes, no?"

I turn slowly and look back at him, giving him my best death stare.

"I said . . . no." Terse, dull, dripping with annoyance.

He either doesn't get it or doesn't care. We ride in silence, him occasionally pressing on the gas or the brakes, consumed by some small clicking I have yet to hear, me wearing my disgust like a burkha, shrouded in it.

Later, in bed, I am still not speaking to him. My anger is less active but still omnipresent, like a constant, low-grade hum. I am also feeling lost and sorry for myself and alone, trying to decipher my own negative behavior with some grace and perspective, in light of what I believe to be generations of female dysfunction. I don't care what he is going through, I want him to *deal* with the issue the way we discussed. I keep imagining Liza Post getting into bed, calling out to Graham from under her covers. "Thank God Taylor is seeing Jason," she would say, as if Jason Zucker, of the Zucker Meat Empire, is the Second Coming. In truth, at this moment I am jealous of Liza and I am wondering why my daughter hasn't found a nice Jewish meat heir of her own.

At precisely that moment Eric snuggles up against me, drapes his arm over my stomach, and starts to fondle my breasts. Is he out of his mind? I am always taken aback by the way Eric—all men, I guess—are able to separate sex from anything that has happened during the day. It would never occur to him to be too angry to have sex. One feeling has no relationship to the other. I, on the other hand, equate sex with intimacy and connectedness. There is not a chance in hell that I will want to open myself up to him after the way he has acted today.

"Go away."

"Come onnn, sweetie . . ." His hands are working.

"Eric, get away from me. You disgust me. Why don't you call Graham? Maybe he'll let you lick his balls."

"Jesus Christ, you are fucked up."

"I am fucked up? *I* am fucked up?"

I want to fight. I want to smash insults into his face. I know I'm fucked up, but I'm trying really hard not to be fucked up, okay? I can't even tell when I'm right to be angry anymore! I want to hurt him and abuse him and make him cry, but mostly I want Alexis to call and tell me she made the whole thing up. I want to start the week over. I want to leave the country. I want to be fourteen again. I never want to be fourteen again. I lift my covers with great fanfare, curl them around my body, and flop down, facing away from Eric. I will not fight, I think, because I will not give him the satisfaction of it and because, suddenly, I have lost the passion for it.

TWELVE

"might come down any day"

By the time my parents make it down the corridor of Newark's Terminal C, it's been a full half hour since the plane officially landed, and every passenger has already deplaned. I am impatient, but trying not to be. For one thing, my worst fear has not materialized; I have not dropped to the floor of the terminal and become familiar with the calves of yet another airline employee. So I will not allow my impatience to escalate, no need to trigger anything that hasn't surfaced on its own. Also, I'm a little preoccupied wondering how Eric will do at Branford. When and where will he meet Russell? How long does it take to actually castrate someone?

As if on cue, the phone rings and it's Lexie. Oh God, please don't tell me she's spotted her dad. He was supposed to stay put till the morning. Lexie has classes straight through on Monday mornings, from nine until noon. Not English class.

"Hi, Lex."

"Hi, Mommy. How are you?" Still Mommy. A good sign.

"Oh, just peachy! I'm sitting here at Newark Airport waiting for Grammy and Pop. The plane landed a half hour ago and every single person has gotten off, including two people in wheelchairs and a child who was traveling alone, but not them."

"You didn't tell me they were coming up. Grammy got on a plane? Wait, you were just down there, what's wrong?" Shit. I forgot she doesn't know about my mother, not to mention the Great Gag Order. There's no way she's going to buy the furniture story, but I have to tell her something.

"Well, you know your grandma and how much she likes a bargain? It seems that Millie Kaufman's son Paul owns a big carpet and furniture warehouse in Manhattan and it's going out of business. So Millie told your grandma she could get everything at cost, and since she's been planning to redo the house, especially the family room and the dining room, she decided to make the trip." I take a breath, and then add, for authenticity, "Of course, guess who has the honor of schlepping her to the store?"

"Oh, Mommy, be nice. It could be fun." She actually believes me. I can't imagine why. Then I get a clue.

"So, Mommy, have you given any more thought to what I—we— um, talked about?"

"Oh, Lex, what do you think I'm going to say? That it's a great idea? That you should hurry up and grab it before it's too late? That you should turn your whole life upside down because this—this *professor* has some-how made an impression on you?"

"You don't have to make it sound so seedy! I'm sorry I thought we were close enough that I could tell you I liked him, but I guess not! I'd be going to school, you know, real school, it just happens to also be that I— I—like one of the professors, what's so wrong with that? If I wanted to sleep with him, I could do it right here, you know!"

Well. Alexis has screamed this last pronouncement. I wonder if the two other people in the gate area can hear what she's saying, since they have both looked my way. One, a Rastafarian type who may or may not actually be Jamaican, I can't tell because he's so dirty, is considering me from his position on the floor, where he has camped out, a woven knapsack and guitar by his side. The other, an airport employee whose shirt bears the label Aramark Food Services, is seated, but has put down his newspaper and is staring at me directly. I smile nervously at both and cover the mouthpiece of my cell.

"Alexis, this is really not a good time." I am actually glad to see the two figures that emerge at that moment from the boarding corridor, which makes me wonder if hell is beginning to get icy cold. "We will have to finish this later; your grandparents are coming right now." There is silence. Then I hear her take a huge dramatic breath, a breath that says she is too big for this discussion, a breath she wants me to hear.

"Fine."

"Okay, I'll talk to you later."

"Tell Grammy and Pop I say hello. And I love them."

I get the dig. She hangs up before I can be the really big one and say "Love you," but I have little time to feel bad. My legally blind father is slowly guiding my tension-filled mother toward me, and I can see that the trip has taken a toll. It was a really big deal for my mother to get on this plane. She hasn't flown for two years, ever since the famous Passover Ordeal; the details of said ordeal are etched into my brain. They were caught in some sort of wind event. They circled for hours, in bumpy conditions. Many of the passengers got sick, she included, and when the plane began to run out of gas, the pilot came on the loudspeaker to announce that they were diverting to Philadelphia to refuel, not deplane, and then they would return to Newark. That had been the last straw. My mother, who had been gripping the armrests tightly, reached up and pressed the call button. The stewardess came over.

"Yes, ma'am?" With deadly calm, my mother explained her position.

"When we land in Philly, I'll be getting off the plane." The girl shook her head and smiled.

"Oh, no, ma'am, no one's getting off, we're just refueling." To this, Estelle Berman, all 102 pounds and seventy-two years of her, responded by grabbing the girl's wrist in a death grip and pulling her close.

"I don't think you heard me." The tension in her voice grew along with the volume.

"When we land in Philadelphia, I am getting off this plane." With that, a lady two rows back shouted, "Me, too!" And then a little girl began to cry. "Mommy, I wanna get off tooo." The stewardess looked nervous as she withdrew and rubbed her wrist.

"I'll be right back."

My mother was sure she went to tell the pilot that some crazy lady was starting a riot, but she didn't care. Suddenly the pilot came back on. "Ladies and gentlemen, good news. We've been given priority clearance to land at Newark. Flight attendants, please take your seats."

As THEY APPROACH, I see that my dad is exhausted, he is shuffling, not walking, and my mom is holding her stomach.

"I've had diarrhea for three days." She kisses me and hands me her makeup case. And so it begins, that subtle transfer of responsibility. Her carry-on holds more than cosmetics, more than cotton swabs, it holds the tension and fear, the anguish and outrage, the very control she needs when no one is around but seems perfectly willing to relinquish now.

"You're here now, Mom, not to worry."

"Easy for you to say, you don't have to fly back."

I lose patience. "Mother, you're dying of cancer. I wouldn't think you'd need to worry so much about the plane crashing." I stop. Did I really say that?

"This is supposed to comfort me?"

"No, but—"

"Never mind, I'm too tired to argue." Oh God, now I really feel like shit.

"Did you remember to get my stuff at the market?"

"Of course. Orange juice without pulp, cottage cheese with fruit, and Instant Cream of Wheat, right?"

"With calcium in the juice, and the small-curd cottage cheese, not the kind you bought last time."

"Right, small curd." (What is it about curd size?)

"And the regular Instant Cream of Wheat."

"I know."

"Not the little packages, the red box. The little packages have extra calories from the flavorings." We are stepping onto the escalator, not a smooth process, with my mother sagging from the blisters created by her two-inch beige pumps (I once suggested she wear sneakers, and you'd have thought I'd told her to travel naked), my father having to tip over so that his head is parallel to the floor in order to see the steps, and me trying to steady and guide them both without cartwheeling down on top of them, propelled by the weight of the most awkward, unusually shaped carry-on you've ever seen. This triangular turquoise case must have been discontinued thirty years ago because of its girth and weight, but my mother swears by it. I get them seated in plastic chairs outside the luggage carousel and I take a deep breath. Think of yoga, good breaths, a warm light at my center core. Then, waiting for the luggage, I sneak a look at my shopping list to make sure I got it right.

Mom's Groceries

Orange juice (Calcium—no pulp)
Cottage Cheese with fruit (Small Curd)
Cream of Wheat—Instant **Red Box**
Ensure (Strawberry)
Turkey bacon
Eggbeaters
Velveeta (do they sell that here?)
Temptee Whipped Cream Cheese
Partridge in pear tree

During the ride home I remind myself to be tolerant and patient and to think before I react. My mother is asking a lot of questions about Eric, where he is and why he has out-of-town business since he never has out-of-town business. Then she moves on to Lexie. Have I spoken with her, is she involved with anyone? I actually turn and look at her for a second while I'm driving. Does she know something? But her face is a mask. That's all I need, I think. My mother's thoughts on how to handle Lexie. In my head, we have an imaginary conversation.

"Well, Mom, we're having a little incident with Lexie."

"An incident? What kind of an incident?"

"Well, it has to do with her plans for next semester."

"Oh, good, I thought you were going to say it was about her hair. I don't know why you can't get her to part it on the side and to stop blow-drying it so straight. Last time it was so plastered down it looked like she had glued it."

"Mom, it's not about her hair."

"Well, good."

"So, she has this professor, for um, English, and he's made quite an impression on her."

"Lovely. She's following in my footsteps with her love for great literature."

"And, well, it seems that Lexie wants to take a semester off and go traveling with him. Um, studying with him, she says."

There would be silence. My mother would need time to digest. And then she would solve everything.

"Oh, honey, I bet she's just not getting out enough, you know, going to enough mixers."

That's the word she'd use, mixers.

"Those winters are just maddening upstate. You know some people need sunlight or they go a little crazy—there's a real live name for it, a disease."

Well. There you go. What did I expect? Would I really want my imaginary mother to evolve from Blanche DuBois into Ghandi? No, that would be too confusing. Better to have dreams imitate life. At least in real life and my fantasies, Lexie and my mom maintain their mutually rewarding relationship; Lexie doesn't see her grandma's faults and she returns the favor. Very productive.

Later I am helping her unpack when I notice some papers, like a report, in her carry-on, but she snatches them away and says they are "cancer articles, silly nonsense." I am suspicious, there is something panicky about the way she grabs for them, but I hold my tongue. I notice that she has brought enough cosmetics to open a day spa. Did she really need a whole jar of Elizabeth Arden's Replenishing Monthly Mud Mask just because she's missing her facial day this month? But I restrain myself, even when she asks to see what masks *I* use. I wish I could instantly produce a concoction of homemade baking soda or caviar oils or, at the very least, my own in-house facialist named Ivanka, but instead I confess that I am all out of facial masks of any kind.

"Well"—she seems sad—"you have to stay on top of those clogged pores. If you don't, oh boy, that's just what they want. You forget about them and they grow into large blackheads and then it's too late to manage them." So. I not only have clogged pores but they're mean. They have an agenda and they are against me. What next? Is she testing me, wondering how I will be able to fight the evils of cancer if I cannot even clean my face properly? And then a funny thing happens. I see that my mother is not really looking at me. She is not suggesting that I have clogged pores or that I am deficient. She looks scared. It's not a look I'm used to seeing. Masks, cottage cheese, a makeup bag from 1932? Such small concerns for someone with such a large problem. Why bother? And it begins to dawn on me; for someone so committed to order, cancer must be the ultimate affront. What could be less orderly than having your very cells mutate and multiply without your consent? No wonder she is so focused on the little things. Right now they are about all she can control.

I no longer feel defensive. Only tender. And right then I know I will do my mother's cancer the way she wants me to, respectfully and, most of all, cheerfully, as if it will have a happy ending. She wants to carry on as if we are engaged in a project, like remodeling a home, an older home, yes, a challenge, definitely, but ultimately a doable one. After all, this is the reason we are giving to explain the visit. I have been quite busy since I left Florida. In addition to dealing with the problem of this Russell, I've resigned myself to the idea that I *do* want to attempt to land the job at the *Sentinel,* and have begun work on essay number two, studiously assuring myself that my interest in the job is strictly professional and has nothing to do with a certain crinkly-eyed, attractive editor. I've also begun to plan my annual Passover Dinner for approximately twenty-four relatives. Even though my parents will not be among them, since it's been decided that a second trip would be too grueling, my mother insists that I not disappoint the kids or the rest of the family. Fine. I do need to focus on something positive after immersing myself in information about pancreatic cancer. I've been collecting data from the Internet, national organizations, and friends, like a crazed research assistant on crack, double-checking statistics, filing info in color-coded folders, double-clicking on every cancer website from here to Hungary. Curiously, this is not unlike a thorough search for the best home improvement professionals, not unlike interviewing contractors, designers, and closet installers. Eventually, and with connections, I was able to make a series of appointments, all crammed into two days and beginning early on Monday, and that's exactly what we do.

First appointment, third floor, Dr. Gerald Cantor. Second appointment, east pavilion, Drs. Jakairan and McCormick. Third appointment, seventh-floor suite, Dr. William Zacharias. We have lunch, between appointments, on the Upper East Side, just as if we are looking at sectionals, not frozen sections of my mother's insides. To the outside observer, my parents and I might be taxiing around Manhattan on holiday, shopping for fabrics and the perfect armoire, rather than a medical messiah who will deliver the miraculous proclamation that (lo!) during the night a cure has been found for pancreatic cancer. I pretended to believe the impossible: If we keep up our constant humorous banter, dutifully search and research my mother's condition, and continue to leisurely lunch, things could turn out okay, and despite the numerous telltale bandages on the inside of my mother's arm, and the growing bruises beneath it as she gives blood no less than five times in forty-eight hours, it is only when the last doctor, the most eminent of specialists, apologizes for disqualifying her from his clinical trial, our final hope, that we all begin to sag.

"But, Doctor," my father is saying, pleading, it sounds to me, "she's an otherwise healthy woman, why not try?"

The doctor is uncomfortable. I can see it.

"She's seventy-four years old," he says quietly, "well past the maximum age for this trial."

"But she's got plenty of years left—"

"Sol," my mother whispers, "let it go."

My father shakes his head. "It doesn't make sense." He is getting agitated.

The doctor tries again. "These trials are based on statistics. I know it seems unfair, but in order to get funding they have to succeed, you see, and so the best profile for success is with a young person."

"Seventy-four is old? You think so? Of course you do, I can see that. But let me tell you something, seventy-four is nothing. Nothing!"

"Thanks, Doctor." My mother begins to get up. She doesn't want to make a scene. The doctor, approximately my age, looks to me for sympathy. Forget it. I am not on his side. I am exhausted. My parents are exhausted. Defeated. Two full days in Manhattan and the news is all bad, the opinions are all negative. Having pancreatic cancer is like having a crumbling roof, rusty pipes, and a septic system that is beyond repair. Nobody wants to take the job. Everyone we've interviewed wants to knock down and start over, not exactly an option. My mother is resigned, reiterating her fear of nausea and hair loss and pain. There is only the barest bit of surface remodeling to be had. We will have to go back to papering her world with the shiniest, most hopeful press releases (New Treatment from Budapest Shows Pancreatic Tumor Reductions) and painting her inside and out with the newest shades of Herbal Antioxidant and the latest in Faux Shark Cartilage. I feel guiltier than ever about dragging her up to

New York. She had known. By the time they find pancreatic cancer it is usually too late, the disease is so progressed that the organ is destroyed and usually other organs, specifically the liver, are infected. When it comes to pancreatic cancer, people don't say things like "Oh, I hear they've made marvelous strides with the pancreas!" Instead, they grimace and shake their heads and mutter, "Such a shame." There is no How To, only How Long.

As we're driving back to New Jersey the clouds roll in and a dull gray film hangs over the day, matching our mood. We drive past a building on the Harlem River Drive that has no windows and a burned-out façade. The whole structure is on a tilt and has red and white signs pasted all over it that say CONDEMNED and KEEP OUT. And just as I am thinking how much that building reminds me of my mother's body she remarks that she hopes there are no homeless people taking shelter in that one because it looks like it might come down any day.

WHEN WE ARRIVE HOME, Eric is there and my mother asks him how his business trip went and again I get the feeling she hasn't bought the lie. Eric doesn't help by acting funny, jumping about staccato-like as he greets them, mumbling something about "mis-zoned property." I don't know whether to be comforted or annoyed that he isn't smoother. I decide on comforted. After I've spent two torturous days in Manhattan, Eric looks like a big, soft, fluffy goose-down featherbed on which to fall. I want someone to hold me and tell me how wonderful I am and rub my feet. Any thoughts of dashing reporters or flirtatious flings are nonexistent. I want only the easy, comfortable clip of domestic familiarity. We are speaking again, but we haven't made love since I came back from Florida and I suddenly, intensely, want to rectify that, *after* I hear about his trip, of course. But we don't have a minute alone all afternoon and evening, so by the time we get into bed later that night I am exhausted and the only thing I am still in the mood for is the news of Branford and Russell.

"Okay, tell me everything."

"The property wasn't at all well located. I'm going to advise the investors not to buy."

"Very funny. You're stalling. Why? Did you meet him?"

"I did."

"And?"

"And he's not my type."

"Eric!" I throw a pillow at him.

"Okay, look, I spoke to him. He's very young, or at least he looks it. He could be one of Jake's friends."

"One of Jake's friends? Are you kidding me? Since when does Josh Fineman have a wife? Or maybe Matt Podell is the new superintendent of schools? What's going on? You were going to put the fear of God into him, remember? Did you at least kick him in the nuts?" I am getting concerned. Did my husband go up to Branford and confront the sleazeball, or did they have a friendly little chat?

"Jules, calm down. It wasn't exactly what I expected. First, he had all these students around him and they really seemed to like him."

"Oh, I can just imagine. Did these students have breasts?"

"No, listen, I heard him teach, I stood outside his class. He was amazing. Relating everything in literature to, um, modern stuff that the kids understood. They were totally into it. And then after, well, all these kids gathered around him at his desk, you know, just wanting to talk to him. Seems like a very sincere guy. You had to be there."

I am stunned. I don't know what to say.

"Eric. Did you talk to him or not?"

"I talked to him. He was taken aback at first. But then he seemed almost relieved. Jules, listen to me, you're not gonna wanna hear this, but he swears he loves her." I wait for the punch line. It doesn't come. I collapse on the bed in disgust. Eric turns over on his elbows, stretched out, facing me.

"I'm telling you. The guy is sincere. His marriage is over, his wife wants out as much as he does. And he knows more about Lexie than you think, like—like little things, how she twists her hair when she's anxious, and how she's a sucker for lost causes. And even though he looks young, he's very smart."

"This is unbelievable. What did you do, take him out for a Happy Meal?"

"We went for coffee."

"You went for coffee? You went for coffee?" I am spitting out the words. "Like civil, reasonable, friendly *coffee*?"

"I knew you were going to react this way. I know you think I didn't want to, whatever, make a scene, but I was there, not you, and I'm telling you, it's not like we thought. Plus I told him how much Alexis means to me, uh, to us. I told him that if he hurt her in any way, he'd have me to deal with."

"Oh, great! That must have scared him off! Who knows, next time you might drive up and force-feed him a doughnut!"

"Laugh if you want, but when I left he knew I meant business."

"Because that's when you . . . what? Showed him your marksman-ship award from Young Judea Summer Camp?"

"I shook his hand, Jules." Eric is getting disgusted with *me*. "And believe me, he got the message."

"Uh-huh. How?"

"By the pressure. And the fact that I held on an extra beat."

"I see."

"You don't believe me? Well, I have news for you—it's true. You can say a lot with a handshake."

You can say a lot with a right hook, I think to myself, but I don't say it.

"So you let this guy know not to mess with you by the pressure of your handshake. What's your backup plan? A foot massage?" Now it's Eric's turn to throw the pillow at me.

"I'm telling you, Jules, the guy's okay. I actually feel much better about all of this. He's had a rough life, no mother, put himself through school—graduate school, too. From what I gather, his father doesn't think too much of the teaching profession. He wanted him to follow in his foot-steps as a plastic surgeon and they had some sort of huge falling-out when he refused."

"Mm-hmm." I am less than impressed. "And the little woman? I suppose he trashed her too?"

"Actually, he didn't. Said they'd gone in different directions. She's a lawyer, ambitious type, travels all the time. In fact, she's heading out to Vail next week, *with her boss,* was how he put it, and I kinda got the feeling there was something going on there."

"Oh, great. So now everybody's running around. What else?"

"Well, interestingly enough, he's Jewish, at least by birth. He's sort of been nothing all these years."

If I were even vaguely inclined to consider this Russell an appropriate match for Alexis, his religious affiliation might have gained him some points, but I am still flabbergasted that Eric is defending him. I wonder if it's a defense mechanism. I was worried about how this might be wounding Eric, and maybe it is, so much so that he has to find a way to make this guy okay so the whole situation becomes wholesome! Which tells me a lot about how much tolerance he'll have for me if I don't manage to "set myself right," as he puts it. I am half-listening to Eric ramble on about Russell's past, wondering how he knows so much about him in such a short time, when something he says makes me sit up.

"What did you say?"

"Private schools all through high school."

"No, before that, about being a loner."

"Um, he likes quiet, used to it, that sort of thing. He has no siblings and he says he's overwhelmed by too much noise—apparently he and Lexie do a lot of solo things, walks and coffee, movies. Not big on the bars or the club scene. Why?"

"Well, I just had an interesting thought." I sit up now, my mind is racing.

"Jules?"

"So this 'nice guy' really loves our daughter? Well I guess we'll just see about that."

"What do you mean?"

"You said you left on good terms, right?"

"Yeahhh . . . So?" Eric is suspicious.

"So call him up. Tell him you've had time to think about it and you're willing to give him a chance, but there's something you want him to do."

"Oh, please. I can't do that."

"Why? Why not?"

"This is ridiculous. I can't just call him up! What's this about?"

I'm up on all fours. In his face.

"Eric, I have a great idea. How exactly did you leave it with him?"

"Um, I said we'd have to talk about it. I told him Europe was still out of the question but that I would try to be—I would try to convince *you*— to be somewhat open-minded."

"Excellent. So now you'll tell him I'm coming around." Eric looks dazed.

"You'll tell him I want to meet him." Now *he* is up.

"You what?"

"Oh, this is perfect. Yes, I want to meet him. Tell him I won't even consider the possibility of accepting him without meeting him. Then I'll call Lexie and tell her we want him to come for Passover dinner! If he doesn't come, we'll know he's the sleaze that *I*, for one, still think he is and Lexie will know it too—problem solved."

"Yeah but what if he—" I was up and pacing now, excited, and inter-rupted Eric mid-sentence.

"Oh, well, that's the beauty of it," I exclaimed. "If he comes"—I eased myself back onto the bed, crawling on all fours to Eric—"he'll get a taste of what being in our family is really like . . . and that should do the trick." I clapped both hands together as if to say "done deal."

"You're serious."

"Listen, this could work, really." Eric is staring at me. I'm pretty sure he thinks I'm nuts, but I've always expected that to happen anyway, right? Maybe I can save our daughter before they take me away. I sense a small opening.

"Look, you know what it's like here during the holidays. Between my cousins and your parents, it's like the common room at Rockland Psychiatric. You said he likes things quiet? Oh boy, is he in for culture shock." I sit back on my haunches and continue. "You know, we could really play up the Jewish thing too, I could make all the old traditional foods that I don't even like—you know, kishka and schmaltz herring and definitely gefilte fish— it is Passover, after all. Oh my God, and all the wine! What is it, seven glasses or eight? Oh this is great! Everyone will be drunk by salad!" I am giddy, laughing and excited. "I say he's out of here before you can say My Big Fat Dysfunctional Jewish Wedding. What do you think?"

"I think it's manipulative. Far out. Risky." Eric is leaning back, watching me, hands behind his head, but he is softening, smiling.

"You don't think he'll freak out?"

Eric hesitates. He is thinking about Russell, and I like the look that comes over him. He can't help but admit that I might have a point. He was one of those "only children." They don't do well in large gatherings, even temporary ones. Eric craved a big happy family, but he's the exception. As much as he may have liked this Russell, he's still been conflicted about the idea of anyone manipulating Lexie.

As a smile forms on his face, I know he's imagining Russell in the midst of our cacophonous family. "What makes you so sure he'll accept?"

That's an easy one. "You, darling," I say sweetly. "Your excellent and thorough assessment of his honest, sincere, and wanting-to-please character." Eric smiles.

"You're crazy." But it isn't a challenge; it's acquiescence. He sits up and pulls me toward him. Ahh, saved by sex. Eric doesn't care if I am a raving lunatic, or a serial killer, for that matter. He's horny.

"And, Eric, do not say anything about this to my mother. She's already implied that she thinks something's going on around here and she knows you are the easiest mark." He looks wounded, but happy. I know he's relieved that I am not pissed at him for blowing Operation Confront Russell. Somehow he blew it but he didn't. He leans in and kisses me and his hands move up under my nightgown. I almost protest. I am thinking about how to make Passover dinner especially chaotic this year when I remember that poor Roberta who lives across the street will probably be alone. Roberta's been having all kinds of marital problems, which she's decided to handle with multiple prescriptions of Valium and vodka chasers. Normally I wouldn't think of having her over on a religious occasion, but now I am bursting with generosity. If we're lucky, she might actually fall down and break something! Between that happy thought and Eric's urging hands, I smile inside and out. And for the first time in days I actually stop thinking altogether and just relax.

THIRTEEN

"don't encourage him, he's too young"

The next day is a good one. I am excited about our plan to have Russell for dinner. Jake is actually pleasant to his grandparents at 6:30 a.m. when he gets up for school (of course, my mother is up and dressed and waiting for him in the kitchen), and we all smile as he declines her offer to make him a nice, hot bowl of Cream of Wheat. Although Jake eats ten meals a day, the first course never begins before noon. And if anyone was worried about him not buying that his grandparents are visiting to shop, it was unnecessary. Jake is far too self-absorbed these days. Why or where his grandparents do whatever it is they do is of no interest to him unless it impedes his activities in some way. After I return from driving Jake to school, my mother "fake" complains that she "hasn't had any attention from my favorite [read *only*] son-in-law" and Eric cheerfully agrees to take her out to breakfast, which leaves me time to be alone with my dad, who looks as tired as he's ever looked. This is not going smoothly for him. I can't even imagine what life will be like for him without his precious "Stell." A vision of him alone and lonely in Florida spreads inside me like a shot of liquid anxiety.

"Dad, do you want some tomato juice?" He is sitting at the kitchen table, methodically counting out his pills. Oh, *now* he takes plenty of stuff for himself: eyedrops morning and night, thyroid, blood thinner.

"Jules, come count these pills for me. Do I have seven? There should be seven."

I look at the pills in his palm, counting six, and tell him so. He insists there should be seven.

"Two big white ones, a little blue, a little white, a big gelatinous thing and two medium-sized yellow ones that are scored. Immediately I see the problem.

"There's no blue one, Dad."

"I definitely took out the blue, are you sure?"

"I'm totally sure, there's no blue."

"Oh, well, then, I must have dropped one." At that moment I know I have a problem. There is nothing that falls on our floor that isn't instantly scooped up by either Lacey or Jasper. They could be two rooms away and they would hear a Cheerio fall on the kitchen floor. Slowly I turn to my right and sure enough, there is Jasper, sitting erect, tail wagging, tongue hanging out expectantly, slightly blue.

"Daddy, what is the blue pill for?" I try not to let him hear the panic as I mentally search for the vet's phone number. The last thing I want to do is stress him out any more than he's stressed already, but the second-to-last thing I want is for Jasper to have some sort of seizure.

"Uh, the blue one? Let me think. The blue one . . . the blue one. I think it's a vitamin, but the bottle is in here." He hands me his leather pouch. I search through the bottles, trying to think of blue pills, but I only come up with Tylenol PM. Surely my dad can't be taking Tylenol PM every day. Finally I see it. It's not a prescription bottle at all. Instead it's a tin. A white tin with a blue brushstroke, not of medicine, but of breath mints— in this case, spearmint.

"Daddy, the only blue thing in here is a breath mint."

"Oh, that's right. I forgot about that. Your mother likes me to have that after my juice and coffee." My mother likes him to . . . for a moment I feel the familiar pangs of rage, then guilt at the rage, but then I smile. Why should I get upset? If he doesn't mind, neither should I. This is their arrangement, their feng shui. They've made it together for over fifty years, and for once I'm tired of being incensed on my father's behalf. Plus, I don't have to rush Jasper to the doggie emergency room, a definite relief. And to think Eric doesn't like it when I suggest he wear cologne.

My parents are supposed to be on a six o'clock flight back to Florida, but when my mother returns with my husband, she is antsy. She is ready to leave this place of bad news and closed doors. There is no comfort here, no wildly odorous bougainvillea to tame or red-haired Latina to instruct or bite-sized poodle to stroke. They decide to pack up and go to the airport and try to get out on an earlier flight. Of course, by the time my mother packs her belongings, it is well into the afternoon anyway. I use the time to make a series of calls. Not only do I call back every single doctor we saw and plead her case, but also I call in the big guns, as Eric would say, the Burt Fogels of the medical world. I have no shame. Every single person I can think of who can possibly exert some influence makes my list. It takes me an hour and a half, and when I'm finished I am slightly ashamed and in a sweat, but I have some hope or at least less guilt, at times it's hard to distinguish between the two.

My parents insist that I drop them at the airport and leave, which I do only after a vigorous protest and their promise to call me when they know their flight. I am barely out of the airport when the phone rings. They have gotten on the very next flight, at three-thirty. I take it as a sign that the momentum is turning toward good fortune. When the phone rings again, I am wondering what she's forgotten to tell me, but I'm additionally surprised.

"When it comes to women, my instincts are always excellent."

I smile. Ted's voice is just delicious. How is it possible that just talking to him on my cell phone makes me feel so naughty and yet so alive? I have never been unfaithful to Eric, and nothing has happened between Ted and me, but I feel like it has. I look around guiltily, as if my fellow drivers on the New Jersey Turnpike must know that I am talking to someone who is not my husband, and even worse, that I'm enjoying it.

"I take it you liked my piece."

"Your piece? I certainly do. But I was talking about the essay."

"Very funny. What a mind you have."

"You should see the rest of me."

"Can we stick to the subject?"

"Are you sure you want to?" Damn. I wish I knew.

"Of course I'm sure. You didn't think my tone was too hostile?"

"I like it when you get angry."

"Ted!"

"Okay, okay. It was perfect, brilliant, I didn't even have to push for you. The committee was salivating. Keep it up. Did you start the second one?"

Wow. I didn't realize I'd be so pleased, that I'd been holding my breath, in a way, for days. I wanted more.

"They really liked it, they really did?"

"They loved it. I knew they would. I told you, I'm always right about these things."

"Oh my God." The reality of it hits me. I've got a shot at a byline at the *Suburban Sentinel*.

"Julie, don't get too excited just yet. There are some very well-known writers vying for the job, some that already work here in one capacity or another."

"Oh." I should've known better. I'd gotten ahead of myself. These things were always political anyway. What were the odds that the *Sentinel* would take a chance on me, a part-time, unpublished nobody? Maybe they already had someone in mind and just had to go through a show of advertising because of some law.

"Are you still there?"

I sigh. "Yep."

"Uh-oh, don't go all depressed on me. Jeez, I didn't realize you were so sensitive. I just want you to be realistic. I think the second essay, if it's really good, will establish you as a solid contender."

I think about the second essay. It requires a response to an opinion that, in the spirit of separation of church and state, no holidays or customs should be celebrated in the schools. None at all. I'd given it plenty of thought, especially since some of my fondest memories of Lexie and Jake in the lower grades were the holiday parties, me bringing in potato latkes while another mom served Christmas cookies and yet another mom decorated for Kwanzaa. The anti-holiday essay ended with the line, "You teach them reading, writing, and arithmetic. Kindly leave everything else to me." God, that bugged me! The author must be a racist, one of those few who had thought it perfectly acceptable for all the children to sing "We Three Kings," but suspiciously kept her kids home due to undisclosed illness on Menorah-lighting day. Well, I'd launched a radical defense. It was a mock memo from a fictitious principal to all second-grade teachers at a make-believe school, instructing them to refrain from all teaching that was not strictly academic. Of course, it exaggerated the end results of such strict guidelines. At the end of the memo, the principal directs that even cheating and name-calling is to be overlooked since honesty and manners are essentially nonacademic subjects. But now I was having second thoughts about the facetious edge, and it made me realize just how badly I wanted to impress the *Sentinel* staff.

"Um, Ted, I think maybe I should run my second one by you, it's a little out there. Is that allowed?"

"Technically? I have no idea. But e-mail it over anyway."

"Well, it's not done yet."

"Whenever it is."

"Actually, I thought maybe before I finish it I could show it to you—like in person." Silence. What am I doing?

"Okay. Good." If Ted was surprised, he quickly covered it up. I should reverse it, take it back, tell him that e-mailing was probably fine. Instead I find myself saying, "Do you think we could meet for lunch?"

AND NOW, as I pull into my driveway, I am breathless at the thought of sharing a booth with him tomorrow at noon, and try to assure myself that my sole reason for meeting him at the Coach House on Route 4 is to further my career. When I look at the clock, I can't believe I've driven the forty-five minutes from the airport. It seems to have taken about ten minutes. My mind must have been on autopilot after our conversation. Thanks to my parents' early departure, I'd even missed rush hour and made it home by four, almost two hours earlier than planned.

Jake's had the privilege of being home alone for so long, since before he turned thirteen, that I don't ever worry about him. He is so responsible that you would think he was the older sibling. If he and Lexie are both home, he is always the one to remember to turn on the outside lights when it gets dark, or to fill the dogs' water bowls if they're empty. So when I pull into our circular driveway I am surprised to see a strange car parked in front of the house. Jake has one or two friends who have their permits and are close to getting their licenses, but the only real drivers he knows are the older boys on the soccer team, and soccer season has been over for months. I pull into the garage and enter the house, expecting to see Kirby, the tall handsome goalie, or Jared, the broad-shouldered sweeper, but the house is silent so I call out, "Jaaayy! I'm home!"

There is a noise above my head something like a stampede and followed by what is possibly a crash and then I hear the slamming of a door and more thuds and I know instantly and with some fear to be suspicious. Random visions of drug paraphernalia being thrown into a closet or bomb-making devices hastily dismantled flash through my head even as the absurdity of Jake being involved in such activities takes hold. I pause, my hand on the railing of the back stairs, incomprehension the only thing keeping me from ascending, when Jake's door flies open and he emerges, followed by neither Kirby nor Jared nor any other member of any boys' soccer team I've seen.

"Hey, Mom, you're home early." He is so astute. And so breathless.

Behind him, blond hair flowing, breasts bouncing, is a girl.

"This is Kate." Uh-oh. I am unprepared. It's a girl. I say the words to myself, but I am still stunned. A part of me wants to laugh and give thanks. There is no greasy, tongue-pierced, trench-coated neo-Nazi on the stair, just a girl! And then it hits me, just a girl, alone in Jake's room, the two of them scrambling frantically when I called out. Wait a minute, when did this happen? It seems like just yesterday he was content to come home from school, dribble a basketball, and fall asleep on the couch with his hand shoved into a bag of Cool Ranch Doritos while watching reruns of *Saved by the Bell*. When did he make the jump from sitcoms to trysts? A part of me rejects the whole idea, denies it. No, Jakie, not you. No stunning surprises. You don't do that, Alexis does that!

"Hi, Kate." I am so cool, I think. I am friendly and smile and avert my eyes just enough so as to pretend not to see that her shirt is untucked on one side and there is lint in her hair. Back to Jake. I stare at him, but he continues past me without looking in my eyes and ushers her to follow him by his movement and, I suppose, his will.

"We were studying and we're just gonna get something to eat, okay?"

Kate brushes past me and I feel embarrassed for a moment, mostly for her, but she looks directly at me, no hint of shame or guilt, and says, "You have a beautiful home, Mrs. Resnick, I love the way the kitchen curves toward the backyard. It would be so great to have a sunroom there."

She is cool, this Kate, which throws me. She should be a little embarrassed, I think, and I want to hate her, but she has good taste so I don't.

"Thank you, Kate. Is that your car outside?"

"Yep. It's only two weeks old. My birthday present. Oh, is it in the way?"

"No, no, I just, I didn't realize you were seventeen. Are you a junior?"

Jake is suddenly there, he has come back to rescue her. He stares at me, and I get the impression he would like to turn me into stone or sand. My stomach literally hurts as he looks at me this way. Suddenly, impossibly, I am the enemy.

"Kate lives in New York, so she gets her license at sixteen, okay? She doesn't go to our school. She goes to Hills. Kate, c'mere, do you want Diet Coke or Sprite?"

"Oh, whatever you're having. Well, nice meeting you, Mrs. Resnick."

I am left on the stair. Am I dismissed? I do not really want to go upstairs, but I feel as if I am supposed to leave them alone. So I go. Rockland County, New York, is just a mile away from our home, but I never realized Jake knew anyone from there. God, I think to myself, what next? After about ten minutes, Jake says good-bye to Kate and walks her to her car (my baby is walking a girl to her car!), and it takes another ten minutes before she actually leaves. I know this because I am eavesdropping from a position at the top of the back stairwell that allows me to hear into the kitchen and see out into the driveway. When he comes back into the house, I take a deep breath and join him in the kitchen. I wonder if he will start or if he will wait for me. I know he knows that there is something to talk about. I'm betting he will play it cool and casual, and I am right.

"Jake," I begin, "we need to talk."

"Um-hmm." Oh, sure. *Now* his mouth is full of Cool Ranch Doritos.

"Jake, what is going on? I come home early and find you with some girl in your bedroom?"

"She's not 'some girl,' her name is Kate."

"How do you know her?"

"I met her at a party. She knows Ally and Brooke from soccer."

So maybe she *is* a sweeper after all.

"Has she been here before?"

"Why? What's the difference?"

"Jake," I sigh, wondering what it is I want to know or say, and knowing instantly exactly what I want to know.

"Jake, look, we never discussed this, having a girl here when we're not home. There are things we need to say, limits, ground rules, that sort of thing."

"So you mean I can't have friends over when you're not here?"

"No, I'm not saying that. I'm saying that this was a bit of a surprise. The two of you came bounding out of your room like you were in the middle of something—"

"Oh, please," he interrupts, "I don't want to hear this." He grabs the bag of chips and starts to leave.

"Just a minute. Jake! You are going to come back here and you are going to hear this." My tone brings him back.

"Jake, I don't know what you and Kate were doing, I'm not even asking you to tell me, I'm just saying that [help, what *am* I just saying?] being alone with a girl, while it may be an opportunity for [what?]—I mean, it has certain responsibilities."

"I know."

Standard answer. Whatever I say, he will answer "I know." I try again.

"Look, maybe you and Kate are just friends, whatever, but you have to think about a lot of things, including"—I pause for effect—"whether or not what you do is appropriate in your parents' house." God, I sound like I'm from *Little House on the Prairie.*

"As opposed to the backseat of a car?"

"So you're saying that you are doing something?"

"That's what you really want to know, isn't it?"

"I want to know that you're being smart, Jake, and safe, okay? Is that so terrible? I want to know that you respect yourself and this girl and us, too. I want to know that I'm not going to walk into my own house and get a big surprise, all right?"

"I'm outta here."

"Jake!"

"Later."

Unbelievable. Who is this child? Yesterday he needed his Gloworm to fall asleep, and today his tongue is hanging out and he is drooling like a baby, but it's not for a Gerber cookie, it's for someone named Kate. Something tells me that nothing has actually happened yet. Maybe it's his edginess and his bravado. I guess I must have this idea that if he'd actually had sex, he'd be more mellow and less tense. But they're doing something. There was an intimacy about the two of them, and they were definitely disheveled. God, how long has it been since we actually talked about condoms and AIDS and pregnancy? In fact, did we actually ever talk this out with Jake, or did we just assume he got it through Alexis Osmosis? Eric will have to speak with him immediately, since it's obvious that I'm the last person he'll talk to about this, which is probably normal. I make a mental note to ask Dr. Bob about adolescent male behaviors vis-à-vis their mothers. At least that will keep me from exploring the undertones of lunch meetings between wannabee columnists vis-à-vis handsome senior editors.

THE COACH HOUSE is a sparse, multiroom, matter-of-fact kind of restaurant, doing a brisk, impersonal lunchtime business, which I find reassuring, until the sight of Ted in jeans, white dress shirt, and blue blazer causes my chest to contract. He is standing in the vestibule, finishing a conversation on his cell phone, when I walk in. I get to watch him and catch my breath, which is good, and observe him, which is better. He is so tan, and the whites of his eyes are like porcelain. He looks like a movie star. Think George Clooney meets Ralph Lauren, but blond. I think every girl in the restaurant and in the world, really, must catch her breath as he passes by. And not just the older girls like me. Alexis told me that she and her friends think Pierce Brosnan is hot even though he's old. Ted has that same boyish cuteness and masterful air. He is smiling as he speaks.

"Then go with the vets, minus the hospital shot, right, the march and that's it."

I feel insignificant. I do not have a staff to call and instruct. I do have a slight wedgie, since I was too afraid to pick at my underwear when I got out of the car, not knowing where he was or if I could by seen by anyone. Ted smiles and raises his index finger to say he'll just be a minute.

"How many? Two? Smoke or no smoke?" The Greek maître d' barks questions and wants us to decide, and Ted waves that we should go in, so

I say, "Two, no smoking," and we follow him, me with my purse and file folder that holds my future and Ted finishing his conversation. As we approach the booth he snaps the phone shut, apologizes, and smiles so wide that if he was a surgeon you could forgive him for mistakenly amputating the wrong leg. ("No, no, don't worry. I should have reminded you that it was the black and green leg that was infected.")

"Hey, gorgeous."

"Hey, yourself. Thanks for meeting me."

"Major hardship. You owe me big-time."

"I figured that." Smile. Relaxing a bit. A little awkward moment over whether we should shake hands, kiss cheeks, or nothing, but the busboy arrives with water right in between us, so we just slide into our booths.

"So," he says, leaning back. I just look at him. My smile is wide, too. It's a little uncomfortable, but in a tantalizing way.

"So," I say back. We are big thinkers, all right.

"So do you want me to take a look first or after we eat?"

"It's up to you."

"I say first. Then we can just talk." I reach for the file and take out my rough copy and slide it over to him. He can see right away that it looks like a memo and he smiles. "Taking a creative risk, I see." I hate watching when someone reads my work. I never know what part they're at or what they're thinking. When Ted laughs out loud, I'm so happy I can't stand it. "What? What part are you at?" His finger is following along down the page and he is saying "Oooh, brutal," but he won't tell me where he is, so I jump out of my seat and go next to him to see. He is coming to the end, and as he does, he turns to me and the closeness is paralyzing. I can smell him. His aftershave and his breath are like vanilla and pine and maybe something citrusy, too. I can see that he is mesmerized, too, and not by the essay.

"Sorry," I say, returning to my side of the booth, and hoping that he can't see me blush. "It makes me crazy when I watch someone read my stuff."

For all his smoothness, Ted is looking plenty ruffled himself, and I realize I don't know anything about him. What is he feeling? What have his past relationships been like? Was he ever married?

"You're incredible." He's looking right at me.

"I am?" Does he mean me the girl, or me the writer? He points to the essay.

"This is so great. I don't know how you can get so worked up about a holiday show, but you totally won me over." I have a moment of disappointment. But then he slides the essay over to me and adds, "I'm beginning to think you're too good to be true." His hand comes to rest next to mine and he doesn't move it and he stares at me and I know he means more than just about my writing and he knows I know this and we have a moment, a very brief moment, and then I pull my hand back and pick up the menu. "Well," I say. "Well." I look down and up again and say, "Thank you, um, thanks." Now we both look at the menus although I'm sure neither of us is very hungry, and over half-eaten salads we make some small talk. I do ask Ted about his past, and in the sketchiest of ways he mentions a failed marriage and a series of meaningless relationships as well as a confession that after years of being single he's finding it harder and harder to compromise his routines, adding that he's never found anyone who made altering those routines seem worthwhile. I find myself alternately wanting to kiss him or comfort him and wanting to escape the terror of this lunch and go back to my nice, safe, neurotic life. I suddenly find myself looking around constantly in case I should see someone I know, and realizing with panic that I don't have a suitable explanation if I should. Ted insists on paying for lunch, and although I'm hesitant, I allow it, because I now firmly want to get out of there. In the parking lot we say good-bye and this time we do the cheek-kiss thing, but in the most chaste, brother-and-sister sort of way. I have a headache. I'm all mixed up. I don't know exactly what kind of fire I'm playing with, but I know it can burn. It takes me an hour to calm down.

That night I push Ted out of my mind and concentrate on things I can control, mainly getting Eric to talk to Jake. But they can't seem to connect; one is always leaving as the other arrives. Kate, however, is quite available and seems to be at our house every minute. She has even stopped by Wednesday evening to drive Jake to a Peer Leadership meeting at the high school. Tonight is my Writer's Group, so I will be out from eight to ten, and Eric has gone straight from the office to a business dinner. I am grateful that Jake has a meeting and that the two teenagers will not be alone in the house. I am grateful for the routine and the distraction of my group. I'm in the kitchen, cleaning up the dishes, when Kate comes downstairs and we have a rare moment alone.

"Do you need any help?" she asks sweetly. Yes, I want to reply. Please return my baby boy to me; I think it's time for his bath.

"No, thanks," I say instead. It occurs to me that Kate and I have never been alone since she is rarely out of Jake's sight. He has taken to following her around wherever she goes. If she goes to get a soda, he is there. If she goes to the bathroom, he hovers nearby. Yesterday he accompanied her to the driveway when she went to get a history book out of her car. And just as I begin to wonder, three, two, one . . . there he is.

"Here you are." The smile on his face is positively dopey. And he can't seem to go more than thirty seconds without touching her. Now he grabs a bunch of her hair and asks if she's ready to go.

"Okie." That's what she says: "Okie," not "Okay." Then she turns to face him by pirouetting on her toes so that there isn't even an inch of air between them. The look on Jake's face tells me he wouldn't know if she only spoke Swahili and wouldn't care, either. They pile out the door and fifteen minutes later, I do too.

That night in bed I urge Eric to make some time and have a talk with his son.

"So you'll talk to him?" I begin sweetly. He puts down his *Time* magazine and looks at me.

"So ya think he's gettin' some?"

"God, would you please try to sound like a grown-up?"

"Hey, it's a guy thing, okay?" He is not ashamed; rather, he is smiling.

"So is she pretty?"

"No. She's a big fat blimp with pimples and frizzy red hair."

"No, really, is she pretty?"

"She weighs 260. Her hobbies are sumo wrestling and all-you-can-eat contests. Oh, and world peace."

"She's pretty, right?"

"Right."

"And he wouldn't tell you anything?"

"Nothing."

"Sounds promising."

"Eric, *please.*" I am starting to hyperventilate. "Don't encourage him, he's too young. And make sure you talk about protection and give him the speech about one minute of pleasure can cost a lifetime and oh God you better scare him a little and mention that we don't know how this girl feels about abortion and how would he like to be a father and give up his plans? Okay? Eric, are you listening?"

"How about we go over the part about one minute of pleasure?"

"Eric!"

"No, really. Just lie there and give me one minute and I promise you a lot of pleasure."

I am on my side and Eric is running his hands up alongside me, over my outer thigh and hip and into the valley of my waist and then slowly up along the side of my breast. His thumb trails over the front of me, and when it reaches my nipple I gasp. Maybe it is guilt over my clandestine lunch with Ted or maybe *because* of my lunch, but I am in the mood.

"I'll give you thirty seconds," I say devilishly, "and if you can't turn me on by then, I'll just have to attack *you.*"

Eric is unexpectedly thrilled, and I am surprised by my own abandon and energy. I rationalize that I must have been stimulated on some level by something. While Eric and I make love, I realize that despite everything that's going on I haven't worried about falling apart in several days. As I drift off into the sleepy night, I wonder if perhaps I've been overreacting about my fragility all along.

FOURTEEN

hold on to him for just a little longer

Driving Jake to school is sometimes like a little gift from the parenting gods. A few moments to forget the crude language and dirty laundry and self-absorption and see only the softness and sensitivity that makes me want to cuddle and stroke him despite his being sixteen. In the predawn light, my little boy has gangly legs pushed up and into his chest on top of his backpack, no jacket despite the frosty morning chill, eyes still partially hooded, and an air of vulnerability as he tries to prolong the night and savor the last few unfocused moments before his day begins. I love driving Jake to school because I know that I am less than a year away from the end of it. I want to savor every hurried morning, every crazy afternoon school line and every car pool. He is so ready to be mobile that I could never begrudge him his independence, but for me it will be sad, another passage out of something into something else. The car is warm and the day is still so blanketed by darkness that I need my headlights, and as I look over at my son I am overwhelmed with motherly instinct. I want to keep him here in this car-womb with me a little longer. There is something about Jake that makes him seem fragile when he's half asleep. I never catch the little girl in Alexis anymore, she is fully grown into herself, but it's different with Jake. It seems to me that men are quick to revert to babies when they rest, able to surrender their serious selves up more effortlessly than women. The demands of the world appear to leave Jake the instant he lies down and pulls a blanket up around him, and even his smell is reminiscent of bunk beds and Band-Aids and Cheerios. These days, these teenage, testosterone-swelled days, I know so much less about Jake than I used to, he is often a stranger. I find that the more questions I ask, the less information I get. One question is okay, but try to ask a second and it is perceived as harassment. What used to be an afternoon ritual of "How was your day?" is now an intrusion. I wonder if this boy-man is growing emotional limbs to survive in the world, just as he once grew fingers and toes in the womb? It seems unnatural to have known everything there was to know about him, how his thumb crept into his mouth when he napped, the way the ends of his hair rolled into tight little curls after a bath, how he liked the butter put on his bread before it was toasted, to have known all this and more, and to know so little about him now. I want to hold on to him for just a little longer. So much so that it hurts.

I steal a glance at Jake as I'm driving and wonder if there's anything else going on with him that I missed. His grades are good and he seems happy to me, nothing appears out of the ordinary. But maybe that in itself is strange for a teenage boy. Have I counted on him to be uneventful? I know that Lexie has trained us to expect her dramatics and I wonder if we've trained Jake to assume the role of the predictable son. Sometime between this crisis and the next I resolve to talk to him, really talk to him. I don't know his hopes or his dreams or his fears and this worries me. Does Jake even have any fears? It occurs to me that there is nothing he's afraid of. Not that he's a superhero or anything, it's just that I can't name any of his overt fears, and this, too, seems awfully strange. Who isn't afraid of something? Even Eric, who likes to fight his fears, has a thing about snakes. I certainly have more than my share. Alexis has a virtual fear itinerary, headed up by peacocks. She has had this fear since she was three, when she claims she was attacked in Van Saun Park, but Alexis is the only one who remembers the incident as an attack. Eric and I remember a vague, distant, and benign "flapping." And we don't think she is as afraid of peacocks as she makes out, anyway. We've noticed that she gets quite a reaction when she tells people she is afraid of peacocks. The girls think it's adorable ("Peacocks, you're kidding!") and the boys get all puffed up, imagining, I guess, that they could definitely protect her from a peacock. Once again, Lexie has found a way to turn a hang-up into something cool, and besides, she is not confronted that often, as petting zoos tend not to be a big part of campus life. Here is how she states her case:

"Think about peacocks," she begins. "Everyone says how beautiful they are, but did you ever see one up close? Believe me, you wouldn't want to cuddle with it. Plus, they are like living jack-in-the-boxes, you never really know when they're going to just throw open all those feathers in your face. A walking horror movie, if you ask me."

If only I could find a way to make Lexie have a dream about a peacock with Russell's face on it, that would be excellent. Actually, a subliminal connection to any creepy, negative image would do. Until then, I will have to rely on Operation Passover. And once again I have started out wondering about my son and ended up focusing on my daughter, and I know I do that a lot. The truth is she has a way of sucking up all the emotional air, appearing more complicated, more needy than her brother. Obviously I do count on him to be the good one and on some level he must know it, but how can he when I am just coming to it myself? Bad parenting, I admonish myself. I need to be more honest with Jake and I will, soon, right after I call Alexis and try to dupe that professor into leaving her alone.

"You want what?" She has now asked me the question three times.

"Look, Lex, if you don't want him to come, that's fine. We were just trying to be accommodating."

"No, fine, I mean, great. I'll ask him. I mean, he might not be able to get away, but, well, thanks." I can picture the quizzical look on my daughter's face, almost hear her wondering what to make of our invitation, and I almost laugh into the phone. It isn't often that we have a chance to stun Alexis. In our last conversation we'd been clearly opposed, and now suddenly here I was, saying that we wanted to meet him. And not just any old time, but next week, and for *Passover*. Maybe Alexis was wondering if Russell would be able to come. Of course, thanks to Eric, I know that his wife is going to be out of town at her boss's ski house, and the knowledge makes me a bit uneasy. I try to reassure myself. This can't hurt Alexis in any way. In fact, we are actually doing a *good* thing. If this Prince Charming is so wonderful, it shouldn't matter how large or loud or loony her family is—and if he can't handle it, better to know now. Alexis would have to agree, I tell myself, but I am still not entirely convinced. What I need now is confidence, not doubts. What I need is a nice list.

FIFTEEN

any baby named Zeus should be able to handle a couple of dogs

1. *Borrow extra folding chairs from Beth.*
2. *Cook and freeze chicken soup (two pots).*
3. *Cancel Dr. Bob for Wednesday of Passover.*
4. *Send funny tapes to Mom (laughter known to cure cancer).*
5. *Find out who Mom thinks is funny.*

Then, as an afterthought:

6. *Refill prescriptions for Imitrex, Xanax, Pepcid, etc.*

With Passover just over a week away, I need to organize. I call in my orders for meat, gefilte fish (I once made the fish from scratch. It took about six hours to make, and a week of apologizing for the smell of boiled fish heads—too bad I don't have the time now, I would love the smell of fish heads to greet Russell at the door), and I start to ready the house. We are Conservative Jews and don't follow the strict rules of removing all bread products from the house, but I am a purist about what we actually eat for eight days, so my grocery list contains some weird things: potato starch, matzoh cake meal, and about forty dozen eggs. I did not get these observant stirrings from my mother, who can actually make a mean Jewish meal but prefers less traditional nouvelle cuisine on the holidays. (Something about all the chicken fat and stewed meat reminds her of a deprived childhood; so growing up we had everything from baked salmon to a most un-kosher chicken parmigiana for Seder.) I took a class at the JCC on the Palisades in Tenafly, New Jersey, and learned how to cook everything from tsimmes, a casserole of stewed prunes that cooks for about a decade, to mandelbrot (think Jewish biscotti).

I AM WORKING on the latest guest list when Eric comes home. Holidays are chaotic at our house, even without trying. Several years ago, after one depressing Passover Seder at the Orchard Hills Country Club when it was just the four of us (I thought it would be lovely but it was just lonely) I learned that I prefer (need?) a lot of turmoil around the holidays, and I don't care to analyze this with Dr. Bob or anyone else. In fact, I like to get a little crazy as the day draws near and the guess list shifts, which is usually because cousin Diane has yet another personal crisis or one of cousin Ellen's kids cracks up the car or loses the dog. I begin by making elaborate food lists, sketching out possible seating charts, and pre-baking and freezing up a storm, although obviously this year will be modified. Certain items on the menu are a given. For instance, my nephew Derek craves my baked stuffed potatoes, so they are perennial, and I make four extra halves for him to take home. And Lexie goes crazy for my flourless chocolate cake even as she fights not to consume the calories. This year I will be adding a smorgasbord of unappetizing, unidentifiable delicacies.

Whether or not my brothers come depends on the physical or emotional status of their respective in-laws. Lyle's wife, Barbara, has been bringing her mother, Arlene, to me since her father died, five years ago, and that has worked out nicely. Stewie's in-laws like to take the family away for the holiday, cruises to the Caribbean and golf trips to the Carolinas, and it's hard to compete with that, but this year they've decided that they need a break from traveling, and Stewie's wife, Gayle, has asked if she can bring them to me along with her dysfunctional brother, Edward, and of course I've had to say yes. No one is really sure what's wrong with Edward except that he's forty-two and still lives at home and pulls at his ears. I guess we all assume that he is bipolar or schizophrenic, but it is never discussed. Gayle's parents, the Solomans, are Old School, in that they don't "air their dirty laundry in public" as Viv Soloman puts it. I don't really like Viv, none of us does, she's always been a bit stiff and phony, but we put up with her because of Stewie and Gayle. Viv professes to love my children, and compliments them often. Since my mom moved to Florida, Viv acts like she wants to step into the role of surrogate grandmother, except she only acts that way at the moment she is seeing them and never makes good on her promises to "get tickets to see a show" or "take them to a museum." In between the holidays and birthday dinners we never hear from her. Gayle's dad, Lou, is a sweet, passive man who seems perpetually out of it but is very bright. "My genius," Viv mutters often, but it's more an expression of frustration than a compliment. When someone asks Lou a question, it seems to startle him. It also makes you wonder about Edward, about that fine line between genius and madness. I confess that I wasn't initially thrilled to have Gayle's family, especially since my nieces—their three daughters, whom I do adore—may not be able to come, so except for Stewie, there won't be any good Bermans to offset the annoying Solomans, but now that we have Russell coming, I'm ecstatic. I wonder if we can somehow push Edward over the edge, just a little, into doing something really weird like grunting or something, just enough to make Russell wonder if the whole family's nuts. Lyle's two kids are both coming, which works out great, since Derek just graduated from college and so did cousin Ellen's oldest daughter, Jillian. Jillian is always a little strange; hopefully she hasn't outgrown that. Lyle's older son, Evan, and his wife, Brooke, have an adorable new baby boy, and it will be great to have babies at the table again. Of course they had to go and name the baby Zeus, which freaked everyone out, including me, but what can you do.

"So what's the final count?" Eric asked, although the actual number would mean little more to him than the number of chairs he'd have to fetch from the basement. Normally, Eric's parents spend every holiday with us, but this year they were intent on experiencing Passover at one of those dilapidated old Catskill hotels, the Paramount, with a group of local merchants and an aging second cousin from Orange County. They'd known better than to suggest we join them, and Eric wasn't even upset. On the contrary, he was relieved. It meant he was really off the hook in terms of responsibility. I felt torn. Normally it would be a real treat to have a break from Helen and Harry, but now I was slightly disappointed. I was counting on the fact that Helen has a nice shriek to her voice.

"Welllll . . . I think we're twenty-four, but that all depends . . ." and I began to give him a rambling account that would confuse a genealogist, ". . . on whether or not Tracy is coming and if Diane is bringing someone. Also, there's a chance that Dana's conference will get cut short, and if she can get a flight she's going to grab one but she won't know till the last minute. Of course I'm also basing this on the fact that Diane insists Tori is coming but she can't say about Mark because they've been fighting again." I could see that I was losing my husband, but I went on anyway, checking my notes for accuracy.

"Oh, and Tori *is* a vegetarian and Ellen thinks Tracy is allergic to *all* nuts and Brooke called to say that she hopes it's not too much of an inconvenience but they don't allow the baby near dogs. I wanted to say that I thought any baby named Zeus should be able to handle a couple of dogs but I didn't. So I guess we need to get those crates out of the basement. I hope I didn't lend them to anyone." I looked up, but Eric had already gone. He pretends not to share my delight in mass holiday hysteria, but we all know he loves it. However, he is purposely distancing himself from Operation Russell and will not join me in my efforts to create as much dysfunction as possible. Plus, he is scheduled to have a colonoscopy tomorrow and has called me three times today to make sure that I will be accompanying him. Eric is never sick, has never been in the hospital, and has never had a procedure stronger than a gum cleaning. He is also on his sixth glass of GoLytely in preparation for tomorrow, which explains his quick departure. I am about to go check on him when my mother calls.

"Hi, Mom, how are you feeling?"

Big sigh. "Oh, fine. Are you getting ready for the holiday?"

This is tricky. A simple yes will not do. She does not like to miss family gatherings. So she'll still want me to do everything perfectly (a reflection on her) but not be too happy about it since she won't be there. I try to convey competence without excitement.

"Everything's under control."

"Did you polish the silver?"

"No, Mom, you don't have to do that anymore, it stays pretty good."

"That's what you think, but you better check that bowl under the Lenox platter, you know, the one you like to use for vegetables. You always forget about that until the last minute."

She's right. "Okay."

"Are you making your candied carrots?"

"Of course."

"Use a little less sugar this year."

"Fine."

"When is my Lexie coming?" She hasn't spoken with her?

"I'm not sure yet, haven't you talked to her?"

"Of course." Okay, then.

"I guess you'll manage just fine without me."

Oh God. That's what it's really about, isn't it?

"Of course not, Mom. You know my matzoh balls never come out right without you and I can't even begin to figure out how you fold the napkins into those perfect shapes." I can *hear* her smile.

"Are you using my china?"

"Your china, your crystal server, and those little salt and pepper swans."

"Julie."

"Yes?"

"Don't forget to call your father."

"On Passover?"

"Not this year, you know, in the future."

Oy.

"Mom, really—"

"It's bad enough he has to spend this Pesach alone with a sick wife, but if you're all together and if he doesn't hear from you . . ."

Oh God. This is not just guilt for now but guilt for later, from the grave.

"Mom, please. You know you don't need to say that."

"I just don't want you to forget, that's all. You have a very busy life up there."

"I'm not the one who moved to Florida."

"Don't be fresh."

"Okay, sorry. Don't worry, okay? Is there something else wrong?"

"What do you mean? Of course not. I have to go now. *Golden Girls* is coming on."

"Okay. I'll talk to you tomorrow, okay?"

"Okay."

"I love—" She's gone. Shit, I forgot to ask who she thinks is funny. I don't think Bea Arthur has cut an album yet.

IN THE MORNING we set out for Dr. Marion's, and I do feel badly for my husband, who looks as if he would rather fight Muhammad Ali than lie down on a stretcher in the doctor's office. We sit in the waiting room and he does a good job of pretending to read a copy of *Time* magazine. I have brought material from my writers' group, and plunge into a script that is a slapstick comedy based on the drug-related antics of a group of New Jersey twentysomethings. By page three I realize that my son would certainly pay good money to see this film, which in fact is quite funny in a commercially trashy sort of way. Eric has gotten up a few times at the request of the receptionist to provide insurance information and retrieve his card, and by the time his name is called I am so engrossed in the screenplay and so used to him popping up and down that I barely notice when he moves reluctantly toward the nurse and says, "Okay, so I'll see ya."

"What?" I say, distracted, as I am in the middle of a very funny bit between the hunk bartender and a disgruntled policeman he used to know and pick on in high school.

"I'm going in." Eric sounds like he's about to parachute into Korea, but I don't notice.

"Okay, honey, have fun," I call out, forgetting what it is he's here for. Two pages and a few minutes later I look up from the script to find the other people in the room staring at me and wondering, I'm sure, if I am really as insensitive as I sound. Luckily my husband emerges an hour later, sleepy but intact, unable to remember anything. Dr. Marion pops his head out and says everything went fine and Eric is in the clear.

"It was the strangest thing, Jule," he mumbles. "I dreamt about your dad."

"You dreamt about my dad while you were having something shoved up your ass? Okay, more than I need to know."

"No," he says thickly, trying to shake off the Demerol, "I dreamt he could see perfectly and he wanted to go up to Branford and talk to Lexie. He said he had something to say that would fix Lexie and your mother at the same time."

"Really? My kind of dream. Did he go?"

"I think so."

"And did he fix everything?"

"I don't know, I don't remember any more about it."

"Well, don't you think you should go back in there and get a vasectomy or something so we can find out?"

Eric isn't too groggy to laugh, but laughing unbalances him and he leans on me as we make our way to the car. "I love you, Jule."

I look at him, my throat tightening, ashamed of myself for even thinking that another man could make me happy. What's wrong with me? Am I really programmed to self-destruct? It must be some kind of rebellion, this looking for danger. When I was younger I always went for the bad boys, the players, the ones that other girls instinctively knew were trouble. Some sort of knee-jerk reaction to being Suzy Sunshine at home? But it never worked. I never felt happy or peaceful—excited maybe, but not happy, not until Eric.

As I help him into the car he says, "The doctor said I have a really clean colon."

"How attractive," I shoot back. "I've always been a colon girl myself." But I get it. Eric gets scared too. It seems none of us is safe from worrying about how it will all turn out.

SIXTEEN

between homesickness and existential despair

When we get home I put Eric to bed and tuck him in as if he were a child. He pulls me close and says thanks, gives me a mushy kiss, and then turns and draws himself into the same fetal position Jake assumes when he's zonked. As I stroke his forehead, relishing the feeling of nurturing him, I have this strong, clear thought: Eric is a good man. I feel lucky to be so sure that he not only loves me but also needs me. This is not a fantasy or an indulgence on my part, it is Eric himself who tells the kids that he "hit the lottery" when he met me. We were on a car trip a few years ago, when he first revealed himself to Lexie and Jake.

"All those years in Spring Valley, in the country, I was pretty backwards. I was kind of a math nerd. Do you know how many hours I spent in that office with Grandma and Grandpa with nothing to do?" The kids did know. Not only had they heard about it, but Eric had taken them there once, which was all it took. After that they begged never to go back. "There's nowhere to sit, it's all disgusting," Lexie said, "and the weirdest people walk in and out of there."

"Can't Grandma and Grandpa ever have us to their *house*?" Jake had asked.

"I don't think so," Eric replied. "They forgot where it is. So anyway," Eric continues, "we had no small TVs or Game Boys, but there was that old adding machine I showed you, and I used to play with that. I was so bored that I would spend hours adding up sums and subtracting. By the time I was six I was a whiz; I started to think in numbers instead of words. I would go into Grandma's office and interrupt her and say something like, "I've been here for 14,400 seconds today.""

"Oh God, how dorky." Lexie smirks.

"That's pretty cool, though," offers Jake, "you know, how you figured out the seconds and all."

"Thank you, Jake. I see you've developed an excellent appreciation of my finer qualities."

"So, what did Mom see in you anyway?" Lexie is right to the point.

"Well"—Eric shares a wink with me—"your mother almost didn't see anything in me at all. I just barely got up the nerve to go speak to her. We were at a party at someone's beach house in the Hamptons, and when she walked in, she was easily the most beautiful thing in the room."

"AWWW . . . !" Both kids in unison. I am blushing.

"I mean it. Her eyes and her smile were sparkling like in one of those toothpaste commercials, you know, with the little diamonds bouncing off them?" I look over at Eric to see if he is pouring it on, just to tease the kids, but he is dead serious. "At least that's what it looked like to me. So there I was, calculating how many steps it would take to walk over to her, and then converting the steps into feet, then inches, then centimeters, and then, before I knew it, I had waited too long and she was on her way out. So I just propelled myself toward her and said the first thing that came into my head." I start to smile as I remember back to that summer night so many years ago.

"What? Wha'd you say?" The kids are leaning on the front seats, demanding to know.

"I said, "You don't think I can let you leave without getting your number, do you?"

"Oh, Dad! That's pathetic!" Lexie falls back against the seat, laughing. We are all laughing. "Why did you even answer him, Mom?" my worldly teenage daughter wants to know.

"He was sooo cute, Lex. Very nervous, but cute." Eric grins.

"Your mom took pity on me. I remember that her friend made a noise like she was about to crack up, but Mom had the grace to ignore her. Instead, she looked right back into my eyes, and without missing a beat she said, '486-2486. That's 212. If you can remember it, I'll be on the other end.' Well, of course she had no way of knowing that numbers were my game"—Eric looks over at me—"and I've always thought that was a bit of fate."

"You remembered the number?" Jake is pleased.

"Hey, what do you think? A telephone number is no match for the Walking Calculator!" Eric invokes the nickname I'd given him early in our relationship, a name the kids have since picked up on and embraced.

I AM REMEMBERING that scene as I make my way down to the kitchen, when something catches my eye through the window at the top of the landing. There, on the lawn in the backyard, are two deer calmly nibbling on the grass. The vision is monumental. We live in the suburbs of New Jersey, fairly close to Manhattan, but our town has been carved out of what used to be hundreds of acres of farmland and orchards, most of which are slowly being developed so that many families of deer are forced into smaller and smaller areas and into increasingly bolder contact with humans. This is not why the deer are monumental, though, for me. They represent whole chunks of my childhood. Spotting deer was a kind of physical mantra for me during an endless string of car trips, vacations, and "going visiting." I see these two deer and I am no longer a grown-up with my own home or even a young mother with two children in the back of a

Jeep, but ten years old, unbelted, sprawled and sticking to the backseat of my parents' blue Buick on a summer trip from Long Island to the Catskills. I am looking out the window for deer, as I did on every long drive if there were any woods to scour. Once I got started, I couldn't stop. I'd spend hours staring out the window, afraid to turn away, afraid even to stretch my poor, strained neck, sure that at the moment I looked away, Bambi and family would scamper across the meadow and back into the trees. And my parents encouraged it. They would say, "Are you looking really hard? I bet there are plenty of deer coming up. You have to concentrate." Years later, in a car with two children and a headache of my own, I understood the appeal of having your kids search *quietly* for deer. But naturally my kids never took to it with the same gusto I had.

The most astonishing thing about seeing the deer now in my own yard is that during all those years when I was growing up, looking out the window of the Buick and then the Cadillac, I never did see a deer. Not one. Ever. Not on our way to the mountains, or to camp, or to Uncle Irv's in Westchester. The only animals I ever saw were cows, hundreds of them, and horses, lounging lazily in fenced fields. And then one day there was that horrible dog, a mangy mutt whose unremarkable existence should have been as inconsequential to my life as one of those slumping horses, but who instead became a permanent character in our family lore.

"Remember that horrible dog?" This is how my mother always begins the story, with a slight shiver, barely able to ask the question, as if the dirty, diseased animal might come back to life just by mentioning him. When I was young, I was so proud to have been there, to have a part in the story, that I always begged her to tell it.

"We had just passed a river," she would begin. My father would interrupt at this point and remind her that she had distracted him, but she would wave him off with her hand and a roll of her eyes and a conspiratorial wink toward me.

"Julie was being an angel, looking out the window for deer . . ." Let's get it straight, Mom, Julie was engaged in a bovine obsession.

"There were several people standing in the river . . ." When my mother details the events, I am transported back to the Buick. I can feel the vinyl seat sticking to my shins, its thick seams making indentations in my knees as I perch, alert for signs of movement in the trees.

"Fishin' for their dinner," my mother remarked, as we passed. No sooner had she said it when from nowhere a black and tan dog darted right onto the highway in front of our car. My dad never even had time to stop. I felt it, a double bump under our car, and then I made the mistake of following the sound by turning and looking out the back. Although my dad had now slammed on the brakes, the dog literally came flying out from under the back of our car in a half twist, straight up in the air, before it landed in the middle of the road. I was transfixed.

"My God, what was that?" My father had pulled over to the side. The people were coming up from the river. We could now see that it was a family. A mother, a father, and five dirty, disheveled children.

"Sol, you have to get out. Good God! Could that have been their pet?" My dad, muttering, pulled the car even farther off the highway. Other cars were coming, and he tried to signal them over to the other lane. The man had reached the dog and was pulling it out of the road, but the children hung back with the woman.

"Let's get out and get some fresh air," my mother said to me, lightly, as if we had merely stopped for a stretch. Even then she pretended that nothing was ever wrong. Was it for me or for her? We stood on the side of the road, ankle-deep in wildflowers and dried-up, wheat-colored grass that tickled my legs, the cool mountain air already becoming oppressive as the morning slipped into midday. Me in my red and white striped Danskin shirt and matching red shorts, white socks, and red Keds, my mother in her Jackie Kennedy green and white polka-dot shift, white patent leather sandals and white, plastic-rimmed sunglasses, a crisp lace kerchief in her thick brown hair. We could have been on the cover of *Look*. Across from us, in a cluster, and in sharp contrast, stood the river family. The mother glared at us, openly hostile. She was dirty, wet, and spattered with muck or slime. In fact they were all covered with the same greenish black substance. There was a little girl who looked close to my age, holding her baby brother's hand, wearing no shoes and a torn sundress that may have once been yellow. I don't think I had ever seen anyone so filthy up close, and I remember thinking of the character in a book I was reading, Ramona something. But I hadn't imagined Ramona as this dirty, just kind of messy. Involuntarily, I leaned back toward my mother, not wanting to get too close to them. These people were . . . different. And then, suddenly, I felt guilty. I couldn't take my eyes off them, but I also wished that I had stayed in the car. I suddenly felt self-conscious that my hair was held in place by my shiny red headband and that my mother's dress was so . . . bright. One of the boys had wandered over to our car and was touching it. He ran his fingers along the blue metal the way I sometimes stroked my mother's mink coat, the way I like to feel soft leather today, lovingly, sensually, and he pressed his nose right up against the back window. Inside, on the seat, was my brand-new Etch-a-Sketch. I had an intense urge to grab it and give it to him, but I was never as noble in deed as in thought, even then, which is why my guilt is endless. I've spent a lifetime trying to assuage that guilt, first as a naïve child, later as a well-intended volunteer, and finally as a writer with imagined purpose.

My dad came over, and he and my mother had a short discussion of which I only heard snippets: ". . . should give something . . . not your fault . . . so poor . . ."

"*Was* it their pet?" I wanted to know.

"Ssh. Get back in the car, now."

I obeyed. But after my parents joined me, I asked again. "Was it their pet? Was it?" We were pulling away and I was leaning forward on the seat, but also watching out the back as the river people slunk back into the gully and became smaller and smaller, watching until they were nothing more than a blur of dust. If not for the heat, which held the smell of the day inside the car, and which was slow to respond to the filtering effects of the Buick's primitive air-conditioning, I might have thought I'd dreamed it all. But I hadn't, and I was still insisting on an answer. "Was! It! Their! PET?"

My father glanced at my mother, who looked back, astounded at my tone. She seemed to draw a deep breath and physically regain her composure. Then she reached up and back and patted my hand.

"No, sweetie, it was just a stray." Then, "Are you looking for deer?"

As DISTURBING AS that memory is, there was something else that came out of the horrible dog story. My father was so unnerved about the dog that he missed the turnoff for the hotel and didn't even realize it. It was not until they had driven for twenty extra minutes that my mother realized she didn't recognize the signs and became agitated.

"Relax," my dad told her. "I just have to turn around. We're not lost."

My mother tensed and sat even straighter in her seat. There was no sign of the next exit. "Sol," she urged, whispering, but at the same time enunciating, "she needs the bathroom," pointing to me (I didn't), "and any minute we'll be passing Roscoe!"

Roscoe, New York, was near the end of the Quickway, and was sort of the unofficial DMZ between the Catskills and the Poconos, as well as between the Jews and the Gentiles, the latter of whom my mother felt were all hunters and fisherman. On camp visiting weekend, some of the parents went to the newly opened Roscoe Diner, but my mother always thought it was "too far to schlep," as she did now. She was already upset that we weren't going to the Homowack, her regular hotel, having agreed to stay at the Concord (so pretentious) so my dad could play golf. From that trip forward, "we'll be passing Roscoe" became an important phrase for my family. We would use it anytime we were lost or if we went too far, no matter where we were. My dad once called from the Hartford airport after his flight had been diverted from Kennedy.

"Hi, Daddy, are you in the airport?"

"Yes, baby, but not in New York, in Connecticut. They had a problem so they made us go here. Where's your mom?"

"She's lying down, Daddy. Will you be home soon?"

"I don't know, Jule. I think they're going to take us up again and then maybe we'll pass Roscoe and then maybe home, okay?" My dad chuckled at his own joke, and I was so proud to understand it!

Even my brothers, who weren't even there when it began, got so used to the expression that they used it, too. When my brother Stewie went to Vietnam, he wrote home in a letter:

Dear Folks,

> *Yesterday we hiked all night, through a village called Quin Hnon, and we didn't stop till we made camp at daylight. They finally let us collapse, just after we passed Roscoe!*

I myself craved an opportunity to use the in-joke, for the deep sense of identity and belonging it engendered, but the first time I got the chance, I used it metaphysically, or tried to, and failed miserably. I was in my last term at college, when I thought I couldn't take another moment of angst. I had doubts about my choice of English as a major, doubts about my sexual behavior, questions about how to break off a relationship with an angry but stunning graduate student.

"Mom," I sighed quietly into the phone, letting my tone speak my pain. Remarkably, she had actually asked me what was wrong.

"I—I don't know . . . I'm just not . . . I'm very . . ." I trailed off, searching for the words to describe what I felt, something between homesickness and existential despair. And then it hit me. I knew how to describe it. Excited, I began, "Mom, it's like, it's like I'm passing Roscoe."

Complete silence.

"Mom?" No answer.

I heard her in the background, as she handed the phone to my father. ". . . talking nonsense . . . thinks she's in the Catskills . . ." My dad got on and gave me a stern pep talk. Told me to snap out of it. I guess I'd stretched the meaning, or they'd forgotten it entirely.

Maybe that's what I should do with my daughter and mother right now. Call them both up and tell them to just snap out of it. As if I had magical powers, the phone rings.

"We accept!"

"Lex?"

"Yes, it's me," she is laughing, "and we accept. Can you believe it? Russell said he would *love* to come for Passover."

Okay, think hard. He's really coming. I guess a part of me thought it was just too outlandish to actually happen. Now it's surreal. I am happy and not happy.

"Great, sweetie. Will you be driving in together?"

"No, I'm going to come the day before, after classes on Tuesday, and Russell's going to come just in time for dinner. Then he's going to stay with a friend in the city and I'm going to stay for the weekend, okay?"

Okay? Great, I think. My daughter will be mine all weekend, and Russell will be long since gone, I suspect. I play it cool.

"Umm, that sounds fine, honey."

"Mom," she says sweetly, her voice cracking a little, "I just want to say thank you. I—I can't believe how great you're being and I—well, I really love—I mean I like him a lot and, oh, well, just thanks." I feel like the biggest shit on the planet.

"Okay, honey, let's just take it one step at a time, okay?"

"Okay. And by the way, did you get the papers I sent about going abroad next semester?"

Stall. Avoid. Ignore. "The papers? What? Oh, no, no I didn't. Oh there's the bell, sweetie." I cover the phone and whisper excitedly to the dogs, "Who's there?" which is their cue to bark loudly. "I have to go, sweetie, okay?"

"Okay, love you, Mommy."

SEVENTEEN

watch out for squirting juice

I make an extra-special dinner for my men, split-pea soup (okay, that's from the deli), steak and mashed potatoes with fried onions and mush-rooms, broccoli (the only green vegetable Jake actually eats), and salad with olives and fake bacon chips. The fake bacon has about 150 chemicals and preservatives, about 149 more than I like to serve, but the guys can't get enough. I have my motives. This is the night that Eric has promised to talk to Jake, and I don't want anyone cranky and looking for an excuse to postpone. After dinner I clean quickly and leave them to their talk. I have bought them pomegranates, because they make a ritual out of eating them together. First they change into old T-shirts, then they spread newspaper all over the kitchen table, then they attack, squirting red juice everywhere. As I leave, I have this vision that the pomegranate is a metaphor for life. You open it up and it's all there before you; an intricate network of won-derful, juicy red fruit, but to get to it you have to work through the bitter rind and peel away the yellow, uneatable parts. Then, just as you are ready to take this big juicy bite, some of the rind gets in the way and you taste it, the bitter with the sweet, which reminds you not to be too complacent

next time. And it's work, the pomegranate, no peach or apple, ready to eat
as it lies. To get to the meat requires some skill as well as tenacity. It takes
a long time, too, a long time to learn the ins and outs, to realize that old
newspapers make a wonderful tablecloth, that a comfortable old T-shirt
can save you aggravation, and to watch out for squirting juice.

I sit at the computer and struggle with the third entry in the *Sentinel*
application. I am beginning to feel like I'm applying to college, only there's
no choice of essay. And this is the hardest one yet. I must respond to an
opinion that is clearly right-wing, an opinion that is anti–special education as it exists now, as catch-all for every yuppie parent trying to give his
or her child an edge. It's an opinion I happen to share. But they want the
other side. Shit. I have no idea what it must be like for the parents on the
other side, it seems pretty easy for them. All you have to do these days is
say you want your child tested, and the administrators are so afraid of law-
suits that they haul out the WISC-III and practically offer to tutor the kid
free of charge in a suite at the Hilton. But then I think, would I really trade
places with them? And when I put myself in those parents' shoes, I realize
it is never fun to have a special need, and I'm on my way. Soon I nail it, and
this time I confidently deviate from a traditional format and revert to my
specialty, rhyming verse.

> *Professionals we currently see*
> *Like branches of our family tree;*
> *His own Pediatric Neurologist*
> *Consults with the Auditory Pathologist.*
> *A Behaviorist on Tuesdays, for an hour,*
> *Self-Esteem Coach, after that, to empower,*
> *Nutrition Counselor monitors gluten and whey,*
> *Social Skills Group teaches him to play.*
> *Lifestyle Manager structures chores big and small,*
> *Personal loan officer helps us pay for it all . . .*
> *And all we ask of his teacher and the rest*

Is five extra minutes to complete his spelling test.
Classes with his peers for art, lunch, and gym,
So he doesn't have to learn everything with kids two years younger
  than him.
That and a report card with a narrative instead
Of another string of Ds in your darkest red.

I title the essay "The Huge Edge" and send it to the same e-mail address as the last two, as Ted instructed. Then I lie on my bed, purposely thinking about anything other than the paper and Ted. I wonder if Eric will say the right things and if Jake will open up to his father, man to man, and I slip into a lovely daydream about saying all the right things. Naturally, I am back on *Oprah* and she is asking me about my new book. No matter that it is my book of children's poems, Oprah sees universal importance in the way my words reach millions of emotionally vulnerable kids and give them a sense of normalcy. "A sense of belonging," she adds. Exactly what I planned, I am saying to her and to the audience. I catch Ted's eye in the front row, and I do not feel guilty at all. In this daydream I belong with him. Oprah is asking me if I knew that my small ideas about life could affect so many in such a big way, and I am telling her that I am flattered and impressed because nobody has asked me that question before and how astute of her, and we are having a marvelous exchange of mutual admiration when she asks me what my newfound success means to me.

"And *so*," she says, "have you redefined your own vision of what success is, or did you always measure it by the idea of selling a lot of books?"

I think long and hard and then I say, "You know, Oprah, being here on this show with you is unbelievable, but I learned a long time ago that it is the one-to-one connections that make me the happiest. What would really turn me on would be to come over to your house, put on sweats, and hang out and get to know each other, maybe invite some other girls over like *Patti* (I know Patti Labelle is her good friend) and *Whoopi* (I have no idea how she feels about Whoopi, but *I* like her) and we would just talk and

maybe share recipes like that potato salad of yours, *with* paprika." I laugh
and wink at her because that is a private joke you would only know if you
saw a particular show. "I guess that's when I feel like life is really good," I
gush, "when I can be myself and be a friend. That's when I'm more than a
successful writer, I'm a successful person."

There is silence, and then the audience bursts into spontaneous
applause. Oprah smiles, turns to the audience, and starts to say something,
but closes her mouth. She looks back at me. This is one of the rare times
that she is speechless. The moment speaks for itself, she decides, so she
merely turns to the camera and says softly, "And we'll be back." Oh, and it
is a delicious sensation to know that I will be asked back many, many
times, and strangely, even in my fantasy, I really do want to be asked back
for "one of the girls" shows, not for the Book Club show, and I wonder
what that means. Vaguely, outside my euphoric state, I hear my own realistic, cynical voice, the grown-up, wounded me, pretending to vomit,
screaming "UGH! Nauseating fantasy! Please!" But I don't care because the
hopeful ten-year-old me who believes in happy endings and Broadway
musicals and pots of gold thinks this daydream is not only wonderful but
also possible. And she has been disappointed enough.

After a time, Eric comes up and I sit up expectantly, but he turns and
goes into the closet, where I hear him puttering around with his money or
socks. Then he comes out and goes right into the bathroom and begins to
floss his teeth. I am getting irritated. He knows I am waiting to hear about
the discussion with Jake. Why is he making it so that I have to ask? I wonder if Ted is the type to make a woman have to ask. I want to wait him out,
but I am too anxious. I follow him into the bathroom.

"So, are you keeping me in suspense?"

"Un thecond." This is very attractive, I think, as a little piece of food
tinged with blood hits the mirror. I have no choice but to wait if I want the
news. When he finally finishes, rinses his mouth and dries it, Eric turns to
me and sits down on the platform of the tub, where I already am. He looks
like he has something to say, and I think, Uh-oh, this can't be good.

"Well, there's no other way to say this." A pause. "He did it."

"What do you mean?"

"I mean he did it."

I am still looking at him, uncomprehending.

"You know," Eric prods, grinning, "the nasty." Then he stands and kind of wiggles his pelvis in place.

"He DID it?" I am stunned. "He did IT? Oh my God! When? How? What did you say?"

"Well, first I said 'Congratulations.' Then I said, 'My boy!'" Eric mimics high-fiving an invisible Jake.

"You didn't!"

"Yeah, I did." Eric looks proud.

"Oh, Eric, you are such a Neanderthal. Oh God, I had no idea. Did he know what to do? Did he use something? Oh my God, please say you asked him if he used something."

"Of course I did, and it turns out he has a supply. You should see some of these things they have today, colors and flav—"

"Oh my God, Oh my God, Oh my God . . ." I can't stop saying it.

"Jule, it's okay." Eric stands up and puts his arms around me. "He really likes this girl and he knows about being careful and I think he figured out how to do it, okay?"

"When? Did he say when?"

"Yeah, he did."

I wait. Eric squirms. "You can't tell him I told you, okay?"

"Oh God, it was here in this house, wasn't it?"

"Yep."

"Okay, when?"

Eric looks at me, measuring. Should he tell me or not? He is undecided.

"ERIC!"

"Yesterday."

Yesterday, yesterday, I search my brain, what was yesterday? It hits me.

"Yesterday? How can that be? They went to a meeting. They left *before* me!"

"Except they didn't really leave. They drove around the corner and hung out on Blueberry Drive till they saw your car go by, and then they doubled back." It is all too much. I collapse on the edge of the tub again, assaulted by this news and by my own thoughts. My son has tricked me and had sex in the same afternoon. I had just talked to him about respect and limits. Holy shit, I am now one of those "last to know" parents. If anyone had asked me a week ago if I trusted my son, I would have said "totally." Now he is a run-of-the-mill ordinary teenager, or worse, he has turned into another "penis," as my friend Amy would say. Eric is grinning again. Plus he is humming "Walk Like a Man."

"Eric, cut it out."

"My boy . . ." he tries to tease me out of it, "just a stud like his dad." He stands, flexing.

I watch him for a minute and then I suddenly realize what to do.

"Sooo," I say, rolling the word off my tongue, "I'm sure you had the chance to talk to him about the girl, right?"

"What about her?"

"Well, you know, the *girl*. It's a two-way street, dear. Naturally you spoke to him about the girl and her pleasure, right?"

The look on my husband's face is priceless. I might as well have asked him to pierce something.

"I don't think that's any of my concern."

"Oh no? And just where do you think he should learn about it? Or would you prefer he be one of those men who thinks that plunging himself in and out of a woman is all she needs to be blissfully satisfied?"

"Hold on! That's not fair. I certainly never learned about it from my father!"

"That's right. You learned most of it from *me,* and who knows how many women before me paid the price of your selfish ignorance, hmm? You don't know, do you? Well, these are different times. You never spoke about anything with your father, but you and Jake are different. And it is your responsibility to cover this. Let me know how it goes."

I feel a little better. Not much, but a little. At least Eric is no longer smiling when I leave the room. He is something of a Renaissance man, which means he will not only want his son to have a lot of sex, but to be great at it, too. Now I need to call the girls.

"No way, our little Jake?" Amy is stunned for a change.

"Are you sure?" Beth, with two little girls, has no frame of reference for this sort of thing. "The real thing, the whole way?" I have them on conference call.

"The whole way, Eric said, the whole way! My baby!" I don't know what I'm feeling, as I say this. I am still upset, but then there's also something else. Pride?

"So, babe, should we send the little bugger some flowers or what?"

"Amy!" Beth is horrified.

"It's okay, Bethie," I say. "What do you expect? Amy is an old hand at stained sheets and hidden condoms."

"Welcome to my world. I'm lucky if they pick up the wrappers from the floor."

"Ugh." Beth and I, in unison.

"Seriously, Ame, did the boys come and tell you, or did they talk to Seth?"

"Are you kidding? They're like peacocks, the way they strut around here. And Seth encourages it. They would give me *details* if I didn't leave the room with my hands over my ears."

"I see."

"I'm sure that's not the norm for every boy," Beth pipes in immediately, sensing my loss.

"Thanks, sweetie. I'm not sure I really want him to tell me, I just hate that Eric gets to share this and I don't."

"Oh please." Amy is having none of my self-pity. "Will you stop looking for things to bother you? Jake is still your baby, trust me. It's just that now he's joined the ranks with the rest of the brain-dead. You won't even want to speak to him for the next two years because he'll have nothing worthwhile to say because all he'll be thinking about now is his penis anyway. And when he's not thinking about his penis, he'll be thinking about how he can get some girl to think about his penis. That's it in a nutshell, no pun intended."

"Oh my God, Amy . . ." Beth and I are cracking up and I can't believe I'm laughing about this.

"Good night, ladies, call me when something earth-shattering happens like Jake asks what makes a woman happy."

"Julie, I've gotta go, too." Beth tries to soften Amy's perspective. "But it's gonna be okay. Don't overstress about this. Sweet dreams."

"Thanks, girls."

EIGHTEEN

how was your sex?

The next morning I am pacing, wondering what I will say to Jake when I see him. Since it's a school morning, I know he will be half asleep and pressed for time, which is good because it means I won't have endless awkward hours to stare at him while I wonder how to act around him now. Not that I can say anything related to the actual fact that he has had sex, since I am not supposed to know. Eric promised Jake that he wouldn't say anything to me and promised to divorce me if I even thought about letting on that I know.

"I'm not kidding, Jule, no funny side comments, no read-between-the-lines jokes, or I'll never tell you another thing, I swear."

So here I am, estranged from my baby, the one I have felt most aligned with in the family, and it is due primarily to what? The fact that I am a woman? It's a simple reality, I suppose, but one that seems oddly discordant in 2003. Not wrong entirely, just strange. I guess the sexual revolution has not transcended the mother-son relationship because as much as Jake feels uncomfortable discussing sex with me, I think I don't really want to sit and discuss sex with him. I mean, at first maybe I would talk to him comfortably enough, but then I think it would get weird and maybe it should, maybe that's developmentally correct, who knows? Well, this is not the time for monumental pronouncements about American Sexuality, it is merely the morning after I have learned that my youngest child has had sex for the first time and I have had too many cups of coffee and my mind is racing and the point is moot besides. At least Jake seems to like this girl and have some understanding of a relationship, even if this is his first. I wonder what number it is for her? I have the thought that maybe this Kate is the town slut and I wouldn't even know it and what would it matter, really? In typical double-standard fashion I think, reflexively, at least I am the mother of the boy. I suppose that whether it is her first or tenth, I am in no position to judge any girl. I certainly do not want to think about my first. In fact, I do not want to think about most of my sexual journey, which I now know was doomed by my mother's illness.

I learned from Joanie Leiber in the sixth grade that I had a clitoris. She was my best friend for about two years and she had two older brothers who were on the wild side. They told her all kinds of great, raunchy stories that were totally inappropriate for her twelve-year-old ears and luckily for me she shared them all. So we were in my bedroom when she explained to me that if you put your finger down there and felt for this little nub and rubbed the side of it pretty fast for a while, you would feel something. I was always eager to try stuff like that, unlike Robin Fetterman, who I tried to teach a few weeks later and who responded, "I don't think so, but you go ahead." Anyway, after a few tries I really did feel something, kind of a numbness and then a tingling and then, well, a burst of something, I guess you could say. Of course I was hooked. We didn't even know what to call the thing we were doing, so we just called it Getting There, and we tried to Get There all the time. We always did it on sleepovers in our separate beds and we even raced each other to Get There. Secretly I was a little worried since I was finding time to do it all the time and Joanie seemed a little more blasé about it than I felt. I loved it. So much so that I became careless. One night I was reading and playing with myself on my bed about seven in the

evening when my mother came in. She had a way of knocking and opening the door at the same time and if you ever questioned her she became
defensive and accused you of having something to hide and since up until
then I didn't, it was easier not to argue. But that night I didn't have a blanket over me, just my hand shoved down inside my unzipped jeans and my
legs spread, my finger working away. I jumped up and mumbled something unintelligible, but mostly I started to die of embarrassment and my
mother looked down and away and then back at me, frozen-like, in shock
I guess. Then, with her hand still on the knob and her body one step into
the room, she squeezed her lips into a tight line through which words
could hardly escape, and said, "I'm off to Selma's for cards, I left the number with Dad."

I was so relieved. I waited for the door to close behind her. I thought
that was it, that we would pretend nothing happened, but I was so wrong.
She turned to go, and then, as if she'd had an afterthought, she turned
back, a hurt look on her face. Hurt and disappointed.

"Oh, and Julie, I just want you to know, you're only hurting yourself."

Eight, nine, TEN! Knockout. And the winner is not me. I have lived
that scene over and over again so many times in the last thirty years that
you would think I'd have some closure by now, that I could file it away like
an old filmstrip in a musty cardboard box, to gather dust and fade away.
But that moment is the single most shameful and damaging moment of
my life, I think, second only perhaps to losing my virginity, which is a completely different story but, in hindsight, so pivotally tied to this one. On
that night in the late sixties, as my mother threw an apricot cardigan
sweater over her shoulders and casually descended the stairs for an evening
of canasta, I became hysterical in my room. I was so ashamed and so *sorry*.
That was what plagued me, that I had somehow done something horrible
to my mother. I was a dreadful, dirty little girl, a disgrace. After crying and
sobbing for over an hour in my room, I needed salvation, absolution. I
called her at her card game and begged forgiveness. Really. I was hysterical
and I think it scared her a little because she ended up trying to calm me

down and telling me it was all right. We never really spoke about the incident after that. In truth, we hadn't spoken about it that night, even, just around it, around the terrible, shameful truth that I had masturbated. Years later I looked back on that incident and felt sorry for my mother, sorry that her sense of her own sexuality was so warped that it would lead her to do psychological damage to the daughter she loved so much. I thought that was very progressive of me, that pity, very healthy. After all, I know masturbation is a normal, natural part of growing up. I came to see that it was my mother who had the problem, not me. But my intellectual understanding was also a ruse concocted by my protective subconscious, I think. And Dr. Bob says pity isn't forgiveness—a second cousin to it, maybe, but that's all. So I guess you could say I'm still working it out.

Is it any wonder that I want to be PERFECT with Jake now, and of course with Lexie, too? That I want to keep my baggage off their feet? This is why I am always thinking, thinking, thinking, working on what I will say. This is why I walk on eggshells with Lexie and why I do not give her ultimatums and threaten to cut her off financially if she doesn't forget about running off with this Russell. And this morning I am thinking that I will be perfectly natural with Jake and keep my promise to Eric not to say a word and that is exactly my plan when I hear Jake's feet on the stairs a full half hour before I expect him. I have no idea why he is up at six-thirty instead of seven and I wonder if he is energized from his new sex life. "Stop it!" I chastise myself. I will say good morning and ask him if he wants some breakfast, that's all. Except when I see him it does not happen exactly that way because he just doesn't look the same to me this morning. In fact, I look at him and my brain is screaming SEX and I am imagining him with a PENIS for maybe the first time and I can't even sustain eye contact, let alone put my arm around him or tousle his hair, because he is now another species. I want to ask him how he's doing, but I am afraid it will come out "How was your sex?" so I turn away in horror at my own thoughts and try to remember that this is still Jake. But I can't shake the feeling that everything is different now, that *he* is different now, or perhaps I have been affected by this more than he. Jake doesn't seem to notice my discomfort and in fact comes over and throws his arms around me affectionately and calls me "mamacita, my little mommy," something he has been doing since he grew taller than me last year. This reassures me, this familiarity, and I think maybe Eric was wrong, but when I ask Jake if he wants me to make him some eggs, he pulls away and says that he's going out to breakfast with Kate before school, and I am left standing there feeling so distant and alone I could cry. I hate Kate.

When I was a freshman in college, despite my wild ways, I had a boyfriend I really loved a lot, but he only played into my self-doubts, because he was so unreliable. Rob was tall and lean, like a wild horse, and just as unpredictable, and I guess that was what attracted me to him as much as anything else, that and a kind of chemistry I've never known since, even with Eric. The closest I've come lately is with you-know-who in the Coach House. But for years the grown-up intellectual in me will always classify my attraction to Rob as infatuation, a fleeting state that couldn't have lasted, which is why it's so unnerving to think that I felt something like that the other day. Deep inside is a part of me that's been longing to feel even one moment of what I felt for Rob. We were true to each other in that feeling, but not in our actions. We both liked the attention we got from other people and liked to party and have a good time. Still, I always felt our relationship was special and apart from any of the flings I had with other guys, which is why I felt so badly about what I did to him, what I did to myself. In my mind, Rob was my first everything, first love, first real boyfriend, first sexual experience. Except that he wasn't.

I had just turned eighteen and Rob and I were in his dorm room. He brought out a small, robin's-egg-blue box with a white satin bow. I opened it to find a friendship ring, a single circle with a sapphire stone at the top, and knew instantly that I had never received anything more wonderful or treasured in my life. I was completely and totally in love with this boy. "You went to Tiffany's?"

I couldn't believe it. Tiffany's was only in Manhattan back then, and teenagers rarely got presents from such an expensive store. I felt so special. We started to make out and progressed to our heaviest petting yet. Finally all our clothes were off, which was a first, and I decided that I was ready to lose my virginity. I told him, "Let's do it," and he said he should have bought me a ring months ago and I smacked him playfully and then he got really serious and said he loved me. I said, "I love you, too," and then we heard a jiggling in the lock and I ducked under the covers as his roommate came in, and although he left again quickly when Rob practically killed him, the moment was broken and we didn't make love. It didn't matter to either of us; we knew it would happen soon.

What happened next is hard to explain. In retrospect, my own actions seem rash and ignorant, and through the years I have tried to revisit the facts in case I have gained additional wisdom as I've grown older, but the process has been unsatisfying. I cannot truly sanction or even illuminate what may have motivated me. Rob wasn't blameless, he certainly wasn't the most reliable or nurturing of boyfriends, but still, as my mother would have said, "For a smart girl, that was a foolish thing to do."

My roommate Lizanne prided herself on being sophisticated and the unofficial avant-garde New Yorker among us, since she came from Riverdale. Although Riverdale is really just part of the Bronx, its location on the Henry Hudson Parkway gives it a North Manhattan status, and of course the Riverdale girls all had frequent, easy access to the city and to Manhattan's private schools, which did, in effect, give them a certain street/fashion/urban flair. When Lizanne saw the ring and the box, her reaction was not what I expected. Instead of squealing with delight, she hesitated, turned the ring over and over in her hands, and said, "Nice."

"What's wrong?" I was confused.

"Ummm, nothing, Jules, I don't think. It's just . . ."

"What? Jesus, Lizzy, you're making me crazy! What!"

"Wait here," she commanded, and fled the room.

Fifteen minutes later she returned with a serious but determined expression on her face and began to explain that she had something she wanted to tell me that she thought I should know. Oh God, I thought to myself, it's stolen. She's going to show me an article from the *New York Times* that says Tiffany's was recently cleaned out of friendship rings.

"I've just spoken with Barbara and Hillary, and we all agree." My stomach turned over at this news. You can't underestimate the importance of the opinion of certain girls when you're eighteen and in college and a consultation with the Kaufman twins lent immediate credibility to whatever Lizanne was about to say. She took a deep breath.

"The ring is not from Tiffany's."

"Excuse me?"

"Tiffany's stopped using this style of box years ago."

"Oh, well, okay."

"I'm sorry, Jule, he must have put it in an old box or something. It's still a nice ring."

"Yeah, it is. Of course it is. Well, thanks."

A smart girl would have let it go, I suppose. After all, he cared enough to want to impress me, he had bought me a ring, and even with my doubts, I felt as if he loved me. Had I taken even one intelligent moment to investigate, I also would have learned that Tiffany's had *never* stopped using that turquoise box with white satin ribbon, which was the ultimate ironic joke. But I was embarrassed. My sophisticated friends had unearthed my boyfriend for a cheap fake, and I was so impressionable that I let them turn me into something small and ugly. Out of their compassion, they decided to cheer me up that night by taking me out. The evening became a series of Tom Collinses and the assorted drug staples of the seventies: pot, 'ludes, and coke. They encouraged me to "have a good time" and "show him," and by 2:00 a.m. I was in the lounge of our dorm, making out with another freshmen, a boy I wouldn't even have looked at sober. I wish I could say that what happened next was a blur, but the truth is, I remember it as clearly as I remember my mother standing at the door to my room, admonishing me that I was only hurting myself. This boy asked me if I wanted to go "all the way," and in my numbed, dizzy state I thought of Rob and the hoax of a ring and I proudly and defiantly said, "Sure," and that was that. To this day, I don't know whether I'm more ashamed of losing my virginity or caring so much where the ring was from. Mostly I'm just sad that Rob wasn't my first.

So I guess Jake is lucky. It appears he will not have a horror story to hide from for the next forty years, he will not have regrets, and that is so pleasant a thought I don't mind that he is going out for breakfast with *her*. Besides, I have much to think about. Passover is less than a week away. More important, I have to make sure that all of my guests are going to be their most annoying, difficult selves. Maybe I should run out of food? No, that would be pushing it. Even Lexie might get suspicious of that. Lexie. The brightest spot is that after the Seder I will have Lexie to myself for three whole days, away from college life and *him,* installed in her old room, sleeping under her old, worn flannel goose-down quilt, cuddling on the couch in the family room in her ripped, comfy sweats. Maybe it will remind her of the old Lexie, the one who was content to let me tickle her back. Maybe it will refresh her sense of family values and tradition. Maybe if the plan doesn't work I will simply tie her up in the closet and keep her there until she comes to her senses.

NINETEEN

I know what I'm doing

Lexie arrives home late on Tuesday, which gives us a full day and a half together before the crowd descends, and which also means she is around to help me with preparing, although she never actually does help me, even though each time I imagine that she will. There is always a reason: she has a cold, a paper to finish so she can enjoy the holiday, errands to run at the mall because shopping in "the wilderness" is nonexistent. I predict that on Thursday afternoon, one hour before our company arrives, after every piece of silverware has been sparklingly set out and each serving platter holds a little Post-it to tell what dish it will be used for, and the smell of slow-cooked brisket has filled the house for hours, she will wander into the kitchen, hair up, eyes sleepy, sweatpants crumpled, and purr, "Hi, Mommy, do you need me to help?" But it has been a season for surprises, and today is no different. After dinner Wednesday night, she helps clear.

"Are you making apple pudding this year? Please say you are and *please* do not make that horrible sweet potato and marshmallow mess that Aunt Gayle likes. That stuff is gross."

Jake is right behind her, actually putting salad dressing away in the refrigerator without being asked. He bumps her with his hip. "I *like* that marshmallow thing." To me, "Can you just make the top without the potatoes underneath it?" Alexis moans.

"Ugh, I can't believe you can eat that. Besides, once a year on Thanksgiving is more than enough. *I* will make the pudding this year if you want." We all stop and look at her. Has Alexis just offered to cook? Jake pretends to fall down and die.

"Very funny. I can cook, you know. Oh, and I learned how to make the best vegetable thing if you need one, I don't even need a recipe, it's really easy."

She has a recipe for a vegetable thing? My daughter? I check to make sure that aliens haven't taken over her body.

"You do? So tell me about it."

"Well, it's called string bean casserole, and you make it with these onion rings from a can."

I have to laugh. Is string bean casserole every child's first recipe? I learned to make it about twenty years ago and stopped after a year or two, shortly after I read the label of the Campbell's Mushroom Soup can that contains the "glue" that holds this casserole together. There's no doubt that it tastes good, if you're Lexie's age and you're proud that you've made something and if you don't really care that there's no vegetable taste, let alone redeeming health value, in the whole dish. But I will say none of this because the girl who looks like my daughter and is wearing her clothes has just offered to make two dishes for me.

"Onion rings? Sounds okay," says Jake.

"It sounds excellent," I concur. I suppose I should be thrilled about my daughter's apparent maturity, but my feelings are more complex. How can she be maturing and making such a huge mistake at the same time? I preferred when she didn't have a clue about the menu but her life's direction was normal and intact, not the other way around. I don't need her to make any damn dishes, I think to myself. I need her to keep her life on track.

I decide that after dinner would be a good time to have a little talk with my daughter. I have to be careful. She thinks I am having Russell to dinner simply as an act of open-mindedness. I try several different benign tactics to engage her in a serious analysis of the situation, all of which fail, evidenced by the sappy smile she wears as we share a piece of my chocolate-chip mandelbrot and says things like, "Yummm, Russell will love this."

"Lex, sweetie, let me be blunt for a sec. Strictly on paper, does the idea of a twenty-year-old junior running around Europe or any other country with her married thirty-year-old professor sound appropriate to you?"

"I'll be twenty-one in a few months. And I won't be running around, I'll be going to school." She licks the chocolate off a finger and says, "Besides, he wants to get a divorce as soon as the timing is right."

In my head, the voices of all the grandmothers and great-grandmothers in the Berman line groan in unison. I can hear "Oy vay" in several tongues: Polish, Russian, Brooklynese.

"Still."

She stands up jerkily, has to move. I am proud for saying "still" and not "Oh, Lexie, that's what they all say."

"I don't care how it sounds. On paper or anything else. Or *to* anyone else. It's not like that. Besides, I thought you were trying to understand. I thought that's why you invited him." Lexie doesn't sound as if she's ever believed me. Like she knew this was coming. She's whining, frustrated, as if she's had this discussion before. She is so defensive so quickly that I wonder who else has been giving her a hard time. Hillary?

"Alexis, I know you feel something for this professor, something romantic or"—I am searching for a word other than *sexual*—"or infatuating, and that has to be playing a part in your decision, but I think if you step back for a minute and see what the picture looks like, what it *is*, you'll see that it may not be the best move for a smart girl like you."

She waits for me to finish, thinks over what I've said, or appears to, and I need to remind myself of the debate medals lined up against the mirror on her dresser at home. My daughter is as skilled at verbal sets and digs as she is at spikes, a formidable opponent who has intuited the subtleties of positioning since she was ten years old. True to her talent, she switches gears.

"Okay, Mom, I like him, I do, and that may be coloring my judgment. There's something comforting and exciting about him all at once. When I'm with him I feel . . . special." The smile on her face makes me happy and miserable at the same time. "He is interested in my opinions and he makes me laugh, what's so terrible about that? I haven't felt this way about any guy, ever, and the guys my age just seem so stupid next to him. But I wouldn't just 'run off with him.' I wouldn't go anywhere with him if I didn't think it had merit. I'm not an idiot. I'm a . . . a . . . a seeker. I just need to do something like this right now. I need to explore. That's who I am."

"Alexis, there are lots of ways to get variety and stimulation without a semester abroad you never planned on! For God's sake, you could change majors or even schools or run for office. Why don't you pierce something!!" Even as I say it I know how ridiculous it sounds. Alexis has never wanted to pierce anything because she never saw the point. She never really rebelled because what did she have to rebel against, liberal use of my charge cards, family ski vacations, and monthly pedicures? I take a deep breath because she is shaking her head, amused and superior. She is a seeker, she says. Good God, help me.

"Look, for all your self-revelations, I think a great deal of your desire has to do with your wanting to be in a relationship. This Russell"— somehow I can barely squeeze his name out between clenched teeth, as if saying his name affirms that he exists, which I would like to deny—"is the first *man* you haven't tired of in two weeks. Or vice versa. You don't want it to end, you're ready for something more so you're trying to figure out a way to prolong things, but that's just not how a relationship works. A relationship grows because two people have things in common and like being with each other, not because they run off someplace where nobody knows them and judges them."

"You're not listening to me." She, too, is gritting her teeth, pushing the words out between them.

"I want to do something out of the plan, what is so terrible about that? I have done everything I was supposed to do—Brownies, sleepaway camp, saxophone lessons, Teen Tour, tennis groups—I was 'with the program' and it was fine, but now I just want to do something else. I think that's the hardest part for you! You just never imagined me doing anything other than what I was supposed to do, what you and Daddy planned for me. Are you embarrassed in front of your friends?"

"No," I am almost shouting. "Are you?" She turns her back.

Oh God, Alexis, I want to say, it's been the opposite! I've been so relieved each time you accessed the program, bettered the program. I guess my mistake was in letting down my guard, allowing myself to imagine you might actually finish it. Before she leaves the room, Alexis turns back, looks at me, and evenly puts the screws in.

"I really miss Grammy," she says, and starts to leave the room.

Immediately I feel guilty, not because she's hit the nerve she aimed for, but because she's hit one she didn't even know was there. I really need to tell her that Grammy is sick and to stop this charade. For now, though, I retreat to every parent's safety net, the one they haul out when they realize they will not win the argument today. I have a few days with her and I want us to get along.

"Look, sweetie, just think about what I said, okay? Russell really is welcome here. We'd like to meet him. But if we're considering your position, then you can at least consider ours. Think about how strange it might actually be. Think about coming back and where your friends will be and where you'll be. Your future and your goals matter, and Alexis, you must think about the fact that he is married. I doubt he could even be legally separated before fall, providing that's his intention. Do you know what that makes you, a student cavorting with a married professor? If the college got wind of it"—I lower my voice—"or even the sorority, there could be sanctions, do you understand?"

Now she rolls her eyes.

"Nobody is going to say anything." Unbelievable. Not just that she says that, that she thinks that. She has told half a dozen of her friends about her plans. Nobody is going to say anything. She will teach the puppy not to bark.

"Alexis, there's one more thing I have to say."

I look down into the water. It must be fifty or sixty feet below this cliff that I am about to dive off of.

"If you have *sex* with him"—I successfully make the word sound like a salad of warm maggots—"that makes you the other woman and it makes him an adulterer. I know you, you are proud and dignified, and I don't care what his wife is like, there is nothing noble about either of those roles, Lexie, not a damn thing. You better think long and hard about what your standards are and who you want to be. Up until now, Daddy and I have been nothing but proud of you, but you're at one of life's forks, and the road you choose will be the road you'll have to walk for a long time."

To her credit, she has not turned away, not broken eye contact, not rolled her eyes even. My stomach sags as I realize she has, of course, imagined sex with him, if not already had it. Good, I think, then I was right to bring it up, right to make her pull it out of the abstract. There is a silence. I hate Russell. Then, in a small voice, she says, "Just so you know, I would've, but *he* wouldn't." She stares up defiantly.

"Oh." I am relieved. Sort of. Maybe I don't exactly hate him.

"He wants it to be right." Okay, more than I need to know.

"Well, that makes sense, don't you think?"

"I guess."

"I love you, Lex."

"Then don't worry so much, okay? I know what I'm doing."

Yeah, right. Why do all children say that to their parents just before they snap on their parachutes and board the plane?

TWENTY

who has crystal service for twenty-six?

Thursday morning at 6:00 a.m., I am setting the table, still unsure of the final count and whether my plan will work. Unfortunately, Roberta from across the street has declined, which I take as a bad omen. Just my luck that this will be the very first family dinner that goes smoothly. Eric is no help, mumbling "all your idea" or some such thing. On the table is a tentative list of ideas:

1. *Slip Russell an anonymous threatening note re his potential liaison with Lexie. If possible, have note self-destruct after thirty seconds.*
2. *Drug Russell with copious amounts of Manischewitz until he is susceptible to the powers of suggestion.*
3. *Teach Lacey and Jasper the "Kill" command between now and the Seder. Use "Shalom" for "Kill" to throw off detectives in ensuing investigation.*
4. *Lure Russell into kitchen and knock him senseless with matzoh ball, finally giving purpose to Grandmother's recipe for "Jewish Hand Grenades."*

I'm beginning to lean toward the direct approach. If Russell looks too happy or the family is inexplicably normal, I will somehow get him alone and then I will put him on the spot. I will say that we doubt his intentions and challenge him to prove his love is true and honorable. I will insist that Eric and I feel that he can only demonstrate this by persuading Alexis *not* to go abroad with him. Compared with my other ideas, this actually sounds reasonable to me.

I hope no one asks too much about Russell at dinner, since all I've mentioned is that Lexie is bringing a friend from school. I want it to be chaotic, not humiliating. Knowing my daughter, with a minimal amount of prodding she will gladly share Russell's vital statistics. I resolve to speak to her about that, and to Eric and Jake as well. We really don't need to divulge this particular piece of private family business to every assorted relative or explain Lexie's latest adventure or justify our sanctioning it. By the time I track down each of them, it is already midday. Eric agrees with me, and Jake just shrugs and says "whatever," but of course Alexis has to climb up on a pedestal and give a speech about how she is not ashamed.

"Nevertheless," I say in my most controlled, reasonable voice, "I have a lot to handle today and I would appreciate it if you could use a little diplomacy and sidestep this issue should it come up."

She rolls her eyes and shakes her head as if we are just so silly, two infants who need to be indulged. "Fine," is her flippant response, and then, as if it is an afterthought, "but if anyone asks me outright, I won't lie."

Jake is watching us, Eric and me, and we are both having the same reaction, which is that we'd like to wring her neck. As she leaves the room, Eric turns to me and says, "So there's matricide and patricide, but I forget what it's called when you kill your child."

"Understandable."

"No, I'm serious. There's a word for it, but I can't remember it."

"I know," Jake pipes in. "Brilliant?"

"Jake!" I'm half amused.

"No, that's close, but it's something else," Eric plays along.

"Finally? Overdue? Helpful?"

"Jake, enough," I say, and to Eric, "She's serious, you know. If she tells my whole family all about Russell, well, you know Stewie and Gayle will just eat it up. I'll never hear the end of it. Stewie will laugh and make those 'whew' gestures of relief that it's not *his* child and Gayle's reaction will be even worse. She won't say anything, you know, she'll just look at me with that sympathetic look that makes me feel like a big loser while I want to strangle her."

"Boy, you guys have an awful lot of violence in you."

I look at Eric and he looks at me. We turn to Jake and in the same breath we both say, "Infanticide."

BY THE TIME the family starts to arrive, the guest list has grown to twenty-six including baby Zeus but not counting my niece Dana, who may or may not be flying down from Boston this afternoon. My dining room table has two aluminum folding tables attached to it to make a long T that extends into my front entrance hall, but it looks so homey and welcoming because of the awkward extension that it makes me smile. I have three matching pale yellow tablecloths, one for each table, and they are offset with pale yellow and pale pink napkins that I have folded into fake flowery shapes and stuffed into crystal glasses. Of course the crystal is a mishmash of mine and Eric's mother's, and some of it is actually that deep pink color (from the Resnick side) and some of it is magnificent, heavily beveled Waterford (my side) and nobody has the exact same size glass because who has crystal service for twenty-six, but it looks perfect anyway. And I have scattered those decorative spring stems randomly among the place settings to give the room what Martha would call "that buds-in-bloom look." Each table has its own water pitcher in which lemon slices float elegantly, its own salt and pepper servers, thanks to my mother, who had three sets of antique swan servers with adorable little spoons, its own Seder plate and matzoh plate, small bowls of celery and salt water for dipping, and haroset, the traditional concoction of apple, nuts, and wine, edible "mortar." The latter is my own homemade recipe, but on the main table I am also forced to put Aunt Mimi's Israeli haroset, even though Aunt Mimi is no longer with us and it was made by her daughter, my cousin Ellen, and not as well as Aunt Mimi used to make it, which could actually be a good thing since it has olives and nobody ever liked it to begin with.

Ellen arrives first with her crew, all the way from Yardley, Pennsylvania, and I am amazed at the changes in the kids since I saw them a year ago. Ellen has two children from her first marriage to Howard, a mealy-mouthed, obnoxious attorney whom she fortunately divorced, and two stepchildren from her marriage to Frank, a pharmaceutical sales rep, and a vast improvement. Because Frank has custody of his kids, they have all lived together in a modified Brady Bunch existence for the past ten years, and although there seems to be an hourly crisis, they have survived quite nicely. Only Tracy, Frank's oldest daughter, who is a junior at Penn State, is not coming because she is on some sort of humane mission to the Deep South to cook meals for homeless families, and we are all properly sobered by this gentle reminder of what the holiday means. At least most of us are sobered. Alexis rolls her eyes and shakes her head—her hunger-strike days are long past—and checks her wrist to make sure she hasn't left her silver Tiffany bracelet at school. Frank's son, Tim, who is sixteen, looks like an advertisement for *Surf and Skateboard* magazine, complete with eyebrow piercing and a streak of green hair, but he has a shy smile and a friendly nature and Jake corrals him immediately, as well as Ellen's youngest, Cory, who is seventeen and a bit more conservative. The three boys head up to Jake's room and within minutes I hear Jake's latest boot-leg Dave Mathews CD and the sound of his drums, which he hasn't actually played since his last private lesson in eighth grade, but which are a magnet for every teenager who enters the room. Jillian, Ellen's daughter, looks a little lost, and I sense that there is still a wide gap between her and Lexie, despite an age difference of only two years. I hope that Lyle will get here soon with Derek and that he and Jilli will have something in com-

mon. Jillian is pretty in a dark sort of way. She could be prettier if she
didn't keep pulling both sides of her straight black hair down onto her face
as if they were curtains to hide behind. She could also be prettier if she
raised her head and smiled once in a while. But Jilli is what I call terminally
serious, and she was deeply affected by her parents' divorce. She and Lexie
have always been worlds apart, personality-wise, and I've tried to explain
to Lexie that Jillian didn't have the luxury of feeling secure and confident
the way she did, and that it's harder for her to relax. Lexie understands, but
her patience has worn thin over the years. Somewhere between the seventh
Hanukkah party and the twelfth Mother's Day, she got sick of trying to
draw Jillian out, and this morning she informed me that she would be nice
to Jilli, but she wasn't planning on spending any time alone with her, not
even if Ellen said something like "Why don't you take Jilli up to your
room, Alexis, so you girls can have some privacy," as if they were nine
years old. At twenty-two, Jillian seems painfully reserved and unsure. She
is a nurse, an LPN, I think, or in training to be, and is living at home. Ellen
and I don't discuss Jillian's personality, but occasionally Ellen will remark
that Jilli "seems to be coming out of her shell." Looking at her as she stands
nervously in the hallway of my home, where she has stood a million
times before, unsure whether to enter farther and tentative about
taking off her scarf and coat, I decide she needs to make a bigger crack in
that shell. Ellen, propelled by her usual self-imposed mania, seems to
notice none of this and is busy ushering her father, my uncle Aaron, to a
place on the couch, where he usually sits for the entire day, with the exception of the meal.

The arrival of Ellen's family starts the chaos, and when someone lets
the dogs in from out back, their barking and jumping accentuates it.

"Oh, Daddy, watch out for the dogs!" Ellen is breathless, steering her
dad to the couch.

"Jule, the house looks great!" Ellen gushes. "What's different? Something's different, I just know it! Here, Daddy, sit here. Yes, here, Daddy, this
is fine. No, I'm sure Julie will say this is fine, so just sit. Daddy, SIT!"

"Eric, the dogs!" I cry. Poor Jilli is standing frozen and looks panicked as our brown Labrador, Jasper, pokes her crotch.

"Mom, phone for you, it's cousin Dana, she's coming!"

"Alexis, help me set another place. Eric, I need one more chair from downstairs."

"Huh, I'm in the wrong chair?" It's Uncle Aaron, who seems to be obsessing about where he sits. I look at Ellen and she throws up her hands and comes over to me, turns me around, and walks me into the dining room.

"I don't know what it is," she half-whispers, half-laughs. "Since his heart surgery he's developed a thing about seats, like if it's a good seat or a bad seat. He's making me crazy with the damn seats."

"Mom, PHONE!"

"Okay, okay. Oh, there's the door, somebody get the door." On the way to the phone, I grab Lexie's arm and plead with her to do something with Jillian, who has barely moved two steps farther into the house, but has at least removed her coat. On the phone with Dana, I hear Stewie and Gayle come in with Gayle's family, and I hear Viv exclaim in a loud, affected voice, "Is this beautiful grown-up girl Alexis? Oh my God, she's stunning! Isn't she stunning, Gayle? She looks just like Allison, I think. Come here, darling, Aunt Viv wants to give you a big hug."

I smile to myself, knowing Alexis thinks Viv is the biggest phony on the planet.

"Your folks just got here, Dane," I say into the phone, "do you want to talk to them?"

She says, "God, no," and just to tell them she'll be there later, and when I do, you would think that Vivian has heard from the Pope.

"Oh, my Dana, I knew she would make it. Oh, Gayle, didn't I tell you she wouldn't let her Bubbe down?"

Gayle and I exchange a look. Stewie has gone to the TV and is already flipping back and forth between baseball games. Before they are all in the door, Lyle and Barbara and Derek walk in. Derek is the same age as Jillian, and is also a bit peculiar, but in a different way. He is very, very bright, highly political, extremely left-wing, and condescending as all hell. I find him alternately funny and irritating. He has the kind of arrogance that needs to be tempered by experience, I think to myself, but his irreverence is often so impressively intelligent you just have to stand back and admire it. Derek has started an Internet firm with two of his classmates from Dartmouth, and will no doubt reinvent communications by the end of the decade. I notice that Jilli jumps a bit as he walks right up to her and says a bold hello. Behind Derek, my brother Lyle is helping Barb's mother and aunt into the house, and suddenly I can't remember Jenny's sister's name, so I just call out "Hello, ladies, I'm so glad you're here!" and hope it will come to me.

There is a kind of assembly line of dishes as my relatives enter. Gayle has brought soup, and of course it is in the pot to make things easy, but Barbara, who has two desserts, has neglected to put them out on plates, so I will have to do it later. Everyone is trying to give me instructions, but Vivian needs my immediate attention since she has brought the most lovely flowers, which, of course, are fresh cut and not in an arrangement, and need to be sliced, watered, fed, and placed in a vase. Lyle has decided to rile up the dogs by play-fighting with them, and the madness is on. This is good, I think to myself, let's keep the chaos coming. I'm hoping it doesn't peak too soon and peter out. Eric's cousin Diane comes next, with her daughter Tori and Tori's volatile, on-again-off-again boyfriend, Marc. We think Marc has a bit of a drinking problem. Last year he polished off two bottles of wine by himself, stumbled away from the table, and took the tablecloth and half the dishes with him. I make a mental note to seat him near the liquor. As I take coats, dishes, and packages, I am buzzing with the joy of this large family gathering. For a moment I forget that in addition to Elijah, we are expecting a very special guest. I am also in danger of over-cooking the brisket, burning the potatoes, and completely draining the vegetables of all nutrients, but I don't care. It's impossible to concentrate on gourmet cuisine when there is so much juicy family interaction about.

Besides, with all of the individual dietary requests, very few of us will be eating the same meal anyway. Diane is on a special diet, *again,* only this time she has to weigh and measure her food and for some reason I had to buy her plain vanilla yogurt, which I did, and turnips, which I forgot, but it's okay, she says, because she can substitute with another root vegetable if I have one. I am not sure what qualifies as a root vegetable, so I tell her to have a look. Tori, the vegetarian, is not a problem, but I was going to make the matzoh balls in the chicken soup, so except for a moment when I wonder if she'd ever know the difference, I plan to make space for yet another pot on the stove. Uncle Aaron is asking for schnapps, which is some sort of liquor, I know, that old people drink, but I have no idea if we have any, and I leave that to Eric to figure out. Derek, I notice, is on his second beer, which I wasn't even serving and he must have found in the back of the fridge, and since Brooke, Evan, and Zeus have arrived, Zeus only wants to play with the dogs and is sitting in the corner near the crates, crying and pleading, "Want to, want doggies, wahhhhhh." And Brooke is mad at Evan for some reason, which is how it should be, since everyone knows that it's always the husband's fault after all.

We are not an early-afternoon-meal kind of family, especially since all the men like to watch any sporting event no matter how obscure or extreme, but we compromise because of the relatives who have a long drive, and eat by six. Russell has been invited to come at five-thirty, long enough after the relatives for them to settle in and close enough to dinner that there won't be too much time for anyone to talk with him alone. At exactly 5:29 the doorbell rings and my heart floats up into my throat and out of my mouth. I hear Lexie get the door, some muffled greetings, the dogs barking to be let out, a man's voice laughing. I make my way into the front hall and I am momentarily nonplussed. Standing in the foyer is quite simply one of the nicest-looking young men I've ever seen. Not just good-looking, *nice*-looking. There is a difference. I see what Lexie sees, he's clearly gorgeous, but I see something else, and I begin to have regrets about my reasons for inviting him. There is a genuineness to his smile, a kind of humble gratitude in his eyes, and I know in an instant it's going to take everything I've got not to like him. Besides, in the two minutes that I have stood watching, he hasn't taken his eyes off my daughter and the look, well, the look is like when Jasper and Lacey hear me coming home and run to the door and their eyes say that nobody better could possibly exist. I wipe my hands and walk into the hall.

Russell looks up, realizes who I am, and immediately leans forward and reaches out his hand to shake mine. Alexis is beaming. "Thank you so much for having me," he says.

"Our pleasure," I reply, going for polite but reserved.

Russell is also holding some flowers in his other hand that he now extends. "I wasn't sure what to bring," he says tentatively.

I take the flowers. They are in a vase. Two points. "They're lovely." I give a little smile.

At this moment Eric comes up with the extra chair. "Oh, hey, how are you!" he greets Russell, as if he knows him. Idiot. He has forgotten that he's supposedly never met him.

I jump in. "Eric," I say firmly, "this is Lexie's friend Russell."

Eric remembers. "Oh yes, um, of course, I figured that. Uh, nice to meet you, Russell, was it?" Oh God, Eric, don't overdo it. "Would you like a drink?" he asks. Good boy.

A timer buzzes as Eric ushers Russell toward the bar, and I follow it. From the kitchen, I listen acutely. It seems that no one has zeroed in on him just yet. I'm wondering what he thinks of such a large crowd. So far he doesn't seem to mind.

By the time I begin to call everyone to dinner, we have filled two garbage pails with plastic hors d'oeuvre plates and forks, wine and beer bottles, and other assorted garbage, and I have emptied the sink three or four times. Dana has arrived to much fanfare, the dogs have been released from bondage, and Zeusie has crawled into one of their crates and fallen asleep clutching one of the dirty, hairy towels that Jasper likes to chew on. Uncle Aaron has switched seats three times, and one toilet has overflowed.

I send Lexie upstairs to get the boys and head to the garage for more ice, and as I open the door I am greeted with the most shocking sight. There, backed up against the door of our Pathfinder, is Jillian, looking anything but nervous and prim. In fact, she is the picture of lust, locked in a deep, soulful kiss and embrace with Derek. Wait, my mind protests, unable to compute all the messages at once. I am happy for Jillian. I am shocked at Jillian. I am angry with Derek. Why should I be angry with Derek? Wait, is this legal? Derek is Lyle's son, Jillian is Ellen's daughter, Lyle and Ellen are first cousins, so what does that make Derek and Jillian? I think it is okay, they are at least third cousins. But so what? They are only kissing, not getting married and having babies.

"Oh, sorry, Aunt Julie." Derek backs off, cool, smiling. Yeah, right. He is very sorry.

Poor Jillian, however, looks ready to disintegrate. She turns, hangs her head, and holds her chest and I am reminded of me, thirteen and ashamed, and my heart goes out to her.

"Oh, don't be silly!" I say warmly. "You two are adorable." I pretend this is all nothing and I couldn't care less. I don't want Jillian to withdraw any more than she already has, or she might vaporize.

"Can you guys help bring in the bags of ice?"

TWENTY-ONE

mother made us sit two and three to a chair

It takes a full twenty minutes from the time I call everyone to the table to the moment we all actually sit down. Eric conducts a modified Seder, where everyone has a chance to read from the Haggadah, the Passover prayer book, in English, and those who can read Hebrew take the other parts. There are several rituals of dipping and drinking, and the busyness of the Seder keeps everyone involved. Before we actually eat the meal, I wish I could say a prayer out loud for my mother, but instead I ask if anyone would like to say something before we begin, and both my kids groan, but Vivian Soloman thinks it's a lovely idea. My sister-in-law Barbara chimes in that we should all be thankful that we're not in China right now or we'd have to eat with masks, and cousin Diane, who isn't used to Barb's unique style of stream of consciousness, asks if Barbara was supposed to be in China, and Barb's sons crack up and Evan is so exasperated he has to ask, "Mother, why would we ever be in China for Passover?" I interrupt and turn to Uncle Aaron, who is the eldest member of the clan, and ask him if he'd like to say something. Ellen looks at me and shakes her head, but Aaron clears his throat and begins, "Well now, let's see, my little Jule of the ocean"—an old pet name I never really understood—"you've done a fine job of bringing everyone together for this holiday. Three generations of family at one table, and everyone has their own chair, not like in the old days when my mother made us sit two and three to a chair—"

"Daddy, you always had your own chair." Ellen is mortified.

All the teenagers start to laugh, and Aaron says, "Laugh if you want to, but those were hard times."

I sneak a glance at Russell and am gratified to see that he looks confused. I hope good ol' Barb will bring up SARS again.

"Okay, let's eat," I tell everyone, and the meal begins. Almost everyone is having soup, although the orders range from extra matzoh balls to no balls, to just carrots. I am a little concerned because despite the number of people, the soup course is unusually quiet. I've been stealing looks at Russell and note that he is losing some of his discomfort and beginning to look far too content.

"So, Alexis," Barb begins, as if Russell doesn't exist, "what's new at school? How come we never met your friend before? Are you and he an item?"

Fire! Evacuate! Run for your lives! I thought we might sidestep this issue at least until dessert. I want to kill Barb. Then I notice Russell's face. He is not smiling; he is squirming. I want to hug Barb.

I look up and across at Eric, and we lock stares and hold our breath. Lexie acts casually unconcerned as she finishes a spoonful of soup. It seems like hours that we sit in dreadful silence while she swallows, licks her lips, and trails the corner of her napkin across her mouth. Then she turns to Barb and replies that Russell is a *new* friend. I am unable to look away from Eric and vice versa. Russell is looking under his seat for the complimentary life raft.

"Oh, how nice. Do you know each other from class?"

"Um-hmm," Alexis says slowly.

"What year are you in, dear?" She's turned to Russell.

Lexie and Russell share a glance. Clearly he's unsure what he's supposed to say. Lexie comes to his rescue. Or so I think.

"Well, actually, Russell is the professor." Silence. From the entire table.

It continues, punctuated by nothing. No dogs choose to bark, drinks are sipped without clinking, and the baby is silent for the first time all afternoon.

"You must mean one of the graduate students, dear, isn't that right?" Vivian offers.

"Oh no, he's a real professor."

I have suddenly become very interested in a piece of lettuce on my plate that is a fascinating shade of green, somewhere between Forest and Hunter. The silence continues until, luckily, Dana pipes in.

"That's no big deal, really, a lot of college students date professors these days. Did you just graduate?" She turns hopefully to Russell.

"Well, actually—"

At this moment, Eric drops his fork into his plate and starts to stand, but before he has the chance, Jake interrupts.

"Actually, he didn't just graduate. He's had quite a lot of time since then, time to do a lot of things, like, you know, get tenure, get married, things like that." Jake looks at Russell defiantly.

I am amazed. This is worse/better than I could have imagined. Lexie is speechless. She gets red in the face and I am not altogether displeased on several levels. There is something chivalrous in Jake's anger. I wonder if Lexie senses it. Plus, Jake has put it out there and for a moment I am unconcerned with the relatives or my plan, because there is a certain relief in hearing it out loud. If Lexie is a little embarrassed and Russell too, well there is some justice in that. But I am the hostess after all. And it wouldn't look right to appear . . . joyful. It's time to change the subject.

"Okay then, I'm sure this is all more information than anyone needs. Who's finished with their soup?" But Lexie will not let the whole subject die. Instead she strikes out.

"What's your problem, Jake? Are you a big expert on relationships all of a sudden? I guess you have so many hot babes calling you all the time that you know what's best."

"As a matter of fact, I have all I can handle right now." The other boys crack up. Who is this self-assured, confident young man?

"Oh, really?"

"Really. And she's not old enough to be my mother, either."

Well. I had no idea Jake had such strong feelings about his sister's situation. I look at Eric and he looks at me and we are both thinking that we should stop their bickering, but the truth is that neither of us wants to rescue Lexie right now because Jake is only reflecting what we've all been feeling, that this relationship is wrong and unnatural. I had planned to make Russell uncomfortable, even if it was only with the size and scope of a large family. I never planned on his having to deal with the pain of the truth, but hey, why not? For some strange reason I have a bit of sympathy for Russell. He does look pained. Plus, I don't want Lexie to freak out and leave the table and take Russell with her. She is regarding her brother, sizing him up and deciding how to respond, and I am about to say "That's enough," and ask Jake to help me in the kitchen, when Uncle Aaron rises abruptly in his place, raises his fork and bellows, "Would anyone like to switch seats?"

WITH THE TENSION BROKEN, the meal continues. Although I always hire my cleaning lady and her friend to help out when I have a large crowd, I still rarely sit down. When you're cooking for twenty or more, it's impossible not to hover in the kitchen and glide in and out of the dining room, and so I am less a participant in the meal than a producer. After the Russell fiasco I hear only snippets of conversation.

". . . this apple pudding is so amazing it should be against the law."

"Marc, try the carrots, maybe they'll help your glaucoma."

"Honey, check on the baby."

"Jule, do you need any help in there?" This last from Gayle, who sounds hopeful of escaping her mother's detailed description of her father's mucus condition, which is thankfully under control tonight. As she enters the kitchen I catch a slice of Viv's voice:

". . . just bubbles up in his throat, great globs of the stuff . . ."

I am taking the sweet potatoes and marshmallow out of the oven when Lexie screams, "MOM!"

Oh my God, I think, she's killed her brother. I hand the casserole to one of the girls and race into the dining room, but I see no trauma, no crisis.

"What is it?"

"Oh, Mom, the dogs are having sex again. *Please* make them stop."

OUR DOGS DON'T really have sex with each other, at least not traditional sex. What happens is that Lacey, the female, lies on her back and spreads her legs and Jasper walks right in and well, you know, samples the goods. They have been doing this since Lacey was two and we brought Jasper home as a pup and we have tried everything to make them stop. I have even considered telling Lacey she's only hurting herself. Although we all think it's gross, we are used to it, and sometimes we forget how much it can freak out our guests. Most of the family is laughing, I see, except Brooke. From the look on her face, I think she's grateful that Zeus is asleep and it appears she feels vindicated about wanting to keep the baby away from the dogs. I notice that Barb's mother, who is eighty-five, hasn't taken her eyes off the canine couple and is actually leaning in and pushing Lyle's arm out of the way to get a better look. Her sister, whose name I still can't remember because everyone refers to her as "sister," has filmy cataracts at least an inch thick on both eyes, and keeps asking, "What's he eating? What's the fuss? I always fed my dog from the table . . ."

"Jasper!" I yell out as I walk over and nudge Lacey's behind. The dogs scatter and I turn to Lexie with a look that says she didn't really need to call me with this, but she just throws up her hands. Russell looks better but not entirely comfortable, which pleases me, and he and Jake are involved in some kind of game with a fork at the table, a snapshot that leaves me ambivalent. What's the deal with Jake, anyway? First he practically castrates Russell in the town square and now they're bonding? Everyone else is still mesmerized by the dogs, and Barb asks, "Who taught them that trick?" and I think, the way things are going in my house, it could have been anyone. The boys are all laughing and hooting and Dana calls to the dog, "Yeah, Lacey, you go, girl!" and her grandmother turns bright red and we are all laughing now, and then I notice that Vivian is not only turning red but also clutching her throat, and with one hand she begins to pound the table, and the easy feeling that was spreading through me turns to panic.

"She's choking!" I scream at the same time that I grab this old woman and wrap my arms around her and make a fist. Except for one moment when it occurs to me that her skinny bones feel like twigs that could snap in my arms, I am on autopilot and not thinking and the millions of examples of the Heimlich Maneuver that I have seen are apparently so ingrained that I perform it reflexively, once, twice, three times, until a tiny brown piece of chewed food flies out of Viv's mouth and into the water pitcher, where it lands with a plop and floats, right between two lemon slices at the top.

Gayle rushes over.

"Mom, oh my God, are you all right?"

"What happened?" Lou has just realized that there's been some excitement.

"We should put her in a good hard chair," offers Uncle Aaron.

Eric comes to my rescue, and Viv's. "Jake, get Mrs. Soloman some water." He puts one hand on Viv's shoulder and the other on the small of my back.

Vivian tries to speak, but she is still catching her breath. The boys have gathered around the piece of food in the water and are examining it, trying to identify its composition.

"Definitely meat," says Derek.

"Nah, I think it's a mushroom," responds Timmy.

"Move it around a little," suggests Evan, who earns himself a look from his wife.

"Oh man," Jake joins in, returning with the water, "that is nasty."

I just stand there, arms at my sides, numb. Vivian is calming down, and as she takes a few sips of water, tears start to flow down her cheeks and she tries to speak again, but we all tell her to stay quiet and just relax.

"Good job, Aunt Jule." Dana comes up and puts her arm around me. "Hey, Grandma, I think Julie just saved your life."

TEN MINUTES LATER we resume the meal minus Viv, who has gone to lie down on the couch in the family room. I steal another glance at Russell, who is getting progressively paler as the meal progresses. Good. It's not like I wished for someone to have a near-death experience (I didn't, did I?), but it certainly didn't hurt the cause. Eric insists that I sit and taste the food and let the cleaning help finish serving. I am still sweating a little. I look over at Viv on the couch, and think of my mother and father in Florida, and I am so angry with everyone and everything. Things change, people die, I'm almost forty-five years old and I should know that, but our family is starting to look like a pile of human leftovers. Tomorrow the onions will be picked out of the string beans and they will be just string beans alone, like Uncle Aaron, who is no longer part of Uncle Aaron and Aunt Mimi, no longer a combination dish. And Jenny and her sister, who never really liked each other, now live together out of convenience, the way you store left-over potatoes and rice in the same bowl, not because they belong together, but because it's easier that way. And what will I be when my mother is gone? I look over at Tori, Diane's daughter, who is frowning at her boy-friend, Marc, now on his fifth glass of wine and doling out bitter commentary on everything from illegal immigrants to governmental conspiracies.

Next to him, Diane is measuring a piece of turkey with a small ruler she took from her purse, cutting the meat into a perfect three-by-five-inch rectangle. Tori catches my eye, and despite my mood we both smile and I think in that moment we are both saying, "Oh well, we're a strange bunch, but we are a bunch. With families you get what you get and you just have to make the best of it." The notion calms me a bit. Suddenly there is a loud sound and a burst of wind and the front door swings wide open, so wide that it passes through three large potted plants and slams into the wall.

"Ish not Elijah or—or anyone, you know, ish jush meeeee!" Roberta is standing in the doorway, arms thrown open, a large red plastic cup splashing liquid on my entry floor as she tries to steady herself and make it over the threshold.

"Eric!" I whisper loudly. He is closer.

Eric makes it to the doorway just as Roberta starts to sway forward, and manages to catch her in time. He guides her toward his seat at the table. Unfortunately she is wearing a brown spandex tube top that begins to slide down on one side with each step. Her hands are busy holding on to the cup and Eric, and although she must feel it slipping since one hand sort of halfheartedly pinches the air in the vicinity of her right breast, she doesn't even come close. As she turns to the table and leans her cup hand down on it, the right breast breaks free and plunges over the top, bouncing in place like an underfilled water balloon, white and droopy, large-nippled and rubbery.

There are gasps. "Roberta! Your top!" I call out. Eric has no idea; he is behind her, trying to guide her into the chair. Jake has fallen off his chair, literally, he is on the ground. The other boys are doubled over, laughing, holding their stomachs, and heading out of the room. Jake, through his whoops, is *crawling* after them. "Oh God," Alexis mutters in disgust. Russell's mouth is frozen wide, really hanging open. It's all I can do to stifle a laugh myself. This should do it, I think to myself. Tori recovers from the shock and reaches right over and pulls up Roberta's shirt. Roberta is all smiles; she is so out of it she thinks it's funny. "Uh-oh," she slurs, "no matzoh hiding in there." Nobody can hold back after that, and the table erupts in laughter.

Tori sits back down, wipes her eyes, looks to her left, and asks, "Anyone seen Marc? He wouldn't have wanted to miss this." With that, everyone turns to the family room. Viv is still on the couch, but Marc is nowhere to be seen. For just a moment it is quiet, no talking, no TV, no laughter. Even Roberta is silent. And then we hear it. At first it might be a faucet running, a dishwasher filling. But slowly the sound becomes familiar and distinct; there is no mistaking it, and recognition comes to almost everyone around the table at the same time. In the powder room to the right of the front door, someone is going to the bathroom. This wouldn't normally be something we'd all hear, but the reason we do is because the person has left the door wide open.

"Who's takin' a whiz?" Roberta shouts.

The rushing water is now punctuated by two loud ripples of gas.

"OH MY GOD!!" Tori wails. "MARC! YOU PIG!!"

I look at Eric. He looks back. We both turn to look at Alexis and Russell. Russell is getting up from his chair, and Alexis is scrambling after him. Everyone else is focused on Tori, who has flown out of her seat and into the bathroom, slamming the door behind her. We can hear her screams through the walls. They do not join us for dessert. I'm not sure if they'll be joining us ever again, or at least Marc won't, since even Tori has her limits. Dana whispers to me that this Passover will be known as the Marc Live Passover. "Join Marc as he leads the family in a medley of favorite Passover sounds . . ." I am praying it will also go down as the Russell Dead Passover. Considering the look on his face, something far more than a cringe, possibly even reminiscent of medieval torture, I'd say mission accomplished. To his credit, he does manage to make it through dessert before exiting with a stiff handshake, a terse thank-you, and very little eye contact. All in all, I'd say dinner was an overwhelming success.

TWENTY-TWO

I'd be dead right now if it weren't for you

The holiday passes, and Lexie and I have three days of late mornings and fattening brunches. She is noticeably quiet about the dinner and barely mentions Russell at all. She does spend several intervals in her room on the telephone, with the door closed, but I have no way of knowing whom she's talking to, or what it's about. By Monday morning I am in the midst of a full-blown, post-hostess depression. Lexie is back at school and Jake has been invisible, having spent most of the weekend at Kate's. This coming weekend he has another USTA tennis tournament, in Westchester, and has informed me that Kate will be taking him. I sigh over my coffee, which is lightened with skim milk instead of my usual half-and-half, a concession to my overindulgence the last few days—specifically my relationship with the strawberry cheesecake from The Cheesecake Factory last night.

Before she left, my daughter was kind enough to inform me that one slice of their cheesecake (even though I removed the crust) has 450 calories and thirty grams of fat. She's very helpful that way. I have an appointment with Dr. Bob at eleven—timely, I think, although it would be even better if he had a subspecialty in liposuction. I am debating whether I need to get dressed yet, and whether I have a spring muumuu to wear, when the phone rings.

"Hello?"

"I'd be dead right now if it weren't for you."

"Vivian?"

"I mean it, I'd be dead. It's Monday so you would have had the funeral already and my children would be sitting shivah."

"Oh God, Viv, don't talk like that." She is really too much. I look around for someone to commiserate with, but Eric is still upstairs so I roll my eyes at Jasper, who decides that I have invited all eighty-five pounds of him into my lap.

"Well, I just wanted to thank you again, dear, for everything. It was a wonderful dinner—well, the first part of it anyway—and your mother would have been proud."

No, Viv, not this morning, I think. Don't bring up my mother, who has called me every day since Lexie came home and asked, "So what are you two girls doing today?"

"Thanks. Oh, and the flowers you brought are beautiful, they still look brand-new."

"Oh yes, well of course. And, Julie, don't forget to put *fresh* water in every day."

I hang up, wondering exactly what *other* water one might put into a vase of flowers and thinking I could use a little fresh water myself. Wouldn't it be neat if *humans* could prolong their beauty and bloom with a little cool water? I have a vision of myself as this fat, bioengineered salmon that is bigger and stronger than ever before, but still spends every minute of her time swimming and fighting to make it farther and farther upstream. Where am I trying to go, and why must it always be upstream? If it's not the kids or myself, it's Eric. It seems like something always needs fixing, unless it doesn't because it's too sick or it chokes and dies. I am starting to feel dangerously low, and it scares me. The idea that I might will myself into an anxiety attack propels me out of my chair. I try to "shake it off," which doesn't work. I try to concentrate on something else, but I keep thinking about concentrating on not feeling low, which is the same as feeling low. Action, I should take some action. I have a new rebuttal to write, so I go up to the computer room and plan to pull up the fourth essay. But first I notice I have a new e-mail from Ted. A delicious lick of excitement develops down between my legs as I sit there, looking at the e-mail, savoring it and wondering if it's personal or business-related, not sure which I'd prefer. I open it. It's an invitation. There is a symposium of famous writers who are speaking together, on a panel, at Princeton University next Friday. Ted has added a note:

> I have to go to this and thought you might
> like to check it out. It's a whole day, with lunch,
> not really my thing but you coming along would make
> it so. If you can make it let me know, Ted.

There is a P.S. that informs me that the fourth essay in the contest has been available for download for days.

I can't help it. The thought of spending a whole day alone with Ted is so exciting that my heart is thumping just sitting here in my pajamas at my computer. I want to go, I really do, I'm just not sure why. Once again I think about Eric, and immediately feel guilty. How can I be excited about another man and love Eric as much as I do? Eric was so wonderful this past weekend, so gentle and supportive. I smile, thinking of his big bear arms and crinkly smile. It's just that . . . Ted is different. Ted is so . . . so alive and edgy and unpredictable. He's good looking, and sexy, yes, and he's so confident, so smooth. When I'm around Ted I suddenly feel like I'm anything but a housewife in the suburbs, I feel like I should be in *People* magazine or on *Entertainment Tonight*. Like I'm prettier and sexier and more important. What's wrong with wanting to feel that way? Maybe going to a writers' symposium isn't automatically betraying Eric. Why shouldn't I have some fun? Before I can think too much about what I'm doing, I e-mail Ted and tell him I'm free to go. Then I download the essay. It's an anti-development piece about lost farmland and McMansions. I am to write in favor of development. I struggle for a while to muster up the right defense. There are the benefits of rising property values and the by-product of excellent schools, but that is about all I can come up with, and because I'm not feeling passionate, the tone is all wrong. I wonder if this is God's way of telling me not to play with fire, by making me inept. I am going for a mix of humor and practicality and instead sound smugly arrogant and bitter, defensive. I can just imagine Ted's voice if I send him this one.

"Uh, Julie, honey, is everything all right?"

On my way to Dr. Bob, I think hard about Ted. Of course, I haven't even mentioned him to Dr. Bob. I am torn between looking desperately forward to seeing him and never wanting to see him again. Maybe I should pay him a visit at the paper. Certainly I have a valid excuse; I'm struggling with my rebuttal. Who are you kidding, I ask myself.

Dr. Bob wants to talk about Alexis. I would rather talk about Jake and boys and their obsession with sex, but Dr. Bob says I've pretty much summed it up.

"We've hardly discussed your daughter, and yet last time, just as you were leaving, you dropped this bombshell about her being interested in an older man."

"Well, I think that's pretty much over."

"Is it?"

"Yes. I mean, I think so."

"How did it end?" Well, here's how, Dr. Bob. My husband and I concocted this really sneaky plan to sabotage the whole plan by pretending that we really liked the guy. And it worked too well.

"Oh, I guess it just ran its course."

"Mm-hmm."

Dr. Bob is good. He's a little sneaky, too. When he doesn't believe me, he just says "mm-hmm" or "I see" and then he shuts up and he sits there until I get uncomfortable and start to babble. But I don't take the bait.

"It seems like you have something else on your mind."

Yes, Dr. Bob, I do. Lots of things. Failure, fear, loss. A handsome reporter who is dangerously intoxicating and a lump of guilt the size of Alaska, but I don't know how to talk about any of it with you. In addition to everything else, I don't want you to think I'm such a mess. I want to be your good client, your easy client, your fun client, even. This is my aspiration: to be the best mental patient on the ward. I should probably get some help for it.

"It's okay to have secrets here, you know."

"It is?"

"Of course. You didn't sign up to reveal your diary. Therapy is about getting perspective, not unraveling. It's okay if you don't want to talk about Lexie. But I'd like to see you get something out of the session. What would you like to talk about?" I feel a little guilty that Dr. Bob understands so well. So guilty, in fact, that I almost tell him about Ted and confess my infatuation. At the last minute, I cop out.

"Well, um, how do you feel about overdevelopment and open space?"

LEAVING DR. BOB'S OFFICE, knowing I have just wasted $150 of my money, Eric's money, I need to do something productive, and what could be more immediately gratifying than the mall? Soon I am in Neiman Marcus, on the second floor. We have a bat mitzvah to attend on Saturday night, the Glucksteins' youngest, and I have an old dress I was planning to wear, but perhaps I could use something new. I would love to head up to Couture, but then I wouldn't be able to go home because Eric would have a fit, and the way I am feeling I would have to shoot him, so to save my husband's life I decide to stay on floor two, where the prices remain in three figures. I'm searching through the gowns by Laundry and Shelli Segal, wondering what I'm doing here. I'm not the best shopper, which is why most of my clothes come from Hartly's Boutique in Westwood, where I can get serious help and attention. Probably I pay a little more than my friends who can spot a Badgley Mishka at thirty paces on a discount rack at Loehmann's, but I don't have the confidence or patience. After several fashion "no's" and probably several thousand dollars wasted, I've learned that it's easier and more cost-effective to call Amy at Hartly's, who knows my size, taste, body shape, and wallet.

Sighing, I turn from the racks and am about to leave, when something catches my eye. It's not a dress; it's the elderly saleslady at the register. At first I think she has dropped something, like a button or a pen, onto the floor. Her torso is bent forward at a forty-five-degree angle, and she holds one hand to her eyeglasses to keep them on. Suddenly her other hand grabs the shelf in front of her and I realize to my absolute horror that she is choking. I look for an instant to my right and left, but this is Neiman Marcus, which must hold the record for fewest shoppers per capita or per department or some such thing, and I am the only one in sight. Without thinking, I rush to this woman's aid and throw my arms around her in what is now a familiar pose for me and I shout, "Hold on, hon, I'll help you!"

Well. I am not exactly a hero and Ms. Rita Sanger, the alleged victim, will not be calling me tomorrow morning à la Viv Soloman, since she wasn't choking at all. In fact, when I put my arms around her she thought she was being attacked and almost had a heart attack. It turns out Ms. Sanger was merely trying to get a closer look at a receipt that was being printed beneath the register. Who knew the receipts came out there? We straighten out the misunderstanding pretty quickly, and I think it is an understandable mistake, but Rita seems to be a little put off, a little over-reactive if you ask me, the way she keeps backing away from me each time I ask if there is anything I can do, and waving her hand at me as I apologize for like the fifteenth time. Of course, *after* the incident there are

suddenly hordes of shoppers and salespeople in the Elegant Dress department who come to poor Rita's aid and who stare at me as if I need to con-
sult the dosage on my meds. I decide rather quickly that my old dress will
be just perfect for Saturday night.

When I tell Eric about the fiasco in Neiman's, he laughs and shakes
his head and says it makes sense in light of the episode with Vivian. I am
grateful he doesn't use the opportunity to make me feel foolish. I call Lexie
at school and tell her the story, and her reaction is slightly different.

"So you mean we can't go to Neiman's anymore?"

Relax, Lex, I think to myself, I probably forced the woman into early
retirement, so she won't be there to recognize me.

On Tuesday, I am wondering if the Passover plan worked, since I haven't
heard anything either way from Lex. I want to hate Russell as much as
before, but mostly I keep remembering the way he looked at Alexis when he
first came in and how she looked at him all night. I remember that Russell
never knew his mom, and since I am a mother it's impossible for me not to
feel a little bad about that. Under normal circumstances I would have tried
to prepare Lexie's date, if it's actually possible to prepare for twenty-two
insult-hurling, meat-choking Berman-Resnicks between the ages of one and
eighty-two, plus assorted drunken boyfriends and neighbors. But I refuse to
feel guilty. His wanting Alexis is a bit of culture shock, too. I force myself to
concentrate on writing, but I still can't come up with a reasonable essay for
the contest. To make matters worse, there is another e-mail from Ted.

> Hey good-lookin' you better get cookin' on
> number 4—it's been a week and the cannibals are
> getting restless. Do you need some motivation?
> Inspiration? Personal attention? I hear a full body
> massage often gets the creative juices flowing . . .

Despite my mournful mood, I smile. I attempt the rebuttal once again, but it quickly becomes clear to me that I am not getting it right. I can't do it. It's all been a waste. I will not get this job and I will disappoint Ted and probably that's just as well because I had no right to be playing in the big leagues, not to mention entertaining illicit ideas about another man. I will just give up and Ted will have to understand. I should cancel the Princeton trip, too, but I decide that I can do that later.

Jake has a half-day of school because of a teachers' workshop, and last night I offered to meet him and take him out to lunch. He said "Sure," and I realized that his willingness is due to the fact that Kate's school does not have a half-day so I will not be taking him away from his favorite pastime and in fact will be providing him with his second-most-important reason for living, food. More specifically, the Turkey Bacon Club Sandwich on Croissant at Friday's.

As I get ready, I am ensconced in a melancholic haze: mother dying, daughter self-destructing, career failing. I am blowing my life big-time. In addition, a full litter of secrets has grown legs inside my own skin. I still haven't even mentioned the job at the paper to Eric. He's never met Ted, so he wouldn't be jealous, but I feel certain that telling him would be more of a betrayal. At least this way I haven't told him anything, so I haven't left out anything. And now that I know I'm not good enough to get the job, it's moot. At least I don't have to wear that failure in front of him. We both know, although we never speak about it, that I can only handle so much anyway. I don't need to enforce it with another failed career move. Besides, Eric would have been skeptical about my ability to handle, let alone win, a high-pressure job involving deadlines, so I've saved both of us the trouble of a series of exasperating arguments and debates. As for Ted, I will just forget him. So what if he makes me feel like Madonna and Maya Angelou rolled into one? I have enough to worry about without cultivating an infantile fantasy. I will not think about him, not even for a second. Later I will e-mail him and thank him for his time and firmly tell him that my working for the *Sentinel* would never work. In case I lose my resolve, I make a short list.

TED

Pros		Cons
that smile I get when I think of him	*vs.*	*the horror when I think of hurting Eric*
that smile on the inside	*vs.*	*the nausea on the inside*
in sync w/ verbal repartee	*vs.*	*out of sync with family, values, everything*
finds me attractive	*vs.*	*I love Eric, our family, being married*

That's it, then. As Dr. Bob says, I am doing an excellent job of conceptualizing my goals.

At 12:20, I am at the high school in our prearranged spot at the side. When Jake comes out I get a few free moments to stare at him as he ambles, smiling and lopsided from the weight of his backpack, toward the car. I love those moments when you can watch your offspring legitimately without their asking you why you're staring at them.

"Hey." I smile as he hauls his stuff in the back.

"Hey."

"How was school?"

"Good, actually."

"Really? How come?" This is great! School was actually good and we will talk about why.

"I dunno." Okay, so I shouldn't have pushed it. I forgot the one question rule.

"Hungry?"

"Yep."

Well. We are not solving world peace with our scintillating conversation, but we are a mother and son spending time together, and that is groundbreaking enough. At Friday's, Jake makes a show of looking at the menu and even contemplates the Jack Daniel's wings, but I know he has been salivating for the Turkey Club. Since I am the mother of the year, *I* order the wings, which I happen to like, but also because I feel so much love for my son at that moment I would order the fried appetizer sampler if I thought that was what he wanted. Jake tells me a story about his math teacher, who is having trouble maintaining authority in the class, and I have a vague memory from back-to-school night of a young, anemic-looking female, new to teaching. She has become arbitrary and punitive in her effort to retain control of her class. Of course, those are my words, arbitrary and punitive, not Jake's. He merely says, "One day she lets you talk and the next day she gives you a demerit. And if one person screws up, the whole class has extra homework. She's a bitch." I validate his feelings of frustration and say the words "arbitrary and punitive" out loud, always parenting, always teaching, thinking one day the vocabulary will stick, hopefully in time for the SATs. Our food comes, and Jake looks the way he did the day we first got Lacey as a puppy, ten years ago. I can still see him, a curly-headed six-year-old, at the breeder's house, sitting on the dirty floor amid the puppy crap and urine-soaked newspapers, as the yellow Lab pup was placed into his arms. As she lunged to lick his face, my baby boy spread his arms and smiled and, with his eyes open wide and shining, laughed the most joyous, gurgling giggle I've ever heard. Pure ecstasy. And I swear he is looking at this greasy sandwich the same way. Ahhh, I think to myself, boys are so simple.

I am two chicken wings into my own lunch when it happens. Whether or not I had any warning or if there was a sign, I cannot say. I've replayed the incident over and over again in my mind, looking for a trigger, but I only remember feeling as if it were an ordinary lunch on an ordinary day with my son. Our booth along the front window of Friday's looked out into the parking lot and onto the exit ramp of Route 17 North, and the scene was far from interesting—in fact, it was rather hypnotic in a monotonous sort of way, a steady stream of cars, the occasional horn. When the young couple with the baby walked toward their car, I barely noticed them. As they worked together to put the baby in the car seat and fold the stroller, I was eating a wing, studying Jake, and while I may have glanced at them, I wasn't really looking at them. The young mother had just shut the back door of the vehicle, a navy blue minivan, and her husband was loading the stroller into the rear, when she bent over, clutched her chest, and began to make short, violent movements of distress. It never occurred to me that this was anything other than a woman choking, I swear. Her husband was at her side immediately, grasping her around the back with one arm and helping her to hold her chest with the other. He looked up for an instant and there was panic on his face and my own body was propelled out of the booth toward the crisis. By the time Jake had a chance to put down his sandwich and shout through his food, "Where are you going?" I was flying through the restaurant's front doors as if a life depended on my speed, which I believed it did. Unfortunately, in my haste, I lost my footing on the rubber mat just outside the entrance and, in an effort to save myself from falling down the four entrance steps, twisted my ankle and lunged for a grip on the side railing. Although I both heard a pop and felt something grind, I continued toward the couple, my right arm lunging along the railing, and when the railing ran out, limping and hopping the remaining ten yards to the minivan. By the time I got there, they were both on the ground on all fours, and I got my first hint that this was not as it seemed.

"Can I help?" I panted breathlessly. "Are you all right?" It came out as if I was crying, which I was, as the pain in my ankle suddenly turned sharp.

"What? Oh, thanks, but I think we've got most of them."

"Most of them?"

"My pearls." The young woman looked up at me. She was clutching a broken strand of pearls in her fist, and had collected a bunch more in the pocket of her coat. On the ground next to her was a baby's toy.

"They got caught on Mr. Wiggles. They were my mother's."

To add to my embarrassment, Jake is suddenly right behind me.

"Mom?"

"Jake, I—uh, tripped. I think you better help me to the car."

"Mom, what's going on?"

"Nothing, sweetie, nothing at all. Just help your mother to the car."

TWENTY-THREE

so when do you see Dr. Bob again?

"Okay, so tell me again, you thought the woman was choking and you just flew out of the restaurant to save her." Eric is laughing, but he has no qualms about teasing me this time, and I detect an edgy concern beneath his lighthearted tone.

"Dad, you never saw anything like it. One minute we're eating and the next she's like *ejecting* herself from the seat, flying through Friday's, crashing down the steps—"

"I didn't crash down the steps, I saved myself from falling."

"Yeah, right, you slid down the banister to the parking lot." It's hard to make a serious point in my favor at the moment, since we are sitting on the couch in the family room and my leg is propped up on a pillow and my ankle is wrapped in bags of ice. I do make a mental note not to have any more children.

"So wait, then, when you got there, you found out that she had just dropped her pearls? That's why she was holding her chest?"

"Are you having fun, Eric?"

"Dad, the whole place was looking at us, it was so weird. I didn't even get to finish my sandwich."

"How did you drive home?"

Jake and I exchange looks.

"Oh, Jule, you didn't!"

"Well, it was an emergency. If we had gotten stopped, I would have explained that, and besides he's a great driver."

"He doesn't get his official permit till next week."

"I know that. What did you want me to do, Eric, call you? Bother you? So you could be as easy and understanding as you're being right now?"

There is some silence as Eric decides how to deal with me. He is right and I'm not and I know it, but I'm not sure he knows I know it. He is wondering how he's supposed to behave, and I realize that I have successfully confused him. He has every right to be angry, but my injured leg is making him think twice about whether or not that will make him a shit. I know that I am the shit, which makes me feel even worse. I never should have let Jake drive me home, but I was too embarrassed to call Eric. Finally Eric looks at me and asks what he thinks is a benign question.

"So when do you see Dr. Bob again?"

If I didn't feel broken before, I do now. I realize Eric's inner stream of consciousness has led him from my immediate problem to pondering whether or not there might be damage of a deeper kind. He is so transparent. Or is he? Perhaps I give my husband too little credit. Perhaps he knows exactly how this question will make me feel, like I need fixing, and so perhaps it is the perfect jab, albeit a passive-aggressive one. Well, I think, good for Eric. He gets to be a shit and not a shit, too.

I AM ACTUALLY scheduled to see Dr. Bob tomorrow, which I should, since I totally squandered last week's session, but I am feeling resentful of needing help with this little choking obsession, and, spitefully, I sneak upstairs and phone his service to cancel my appointment. I'll show Eric who needs fixing! I meet the girls instead.

"What do you mean, you're trying to save everyone?"

I am purposely sitting at a table in the back, even though I had to hobble there on my bad foot, but I don't want to see if anyone is in any trouble of any kind.

"Just what I said. I think they're all choking. In the stores, restaurants, everywhere."

The girls exchange looks and I say, "See, you didn't realize just how nuts I could become, did you?"

"Gee, call *me* crazy." Amy is dripping with sarcasm. "It's just a guess, but could you possibly be trying to *save* all these strangers as a way of dealing with being unable to save Lexie or your mom?"

Beth is smiling and of course Amy is right and it's sort of annoying since I am the one who's supposed to be so analytical and all, but I'm actually glad I passed on Dr. Bob and want to take out my checkbook and write her a check for a hundred and fifty dollars.

"Now," Amy says, "can we please order some food before I solve the Meaning of Life or at least before we have to hear about your son's sex life, or"—pointing to Beth—"*your* mother's balls or, God forbid, the reverse?"

"Oh please, no more." I laugh. Not that I would mind talking about Jake, but how much airtime can one friend monopolize? I turn to Beth.

"Tell me about the girls. How was the dance competition last weekend?"

"Oh no, don't get her started on that. Didn't you know that all the *other* mothers are disgustingly competitive and spend obscene amounts on costumes and make *their* little girls into disgracefully mature sexual objects? But not our Bethie, oh no! She would never stoop to that!" I glance over at Beth, who is looking sheepish.

"Well, it's true—it is disgusting but it's like you can't escape it, you just get sucked in. I mean, what am I gonna do? These other girls are in strapless sequins. Can you see me putting Heather in a Peter Pan collar and pleats? But really, it burns me. Very JonBenet, you know." I look at Beth, pat her hand, and smile.

"Your girls are perfect, babe, healthy and normal."

"Don't worry, Bethie, we love you for your principles."

Beth puts her head in her hands and rubs her temples. "Oh, but I cave so quickly! What's wrong with me? Remember what happened to me on visiting day at dance camp? I swore I would wait my turn to see the girls. I swore I'd never get involved in that parent stampede, that I'd act civilized. But the minute they opened those gates and the parents started to rush in and I visualized those other girls getting to see their parents first, I abandoned all reason! I started elbowing mothers out of the way and stepping on feet! I was like, 'Out of my way, bitch!' I was no longer me, I was some crazy person. I was like . . . like . . . AMY!"

"Why, thank you, darling," Amy says sweetly. I laugh.

"You know what I mean," Beth apologizes.

"Yeah, Ame," I offer, "she means violent but in a good way."

"No, I don't really mean violent. I just mean assertive."

"That's our Amy."

"Damn straight. And proud of it, too. I say, if the bitches wouldn't get out of your way, fuck 'em. They deserved an elbow. Your problem is you feel guilty about it."

Well. Beth and I exchange a glance. We are thinking the same thing. Maybe. Maybe Amy is as tough as she sounds, or maybe it is part bravado. Maybe it is always easy to be tough on other people's problems. Meanwhile, we hear very little about hers. Besides, any girl who can lose herself in those lusty eighteenth-century English romances is not as tough as she claims. I whisper loudly to Beth, "Methinks the lady doth protest—" Amy balls up her napkin and throws it at me but she's grinning. Just being with the two of them has made me feel more hopeful than ever before.

At home I return to the computer to e-mail Ted and remove myself from his life and consideration for the job. I am about to go online when I decide to read the essay one more time. Just to see if it is still so impossible. The girls have given me confidence, if not that everything will work out, then in me, and before I know it, it's after five and I've written a humorous defense of faux Tudors and mock chalets and made suburban sprawl sound like a friendly, organic, and innocuous ally of Good Old Family Values. I almost believe it myself. With some trepidation, I press send, and through the wonders of Microsoft Windows I am instantly back in the game. Subliminally, I send a "take that" to my husband, who not only doesn't think I am strong enough to tackle the game, but could not even figure out, as my friends did, that I was symbolically trying to save the world.

THAT NIGHT, after dinner, I begin to clear the dishes, and as I bend down to open the dishwasher the lights go out. I hear a clinking sound and look up to see my son with a cake in his hand, its flickering candle illuminating the grin on his face. Behind him, my husband carries a box, a glass, and a spoon. What in the world? It isn't my birthday for two weeks. As I approach the table, a puzzled look on my face, Jake smiles, glances down at the cake and then up at me. I look down and on the cake, above the candle, are the words CONGRATULATIONS HM. I have no idea what it means, and then they begin to sing:

> *"Congratulations to you,*
> *Congratulations to you,*
> *Congratulations dear Heimlich Mom,*
> *Congratulations to you."*

Oh my God, I'm going to kill them, I think, and I say so, but I am laughing and so are they and then I realize it's a cheesecake, which would preclude getting mad about anything. Then Eric flicks on the lights and says, "Quiet, please." He takes the spoon and clinks it against the glass.

"Attention, attention. Have no fear! Heimlich Mom is here! Don't worry," he shouts to an imaginary audience, "your prayers are answered. There'll be no deaths by choking here! Come on, honey, flex those hands for us, show us your tools!" He hands me the box, which I open, smiling like a good sport. Inside is a T-shirt that has the same letters, HM, set into a diamond-shaped logo, like Superman's.

"You are both crazy, you know," I say. They are grinning uncontrollably.

"When did you have time to do this?"

"Oh, honey, if you have time to save the world, one choking victim at a time, we certainly have the time to get you the clothes to do it in. Every self-respecting suburban superhero should have the right outfit."

There are few moments in life when, despite the struggles and the angst, you get to experience pure joy, when it's as if all the planets are in the right houses and you have settled into your one true spiritual and physical axis. I want to freeze-frame my family, the whole room, and the immortal mood. Trying to describe how I feel would break the spell, so I keep it to myself, stowing the feeling away in my cheeks to savor later, when I can loll in the pleasure of it.

"Well," I say, clearing the lump in my throat, "there's cheesecake here. Somebody get the forks and let's eat."

And then, as an afterthought, "Oh, and don't forget to chew before you swallow."

TWENTY-FOUR

the audience would be screaming

Wednesday morning is ordinary, which should be a tip-off for me. My ordinary days need to come with scary music, the kind that creeps in on straining stringed instruments with a background bass, the kind that grows menacingly louder: Music for the Seriously Oblivious. The most extraordinary things always happen to me on ordinary days, and yet I am never prepared. Today I'm paying bills, a monthly event. I divide them into two piles: Medical, which require a system of cross-checking with insurance forms; and Other, which require only that there is money in the checking account. Luckily, Eric's real-estate deals have provided us with enough of a permanent annual income so that there is always enough in the checking account, although this wasn't always the case. Still, the stack of bills, and the stamped envelopes of money they end up as, always makes me nervous. Each month I marvel at the volume of our needs: water, heat, electric, taxes, autos, mortgage, tuition, health, life, landscaper, lessons, cleaning, on and on. And that's before food, clothes, and luxuries. Every time I sit down with the bills, I fantasize about chucking it all to run an inn in Vermont. Eric would show our guests to their rooms and dabble in local real estate, and I would bake blueberry pies and write. Sure. But first I will answer the seventeen voice messages on my cell phone, surf 845 channels on our digital iO cable TV, and call the repairman to come and fix our central vacuum system. An hour later I am almost through with the medical bills and I see that our ailments fall into three distinct categories. Eric's are all preventive: a yearly physical, a full-body check at the dermatologist, and a round of blood work associated with the physical. I find this amazing and a little annoying. Eric turned fifty last May and has nothing wrong with him. Except for one stomach virus and a bout of vertigo eight years ago when the real-estate market crashed, he never has. I, on the other hand, have a list of medical bills for chronic illnesses: an office visit to the top gastroenterology group from Mount Sinai, a bill for a sigmoidoscopy from the same group, plus a separate charge for lab work of the best-left-unsaid kind, all of which resulted in a catchall diagnosis of nonspecific irritable bowel syndrome. There are two bills from the ophthalmologist, who has detected early glaucoma, and one from the gynecologist, whom I saw when my July period continued through September. Luckily, Jake has his own distinct set of bills that are less serious than mine and less neurotic than his father's. Dermatologist for acne, orthopedist for possible hand fracture (it wasn't), and one from the pediatrician for a nasty sinus infection that had him actually lying down on the table while he waited for the doctor to come in. After that visit, Jake informed me that he was too big to go to the pediatrician and I could see why, although reluctantly. Somehow Jake's teenage body doesn't fit in anymore with the bright rainbow colors, Golden Books, and colorful toys, not to mention the infants and babies. During our last visit, one toddler kept running up and down the aisle in the waiting room, tapping people on either side of him as he went. Every time he got to us at the end, he would slap Jake on the knee and announce, "You're it." The memory of that toddler and Jake looking so out of place lingers. It feels as if the passages are coming more and more rapidly these days, like a factory line on warp speed, I am Lucy trying to stuff cherries into chocolates, but instead I'm stuffing moments of my children's lives into the present. And they are going too fast and I'm heading off unfinished, frantic to get an impossible job done right. There is barely enough time to enter one phase, let alone master it, before I'm exiting it. The other day I thought Eric was home from work early because I heard his voice in the kitchen, only to come down and find that it was Jake talking on the phone.

I notice there is one medical bill left: patient's name, Alexis Resnick. I forgot that I took her to the gynecologist before she left for school. She had been trying on clothes in her room and I noticed something on her breast, some small bumps that gave me concern. I asked her about it and she thought she had always had them but couldn't be sure, so I decided to take her in. I have a female gynecologist, for which Lexie was grateful. On unfamiliar turf, she had some questions.

"She doesn't have to, you know, look inside me, does she?"

"I don't think so, babe, not if you're not sexually active."

"I should be so lucky."

"Lex."

"No, really, do I have to tell her I'm still a virgin? It's embarrassing."

"Oh, come on, Lex, you're nineteen and you've never had a serious boyfriend. You can't really believe you're in such a minority."

"Mom, I'm telling you, you don't have a clue. Practically everyone has had sex already. Even the nerdy girls at my school have had sex. I'm like an object of curiosity, like a"—she pauses to think of something obscure—"a red rock from Mars." She emphasizes "Mars," as if to suggest that she is a native.

"Or you're like a shooting star," I say, "rare but special."

"Or a two-dollar bill," she shoots back, "which is pointless and obsolete." She smiles, satisfied, a winning smile.

We are playing the game full force now.

"Or a four-leaf clover," I offer. "Hard to find but lucky!" I smile back, thinking that was a good one.

She turns sideways, stops and looks at me challengingly.

"Or a truffle!"

"A what?" I start to laugh.

"A truffle! A disgusting, moldy, black mushroomy truffle. They're very rare all right, and they only grow on certain sides of a certain tree in a certain part of . . . France, I think. So that's me, you see, a very rare, very special fungus!"

I crack up at this and tell her she's the most beautiful fungus I've ever seen.

When Dr. Hurst calls her into the office, Lexie asks me to come with her, and when she sees the stirrups at the end of the examining table she remarks that she's not entirely certain that she needs this exam. Dr. Hurst is warm and smiling, with a soft voice that puts Lexie at ease. She examines her breasts and declares them to be perfectly fine and we are both relieved. Then she turns to me and says, "Julie, it's great to see you again, but would you mind leaving us alone for a moment?"

"Oh sure!" I say quickly, flustered, and begin to gather my coat and purse.

"No, no, it's okay." Lexie smiles and says to the doctor, "I don't need any birth control or anything, if that's what you want to ask me."

Dr. Hurst, whom I have known for fourteen years, smiles warmly at Lexie and looks back at me. I'm not sure whether she's waiting for confirmation or for me to leave.

"It's true," I say. "Alexis is not sexually active and she knows that if she is, it's okay and she can tell me."

"That's nice," Dr. Hurst says sweetly and evenly. "It's great that Alexis knows that. Now, would you mind leaving us alone for a moment?"

I look at Lexie and she at me, and we share a look that says "whatever, no big deal" and I leave the room, my feathers slightly ruffled. When she comes out she tells me that Dr. Hurst hears the same thing from many mothers and always insists on a private talk with older girls, and that she is really nice. I wonder about this and decide it is ultimately a good thing. Also, a little part of me wants to cartwheel through the office building. After all the years of weeding through the yuppie pressure of the right

teacher at the perfect school and the necessary classes for everything from
music to religion to math—does she really need Preschool Pilates or private Bumper Bowling lessons, or should we spring for the Logic Coach in
elementary school to groom her for the Gifted and Talented Program in
fifth grade so as not to ruin her chances for an Ivy League education and
destine her to a life of impoverished misery?—after all of that, I want to
shout, Look! Over here! Great parenting over here! Daughter still a virgin
post–high school!!! I restrain myself.

AT THE KITCHEN TABLE I have left the world of our ailments and am
working on the household expenses when I get to an unopened envelope
from Branford College whose return address reads Office of Academic
Affairs. I tear it open, and written in bold at the top is the word Confirmation. Underneath it states that Alexis Resnick, social security number
158-54-3026, has applied for the Semester Abroad Program in London,
England, for the upcoming fall semester. There is a required deposit of six
hundred dollars to hold her place, which must be received by May 1. Well.
I lean back, wondering what to do, and am grateful that at least the deadline is still a few weeks away and I'm hopeful that Alexis will come to her
senses by then, and it is at precisely this moment that the audience, if there
was one, would be squirming in their seats, covering their eyes and yelling
"NO!" and "WATCH OUT!" Instead of the stringed instruments and
drumbeat, there is the ring of the phone.

    "DON'T ANSWER IT!" the audience would be screaming. Of
course, like the B-actors in *Halloween* or *Friday the 13th,* I don't sense anything wrong.

    "Hello?" There is a strange whine. I repeat myself.

    "He-llo?"

    "Wha di joo doo."

    "What? Hello? Who is this?" The whine turns into a wail.

    "WHAT DID YOU DO?" Crying, sputtering, coughing.

Instinctively I turn to the caller ID, but just as I do, I know, and my stomach begins to knot. The small, inky screen confirms it. The whine belongs to my daughter.

"Lexie! Jesus Christ, what is it? What's wrong?"

"What's wrong? You want to know what's wrong? I want to know what you did—how you did it—how you could do it . . ." Her voice is choked with tears, and she trails off as she begins to cough.

"Lexie, honey, please. What are you talking about? You're scaring me. Please, honey, what's going on?"

"Like you don't know. He's gone, Mother, just—gone. And don't tell me you and Daddy didn't have something to do with it. We were fine. Everything was fine. And now he's just gone." So this is about Russell. I feel instantly guilty.

"What do you mean, gone? Lexie, do you mean that he broke up with you?"

"YES! NO! I mean he left me a note. He says that he loves me but that he realizes it can never work and he's leaving. He's left school! Just like that! I went over to his apartment and it's empty. I asked in the English department and they said he had a personal problem and he and his wife had to leave. They won't even tell me where he went! And I know this has something to do with you, I just know it. And I want you to know that I HATE YOU! Do you hear me? I really hate you—both of you!"

And then the phone goes dead. I begin to panic. She was hysterical. I can't imagine that Russell would do something so drastic just because of our little dysfunctional family. Was this my fault? I need to call Eric, but first I try to call Lexie back. She has scared me and I need to calm her down. Five rings, six, seven, ten. Either she's not picking up or she's run out. I hope it's the first. I put the phone back and am about to pick it up when it rings again. I snatch at it.

"Lex?"

"Hello?"

"Yes?"

"Mrs. Berman?" Someone for my mother?

"No, who's calling?" I am annoyed.

"This is Dr. Zacharias's office, at Sloan-Kettering."

Whoa.

"What?" Oh my God.

"Will she return soon?"

"Mrs. Berman is my mother. She's in Florida right now. Can I help you?"

"Oh, then you are Mrs. Resnick?"

"Yes, yes."

"Well, I have instructions to contact your mother. Dr. Zacharias would like to see her this Friday at 2:00 p.m., if that's possible, which I hope it is, because he's fitting her in."

"Oh, yes, I mean I'm sure that's okay. I have to get her up here, that's all. Did the doctor say exactly what it's about?"

"Yes, dear. To begin her treatment."

"Really?"

"Yes really."

"The experimental drug? The clinical trial?" I couldn't believe it.

"*Yes, yes.* Remoxilin. I have some instructions. Do you have a fax?"

"Of course." I give the number, numb.

"All right, we'll put her in, then. Friday, at two."

"Yes, definitely! Oh, thank you, thank you so much."

Extraordinary. Was it the voodoo coffee mug with the little smiley faces? Unsure whom to call first, I try Lexie again. Still no answer.

"JULIE, DEAR, don't get excited, but I'm not going to come up."

You've got to be kidding me. I say it out loud.

"I'm not kidding. I'm tired. I have an incurable disease and I don't want to torture myself at the end of my life."

"Mom, please." I am almost crying. I want to say, *What's wrong with you and so what if you're tired, this is your chance.* I want to say, *I killed myself to get you into this trial and why won't you FIGHT,* and also that Lexie will be devastated and she is already devastated and I am rambling in my head, hysterical in my head, and so I don't say anything at all. Before I can compose a coherent response, my dad gets on the phone.

"Julie, you don't have the big picture. Mom's gotten very weak. She's nauseous already, and Dr. Palmer has her on a sedative for nerves. She can't do it." And there it is. It's the way he says it, so final, in his "no buts about it" voice. Like when my hamster fell out of my cousin Martin's hand and landed on the cold basement floor. It happened so quickly. "I'm sorry, Julie, but the little guy is gone. Now let's get a Baggie and we'll bury him out back." The hope goes out of me quickly, too, like a break in a water main, just as when I was eight years old, feeling the first crushing unfairness of loss. If only I could go back in time. I wouldn't take him out of the cage, I wouldn't let Martin hold him, and I wouldn't think everything my mother did was so wrong. I hang up the phone, put my head down on the table, and cry. When Eric comes home I am still there at the table, sobbing. I tell him everything and he just stands there forever, rubbing my head.

"Try her again." It's nighttime and I've washed up, and Eric has ordered dinner in and even Jake is especially *present,* doing his homework on the downstairs couch instead of locked away in his room. We've been taking turns trying to reach Alexis for hours. Eric does so again, there is no answer, and he decides to give up.

"Let's let her be, Jule. We'll call tomorrow. You're exhausted, it's been a draining day for everyone, and she probably just needs some space."

The next morning Eric phones from the office to say that he's reached Lexie on her cell phone. This is the day I'm going to the writers' symposium with Ted, which Eric knows. That is, he knows I'm going to Princeton to listen to some writers. He knows I'm going with someone named Ted. He may, for some reason, be under the impression that Ted is the kindly, seventy-two-year-old widower from my writers' group.

"I didn't know if I'd catch you. I used Dick Merrill's phone because it has an Orange County area code, and she fell for it. She said she wouldn't have answered it if she'd known it was me."

"Nice. Did you get into it with her?"

"Well, I think I was able to convince her that we didn't have anything to do with Russell's disappearance, but she knows that something's up. It seems she's been telling your mother everything about Russell and even sending his novel or whatever he's writing, down for her to read. So now she thinks that maybe Grandma betrayed her, you know, because you're always saying how difficult she is and all. She thinks maybe your mom called Russell and threatened him or something, and she's hurt by that, too."

She's been sending my mother Russell's novel?

"Oh no. My mother wouldn't do that. First of all, she's too weak, remember? And besides, I'm sure she was only trying to—actually, I don't know what she was trying to do. I can't believe she knows about Russell and didn't say anything to me. Oh, but I don't want Lexie to doubt every relationship she has!"

"I know. That's why I'm telling you. She was pretty dramatic, even for her. What do you want to do?"

This time I don't hesitate. "I'm going to tell her everything. I don't know why Russell left. I can see where our family might have been over-whelming, I mean, he looked uncomfortable, but even I didn't think it would be enough to drive him away. I'm going to tell her about Mom's cancer and at least clear that up." Then, "And you're sure my mother knows all about him?"

"That's what she said. Okay, I'm going to make a few calls, too. Maybe I can find out something."

"Fine. One thing—what did you mean when you said she was pretty dramatic?"

"When?"

"Before. You said, 'She was pretty dramatic, even for her.'"

"Um, nothing, I don't know."

"What, Eric?"

"It was stupid. It didn't mean anything."

"Then just tell me. Come on."

"She said that she was through with love and 'everything.' She said now she knew why so many of the great authors chose to leave this world."

"Oh God."

"She was kidding, Jule."

"Oh—God."

"C'mon, I'm sure she was just being . . . Lexie."

But I'm not sure, not at all. I don't even know what that means anymore. After all, I am about to get into a car with Ted Ruben, flirt extraordinaire and seriously tempting bachelor, presumably for a day of perfectly respectable intellectual pursuit but more likely as a flimsy cover for certain less moral thoughts, fantasy thoughts, that have dropped by in recent dreams. Am I just being me? And which me would that be, exactly? If I don't even know what *I'm* capable of, how can I know about Lexie?

THE DRIVE FROM North Jersey to Princeton highlights the infinitesimal percentage of our state that the rest of the world thinks is the lion's share; an unpleasant, ugly montage of factories, refineries, and industrial parks. The average New Jerseyan is acclimated to this stretch of road, pays no notice to the smoke and smog, barely registers a grimace as the smells seep into the car. In short, the hour-long trip from exit 18 to exit 9 is not so offensive, merely boring. Today, however, in the car with Ted, I am anything but bored. In the back of my mind are Lexie, my mother, Eric, but they are on hold. I know they will be there later, at four or five o'clock today, and I have allowed myself a break, to recharge, I tell myself, to survive, a little voice says. Ted is wearing casual black pants, a fancy white

T-shirt that I'm sure has some silk in it, and a faded blue denim jacket. The overall effect of his blue eyes and blond hair against the white and blue jeans is devastating. I'm thinking Hamptons meets Kansas cornfields. I wouldn't be surprised if the Calvin Klein photographers showed up at any time. I'm trying not to notice the energy that comes off him, so close, as we are just inches apart in his black BMW with the soft saddle interior. I keep staring at his driving leg, trying to quell the urge to reach over and feel if it's as hard and muscled as it appears. In contrast to Ted's stark and simple colors, I'm wearing a soft peach T-shirt and a white cashmere cardigan with my all-purpose Sarah Arizona multicolored long skirt. This skirt has taken me everywhere from PTO meetings (paired with a long crew sweater and pumps), to the theater (topped with my beige calfskin blazer and boots), to the Bahamas (over bathing suit and flat sandals). I like it for today, because it looks benign and appropriate, but there is Lycra in the T-shirt that makes me look suspiciously younger than I look and sexier than I usually feel. Right now I'm wondering if my nipples are visible through the thin shirt, and I'm unobtrusively trying to steal a glance down at my own chest, which isn't easy, because Ted seems able to drive and look my way and smile about every third second.

"I love it when my job involves doing something I actually want to do. Business with pleasure, you know?" He grins at me again. Is it an evil grin, or playful? I guess I'm a little rusty when it comes to this game.

"Oh it's great!" I say. Very quick and witty. I try to make up for it.

"So, who did you say is speaking today? I remember Mary Higgins Clark, of course, and her daughter, but I seem to have blanked on everyone else."

"That's because you remembered the most important thing—that you were going with me."

"Oho, we're awfully impressed with ourselves, are we?"

"Not really. The most important thing for me was that you decided to go."

"Ted." I look down. I smile, of course, because he says it so soulfully, but I am uncomfortable. I don't know exactly what I want this to be, or to mean, or to anything. It's at this moment that he decides he can drive with one eye *and* one hand, and reaches across for mine.

"Jule, you can't tell me you don't feel it. The way we click when we talk, when we think, when we're together. I know you do." I should remove my hand. I don't. It feels nice, different. I can't say it's any larger than Eric's, but it's not Eric's, it's foreign skin and knuckles, foreign nerve endings. I think of what it would feel like on my naked skin.

"I'm a little mixed up right now. It's not really fair to you."

"Mixed up is okay. Everyone's mixed up. Eventually, it gets figured out."

"Well, not necessarily, not for me. I do mixed-up really well. I don't think I've done 'figured out' yet." I laugh, but it's a sad one.

Ted releases my hand, but only because he has to turn into the complex at the Princeton Forrestal Center and head toward the Hilton.

WE CHECK IN at a desk that's been set up for this event and I notice that Ted has registered me for the event as part of the *Sentinel*. My name tag says Julie Resnick, and under it, in italics, *Suburban Sentinel*. I wonder if he's breaking any rules, and it hits me that spending the day with me really must have meant a lot to him. We haven't spoken any more about what was said in the car, but Ted looks happy, as he always does, and in charge.

"Let's go," he says with a broad smile, as we head down the hall toward the Imperial Room, where the seminar will take place. We walk down corridors seemingly made for mini-conventions and business meetings, some with glass windows and curtains, some merely with large oak doors proclaiming Roosevelt or Coolidge. The Hilton is nothing if not patriotic. We are coming to the end of a corridor when Ted looks behind him and then grabs my hand, and before I can protest, he pulls me gently into one of the conference rooms. He is smiling as he says "Ssh, just one second." He continues to smile as he closes the door behind us, plunging us into almost total darkness. There is some light coming through the sides of heavy drapes on two walls, enough that I can see a conference table shaped like a U and a cold setup for coffee and tea. "What—" I begin to ask, but Ted eases my back up against the wall, looks into my eyes, and says, "I've wanted to do this for so long it hurts." And then he is very softly kissing me and I am not stopping him, in fact I am thinking that his lips are so soft and sweet and his tongue fits so nicely and nobody is drooling or pressing too hard and I feel his arms relax as he holds my face in his hands, and my hands, which have been aimlessly back and hanging, now move up and hold his upper arms and pull him closer. We are kissing harder now, more deeply, and not just with our mouths but with bodies, our lower bodies somehow coming together and touching now, too. And it feels so good; I have to say it feels wonderful, but just as suddenly it doesn't. Suddenly I go from wanting the feeling never to end to wondering what the hell I'm doing and how I can extricate myself from this oppressive, uncomfortable embrace. In mere seconds his arms are no longer enveloping branches, they're prison bars, his tan is not sexy, it's phony and overdone, he is not George Clooney, he's George Hamilton, and I feel creepy and sleazy and do not like myself at all. It isn't Ted, it isn't anything he did, it is just me. I open my eyes, still in the kiss, and look at the conference table and start wondering who will be sitting there later. An insurance company? Smokenders? Travel agents in training? I think about how ridiculous we are, standing here in Princeton, for God's sake, kissing in the middle of one of these generic meeting rooms. Me, a married housewife with more wrinkles than estrogen, and Ted, a fifty-year-old bachelor with obvious commitment issues. And I start to laugh. Well, not laugh exactly, but giggle. At first Ted thinks it is a sexy giggle, a playful I-want-more giggle, but I wave him away, walk toward the U-shaped table, and lean down, laughing out loud.

"Julie?" He is concerned, taken aback.

"Oh, Ted." I manage to catch my breath. "I'm not mixed up any-more." He looks hurt, really wounded.

"It's not you, Ted, you're great, a great kisser," I assure him. "Really, it's just that, well, I think after forty-five years I finally *am* doing 'figured out.'"

TED AND I never make it to the seminar. He is wonderful about it, really, understanding that I have my priorities and never once accusing me of leading him on or teasing me or anything. In fact, he says he really cares for me and respects my loyalty to Eric and my family. We decide to just head home, despite all the mutual understanding, because at that point neither one of us feels like attending anything. I tell Ted he doesn't have to worry about me being considered for the job at the *Sentinel,* and he is a real gentleman, saying that one has nothing to do with the other, but I think we both know it could never work, that the last thing either of us needs is to work in the same place. Still, Ted makes me promise to submit the fifth and final essay, and I get the impression he doesn't want to have to explain to anyone else why I would drop out, so I think it's the least I can do, and promise to try.

IN THE AFTERNOON I continue to worry about Lexie, but she will not answer my calls. Despite several messages that run from anxious to tearful to stern, there is no response, and I begin to function in a sort of auto-mated stupor. I make breakfasts and dinners, run errands, and try to write the fifth essay, but it's a total waste of time; my heart is not in it. I cancel Dr. Zacharias, much to the secretary's chagrin. I do not say anything to my mother about Russell, because I do not want to fight with her, and even though I can't believe she didn't think she should tell me, the mother, about him, I believe that in some convoluted way she was only trying to be a good grandmother. Eric works, comes home, watches TV, or looks at the screen at least, and we talk about nothing. Jake is in his own world, back to being appropriately oblivious of subtle changes in his parents' emotional stability, and Kate is less visible. In fact, now that I think about it, he has mentioned another girl, someone from the Peer Leadership Club at school. Janey? Jacey? I'm not sure. Alexis does not return our calls. I believe she is punishing us, and try to push all horrible thoughts out of my mind. After two more days I can no longer quell my own fears regarding her dramatic references to artists and suicides, and am stressed to the point where I dial her best friend's mother in Dix Hills and explain that we had a sort of family fight, and ask if she could just make sure that Hillary has seen Lexie since Tuesday. Luckily, Hillary's mom is happy to oblige and does not react as if we are a mutant strain of parents from the planet New Jersey. But I have to admit I'm taken aback when she asks, sympathetically, "So was the argument about her and that professor?"

Great. How many families are privy to our daughter's proposed indiscretion? How many dinner conversations have started or ended with "Well, at least she isn't running off to Europe like the Resnick girl."

"Well, uh, yes, it was. So Hillary told you about that?"

"Oh sure, she's going to miss Lexie so much."

"Well, it's never been definite that she was going. I mean, we had hoped to change her mind."

"Oh, I thought—well, I really don't know all that much about it. I know that Hillary would love it if she did change her mind. And then she'd stop pestering me about that ticket to England over fall break."

"Ticket to England?"

"Yes, to visit Lexie. October tenth, I think she said."

"I see." Plans and developments, more I didn't know. It is so wonderful that Hillary Glick's mother from Dix Hills is more informed about my daughter's fall semester than I am. Well, I have a news flash for you, Mrs. Glick: Change in Plans! Professor Nowhere to Be Found! I feel like a family from a Lifetime Movie Special. The kind that thinks they are a typical American family until it is revealed that the teenage daughter is a closet crack addict who robs banks after cheerleading practice. And now I take whatever joy there is in knowing that Debra Glick is not privy to the latest chapter in Lexie's life story, titled "Betrayal."

"Well, thank you so much for your help. I—I guess I'll call you back tonight. Will you have a chance to speak with Hillary by then?"

"Oh, why don't you just hang on and I'll buzz her on the other line?"

"That would be very nice of you."

On hold, I start to imagine all sorts of outrageous things. Hillary saying, "Gee come to think of it, no one has seen Lexie all week," or "I don't think anything's wrong, but she did give me her favorite necklace to take care of," or how about "She's fine, Mom, but I promised I wouldn't let her parents know that she's okay." The last would be the best news, I think, although the most embarrassing. I make a silent pact with God. I can stand being humiliated if only she is safe and okay. Suddenly there is a click and Hillary's mom is back.

"Good news. She's fine, attending her classes and everything." I realize I've been holding my breath, and it suddenly comes out in a rush. Before I can speak, Hillary's mom goes on. "Um, there is something else. Hillary says that she refuses to go out, I mean socially, you know, with the girls. Not that I think you should worry," she rushes on, "but I guess I'd want to know that." There is a slight pause. I should thank her, I know, but I am suddenly so sad. "Thank you so much," I finally squeak, "for everything."

"Oh, not at all, I'm just glad I could help and that everything's okay. I mean, it's a full-time job, isn't it, worrying about these girls?" No argument there.

TWENTY-FIVE

just back away, ma'am, for your own good

O nce we know that Lexie is safe, Eric and I agree that we can handle a few more days of the silent treatment, and decide not to contact the New York State Police, the FBI, and the cast of *Without a Trace*. We also agree that her reaction is nothing more than an exaggeration of the way she used to react when she was three years old and didn't like a rule.

"That's not fair! You're mean!" She would grab her stuffed animal, hug it to her chest, and proclaim, "I'm never speaking to you again!" And flounce dramatically out of the room.

Her absence and the edict would last exactly five minutes. Now, at twenty, it is to be expected that she will have more control, so we make up our minds to ride it out. To help, we have the diversion of the Gluckstein bat mitzvah. On Saturday night we make our way out the door. The party is called for seven-thirty, but we don't arrive until close to eight, even though the Woodcliff Lake Hilton is only ten minutes from our home. You don't arrive on time unless you are very close friends of the family, that's just the way it is. It is a black-tie affair, and I must say that Eric and I look exceptionally sharp tonight. He has gone to see Charlie at Neiman's for a new tuxedo tie (at least one of us can still shop there), and even though my dress is old, I got it at Hartly's, so it looks like new. It is a shockingly clingy, long black jersey that accentuates all my real curves and a few I've enhanced for the evening. The bat mitzvah has a theme, "Outer Space," which is somewhat unusual for a girl, but Zoe Gluckstein is a science freak who attended Junior Space Camp over the summer and plans to be the first woman on the moon, which I think is refreshing. At least it's a break from the typical girls' themes of "Breakfast at Tiffany's" and "MTV Cheerleaders." Our seating cards are miniature space helmets whose visors lift up to reveal the table name. We are seated at table The Milky Way. Eric and I work our way through the cocktail crowd to the bar and stop to congratulate Marjorie Gluckstein, who is surrounded by well-wishers and looks positively regal in royal blue silk. As we're talking to Marjorie, Zoe, looking like a princess in a slightly paler shade of blue chiffon, darts by on her way to the children's cocktail room. Eric and I exchange glances and I know we've had the same thought: cocktail franks. If we follow Zoe, we're sure to find the children's hors d'oeuvres, our favorites.

By the time we're summoned into the main ballroom, I've learned that we are sitting with Amy and Seth (thank God), Diane and Alan Lederer (boring), Janet and Michael Spiro (good for laughs), and two of Bill Gluckstein's friends from Long Island. I am a little disappointed because there are a number of people from town I would have liked to sit with, and being put with the host and hostess's friends from out of town implies a certain lack of importance or at least standing, a subtle one, but a suburban reality nonetheless. Eric reminds me that I choose to be less connected to "a group," that I have extricated myself from "the ladies who lunch," and that I prefer to be "an independent," and he's right, I do. I feel suffocated by what I called "the Rolodex set," the women who have to go through a Rolodex of social calls each morning, planning their Saturday nights twelve weeks in advance, making sure to cycle through the neces-sary networks. Some of them don't have one meaningful friendship even after twenty years in town, but they give the appearance that they do. They think of themselves as so close to so many, and couldn't possibly "be separated from each other" at a social event and they are always together. Still, I can't help feeling a bit slighted. And it doesn't help that Amy sidles up to me as we find our places at the table, which is in a corner, an additional slight, and says, "So, what are we, at the reject table tonight?"

IN THE CENTER of the dance floor sits a large spaceship made of cardboard and silver Mylar, and within minutes it begins to spew steam at its base. The lights in the room go black so that only the rocket is illuminated. The sound system begins to thump out a disco bass beat, *bomp, bomp, ba da da, bomp, bomp, ba da da, bomp*. Then there is a sound like airplanes flying, neeaaaaarrrrr . . . neeaaaaarrrr . . . and the deejay's voice, low and breathless, practically consuming the microphone:

"Ladies and gentlemen, it gives me great pleasure to introduce to you . . . a very special family, a family that's out of this world, your hosts for this evening, c'mon, I want you to put your hands together foooor-rrrrr . . . THE GLUCKSTEINS!!! BOMP, BOMP, BA DA DA, BOMP, BOMP . . ."

Amy is poking me in the ribs, saying, "Oh my God, can you believe this?" and suddenly the doors of the spaceship open, and out come the Glucksteins. Bill, Zoe, and little Danny are all wearing silver space suits, but Marjorie is in her blue dress. Deejay Sherman is motivating the crowd.

"C'mon, y'all, give it up for a very special family! Captain Bill, First Mate Marjorie, Officer Danny, and your pilot tonight, she's gonna take you to the stars, let's hear it for . . . ZOE!!" The kids all crowd around and are dancing, but the adults hang back a little. We are used to decadent displays, but the Glucksteins have taken their theme to a level even we are a little ashamed of, and I hope the rabbi and his wife have declined to come. The deejay will not let go.

"Hey, people, do you love this family? Who loves this family? I need everyone who loves these people and this family to crowd around and show them how you feel!"

Now we are all a little uncomfortable because it is the Glucksteins' big night and we don't want them to feel a lack of affection, but after all, not too many of us anticipated that attending their daughter's bat mitzvah would obligate us to express our undying love. Luckily, Marjorie and Bill seem to have enough relatives to fill the void, but we are thankful when the frenzy begins to wind down and the volume eases and Sherman the deejay kindly informs us that our first course is being served.

As we sit, the caterer wheels out a huge table with a mutant challah the size of Ohio on it. Sherman asks for a moment of silence as Grandpa Hy says the Motzi, the blessing over the bread. In a gravelly voice, Grandpa Hy completely botches the prayer, then makes a desperate stab at saving it by uttering some prayer, any prayer, and ends up reciting the last line of the Boray, the blessing over the wine. There is a moment of silence and Marjie looks like she wants to die. Some of the kids are giggling, and luckily Sherman, the black, twentysomething deejay, steps in, signals the music, and proceeds to thank Grandpa and recite a flawless Motzi in about five seconds flat. I am thinking about the sadness and hypocrisy of the moment when Amy points to Sherman and says out loud, "He's worth every penny of the seven thousand they're paying him."

We all get up to dance the hora, and even though Eric and I are among the last ones to leave the floor, I have an empty feeling. I feel less a part of this affair and more of an observer than I do at others. Perhaps it is our fringe relationship with the Glucksteins or the sheer number of people in attendance, or perhaps it is a sense that this phase of life, the whole bar mitzvah and bat mitzvah scene, are a thing of the past. I'm not sure whether that's a good thing or not. I love parties and traditions and the way they have the ability to suspend problems, if only for a night. Even here, somewhat removed, I notice a camaraderie between people who might otherwise pass each other in the supermarket with barely a nod. But on the dance floor they are transformed. The way they laugh, spin each other around, touch each other, you would think they told each other their deepest secrets year-round. They look so real to me, these people I know, these people who are not real, and a part of me wishes I could freeze them, happy and open and real, so they could stay that way, so they could see themselves that way. If they had a picture of themselves, they could put it up on the fridge, the way they might put up a picture of a girl in a bikini, to remind themselves to diet. Only this would be a reminder to be real and carefree and to remember what matters.

DESPITE MY LACK of exuberance, we stay until the end and fall into bed at about one-thirty in the morning. Of course Eric wants to make love, but neither one of us has the energy to be on top so we end up falling asleep in the middle of something that is half sex and half cuddle. In the morning I am a zombie, tumbling into my pajama bottoms and sheepskin slippers in search of an elixir, caffeine. The dogs are nearly apoplectic when they hear me on the stairs, and as I head to let them out, I catch sight of myself in the mirror near the back door, and just that briefest glance compels me to do a double take. No, don't look, the protective, nurturing voice says. Oh, go ahead, how bad could it be, asks the resident masochist. I'll just walk right by, I think, but the temptation is great. As I stand, debating, a superhero appears in my kitchen. He looks like Mr. Clean on steroids, and he is pointing a gun at my chest.

"Okay, ma'am, stay AWAY from the mirror, just back away, that's it, c'mon, now, just back off and nobody gets hurt. No, ma'am, please, PLEASE whatever you do DON'T look in that mirror. Don't do it . . . NOOOOO!!"

I blink my eyes and shake my head. Too late, Mr. Clean Man, I have to look. I have to see exactly how much time and Lancôme will be needed to neutralize the effects of forty-four-plus years and another night of anxiety and alcohol-tinged dreams. Even my hair looks tired and cranky, and instead of Chestnut I'm thinking Mud Brown. What has happened to my face, I wonder. Where is the cheerleader face, the girlfriend-of-the-captain-of-the-basketball-team face? Where is my teenage model face? Yes, that's right, I was a teenage model—well, a modeling student, really, not a paid professional. My brother Lyle had a friend who got married and his wife, Trina Jean, opened the Trina Jean Modeling School and my mother enrolled me in Trina Jean's very first class. There was an elaborate contest to mark our graduation, which I lost. The winner was a twenty-five-year-old Asian girl and the first runner-up was an eighteen-year-old dancer. Since I was only fourteen at the time and quite underdeveloped for my age, and since I knew I was merely cute and perky, not glamorous and sexy, I was not upset in the least. My mother, on the other hand, was crushed.

"They should have had a separate age category for that China girl," she hissed, "and between you and me, that other one's breasts are so big she looks like a cow."

Two weeks later I am in the kitchen having a snack when my mother walks in, beaming, and hiding something behind her back.

"Guess what?" she gushes. "Trina Jean called and said there was a mistake! There was supposed to be a *second* runner-up as well, but the trophies weren't ready so they couldn't announce it, but when they counted up all the votes, you won! Look!"

And she proceeds to produce the largest trophy I have ever seen, at least two feet tall, a gleaming affirmation in gold and red.

"Great," I reply, insufficiently, as the look on my mother's face changes instantly from elation to disappointment. Guiltily, I struggle to reverse my anemic response.

"It's so . . . um . . . big." Somewhat appeased, she sets it on the counter and takes out the can of Pledge.

"Well, of course it's big," she prattles, as she begins to spray some foam onto a cloth. "Winning a modeling contest is a big deal. Shall we keep it on the mantel in the front hall?"

LOOKING AT MYSELF this morning, I can barely grasp a filmy memory of those days of perfect skin and budding breasts. They are clearly gone, a fact that even this distorted, grainy, back-hall mirror confirms. My shapely almond eyes sport extra skin in the folds above the lid, and crusty dry pieces at the corners. I smile at myself, trying to invoke the glimmer and brightness I've been told the gesture creates, but I see nothing lustrous, only ever-deepening lines that extend from the sides of my nose down to the corners of my mouth and threaten to channel even farther down toward my chin. They form a boundary around my lower face and push my mouth and nose into a sort of pouch, and suddenly I remind myself of Zira, the simian woman from *Planet of the Apes*. Not a good morning for a mirror, I think to myself. Just back away, ma'am, for your own good.

And then I have a disturbing thought: I wonder if I look different to Eric. I don't mean different in the sense of totally unchanged. Obviously, Eric cannot help but notice that I'm not twenty-two anymore. He certainly sees the loosening of skin and the changes wrought by gravity, and I've not given in to the temptation to hide just yet; I wear my nakedness as proudly as I did when we were first married. So surely he has noticed all of these things. But I mean something else, something deeper. I wonder if I have lost the prize appeal, the brass-ring effect I had for him. Suddenly my guilt is palpable. Eric's given me no reason to need a fling or a kiss or the reassurance that I'm attractive, no reason to feel insecure, I've done that all by myself. How can a person feel so badly about everything this early in the morning? In a valiant last effort to greet the day with some semblance of composure, I bend forward, tousle my hair and pinch my cheeks, and then flip my head upright and look immediately at my reflection, and I do look a bit better. I decide to quit while I'm ahead. Then I grab a paper and pen.

1. *Make appointment with dermatologist to discuss Botox, collagen, silicone, and any other innovations including but not limited to plutonium.*

2. *Search Web for latest youth research—see www.PonceDeLeon?*
3. *Call Mother and ask her advice on looking younger. (This will perk up her spirits, but may be too labor-intensive for me of the "mean pores.")*
4. *Kiss Eric every three minutes until one of us is dead.*

As if he can read my mind, Eric descends into the kitchen and says, "Let's try Lexie."

We stare at the phone. I want him to call, and he wants me to do it. I say that I'm the one who called Hillary's mother, so it's his turn. He looks as if I have just asked him to go to the store and buy Tampax. Whenever I ring Lexie in her room, I never know if it's a good time, a time when she can listen. Sometimes there are one or two friends in the room with her, and often there are multiple knocks on the door in the middle of our conversations. The sorority house is less a house than a terminal. I talk to Lexie several times a week about nonsense, and don't mind the interruptions when we're chatting about a tough exam or a new diet, but this morning we will want her attention. Eric's face is unchanged; it harbors undisguised pain. I used to get that look myself, when I had to call home from college. In those days, before cell phones and calling cards, calling long distance was a big deal. I called home weekly, on Sundays, whether I had anything to say or not. Mostly, I remember feeling a lot of pressure to be entertaining. After all, my mother waited all week for that call! There had to be funny tidbits, interesting events, and reports of challenges met and conquered. Our phone calls always started the same way, with my mother asking, "Hi, darling, how are you?" But it wasn't a question, really, only a greeting. What she really meant to say was, "Hi, darling, what's good with you?"

Sometimes I would make things up, a boy I was dating, a class in which I was especially brilliant. Other times I'd merely embellish.

"The football game was amazing! All of us painted our faces and cheered till we were hoarse, and when we won in the last two minutes, everyone in the stands went crazy!"

Occasionally we would speak midweek, but that was a rarity. One time I called on a Tuesday after I'd been invited to a formal at a fraternity because I needed my mother to send me a dress. I asked her to send the strapless black chiffon with its tube top and handkerchief bottom, but she sent me the yellow satin dress I'd worn as a bridesmaid to my cousin Ellen's wedding instead. I was angry when it came because I knew I'd have to wear it since there wasn't time to have the other sent. As usual, when interrogated, my mother became offended.

"But you look so lovely in the yellow dress. The black one is so 'whoorish.'"

"I didn't ask you to decide, I asked you to send me the black dress."

"Well, I would have, darling, but I just couldn't, it didn't smell fresh. Besides, I just couldn't imagine you going to something as traditional as a fraternity dance in that other costume, not when you have something as lovely and appropriate as the yellow. But I can't say I appreciate your tone, you make it sound like I'm some horrible enemy. Excuse me for wanting my daughter to be the belle of the ball. I'm sorry you're so upset, but I still think you'll thank me when you see what the other girls are wearing."

Deep breaths don't help. Counting to ten doesn't help. Digging my thumbnail into my thigh helps a little.

She goes on. "Anyway, that black dress is a little ... *revealing,* don't you think? You don't want to show too much, better to keep them wondering, right?" She attempts a little laugh. It fades quickly with my silence.

I remember all of this just from looking at Eric's face as he contemplates calling his angel, his sweetie girl, who may be angry with him. His lip curls into a wrinkle of distaste, his eyes squint in an effort to see less of the phone (which he suddenly regards as an instrument of torture), and his head wiggles from side to side as if whining, *Do I have to?*

"Oh, all right," he says instead. And just as he reaches for the receiver the phone rings, as if in a divine gesture to save him from the disagreeable event. He is so ecstatic that he grabs at the phone, smiles broadly, and answers with a jolly "Good morning!"

I laugh to myself. Lucky. But just for a moment. I watch my husband, smiling, and I notice his face has lost some of its color, his voice has dropped off from its original upbeat lilt and he has turned to the side. He holds the phone close to his face, as if he wants to keep it private. He murmurs, "Uh-huh, okay, I see." When he turns back toward me and lifts his head, I see it in his eyes. My stomach drops and I think I make a little noise. "Hold just a sec." He says it in a dead voice, covers the mouthpiece with his palm, and says to me, "Babe, it's about your mom."

TWENTY-SIX

a good, anesthetizing daughter

By the time I get to Florida, my mother is in a semi-coma. Apparently she has been getting weaker and weaker but has refused to go to the hospital, so my father has been taking care of her at home with the help of hospice nurses. They are the ones who told him to call the family. Eric will come tomorrow with the kids. Lexie is driving home tonight, and the three of them are on a 7:00 a.m. flight. Lexie reached me on my cell phone, devastated, falling apart. It was bad enough for her to be shocked like this by her grandmother's illness, but she felt horrible and guilty about not speaking to us when all this was going on.

"I was going to tell you, honey, even though Grandma had this crazy idea that you didn't have to know. I'm sorry you had to find out like this."

"Oh, Mommy, I feel so bad, I'm sorry I've been such a bitch." She is crying.

"Alexis, listen to me. You have nothing to feel bad about. I'm the one that feels bad. We have a lot to talk about. You haven't done anything wrong. I'll see you tomorrow, okay?"

"Okay. Are you all right, Mom?"

"I'm fine."

MY MOTHER HAS DRIFTED in and out of consciousness all day. Sometimes she saw me and smiled and said things that didn't make sense. Once she made mention of some jewelry in the bar: "Take a drink, okay? Liquor and the diamond studs. One after the other." Another time she said the teacher was okay. "He is okay, that one, a good teacher, your grandmother thinks so and she has a way with words . . ." Late in the day she even told me that my book was going to be published.

"Keep writing. Tell Amy. New name, you'll see," she said. By then I'd stopped trying to make sense of her words. But several times she told me to take care of my father's eyes. In a perfectly logical sentence. So I said I would, not knowing exactly what that meant I should do.

My brothers and their wives arrive in the evening. They each take a turn going in to see her. At about 10:00 p.m. they go to the Marriott Courtyard a few miles away, because there isn't enough room in the house for the nurse and all of us. A half hour after they leave, I'm sitting in her room, admiring the fact that the room smells great. I mean, there's a commode, a bedpan, all kinds of medicines, antiseptics, a hospital bed, and an apparatus hooked up to catch her fluids, and the room still smells like flowers and fruit. The nurse is watching TV, a rerun of *M*A*S*H*. My mother hasn't even opened her eyes for hours, and then suddenly I hear this whisper and she's calling me. "Julie." I go rushing over to her face and I lean down and I am almost frantic wanting to hear what she has to say, and I tell her it's me, I'm here, and she is trying to tell me something and I know this is her final message to me and she says something but I can't make it out. "What?" I ask, and "What?" again, and it sounds like she says "bowfeen" and I don't know what that means and she says it again and finally, finally, I understand. It is not a message, not a vow of love or a last droplet of wisdom. It is a request. Morphine. She is in pain.

The tears flow down my face, and even as I move into action, the truth is, I feel cheated. I am panicked for her, too, distraught that it must be excruciating, but also disappointed. I was expecting something monumental, life-changing, from her lips. And then of course I am ashamed. My mother is dying and I'm thinking about myself. Nice. I grab the nurse and say Jesus Christ she's in terrible pain and the nurse says she isn't allowed to give her another morphine suppository but if I want to I can. I look at her for a minute like she's crazy, like the thought of giving my mother any kind of suppository is impossible, but even as it horrifies me I know I'll do it. Even as I shake my head no, I realize it will be my last act as a good daughter, a good, anesthetizing daughter, an extension, after all, of who I've been my whole life. And when I do it, I can't help but feel a little disgusted, even now I can feel my jaw contract into a grimace at the thought of it, but then I see her face relax and I feel better, and I lean over and brush the hair off her face and say, "It's okay, sweetie, sshh, it's okay," the way I would to my daughter.

And it is okay. A little while later, as I sit near her, she takes a strained, crackling breath and then she doesn't take another. After about twenty seconds it hits me that no other breath has come, and I scream for my father, who almost kills himself stumbling blindly toward the room. He throws himself onto the bed with her and I lie to him and tell him she took a breath, a small strained one, just as he got there, so he will think he was with her when she died. And then together we just sit there and watch her go.

By the time the medical examiner comes to pronounce her dead, it is just past midnight, 12:24 a.m., to be exact, on May 1. And I have not only lost a mother, I have gained a year. It is my forty-fifth birthday.

I WILL ALWAYS remember that night like a scene from Edgar Allan Poe, all moonlit shadows and rising smoke. Grown children moving as airily as ghosts from room to room, couch to sofa, daydream to disturbed sleep. At once curled up next to each other, feet to feet on the formal sectional, as cozy as five-year-olds watching Saturday morning cartoons, and then strangely awkward for the forgotten intimacy, the nearness, and the reason for being there. My father slept, or at least pretended to, and we let him.

In almost no time it is late morning and my family arrives. The funeral is tomorrow, so we have practically the whole day to touch each other as we move about, making calls and arrangements in this house of memories (here is where Jake was toilet-trained and Lexie shed her swimmies and Eric invented an orange picker out of an old mop and one of my dad's indoor putting cups). In the afternoon, Lexie and I have time for a talk.

"Mom?"

We are lying on the bed in the guest room, where Lexie has installed herself and her things since the nurse has left. "Hmm?" I am on my side, eyes closed, stroking her hair like when she was a little girl.

"Men really suck, don't they?"

I think about this for a moment. I open one eye and look over. I am reminded of the time we adopted an abandoned puppy from the shelter and it ran away after we spent six hundred dollars on veterinary care and nursed it through a bad stomach, worms, skin lesions, and housebreaking. The look on Lexie's face now is the same look she had after all the fliers produced nothing and no call ever came. At four years old, she couldn't understand how the dog could just leave. "Didn't he know how much we loved him?" she had asked. Now, I want to hold her in my arms and tell her that all dogs don't run away.

"Big-time," I say instead. And then I turn her face toward me. "Except when they don't." She smiles.

"You know I told Grammy all about him." I hold my breath as she gets up and fidgets about the room, arranging her makeup on the night-stand, hanging up the outfit she will wear tomorrow. Usually, I love the way her room looks when she is home for a visit and the suitcase is open on the floor, spilling its contents as if pouring her back into our lives, if only for a little while. When she is getting ready to go back to school, the suitcase seems like an enemy, a black hole sucking up the life-force with the laundered shirts and folded jeans. This small travel bag seems hostile, too, out of place, offensively heralding this horribly abnormal visit. I stay silent, wanting her to go on.

"Yep. I don't know how it happened, but she seemed really interested in his novel, so I started sending her some chapters and then," a wry little laugh, "she really liked it. So I sent her more, almost the whole thing." Alexis stops unpacking and turns to me. "I guess she figured out that a kid couldn't have written it, so she kept pushing me for details and, well, finally I just told her everything."

"Everything?"

"Well, pretty much. I mean, I told her he came for Passover and all. And that I—I . . ." My daughter turns away, coughs a little, and says softly, ". . . that I thought I loved him." I get up and go to her and hug her from behind. "Oh, honey." And then, "I am so sorry."

"It's okay. You didn't do anything. Nobody did. I just wish I knew—" She stops short and turns to me. "I don't understand. I never saw it coming. I know you think I'm stupid, but I swear he loved me. I swear it." She breaks away.

"Alexis, I have something to tell you." Oh God. Don't think. Just spit it out.

"What?" She is wiping her nose.

"On Passover, I was sort of glad that it was so chaotic. I hoped it would be chaotic." There it is. I wait for the lightning bolt, brace myself for it. There is silence. Then Alexis turns to me.

"You mean so Russell would freak out? I know."

WHAT?

"You—you know?"

"Yeah. Dad told me on the way down. I don't blame you. I think it's pretty funny. I mean, inviting Roberta was a bit much, but it's not a big deal." She is completely unconcerned.

"And you're not angry?"

"No, why should I be? I love our family. The whole crazy dysfunctional mess of it. I would never hide it." She looks at me, realizes I'm stunned.

"Oh, Mom, that's not why he left. And if it is, then I still had it wrong. But we talked about it after, and Russell had a good time. He was a little freaked out, of course. Especially when Marc, you know, in the bathroom—well, uch!—I was freaked out, too, weren't you?"

I laugh.

"No, it wasn't the family. I don't know what it was. I thought I knew him, do you understand? Like, like totally!" She looks so pitiful as she goes on. "Even *Grammy* liked him, and she never met him!"

"Grammy liked him because you liked him. She loved you so much."

Alexis looks back at me. "Grammy said anyone who could write like that had a piece of God in his soul. A piece of God! And do you know what I got? A piece of paper with 'I'm sorry' scribbled on it."

"Lex, sweetie."

"This is like a bad movie where somebody has a terrible secret or something. Nothing makes sense. I feel like there's something wrong with me. I guess I am the worst judge of character that ever lived."

"No, no, you are not. You are wonderful and trusting and genuine."

"And stupid."

"Not at all. You are exactly who you should be and what I want you to be. This, this . . . man is the loser, not you. I don't know why he left any more than you do, but he fooled me, too. I have to tell you, I was convinced that he loved you, too."

"You were?"

"Um-hmm."

"So why—I mean, you seemed so angry."

I think about this. "Not angry, scared. This was so out of the norm. I didn't want you to ruin your life. There were so many things that could have gone wrong."

"Except for what actually did. That I could be such an idiot."

"If he was able to fool you, if that's what it really was, then that's because it's easy to be manipulative when you're so much older. Think about it—if you wanted to, couldn't you convince a nine-year-old of almost anything?"

"I suppose."

"But you would never do that, because why would you? Why would you ever cause someone else pain when you are lucky enough to be so beautiful and trusting and sincere?"

WE ARE SILENT for a while. Lexie asks me how she will ever be able to tell the difference between a good guy and a bad one, and I tell her she will learn like everyone else, with some hurt and betrayal, but she will also know goodness and kindness, and she shouldn't be afraid to trust her instincts. And I tell her again how her essence is finer than any happiness Professor Russell will ever know in his whole life.

She goes into the bathroom to wash her face and calls out, "I think I lost two pounds this week."

"Stress?" I ask, half-joking. "Join the club."

She laughs. Then she stands in the doorway of the bathroom, facing me, her hair held back by a headband, a cotton ball in her hands. I start to leave the room and she remarks, casually, that she'd still like to go abroad, only not for fall semester, but this summer, with Branford's six-week immersion program in London. I tell her I think it's a wonderful idea, and I do. It will be good for her to get away. She adds that she's sorry she always "forces me to handle so much stuff." I tell her it is my pleasure. I am half kidding.

Then she says, "No, really, I mean it."

"So do I," I say, dead serious.

"You know, when I freaked out at you and stopped talking to you, Hillary was really blown away. She said she could never tell her mom bad stuff because her mother can't handle it."

"Really?"

"And I was thinking about how you never make me feel like I have to keep things in, you know, how you really mean it when you say I can tell you things."

"I guess I do mean it."

"Well, it's great, it's not just bullshit, you know, like 'you can tell me anything but not that.'"

Suddenly I get that old familiar pain. It's a stab of Lexie-itis.

"Uh-oh. Don't tell me there's something else." Please God.

"No, of course not, I was just giving you a compliment."

"Well, don't do that, it scares me." But I am smiling. Big-time.

TWENTY-SEVEN

when reason fails

There are certain things you have to do when you are the only daughter and your mother dies. One of them is to pick out the clothes she will be buried in. If you have sisters, I guess you have someone to do this with, but brothers merely stand around looking nervous, wringing their hands and waving off the idea, as if the job requires a uterus or experience with Barbie dolls or both. So one minute I am exchanging tender phrases with my daughter and the next I am standing alone in my mother's room, in the center of her walk-in closet, debating about the most extraordinary things. I decide that my mother was always more comfortable in her "club" clothes, the ones she wore to play cards. So that would be it, a nice, casual everyday outfit. The shirt was no problem, she loved red, and there was a nice, comfy-looking red shirt hanging right there, looking freshly pressed. The bottoms were a different story. I thought the shirt would look great with a pair of soft white pants, but white gets dirty so easily, you know, and you really can't wear it all year round. Then, I pulled out a pair of jean culottes. Jean culottes? They looked okay, but jeans? Did they send the right message? I mean, my mother liked nicely pressed jeans, but not for every day, so they were out. Then I saw a skirt she liked a lot. A skirt was nice and neat, I thought, she could belt it, but wait. A skirt was fun to wear for a couple of hours, but it wasn't nearly as comfortable as pants. I didn't think I would want to spend eternity in a skirt. I went on like this for nearly an hour, and now my brothers were *waiting* for me, so eventually I started to panic. I kept thinking of my own closet and what would happen if Lexie had to go in and pick for me. Would she have a clue as to my favorite outfit? What if she picked my black Capris, which showed a panty line unless I wore them with a particular pair of underwear? What about my brown Lycra bootlegs from BCBG? Would she realize that the catch was broken on the side buckle? That would be awful, to end up in heaven forever with broken pants. I thought about leaving a Clothes Will, this was obviously a major subject that needed to be addressed. I looked back at my mom's closet and examined her nightgowns. Very comfortable, but so . . . underdressed. This was becoming a nightmare, as well it should be. I finally settled on a bright blue button-down shirt and red shorts that looked crisp and bright. It was a huge mistake.

AT THE FUNERAL HOME, my father, my brothers and I, and our families sat in the small family waiting room. Just before it was "time," the funeral man leaned in and said that someone had to verify that the person in the coffin was my mother. Actually he said, "verify the body," just like on TV. I think he missed the sensitivity class at Mortuary School. My dad, being practically blind, was out, and Lyle turned white and said, "No way." Stewie looked at me and said—too quickly, I thought—"I'll go." Stewie and my mom had been really fighting lately, and I had the thought that he would look down at her and feel some sort of satisfaction, which is so unfair since he spent his life trying to win her affection, an affection she felt but could never display physically the way he needed. But at the time I didn't want him to be alone with her, so I said, "Me too." Plus, I had remembered that I'd brought a deck of cards for her, with a special note from me inside. The cards were for the canasta game in the afterlife, I guess—you know, it's always nice when the new person actually brings the cards—and the note was to show her new friends that she had a family who loved her. I see now that I was trying to continue my role as the good daughter into her future, attempting to send the serotonin with her. But also I was sincerely feeling so much love for her, for all the things she did right and for the way she loved me as well as needed me. I could feel that. So I was not prepared for what happened when the man led us into the anteroom. They only open the top half of the coffin (look at the things you learn when you verify a body), so the relatives see only the deceased's face, which clearly belonged to my mom. But the blue shirt I had picked for her was All Wrong. I know it sounds crazy, but I was there and I can tell you it was absolutely, totally, a hundred percent wrong. I had reversed the color scheme. My mother always wore red to her face, not blue, and in fact I had never even seen that blue shirt before. It was not her color, it couldn't have been more off, and I suddenly feared it might not even be her shirt. Oh my God, what if she got up to heaven in a borrowed shirt? What if it belonged to someone who was already there? Would she have a black mark against her before she even settled in? Would the rightful owner be indignant and tell everyone that my mother had some nerve if she thought she'd be wearing *her* shirt for all eternity and demand it back right then and there? Would my mother have to spend her afterlife naked because of my gross error? I was more affected by this than by seeing her dead face, if you can believe that. Or perhaps not. Perhaps this was my displaced horror at the finality of her dead face, I don't know. I only know that I was horrified. My brother had to lead me back to the family room, drag me really, as I was transfixed. I couldn't take my eyes off her and couldn't move away.

"Jule, you shouldn't have come in, I know, I know, her hair is so gray."

"It—it's not her hair."

"Okay, okay, just come on."

"No, wait. I—we have to do something, we have to fix it."

"Jule, don't freak out on me now. She's gone. She's not in pain, c'mon . . ."

"No, Stew, it's not that, it's her clothes." I whispered this firmly.

"Her what?"

"Her clothes. I put her in the wrong clothes."

"What are you talking about?"

"She would never wear that blue shirt. I don't know what I was thinking, but it's all wrong."

I think Stewie was about ten seconds away from losing it too. He thought I was having a breakdown. Maybe I was.

"Jule, what do you want me to do?" He was pleading with me now. You could see the people gathering in the outer room, filing into pews.

"I don't know." And I didn't. So, submissively, I dropped it. Because I knew that there was nothing anyone could do. And because I could hear my own mother's voice saying, "Come on, everyone's here, it's about to start." And because it doesn't look nice to make a big scene at someone's funeral, even if that someone is your mother, and because when you are at your mother's funeral you are not yourself. The day before, perhaps you are a person who sends back the eggs because they are runny, or demands a new hotel room because you asked for a king-size, not two queens. The day before, you are strong, you are not the bereaved. When you are the bereaved, your body undergoes a physical metamorphosis. That is probably where the expression "heavy with grief" comes from. Your feet drag, your eyes itch; you are not a mover and shaker, you are a slumper. You go with the flow, no matter how much your inner undertow tries to drag you back.

For two weeks I stay in Florida, fighting that current as I sit shivah, sort through my mother's things, and find someone to live in the house with my dad. He protests, of course, but Lyle, Stewie, and I win out. He can barely see, hasn't cooked himself a meal in forty years, and doesn't even know the washing machine from the dryer. I interview three to four women a day. The most promising prospect is a light-skinned black woman of about forty, with a college degree, tortoiseshell glasses, and a suit that looks like it was custom-made on Madison Avenue. Unfortunately, she wants $350 a day. I ask her where she buys her clothes and promise to call. Most of the other applicants are from the Caribbean, sporting far inferior qualifications. I have mental pictures of my father eating greasy chicken bones and showering once a week, but by the last day I have lowered my expectations and am willing to settle for someone with all her teeth. The second-to-last interview is with a woman who has been with the same family for six years. Unfortunately her elderly charge has passed away. I open the door, hoping for a young grandmotherly type. At six feet tall, Gigi Legagneau is a vision. A French Canadian with flaming red hair, white skin painted a multitude of colors (blue around the eyes, orange circles on the cheeks, pink lips) and more costume jewelry than a flea market. She wears an off-the-shoulder white peasant blouse, a loose, mid-calf-length Aztec print skirt, and spike-heeled red sandals. She is at once part floozy, part cowgirl, and, though perfectly tasteless, a beautiful drop of sunshine. My father takes to her immediately, not merely because she likes to drink Bloody Marys in the afternoon or because she is a confirmed Marlins fan, but because, I notice in wonder and horror, she flirts with him. She calls him "Sol Doll," a nickname that makes him beam. She is hired on the spot.

Two days later at home in New Jersey I have a sort of breakdown. It has all happened so fast, out of necessity, true, but still, too fast. I don't even remember the funeral, the shivah. Somewhere in Florida, I fell into a sort of emotional black hole and I got good and lost. I barely ate a thing after she died. Everyone said it was a reaction, and I guess that was true. I wasn't hungry, which is amazing, food being integral to my state of mind, but everything I put in my mouth tasted like papier mâché. So I stopped eating but continued to do all the chores impeccably, and now I'm wondering if I made a mistake. When you make a wedding or a bar mitzvah, you're too busy to eat, so the caterer saves you a plate with a sampling of all of the wonderful treats that you missed, and I wish now that someone would have saved me a shivah plate, a little tasting menu with a piece of lox, a slice of rye, a couple of rugelach. It might have brought some closure. Instead, I stayed too full to eat, too full of grief or fear or guilt. As if I'd swallowed her death whole and it just sat there inside me, too big to digest. And now I am inconsolable, not sleeping, not functioning, I cannot rebound. I have lost eleven pounds. Because no matter how well I did every other task, I am appalled that I have sent my mother to heaven in the wrong clothes. I keep saying to anyone who will listen, "She never wore blue to her face." I call my mother's friends and ask them if they have ever loaned her any clothes of any kind, and press them when they waver, tenderly, and ask me in concerned voices if I'm doing okay.

"I'm fine," I insist. "I just need to know if you're sure she never borrowed a shirt, a blouse, nothing blue?"

I don't have the strength to see Dr. Bob, but my internist has prescribed an antianxiety drug for the waves of panic and gripping fear which take turns visiting my chest cavity, a part of the body, I remark to him, that is well named. Amy calls every day to remind me of something wonderful I did for my mom.

"Hello?"

"I just remembered that day at the restaurant on Long Island," she begins excitedly.

"Yes."

"Remember she had a headache and they wouldn't give her any aspirin or Tylenol, so you snuck out and drove to the drugstore and came back with aspirin for her?"

"Uh-huh."

"That was so great of you. How many daughters would do that?"

"I don't know."

"Julie, come on. You have to stop this."

"Okay. I'll talk to you later."

"Wait, wait, wait. I know! Her birthday in Florida, remember? You sent that singing telegram with your own personal words? Oh my God, I almost forgot about that. Remember how much she liked that? She said all her friends were so impressed that you customized that song! What was it, something about her famous Passover chicken parmigiana?"

"Yep."

"Julie, please, you're making yourself crazy."

"I know."

My husband also repeatedly tries to tell me that I was a wonderful daughter, that my mother loved me, that I should have no guilt. I love Eric, I am sure of that now, although it took kissing a veritable stranger in the conference room of a hotel for me to see it for sure, but I will not even let him in, for comfort or absolution. Even my children, who don't get it, are trying. Lexie is back at school, in the middle of finals. When she calls I hear Eric say, "I don't know why it's such a big deal what she's wearing," but to me she says, "Don't worry, Mom, she doesn't know," which is sweet but makes me hysterical because I know she's wrong.

Jake even offers, "Hey, Mom, I like blue and red, it's like the flag." And I think, Oh God, I will never make peace with this, and then one morning Beth is there, in the flesh, in my room. She has been out of town for a few days, at a dance recital with the girls. She knew I was upset, but she thought I'd be better by now and has only just been told by Eric how far gone I am.

"Julie, how come you're not getting over this?"

I don't know how to answer her. I am not rational or intellectual. I am stuck, desperate, heartsick.

"How, Bethie?" I confess. "How can I get over this? I put her in the wrong clothes. A blue shirt and red shorts, she never, ever would have worn that, and now there's nothing I can do, nothing." There is a moment. Then two. And then she speaks.

"You know what, Jule, you know what I think? I think she's changed by now."

"You—what?"

"That's right, I think she's changed by now. I think she got up to heaven, looked at herself in the mirror, and called her friends over and said, "Look, look. My daughter was so upset at my passing, she wasn't thinking straight. Look at the cockamamie outfit she put me in!"

Is it possible that I feel a dark cover begin to lift? She goes on, "And then she went over to the nearest boutique, got herself something she liked, and changed right out of those clothes. She's probably been out of them for days."

"The nearest *discount* boutique, don't you think?" I join in, beginning to warm to the idea.

"Right, the one with all those Leon Levin shirts she likes."

"And with salesladies named Vera and Sydelle?"

"Absolutely. And don't forget belts! Alligator and ostrich and . . ."

I can see my room. I can feel my arms.

". . . wide ones decorated with rhinestones and . . ."

And I am smiling. And now I can have my regularly scheduled bout with grief instead of the psychotic one. Beth has joined me in the crazy place, instead of trying to talk me out of it. And it hits me that this is an excellent way to deal with someone when reason fails.

IN THE MORNING, as the day dawns bright and sunny, just the way a day in late May should, I am rejuvenated. I have been at the computer since dawn, working. Not on the last essay for the *Sentinel*—I have long since missed the deadline for that and come to terms with it. I'm sure that Ted, too, has gotten the message, as I have repeatedly ignored and erased his e-mails, and not returned his calls. Timing is everything, and obtaining a high-pressure job in the middle of a highly stressful transitional stage is never a good idea. The same is true for a love. It's highly possible that at another time in life Ted would have been "the one," but the only lover I want right now is at this very moment singing off-key Mick Jagger in the shower upstairs. Instead, my experience with the *Sentinel* has prompted me to probe even further into the perils of preteens, both humorously and tenderly. The result is a series of narrative rhymes that are poignant, funny, and relevant, tentatively titled "Diagnosis *Du Jour*," after the title poem.

When Eric comes down, he notices the change. I am energized by my work, by creating, and it shows. Eric also knows that when my work is going well, I write in the morning and begin to cook in the afternoon. Not just ordinary meals, either, but gourmand productions from *Bon Appetit* magazine. By 10:00 a.m., I have defrosted pork chops, and butter and eggs are coming to room temperature on the kitchen counter. I have also written out an elaborate shopping list that includes fresh herbs such as marjoram and cilantro. He looks so happy I am reminded of Jake and his Turkey Club at Friday's.

"Yes, oh, caveman hunter of mine, you'll be eating well tonight."

Eric comes over to me and puts his arms around my waist.

"I see dessert items as well as meat, so things are back to normal, I take it?"

"I think you know me just a little too well."

"Speaking of dessert, I want to make some plans for your birthday."

"Oh, please . . ."

"Jule, c'mon, you did have a big birthday. We have to celebrate the good things, too."

I want to protest that it is too soon. "Who said? Is there a law that says I have to celebrate my birthday? You want to mark the occasion, how about we call it what it really is now, a deathday?"

"Oh jeez."

"I bet Hallmark doesn't have a card for that yet, do they? I'm sure it's only a matter of time. They already have Pet Sympathy and Susie's Other Mommy cards, why not deathday cards? They could say, 'Thinking of you on this sad anniversary.' No, that's too depressing. Maybe they could be more upbeat, kind of like birthday cards. 'Even though your loved one is still dead, you're getting better!' Or how about those cards with the photographs of those gorgeous, hot guys with bare chests and the top button of their jeans open? Then the message could read, 'Your loved one is dead, but this guy's not. Just a little something to perk you up on this special day. Happy Deathday.'"

"You are really sick when you wanna be, I swear."

"I'm not sick, I'm funny."

"Yeah, like a car accident." I am wrong to be so biting, I know. I try to make amends.

"Sorry, okay? I just can't help it. She died on my birthday, Eric, on my *birthday*. Don't you think that is sick?"

"I don't know. I guess maybe, but you know what? I don't want to think so much, okay? Everything can be sick if you look at it that way. I just want us to celebrate your birthday like a normal family."

I look back at him. I don't know whether to crack up or make a snide remark.

"Don't even say it," he says.

I smile and shake my head. "We'll celebrate, okay? How about at the end of the summer? After Lexie gets back from London?"

"It's a date."

TWENTY-EIGHT

this is not a shock, it's an earthquake

The summer goes by with an easy cadence of predictability. I continue with Dr. Bob, making progress on losing my resentment and anger. In one of our last sessions he asks about the last moments of my mother's life, and I find myself talking about the physical details for the first time, the ones I am reluctant to share with anyone. I describe her inner arms and the backs of her hands, both of which were so purple and bruised I will never forget them. And the clear plastic box, hanging out from under the hospital bed, that held her extracted urine, only it wasn't yellow, it was bright red, and as disgusting as it was, I couldn't help looking at it every time I went in. I think I was looking for a sign: maybe it would clear up, turn back to yellow, and it would be a miracle and she would get well. Dr. Bob waits while I pause, get a tissue, and blow my nose. I tell him that I guess I was a good daughter even if I did have selfish thoughts when she was in pain, and also that I thought it was inappropriate for a daughter to give her mother a morphine suppository. I mean, maybe in some societies, ancient or primitive ones, where it's natural for the young to care for the old, it's no big deal. But it was for me.

"What do you think?" I ask him for a change.

"I think you're working it through. I think you don't want to be angry and disappointed that you never had the mother you wanted. And I think you don't really want to be responsible for anyone else's total happiness anymore, and you want the right to say 'No, that's too much.'"

"Some things just are too much."

"Of course. But you've been doing it so long, it's what you're programmed to do. Sounds like you realize that and want to change. Sounds like maybe you're getting tired of planting corn." He pauses. And smiles. "But, more important, what do you think?"

I want to answer Dr. Bob's question. He's right, I suppose, about my role as wish-fulfiller. It's a shame. My mother loved me so much but the need was stronger, rushed to the front of the line, like Beth at camp visiting day, elbowing everything in its path. Dr. Bob's also right about the anger; I want to lose it. But first I have to say what's on my mind, what's been on my mind for weeks. What do I think? What do I really think?

"I think," I say quietly but firmly, "that no matter how much pain I'm in, if I know I'm dying, I will damn well find a way to tell my children I love them before I go."

And that is how I leave it with Dr. Bob, and perhaps with my mother as well. I write all summer, I exercise, I build myself up physically and emotionally. It is hot during the day, breezy at night; the neighborhood seems to be at rest. Eric and I have leisurely breakfasts, easy walks after dinner, Jake is even semi-human to be around. He has a summer job as a tennis assistant at a local day camp and has started to get that tan, lean, lifeguard look that only sixteen-year-old boys with twenty-inch waists and bulging biceps can achieve. He has his driver's permit and his smile is back. The girls are everywhere, on the phone, in the driveway, at the door. Lexie has gone to London and is studying Shakespeare. She travels with friends each weekend. Last week she called us at 7:00 a.m. (noon over there) from France. "I just had to call," she crooned. "I'm at the top of Montmartre, on a hill. It's so beautiful. The artists are drawing and the balconies all have red and white striped awnings and I'm having a croissant. It's perfect." She sounds happy but subdued. It's almost perfect, I think. I'm glad she's not morose. Thank God for her cultural and intellectual appetite. But she has lost a little bit of innocence, too soon, I think. The pitch of her voice is a tinge off, her laughter an octave lower, nuances only a mother might detect. Perhaps she will meet a Pierre or a Jacques, someone good and true, to renew her faith, if not in men, then in herself. A week before she is scheduled to come home, the phone rings.

"Hi, Ame, what's up?" It's not often Amy calls from work.

"Listen, don't ask me any questions right now, but I need to sit down with you and Eric. Can I come over tonight?"

"Is everything okay?"

"Absolutely. I just, um, need to talk to both of you."

"Of course. You're so mysterious. We are not buying any bull mastiff puppies, okay?"

"Okay. I've gotta go. I'll come by after dinner, like eight?"

"Sure. Fine."

ERIC THINKS AMY has a problem with one of the boys, maybe a real estate issue, or why would she need him to be there? But it doesn't make sense. Amy would have given me a preview. By the time she appears at the door I am intrigued.

I always forget that Amy leads two lives. Seeing her in her work clothes reminds me that she is a dedicated, powerful force in the business of publishing, and she looks every bit the part. A chunky tortoise rope necklace and brown pumps offset her sleeveless powder blue turtleneck and paisley knee-length skirt, a far cry from the rolled sweats and men's undershirts I'm used to seeing her in at home. In one hand is a leather briefcase, in the other her glasses. For a minute I think she's come to list our house or sell us insurance. I can't help but kid.

"Sorry, I was expecting my friend Amy."

"I know. I haven't had a chance to change. At least I know you'll let me take my shoes off."

"What's up?" We move toward the kitchen without thinking. Lacey and Jasper will not let Amy alone, they smell her dogs. "Enough!" she commands, and miraculously they walk away. Eric is actually rinsing a dish in the sink, which happens maybe once a week, but of course his timing is impeccable.

"He knows where the sink is?" Amy remarks, as if he isn't there. She's teasing him and he knows it and he smiles and goes to give her a kiss. "I always wash the bowls after I pee in them."

"So, are we like sitting down formal and all?" I am looking at Amy.

"I think that's a good idea."

Eric and I exchange glances and sit down. Amy puts her case on one chair, sits in another, and pushes each shoe off with her toes. She takes a deep breath.

"Well," she says. "This may come as a bit of a shock," she continues, slowly but deliberately. "It's about Russell."

What? This is a *shock*? This is not a shock, it's an earthquake.

"What?" My face is twisted. "Russell? You mean our—Lexie's—you mean . . ." I don't know what I'm saying exactly.

Eric jumps in. "What would you have to do with Russell?"

Amy looks at me strangely. Sympathetically?

"A few months ago your mom called me. She asked for my address. She said she wanted to send me something. Part of a novel, she said." She waits, but I am still confused. "At first I thought it was *hers,* but she said no, it was a friend's. I didn't think anything of it, you know, I mean it was your mother and when it comes to literature there's no one I'd rather BS with, so I was sweet and polite and everything, but I get like hundreds of people wanting to send me stuff from their brothers and manicurists and the guy who mows their lawn. It's all junk really, you wouldn't believe how bad. So I just gave her the address and forgot about it."

"My *mother* called you?"

Amy looks down, embarrassed. "Right." This was unbelievable.

"So go on." Eric leans forward, intrigued.

"So a few weeks go by and then my assistant, Annabelle, comes into my office and says there's something she thinks I should read. And, well, to make a long story short, it's the pages from your mom, only the author is Russell Fraser, an unknown English professor who of course is not exactly unknown to me."

"Why didn't you tell me?"

"I didn't know what *to* tell you. I mean, on one hand, I was tempted to throw it in the garbage, but Annabelle was insistent. She'd never read anything that touched her like this before. It was a romance, but historical and modern all at the same time. She couldn't believe a man wrote it. She said it reminded her of *Memoirs of a Geisha*!"

"But when we had lunch, I mean, did you already know? And what about after? When my mother died, did you know? When I was all messed up?" I can see by her face that she did. "Even then you didn't say anything?"

"You were messed up, you said so yourself. What was I going to do? Say I was interested in a novel given to me in secret by your dying mother and written by a guy who had broken Lexie's heart? Tell you I thought it was the best thing I'd read in a year?"

"You're kidding."

"I'm not."

"It's that good?"

"It's so good I start to cry if I think about the characters too long." We both lean back in our chairs—me, stunned into a slump and she, relieved to get it all out. Eric is the only one still sitting forward.

"Are you going to represent it?" he asks.

"I signed him last week. It's already in a bidding war. That's why I had to come and tell you." She looks at us purposefully. "You have to under-stand that this is highly unusual for a first novel. That's how good it is. It's not only going to be published, but I can guarantee it's going to be huge. We're talking subsidiary rights, foreign rights, film, the whole thing." She lowers her head. "I'm going to go up a notch in the industry, too. That's the way it works. If I'm right, then this will be a major coup for the Charlotte Sanderson Agency, a blockbuster, delivered by a handsome, well-spoken, sensitive, and straight young male writer. The talk shows are going to have a field day with him."

I'm a bit numb. My usual stream of consciousness is remarkably silent. I have no thoughts at all. Instead of filtering a multitude of reactions, I try simply to *have* them. Do I really care about this Russell's success? What difference does it really make? Except that maybe Alexis will have to see his face and weather the reminders of him. That shouldn't be too bad; he's an author, for God's sake, not a movie star. How visible could he be? Do many people really know what John Grisham looks like? Or Tom Clancy? And what about my mother? What in the world was she thinking? Jesus Christ! She can't help her family evolve emotionally, but she opens the doors of success for this heartbreaker? Some help she is! How am I ever going to lose the anger if she continues to harm me from the grave?

"There's more." Amy reaches down and unsnaps the leather case. Pulling out an envelope and removing several thick pieces of paper, she asks, "Jule, did Lexie ever mention anything about the novel?"

I try to think. Brilliant, she said. Wonderful, I think. Words by a twenty-year-old hopelessly in love. Nothing concrete. And then, "Oh yes, I think she said something about it moving from generation to generation. *Across Time,* I think she said it was called."

"Right." Amy looks at me, then at Eric. "So when it came time to sign him, Russell had only one stipulation. The title. He was insistent. The title was the only thing he wouldn't edit or change. It had to stay. If not, he was willing to throw the whole deal away."

"Okay, so he likes the title."

"Yes, he does. Very much. Because he changed it, just like he changed the name of the main character, who was originally called Jessa." With that, Amy slides a large piece of paper across the table toward me. I can see it is a mockup of a book's cover, with a color illustration. There is a girl running up a country hillside, long dress and brown hair flowing behind her in the wind, a distant city on the horizon. At the bottom in jagged script is the title: *Alexis Across Time.*

I tilt the page slightly toward Eric, but it's not necessary, he's read it just fine. I look at Amy. She slides something else our way. It is another page, with a short paragraph at the top. *This book is dedicated to Alexis, who, like the heroine in this book, has the power to heal with her laughter and love with her soul, and, if there is a God, to forgive. It is a book of second chances. If only life could imitate art. —R. Fraser, August '03.*

Amy is smiling. She tries not to and then apologizes and says she really can't help it and what do we think and she's met with Russell several times and the bottom line is he's just a great guy. Eric says, "That was my first impression of him, too." Amy rewards him with a look that says he's obviously brilliant, and I think, *Oh sure, when he agrees with you he's Einstein and all other times he's an idiot.* But secretly, deep down, I am starting to feel it, a little hopeful sliver of happiness for my daughter. I haven't wanted to admit it, but she had fallen hard, with all of her innocence and trust so tied up in the giving of her love I wasn't completely sure she'd be left unscarred. And now Amy was opening up the possibility that it hadn't been what it seemed, her judgment wasn't off, and just maybe the light could shine again in her smile and this Russell could be redeemed.

"Why on earth, if he felt this way—*feels* this way—did he just abandon her?"

"Well, that's the thing, he didn't abandon her at all. He had no choice. But he wants to tell you about it himself. He wants to meet with you both and explain. I told him I would try to arrange it."

FRIDAY AFTERNOON, Eric and I are sitting in the Palm Court at the Plaza Hotel in New York. We are both nervous. Eric is whittling a toothpick with his thumbnail, no easy task, and I am folding and refolding my napkin on my lap.

"Don't make it too easy for him," I remind him. "Just let him talk. You don't have to fill every silence."

"Yes, dear," he mocks me.

"This better be good, that's all I know," I say for the hundredth time this week.

I can sense that Russell is coming before I actually see him. That's because the heads begin to turn. Not just young women but matrons stop talking and turn to look at him. He is damned good-looking, there's no doubt about that. And the Palm Court is not an easy room. Not only is it full of well-dressed New Yorkers, but it's light. There's no soft barroom haze to hide behind. If your roots need a touch-up or, for that matter, your Jimmy Choos, everyone is going to know. So turning heads with just your natural complexion and a worn pair of Dockers is something of a feat. To his credit, he doesn't seem to notice, there isn't an arrogant flip of the hair or a shy smile delivered slyly to the hostess, he is just earnest, solemnly looking for Eric and me and upon seeing us, focused on making his way to our location.

"Thank you," he says, pulling out his chair and sliding into it, "for seeing me."

We lock eyes, he and I. For the first time, really, since my kitchen. He is shy, but there is something self-possessed about him, too. A man who knows what he wants, is the phrase that comes to mind.

Eric shakes his hand. "You're welcome."

Russell squirms for a moment in his chair, and then seems to settle in. "I want to try to explain what's happened. It's crazy, really, the way things have gone."

We are silent. Good boy, Eric. Let him talk.

"Well, first of all, I love your daughter. I never stopped loving her. I can't explain to you what happened when I met her. We—she—it's like, we just fit. We don't even have to speak, we just belong together." He takes a sip of water. "But, as you know, I was married"—the past tense is not lost on me—"and she was my student and, well, that couldn't have been a worse combination. I knew it all along, but I had this fantasy that we could somehow make it all work out." He looks straight at me. "I shouldn't have let things go on, not without a plan. It's my fault, all of it, but I couldn't stop seeing her—Alexis—I just couldn't stop. I couldn't imagine not seeing her. So I put us both in a precarious position. My wife, Glenna, is extremely proud. When she found out I was seeing a student, she went crazy. It's not that she even cares about our marriage or me; it's just that she can't stand losing to anyone, least of all some student, a kid. We met when we were both in school, both working like crazy to be at the top of our classes. I was just lonely. I haven't been very successful with women, with relationships in general. I guess you know that my mother died when I was six and how things went with my father after that." We don't even have to try to be silent, Eric and I, we truly are riveted.

"Well, I guess I underestimated my wife's reaction. Glenna's an attorney, a ruthless one, excellent at her job. She came from nothing, a very poor family, and she's put herself through school and law school and she sees everyone else, especially the kids at Branford, as spoiled, pampered rich kids who don't deserve a thing." I am starting to get a sense that Russell has not had it so easy.

"Anyway, Glenna hates living in upstate New York. She's been offered jobs at the top firms in Syracuse and Albany, but she's had her heart set on New York City and it's only been me wanting a small college town that's been standing in her way. She knows my father is a big-time doctor in the city, and it drives her crazy that I don't want his lifestyle or, for that matter, anything to do with him. She's been frustrated with me for some time; in fact, she's been having an affair herself. But when she found out about Alexis, she threatened to go to the dean and have me censured, probably fired, and worse, she wanted to have Alexis expelled for some rule she found about behavior and an honor code. She said even if she didn't win legally, she'd splash Alexis's name and reputation all over the local papers and the school newspapers until everyone knew her as the slutty coed who was"—he hesitates for the first time—"who was sleeping with her professor."

"Jesus Christ." Eric is stunned.

I just hold my head.

Russell's face is cramped with pain. I can't help but believe him. In fact, I find myself feeling sorry for him.

"Glenna gave me an ultimatum. Leave Branford with her immediately and come to New York and she'd do nothing about Lexie, and with my credentials intact I could continue to teach. I didn't see that I had a choice. So you see, the whole thing was a mess. I couldn't see any way out."

"Did you ever think about telling Lexie the truth?" Eric, always the straight arrow, asks the obvious.

"I did, God knows I did. But you know Lexie, she would have tried to handle it. Can you imagine how you would have felt about me then? If she was involved in a scandal and had to leave school and screw up her education? And for what? To be with a guy who now had no job and maybe no chance of ever getting another one?"

"Do you know how badly you hurt her?" I think he does, but I want him to hear it.

He hangs his head. "I know. Jesus, I know. I didn't know what to do."

"So why now? What's changed?"

He looks up. "Everything. The book has changed everything." We wait.

"It's like a miracle. When Amy called, I was at my lowest. I was teaching all summer at NYU, remedial freshman English. It was all I could get. Glenna had gotten this job with one of the most prestigious firms, but she was working thousands of hours and wasn't getting any of the gratification she'd gotten upstate and she was even more miserable than she'd been in Ithaca and she blamed me for everything. Now that she had me hostage, she didn't even want me. She started seeing her new boss, I know that, and was getting a reputation at the firm, the same reputation she threatened to give Lexie at school. I knew I couldn't take it much longer. I had thought about throwing in my career and taking a job, any job, and just letting the chips fall. At least I knew with me out of Branford and Lexie finished with the year, she would be safe. And then Amy called. It was like a dream, the agency, and the publishers. Suddenly the money is there, and the future. I'm getting calls to teach graduate writing courses at Ivy League schools, and the book isn't even in print yet. And that would be a miracle. To be able to teach and write, that's all I want. And one more thing. I want Alexis to be there with me. I need her to be there." He gets choked up then, coughs into his napkin, and goes on.

"I filed for divorce four weeks ago. Glenna won't fight it. I promised her a very generous settlement from the proceeds of the book." He lowers his voice. "And I also threatened to write my next book about a backstabbing female attorney who sleeps her way to the top. Not that I ever would. If she knew even one thing about me, she'd know it, too."

Eric and I sit silently. Wow, my heart says. Whoa, my brain says. But for once my heart wins out. I begin to smile. I think I like this Russell. There's only one thing left to say. Eric looks at me and I nod my head. I'll let him do the honors.

"Russell, do you have a car?" Russell looks confused.

"I do," he says.

"Good." Eric is smiling. "Lexie arrives home on Sunday morning. We'll expect you that evening at about six."

TWENTY-NINE

only the finest for my girl

All day Saturday I glide around in a sort of goofy, happy daze, not just because I am anticipating Lexie's happiness on Sunday, but also because it is the night that Eric is taking me out to celebrate my birthday belatedly, and I do not feel guilty about it. I thought I might fixate on the pain it would cause my mother to see me being happy about the day that commemorates not only my birth but, now, her death, and instead of imagining the hand of God coming down to strike me dead in the restaurant, I am wondering what I might *wear*; would the apricot turtleneck go better with the brown slacks or the black suede skirt? All things considered, I am on a much healthier path. And I have to admit, if my mother hadn't sent the manuscript to Amy, it's possible none of this would have happened. So, in her own way, she helped to make things right. With barely a glance in guilt's direction, I look forward to the evening. No doubt Eric would live up to his promise and take me to the fanciest or trendiest restaurant in Manhattan. We have much to celebrate.

Which is why I'm a little surprised to learn that we are leaving at 7:00 p.m., on the early side for a truly hip New York City dining experience.

Most of the restaurants don't get crowded until after 9:00 p.m., and if there is a great bar that caters to the singles set, the scene won't really sizzle till much later. But Eric is smiling and humming and saying, "Trust me," and he likes the city scene even more than I do, so he must know what he's doing. When we are all dressed and ready to go, he says, "Whoa, can we cancel and just stay home?" which means he likes how I look.

I have shed the turtleneck idea for a skintight black Donna Karan slip dress with a built-in bra so that the back is all open and crocheted and plunging. My hair is loose and my jewelry simple and the effect is dramatic, not to mention curvy. When we get into the car, the dress rides way up on my thighs and Eric asks how he is supposed to concentrate on driving when I'm practically naked and I suddenly wonder if he is over-complimenting me to make sure that I don't chicken out.

"Honey, I'm glad we're going out, really, you don't have to overdo it."

"Jule, you really look incredible. Not just for forty-five, either, don't you know it?"

Eric is so nice and sincere that of course I start to cry. As we pull out of the driveway he says to me, "There's just one thing I need you to do."

"Mmm?" I am dabbing at my eyeliner.

"I need you to wear this."

I look over at my husband, who has pulled out a sort of homemade hood from under the seat.

"What?"

"It's a surprise, where we're going, and I don't want you to see till we get there."

"Oh, Eric, you have to be kidding me."

"Please?"

I look at the thing in his hand. No wonder he was being so nice.

"It's going to ruin my hair."

"No, I thought of that. I made it out of this light fabric, and extra big, so it won't bother you."

He made it?

"You went to all the trouble of making this?"

"Yep."

"Okay." So I can be a sport. At least he isn't boring. What husband goes to the trouble of making a hood so his wife will be surprised? And as he promised, it is surprisingly light and comfortable and I can't see a thing, which is kind of weird. For about twenty minutes I try to figure out which route he is taking to the city, but Eric makes a series of sharp lefts and rights, on purpose I think, and after a while the darkness from the hood is strangely calming and I close my eyes and just relax. We talk a little, and then Eric puts on music and we sing together, even though the hood muffles my words, and I am really having a good time. I tell him it feels like we're driving forever and he says well you know how it is on Saturday night and after what seems like an hour or so the car slows and pulls into what must be a parking lot. Eric says not to move and to wait for him to come around. I feel a little ridiculous and I hope no one on the street can see me in this stupid hood, but I listen. He opens the car door and helps me out.

"Okay," I say, a little weary, "can I take it off?"

"Almost." His voice is strange. Nervous but excited. He walks me a few steps murmuring, "Just over here . . . just a little farther . . . almost there."

Then he stops, turns me slightly to the left, and moves to stand behind me. He says, "Okay, I'm gonna lift it off and you just look straight ahead, okay?"

"Okay, okay, c'mon already, I feel ridiculous."

"Okay." Eric takes a deep breath and I can't imagine what could be such a big deal, but I am about to find out.

The hood comes off and it takes a minute for me to adjust to what I see. It is almost dark because, as I soon learn, it is about 8:00 p.m. and we really did drive for about an hour. Only not south to the city and the glittering nouvelle cuisine of Manhattan, and not east to Port Washington or even Long Island City and the eclectic waterfront seafood bistros, nor did we head west to the charming, wild-game-laden country inns of New

Jersey's horse country. No, we headed north. North, on the New York State Thruway, past endless stretches of dilapidated and blighted rural townships. North, through barren, fire-ravaged hillsides and peeling barns that dot overgrown farms, and farther north still, past the occasional mall and miniature golf course and the once-glorified hotels of the Borscht Belt, into the minuscule community of Roscoe, New York. All of this I did not see, but know as well as if I had made the trip in daylight at thirty miles an hour. I know because I have made the trip so many times in my mind as well as my car. And there I stand, just feet from the highway, gazing up at the structure that has held me so captive I've had to pass it by, not even able to bear stopping for the rush of memories it invokes: the Roscoe Diner. This is where Eric has taken me to celebrate my birthday. And I am speechless. I must confess I have a moment of disappointment. It takes a lot of effort to look great when you're forty-five, and I suddenly realize that the only people who will see me in my dress will have names like Zeke and Zeb and Darcy. But, oh! The Roscoe Diner. It is rich. So meaningful and so significant. And Eric knows it. I've been worried that his feelings for me might be changing, that I'm losing my appeal, and here he is, waiting anxiously, waiting to see if he was a hit, as if my reaction is the most important thing in the world.

"Well." It's all that I can muster. I want to get it right, let him know that it is not just a hit, that it's a grand slam.

"'Well' good, or 'well' bad? Or, 'Well what the fuck is wrong with you, Eric, you stupid idiot'?"

"Oh, Eric," I say, turning to him, and then I take his face in my hands and give him the kind of deep kiss you give a boyfriend with whom you haven't had sex yet, but probably will if he doesn't blow it.

"So I guess that's well good." He is relieved.

"No it's better than well good. It's well *amazing*. It's well, 'How did you ever think of something so perfect?'"

"Because I am the perfect man. I've been trying to tell you that for years."

"Okay, now it's becoming 'Well, don't push it.' So are you going to feed me after blinding me and kidnapping me?"

THE ROSCOE DINER is divided into two sections. When we walk up the stairs into the entrance we can see that the side with tables, the fancier side, if you could call it that, is dark and obscured by a large, accordionlike divider, and only the right side with the booths is open. But even that side is empty and I look at Eric and start to smile. We are the only people in the whole place.

"I guess they don't do a big dinner business in August," I giggle.

One tired waitress looks up from the end of the counter as we come in (this must be Darcy, Zeb's sister) and does a kind of a double take and then looks around her, as if she is wondering if *she* is in the right place! As if maybe while she was daydreaming she was transported to a different restaurant, with polished oak floors and linen tablecloths and wine lists, where folks in designer dresses and salon highlights come to eat.

"Hi, folks, you here for dinner?" She sounds doubtful.

I am pinching Eric at this point. We must be a sight, he in his Zegna suit and me in my Donna Karan. Darcy waits for our answer.

"Actually"—Eric's voice is booming as if he is the mayor or, at the very least, the master of ceremonies at Jake's soccer dinner—"it's my wife's birthday and this is where she wanted to come to celebrate. Would it be possible for us to sit at a table in the other room instead of a booth?"

What is Eric doing? The entire place is empty, so why would we need a table instead of a booth? If he takes out a twenty and gives it to Darcy, I will die. I poke him and mumble something about a booth being fine, but he shoos me away.

"Tut-tut," he says dramatically. "Nothing is too good for you tonight."

"'Tut-tut'?"

I look at him like he is nuts. Darcy is looking back and forth from the kitchen to the darkened table section, and finally shrugs her shoulders as if to say "Why not?" She grabs two menus and begins to lead us to the other section. Eric begins to follow, then turns back to me. He whispers, "See, stick with me baby, only the finest for my girl."

I am cracking up, enjoying myself as my strange husband bows ceremoniously and motions for me to go in front of him. "After you, madam," he gushes.

I am trying to remember everything, Eric's overdone acting, the waitress's face, so I can tell the kids. Then something happens that is so unexpected, so stunning, that despite its well-intended point, despite its happy result, I will always associate it with at least a tinge of terror. The sheer shock of the moment will be as ingrained in my memory as any other sensation. The dark side of the Roscoe Diner illuminates suddenly and thoroughly and with such harsh intensity that I am momentarily blinded and I let out a sharp cry as I shrink back instinctively and land firmly on my husband's right foot. I am not in an empty space at all. Packed along the three walls that make up the interior perimeter of the fancier section and up along the sides of the chilled pastry shelves are people. And not just any people, people I know. Darcy the waitress is staring at me, no longer tired, but smiling, clasping her hands together in delight at my expression just as two flashbulbs go off and I hear the word

"SURPRISE!"

In the seconds before total understanding, I have two thoughts: one, we are under some kind of terrorist attack, and, two, I have to hold in my stomach so it looks flat in this dress. I also understand why people cry at surprise parties. The feeling is not unlike coming home to find your house ransacked or, worse, the intruder still inside: total shock and a trace of outrage that you could be so duped. It is a violation of sorts. If you can be tricked about this, perhaps you've been tricked before. Perhaps there are multiple layers of deception in your life. I look back and forth from the crowd to Eric, who has his arm around me and I don't know what to say or how to act. I can hear people saying things like "Oh, she's crying," and to

Eric, "Did she know anything?" but I am stuck in a slow-moving haze of my own emotions. I can see Amy and Beth, and also Margie Gluckstein, and there's Stewie and Lyle and Barb and Gayle. There must be sixty people in the room. Music begins to play in the background and I take note that Eric has hired a deejay. I see his assistant, Brian, who appears to have brought a date, and Laura and Bob from the club. The next moment I am engulfed by the Feldensteins, our neighbors, who are laughing and kissing me and saying, "Happy birthday, are you surprised?" To my right, Amy makes a face, she can't stand Tobi Feldenstein, and I start to come back to myself as I wink back at her, but I can't get near anyone because there is literally a mob pressing in to greet me. Then I hear someone say, "Let the kids through," and my stomach does a little bungee jump and I realize I had been subconsciously scanning the crowd, half-wondering and half-hoping, and before I can fully imagine it, they are there. Both of them. It's unbelievable but true. Alexis is home a day early and looks fabulous in a short black skirt and a red halter. Could she have matured so much in six weeks? I remember that we have such wonderful news for her, and I look at Eric and his smile is enormous. And then there is Jake, wearing his most devastating, sheepish grin, and as the kids come toward me they are smiling, and the photographer is snapping, and we are all hugging, and I am crying again.

"You knew about this?"

"What do you think?" Jake laughs.

"Of course," Lexie adds, "since I left."

"Alexis, what about your exams? You didn't miss them?"

"It's okay, Mom," she assures me, "school really ended on Wednesday. We've been staying with Aunt Gayle and Uncle Stew since yesterday."

"We?" I look around.

Lexie signals to someone, waves unsuccessfully to get their attention, and then cups her hands in front of her mouth and yells over the noise, "Matt!" She waves again, and this time a handsome young man with blue eyes and broad shoulders, wearing a button-down blue shirt and khakis, waves back and begins to try to make his way over to us.

"Matt?" I ask my daughter.

"He's cute, isn't he?" she whispers. "I met him in Amsterdam. He's from Merrick." I consider this. He is cute, actually, and *young*! This one can't be a day over twenty-one, and I suddenly realize I'm upset. We have wonderful Russell news and we do not know this Matt and how bizarre that I am suddenly rooting for Russell, when Jake leans in and says, "I guess she's over the old guy."

"I heard that," Lexie shoots back, and for a moment there is a flash of pain in her eyes. "And no, I'm not. But I'm not dead, either."

"Sorry. I was just being funny. I didn't mean it." Jake suddenly has a sensitive side.

"It doesn't matter. Besides, Matt is just a friend."

I am listening to this exchange between my kids, and even though it is my big birthday party, I wish everyone would just keep quiet and go entertain themselves so my kids will keep talking and I can keep listening. Things are going to get really interesting tomorrow, I want to say. But of course my guests all want to talk to me, and a private conversation is impossible.

I look at Lexie and ask, "Are you okay?" and she says, "Totally. Let's party."

By 1:30 A.M., the last of the guests have left, and we head home with Lexie and Matt and Jake in our car. It takes us barely an hour at this time of night, but even so, when we walk in the door it's almost three in the morning and everyone is wiped out. Eric grabs the mail, which we forgot to get today, and throws it on the counter. "Tomorrow," we say at the same time. We install Matt in the guest room, and I change into my pajamas and knock softly on Lexie's door.

"Enter."

"Hey, just wanted to say sleep tight and thanks for coming home early."

"Are you glad Dad made the party?"

"I am. Especially for him. He thinks I'm making too big a deal out of Grammy dying on my birthday, so I'm trying not to focus on it."

"You know, I don't blame you. What a raw deal. It's like Grammy's been messing with your mind all these years and now she even screwed up your birthday. I mean, she couldn't have held out another day? I think it's really big of you to get over it." Who is this child? And now I find myself defending my mother. First Russell, now her.

"Oh, I don't know, I don't think Grandma ever meant to hurt any-one, she loved us so much and needed us so much it just scared her to think of us as flawed or imperfect. Like if we had flaws we'd somehow dis-integrate or fade out. You know, love is a powerful thing, it makes you do crazy things." I walk over and give her a kiss.

"G'nite, Mom. Happy birthday."

"Sweet dreams."

IN BED, Eric and I snuggle into each other like newlyweds. I love the smell of his chest, musky with sweat and the remnants of cologne. "Happy birth-day," he mumbles into my hair and I wiggle closer, getting drowsier by the second. We fall asleep that way, holding each other, drained, content, and I do not wake up even once until daybreak.

The morning is heavenly, a perfect combination of sleepy teenagers, French toast, and the *New York Times*. Alexis and I do our standard recap of the party, detailing who was wearing what and focusing on who shouldn't have been, and the boys groan and discuss the upcoming foot-ball season. Matt asks if he can take the dogs for a run, and Eric and I invite him to live with us for the rest of his life. Then we exchange a glance and ask him exactly how and when he is going home to Long Island. His friend from Woodcliff Lake is picking him up at two o'clock. Jake gets a phone call, which leaves Eric, Alexis, and me alone. Eric remarks that this is the first morning in over a year that someone in the family isn't having some kind of crisis. Alexis asks him if he thinks he's really so normal, and Eric responds, "Damn straight."

"Daddy, you need to get over yourself. You have your share of issues, too. Besides, you should know by now that parenting has its ups and downs. You should learn to roll with the punches."

Eric groans, and this time I have to pipe in.

"Please, Lex, you know how I feel about clichés."

"You mean you don't want to hear that I was lost but now I'm found?"

"You're killing me."

"My ship was adrift on an ocean of uncertainty."

"Nine-one-one!"

"I was searching for meaning . . . looking for truth . . ." I can't take it. I break in.

"Actually," I say, "you were passing Roscoe." I turn to Eric and smile. He smiles back.

"Oh, please," she says jokingly. "Dad explained all that to me when I asked him why in the world he was making your party at the Roscoe Diner, and it was kind of cool, but let's not turn this into a family mantra." I sigh and shake my head, shrugging at Eric as if to say, *Where does she get these dramatic expressions?* Eric jumps up suddenly, remembering yesterday's mail, and begins to simulate a mantra as he flips through the junk.

"Ohhhmmm, more bills, ohhhhmmm, make them go away, ohhmmm, for you and for you." He is distributing the mail, chanting, and driving Lexie crazy.

"Dad, enough!"

I am about to intervene and throw my napkin at him, but the letter in my lap stops me. It is fat, bulging even, and the return address says North Jersey News, which is the group that owns the *Suburban Sentinel.* They must have sent me back my essays. I slide my finger through the back as I walk out of the room. For now, I'll just throw them in my desk so I don't have to explain. When I pull out the documents I become confused, because they are not copies of my work after all. There is a letter and then some sort of contract. I am staring at the letter, reading, but uncomprehending, when I realize that it is a letter of congratulations and an invitation to join the staff as one of two columnists who will participate in a new weekly column, *Suburban Sparring*. Attached to the contract is a handwritten note: *Five-shmive. I told them if they didn't hire you based on the four you submitted, you'd be snapped up by the* Star Ledger *within the year. Welcome, T.*

I turn back to the kitchen, look at my daughter and husband, who are oblivious, and words fail me, but my heart is racing and my blood is warm and singing and my smile is returning, maybe for the first time in a long time. "You guys," I croak, "I have something to tell you."

When I am done telling them and Eric stops hugging me and Alexis finishes her singing and dancing medley of "I Am Woman" and "She Works Hard for the Money" and goes to find Jake, I collapse in a chair and Eric finally asks me why I didn't tell him anything about it.

"Oh, Eric, I was worried you'd think it was too stressful, that it was unhealthy for me, and then I figured I didn't get it so what was the point of even mentioning it."

"I would never encourage you to settle, don't you know that? You can do anything, you're strong and sensitive, too, but mostly strong."

"Thanks." I don't know what to say. I love this man so much.

"We're a family, Jule, and we're a good one. No matter what crisis is on the horizon, no matter who temporarily loses their sanity, at the end of the day, always, we have each other." As if on cue, Lexie comes downstairs, announcing that she can't find Jake anywhere, just as we hear Jake's heavy limbs, hard, coming up the garage stairs. He comes bounding into the kitchen, looking anxious and a little wild.

"Hey, I've gotta ask you something. Wait, wait here, I'll be right back."

Jake flies out to the garage and we all look at each other. In a minute he is back, and we can hear him talking to someone. Then he is in the kitchen, and next to him, hair in her face, tears running down her cheeks, is Kate. That Kate. My brain is having a little trouble processing the item in her hand, a suitcase.

"Okay, look, Mom, Dad, I didn't know how to ask you this, but, um, you said I should always be honest, right?" We are now a family of mutes.

"Well, Kate has been having a tough time, at home, you know, and well, I sort of told her . . ." He breaks off and looks at Kate, who completely dissolves into tears and runs out of the room, suitcase in hand. Mind you, she doesn't run out of the house and into the driveway, but up the back stairs to Jake's room. Jake looks pained as he turns back to us.

"So, I mean, I'll explain it all later, but what I really need to know is if it would be okay if she moved in here for a while. I mean, I know I should've asked you first, but, well, what do you think, is it okay?"

Is it okay? Is it okay? How are we supposed to think when Lexie is laughing hysterically as she walks out of the room? As she reaches the doorway, she turns and, with a big smile on her face, announces that she is going back out to look for Matt. Then she says in a falsely sympathetic voice, "Sorry, Dad, but you did have a whole morning without a catastrophe."

And as she turns she pumps her fist and exults, "Finally! I am *so* the good one!"

WITHIN THE HOUR, Matt leaves and Kate unpacks, but only after I insist on calling her parents, who tell me it is fine with them if Kate stays with us. Really? I look at Eric in disbelief. What do we do now? We spend most of the afternoon debating this, and before we know it, it's six o'clock and then the doorbell rings. Eric takes my hand as our hearts jump out of our chests and I am half thrilled, half terrified by what is about to take place, especially when Eric whispers, "Here we go." Then we give each other's hands a squeeze, look into each other's eyes, and yell in unison, "Alexis! Get the door!"

THIRTY

Alexis would look lovely in lace

*O*prah is holding up a copy of Alexis Across Time, *and I am in the audience holding Lexie's hand. On stage, Russell looks adorably uncomfortable as she gushes over the book. ". . . truly the most intense, passionate love story I have ever read. It makes me sorry we stopped the Book Club, don't you agree?" Oprah turns to a panel of women, her friends, and they all chime in approvingly. Then she turns to the audience and says, "I understand the inspiration for this romantic novel is in our audience today. Alexis, where are you?" I gasp as the audience murmurs and looks around, and suddenly my baby is standing and we can see her on the monitors and Russell finally looks a little more relaxed as he smiles and beams as he catches Lexie's eye. I turn to my mother, who is on my right (hey, it's my dream, I can have my mother in it if I want), and pat her hand. "Alexis would look lovely in lace," she whispers. "I see a twilight ceremony in the fall with ivy, they're both so academic, think of the symbolism, and you could pick up on the ivy with pale green bridesmaids' dresses and a first course of butter lettuces with grapes . . ."*

In the morning light, I hold the dream close and smile. I am not so angry, not so fragmented anymore. I have survived quite a year and I've emerged less obsessed with being good or liked or worthy—in fact, less obsessed period. I am beginning to forgive my mother and myself. But mostly I am enjoying what I have without fearing it will vanish if I do. I think about getting up and making a list of all that's good, but instead I just lie back, close my eyes, smile again, and let my life's blessings wash over me in no particular order. There is Playfulness, with a husband who makes me homemade hoods so I will be surprised, Unconditional Love from a daughter who feels allowed to drop emotional bombshells, and Tenderness, given by a son who calls me "mamacita" as he learns to be a man.